THE MARKED BOOK ONE

MARKED FOR GRACE

K.C. HARPER

MARKED FOR GRACE

K.C. HARPER

MARKED FOR GRACE
The Marked, Book 1

CITY OWL PRESS
www.cityowlpress.com

Cover Design by MiblArt. All stock photos licensed appropriately.

Edited by Lisa Green.

For information on subsidiary rights, please contact the publisher at info@cityowlpress.com.

Print Edition ISBN: 978-1-64898-298-9

Digital Edition ISBN: 978-1-64898-299-6

Printed in the United States of America

PRAISE FOR K.C. HARPER

"*Marked for Grace* was such a fast-paced, sexy read…the romance is a slow-burn steam-fest that I'm excited to follow through the series. Such a great debut!" — *Regina Black, author of The Art of Scandal*

"Gritty, intense, and clever, *Marked for Grace* is an immediately addictive, fresh spin in the paranormal romance genre. Just when you think you know where the story is going, it twists in unexpected directions and begs you to turn the page." — *Kristy Gardner, author of The Stars in Their Eyes*

"The characters Harper builds and (emotionally) tortures continually stun me; reading feels more like living amongst them than simply observing from the distance of the page. I can't wait to start gifting this book to every book lover I know for birthdays and holidays." — *Eve, Ink Stains on My Sheets*

"Harper delivers a unique, spell-binding story that blurs the lines of good and evil, right from wrong. There were twists and turns along the way seamlessly interwoven with romance and battles that kept me reading page after page, chapter after chapter." — *Jennifer Thé, gothic horror author*

For Nana.

AUTHOR'S NOTE

I cannot thank you enough for picking this book up. It's my intention for people to feel safe when reading, and for that reason, I've included a list of content warnings which are available on my website: https://kcharper.com/content-info

If you have any concerns about the content in this book, please be sure to check this page out first. Thank you again and happy reading!

CHAPTER 1
GRACE

It was one thing to stare at the dead, another entirely when they stared back.

Grace was seated in the cold, red pleather booth of a small cafe adjacent to the hospital where she worked. She twisted her long umber-colored hair around her finger as the thump of her heart rivaled the wailing sirens from an ambulance parked nearby.

Canting her head, she peered through her reflection in the window to her right. Blood coated the sun-lit sidewalk across the street, dripping from a man's hand where it hung from the gurney. His translucent soul hovered near the emergency entrance, its unblinking stare fixed on her. It didn't speak, didn't move. Nothing. Just existed.

Someone dropped into the seat across from her and she jumped. "You scared me to death, Noah," she said to her best friend and roommate.

He frowned. "Not sure why since you invited me here."

She waved a flippant hand. The vanilla and burnt coffee aroma dominated her senses while steam from an espresso machine behind the counter shot into the air.

Removing his gray parka, Noah hung it from a hook beside the table. "When did you get here?"

"A few minutes ago, so I can't stay long. My break is almost over." Her gaze drifted to the familiar, rippling glow of the two gold cuffs embedded along the soul's right arm, but whether they were a gift or a sanction, she didn't know.

She wanted to look away, but the dead commanded her attention like lightning striking down beside her. Even four years after her Sight appeared, their presence still affected her. No, they affected her *more*. It wasn't that she feared them, but she feared what they meant.

Lights from the ambulance painted the snow, the building, and everything else in the vicinity with a chaotic, staccato spray of red and white. The paramedics performed CPR on the too pale man while they wheeled him inside, but their efforts were for naught. He was well beyond saving.

Noah was midway through placing the lunch Grace had forgotten—and would desperately need before her shift was done—on the table when her hand shot out, snapping it from his grasp. She clutched it to her chest like a desperate lover. "You're a lifesaver."

The lines of his olive-toned skin creased when he laughed. "Easy, Gracie. I'd like to keep my arm."

"You assumed the risks when you agreed to bring my food, delivery boy. You know my hunger's an emotion."

"A dangerous one."

She offered a sharp nod before her attention returned to the soul. Its expression flat, unsmiling. It didn't look happy. Didn't look sad or scared. Didn't look anything. Like all the others she'd seen, it bore no signs of emotion, and she wondered if it had any awareness at all.

Noah followed her line of sight. "What is it?"

Her mouth ran dry. "One of them."

He looked away and shuddered.

"Pfft," she scoffed. "I don't know why they bother you. It's not like you can see them."

His honey-brown eyes settled on her. "That almost makes it worse. I hate knowing they're there."

She ran her palm over her baby blue scrub pants, smoothing the material again and again, thankful she had at least one person who knew her truth and believed her. "And yet you always ask about them."

"Because that," he flourished his hand toward her face, "is impossible to ignore."

She snickered.

He peered in the soul's general direction again. "Does it have any of the markings?"

"Just two."

His lips pursed. "I wish we knew what they meant."

"You're telling me." She curled the sleeve of her wool coat in her grasp, exposing the fair skin of her wrist. On some messed-up level, she figured becoming a nurse would make it easier. Like being around the dead would either give her answers or force her skin to thicken. Neither had happened. If anything, the oppressive questions had only grown deeper, more unnerving—worse. Her leg bounced under the table. "They *have* to mean something."

He flicked the side of his menu with a finger. "If that's true, logic dictates someone was meant to see them."

Her stomach torqued into a knot she wasn't sure could ever be undone because if he was right, then she had a purpose. But if he was wrong... "What if I'm losing my mind, Noah? What if this has all been in my head?"

"Don't go there."

She threw her hands up. "How can I not? If anyone at work finds out, I'll be deemed unfit to practice. I'll lose everything, my nursing license, my career," her voice hitched, "the house."

"You're not losing your mind, you're just upset because you're hungry, now take a breath, Gracie."

She did, sucking in deep and slow, then followed that one by another and another. "I can't tell anyone without risking everything, but then if I don't, I'll never find answers." And the idea of going through life without those explanations, knowing she was alone in this was more painful than she cared to admit.

Noah's gaze pinched at the corners as he reached across the table and gently squeezed her forearm. "It's too bad they don't share it with you."

"That might be difficult when they don't speak."

His brow furrowed. "You know what I mean, smartass."

She released an explosive exhale as a small smile tugged her lip. He always knew what to say to smother her wildfires. Withdrawing her arm, she gave him a spirited pat on the head. "You'd think I'd be used to them by now."

"I think there are some things we can never get used to," he replied, fixing the hair she'd mussed. "We could scour the internet again. There might be something new."

Sweet lord, anything but that! Her eyes rolled so aggressively it hurt. "And maybe while we're at it, we could join one of those ghost hunter's clubs."

"I'm fairly confident you're mocking me."

She offered him a tooth-baring grin while a raucous group of teenagers guffawed at one another across the café.

"Why are we friends again?"

Grace smacked his elbow. "Because I'm so lovable."

"Clearly," he grumbled as he rubbed his wound, then straightened. "Oh! Did you get my email?"

She fidgeted while the sharp scent of burnt toast filled her senses. "I haven't had a chance to check it yet. Why?"

"Some real estate lawyer named Gerald Martin came by. He's representing this company, G.R. Incorporated. They're considering building a business development in the area and are inquiring with homeowners about selling their properties. He left me his card and a bunch of documents. I sent pictures of both for you."

She pulled her phone from her coat pocket then brought up the file and scrolled down, eyes flying wide when they landed on the offer amount. "Holy crap!" Her brows climbed so high on her forehead it was a wonder they didn't slip free because the proposal was *well* above market value.

"That's what I thought. It'd more than cover the remaining mortgage debt."

Grace chewed the inside of her cheek as a waitress shimmied by, a tray of steaming drinks in hand. She shook her head and closed the message. "It doesn't matter how good the offer is, some things are more important than money. That house was Mom's." Her vision blurred when she fought back the tears stinging her eyes, the conversation an excruciating reminder of the night her mother died—a blood and agony-filled night she refused to think about.

Noah cleared his throat and looked away. "You're still good for your graduation lunch tomorrow?"

Heat flooded her body as she blinked her sight clean. "Everyone knows I graduated two months ago, right?"

"They sure do, but that's what you get when you have friends who do shift-work."

"Disorganized planning?"

He snickered. "Exactly!"

A series of piercing sirens drew closer, reverberating off the buildings and amplifying the sound. Her head snapped toward them. Several ambulances whipped into the hospital's lot accompanied by a slew of Arillia City Police vehicles. The hospital's P.A. system crackled, the announcement muffled from inside the restaurant.

She scrambled out of the booth, snapping to her feet. "I've gotta go."

Noah's voice was lost in the cacophony as she bolted from the café, aiming for the entrance of the E.R. A car whipped across her path, and she jolted to a stop. It passed so close its wind snapped her clothes. Her heart lurched when the distinct cry of metal-on-metal filled the world as the vehicle side-swiped one of the ambulances. Its tires screeched before it crashed to a halt and smashed into a concrete garbage can. Glass exploded from the windshield, tinkling across the ice-covered ground like freshly fallen snow.

A bloodied man exited and took three steps before dropping to his knees. His hands were clasped over his stomach like they could hold back the torrent of blood that leaked between his fingers. His shoulders heaved from his labored breathing. He was pale. Too pale.

Help, he mouthed.

Grace made for him and threw his arm over her shoulder, taking as much of his weight as she could. Her teeth clenched from her effort while she guided him toward the doors. The first wave of paramedics burst from their vehicles, rushing past with their bloodied patients, each of which was escorted by an officer and cuffed to their gurneys.

The distinct scent of copper saturated the air, heavy and clawing. It burned her throat like a sharp mineral acid and made her voice thick when she called, "What happened?"

"Gunshot wounds," one of the paramedics said.

"Bar brawl," an officer added, hand on her gun, eyes trained on the patient she followed.

Grace swallowed hard as Angie the Charge Nurse pushed outside, barking orders when she pointed to one of the lesser wounded men. "Get him to E.R. room four. Move that car out of the way and for the love of all that's holy, turn those damn sirens off!"

One of the prisoner-patients with a jagged gash across his cheek offered Grace an air kiss. "Hey there, blue eyes. You can take care of me if you want."

A poisonous shiver prowled across her skin. "That's Nurse Crawford to you. And you'll be dealt with when your friends stop bleeding."

The man she helped stumbled. She held tight but his momentum was too much. "He's going down," she warned. Several people lunged to catch him, too late. He collapsed, grunting when he landed hard. His hands dropped limp by his sides and his eyes rolled back in his head before they fell shut. Blood slithered from his slack mouth, crawling across his jaw like a life-stealing snake.

Grace cursed when she knelt by his side, searching for a pulse, and finding none. Setting her palms on his chest, she started compressions. "I need help over here!"

Dr. Rodan Brookes, a man in his late twenties, crouched across from her. His long-sleeved white lab coat skirted the ground while his keen, hazel stare took in the scene. He pressed his blue latex-gloved hands over the man's wound.

"He's lost a lot of blood," Grace told him. Her shoulders and back ached from her efforts while the chill from the wintery ground seeped into her skin, taking root in her bones. *Come on. Don't die on me. Come. On!*

"We need another gurney here," Dr. Brookes called over his shoulder before coming back to her. "Do you need to swap out?"

Grace heaved a breath and nodded. She pulled her hands from the patient's chest and pivoted to put them on his stomach but jerked back when his soul materialized. A diaphanous mist rolled from the body. It torqued and roiled as it took shape until it stood fully formed before her.

Her hands trembled as she stared, because its forearms were *covered* in markings. On the right were three golden bands, while on the left were seven blacker than coal, thickly scaled serpents. Each coiled around the arm, climbing higher and higher, binding.

She'd seen them before, but never that many on one soul and something about it felt wrong, so damn wrong. She couldn't say why, but it was a pervasive, indisputable sensation that's shadowed limbs spiralled around her and tightened like a vice, whispering of darkness.

"Here!" Angie called as she wheeled an empty gurney their way, snapping Grace back to her surroundings.

Dr. Brookes' stare was locked on her, narrowing when it flicked to the space above their very dead patient and back again. There was something strange in his expression but what it meant, she had no clue.

Biting her lip, Grace squirmed under his scrutiny. Or suspicion? God only knew. Regardless, she couldn't let him see something was…off about her. Needing his attention anywhere else, she threw herself forward and pressed her hands to the patient's stomach. *Please don't notice. Please don't notice.*

"I'm calling it." He leaned back and snapped his gloves off before shoving them into his pocket.

One of the injured men launched a brutal string of epithets his way.

The doctor checked his watch. "Time of death: Seventeen hundred hours and fifty-eight minutes."

Against every instinct, Grace lifted her eyes to his, but if she'd hoped for reassurance, she found none.

His jaw was clenched, movements rigid when he pushed to his feet. "We're needed inside." He pivoted on his heel and pulled his phone from his pocket as he stalked away.

He couldn't know anything. It wasn't possible. She was just reading into things that weren't really there. Fitting under the circumstances. She swallowed hard and removed her blood-soaked hands from the body. Releasing a shuddering breath, she took one last fleeting glance at the soul, then moved on.

AT THE END of her shift, Grace shuffled her way to the change room, barely able to lift her feet from exhaustion. She struggled to strip off her blood-stained scrubs then hopped in the shower trying not to, but unable to stop replaying the haunting moment with Dr. Brookes earlier.

Rolling her shoulders, she tried to release her taut muscles and failed miserably. She turned off the water, dried and dressed before rubbing her hands along the back of her arms to warm them–a useless effort since the cold had burrowed soul deep. Giving up, she grabbed her belongings and left, turning down the hall toward the staff exit.

She bit the inside of her cheek when she spotted Dr. Brookes speaking with two imposing men by the door. Both were tall, well above six feet. Their backs were to her, but their broad, solid frames and clenched fists made the tension that pulsed from them nothing short of menacing.

They turned at her approach and the weight of their scrutinizing stares almost crushed her. The first had a shaved head, chest-length dark beard, and offered her a glare that made her think it was personal; the second's chestnut brown stare pierced her, hunting her every move. The intensity he put off was a bizarre mix of threat and intrigue. To say he was gorgeous would have been an understatement, and the weight of his attention sent the heat of a blush crawling up her cheeks. He lifted his hand and raked it through chin-length blond hair, exposing the inside of his wrist.

Her heart shuddered in her chest. A mark, one she'd never seen before. It was similar to, yet wholly different from the ones on the dead, though this guy was very much alive. Did he see things too? Did he have the answers she wanted? The answers she craved?

The questions danced at the tip of her tongue, threatening to burst free, but a nagging caution told her to keep moving, fast. She couldn't override it and it set her teeth on edge. She nodded to acknowledge them, praying it covered any reaction she might've had before she slipped past the three and out into the night.

The wintery air hit her like a wall, and she drew her coat tighter to block the chill as she advanced, her legs pumping hard. Pulling out her keys, she unlocked her car, shoulders sagging while the familiar icy bite of the driver-side handle stung her skin. She was halfway through opening the door when someone reached past her and slammed it shut. Her body went rigid, and she sucked in a sharp breath before she whipped around.

The blond man loomed less than a foot away, eyes narrowed as he edged closer. His heat brushed her flesh when he penned her in. "Good evening, Grace Crawford. I believe we need to talk."

CHAPTER 2
GRACE

Grace backpedaled and collided with the car. Her chest heaved with frantic breaths, and she trembled so wildly, her hair shook in the periphery of her vision.

The blond stranger towered over her, standing so close she was forced to look up at a painful angle. His stare roved her face, lingering on her eyes and lips before it dipped lower. He assessed her with a tinge of some emotion she couldn't quite place while his strong jaw worked, muscles pulsing under the movement.

Her gaze darted between him and his friend with the shaved head who skulked from the shadows. "What do you want?"

"Who are you?" the blond questioned, tone rough, sandpaper brushing stone. It burned her skin with its accusation.

"You *just* said my name," she replied, the bark in her voice surprising even her.

He furrowed his brows and honed his glare. "You know what I mean."

Shaved-head guy took several steps forward, edging closer. "What Sect are you from?"

Her head snapped his way. "*Sect*?"

His boots crunched on the snow and ice-coated ground before he came to a stop beside her, the two men boxing her in. "This isn't your territory."

Pulling her coat tighter, she crushed herself against the car to put as much distance between them as she could–which was literally none. "What the hell are you talking about?"

"Don't play stupid. You know the rules. You need to get a transfer to the chapter." He chucked his chin to the blond. "Ben and I know you didn't do that."

Sect? Territory? Chapter? What in the sweet lord was going on? She shook her head. Were they out of their minds? She needed help. Her gaze flicked around the parking lot while she prayed for someone, *anyone* to walk by.

"I have no idea what you're talking about, so if you don't mind, I'll be going now." She reached behind her, hand fumbling furiously against the door.

"No," Ben said, the word hard, final, and it rocketed her heartrate to a dangerous level. His head cocked, hair shifting with the movement before he nodded toward his friend. "Trevor and I need you to show us your wrists, Grace."

Her *wrists*? Could things get any weirder? "I'm not showing you anything." Latching onto the handle, she popped it open. Before she could move, Ben reached past her and shoved it shut...again.

Trevor's slate-colored eyes were sharp when he crossed his arms over his chest like some kind of enforcer. "We're not asking,"

Grace slipped a key between the ring and forefingers of her right hand. One good hit would hurt. That was all she needed. *One good hit*. Ben latched onto her left arm. She struggled against him and opened her mouth to scream.

Trevor's palm clamped over it, muzzling her. "I wouldn't do that if I were you."

To hell with that! She swung, aiming for his ribs but he was fast. *Too fast*. He dropped his elbow and it collided with her forearm, blocking her with so much force, she winced and lost the grip on her keys. The clank when they hit the ground struck her like an undertaker driving the final nail in a coffin—a coffin that sealed her in.

"Enough, Trevor!" Ben growled. Trevor took half a step back, giving up ground, but barely.

Ass!

Ben's thumb traced a cool path across her exposed skin, his touch disconcerting in its gentleness.

"What are you doing?" she demanded and jerked her arm back, but his grip locked tight–a shackle holding her in place. A prisoner. She was a *prisoner*. She gasped for air and her legs grew weak.

Trevor's laugh was caustic. "You're caught, little mouse."

Ben dragged her coat sleeve up. His eyes narrowed on her flesh, brows furrowing deep.

Trevor's his hand fisted around his beard. "What the fuck?"

Ben grabbed Grace's other wrist, exposing it so fast she flinched. "Nothing," he uttered to himself before his stare locked on hers, hunter on hunted. Releasing her, he ran his hand through his hair as the edge in his voice lessened. "Who are you?"

She peered past him and scanned the lot. Still no one. Oh, God. She should try and scream again. Maybe if she did it fast enough someone would hear.

He must've noticed that thought simmering behind her eyes, because he said, "We're not gonna hurt you."

Her hands clenched by her sides, and she frowned. "Your interrogation tactics would suggest otherwise."

He shook his head. "Then let's start this over. You're Grace. I'm Ben Jones." He chucked his chin to the left. "And that's Trevor Richards."

Trevor shifted, rolling his neck on his shoulders. "Rodan said she has the Sight."

Dr. Brookes. That son of a bitch! If she ever got out of there, she was going to kill him…or hide. Probably hide.

"She does," Ben said. "She saw my Mark back in the hospital."

"You sure?"

"I'm sure." With slow progress, like he didn't want to startle her more, Ben pulled up his sleeve. The sinewed strands of his forearm muscles flexed as he moved. Her gaze slid down the same instant her heartbeat kicked up.

"Careful, Ben," Trevor said, voice tight. "We're on thin ice here."

Ben inclined his head before he asked Grace, "What do you see?"

Her thoughts careened in a thousand directions at once because if she answered him, she'd confirm his suspicion that she *could* see. But it was obvious that at least, on some level, they were like her. They held information. Information she'd longed for since she'd gained her Sight. Information she'd started doubting even existed. Yet with the moment before her–with Ben and Trevor before her–she wasn't convinced she wanted it anymore.

But Rodan knew what she was. Knew *who* she was. He'd sicced them on her. He was a doctor. His word carried weight in the hospital. If he wanted, he could lob an accusation, destroy her in more ways than one. She stood at a precipice. She could lie, try to convince them they were wrong. If she was lucky, they'd leave, but then she'd lose an opportunity that might never present itself again. If she was honest, she could find what she craved: Answers, belonging.

She shifted, rocking in place while she swallowed hard. Some recessed part of her mind—her soul—recognized that once she opened that door, there'd be no going back.

Yet keeping it closed no longer felt like an option, either.

Her mind made up, she released a quavering exhale and prayed she wouldn't live to regret what came next. Setting the tip of her finger to Ben's wrist, she pointed to his intricate design. "I see white wings that are spread wide. The feathers are overlapping, and they arch at the top and bottom to create a circular shape."

A cold silence stretched until Trevor broke it. "Ben?"

Ben scrubbed the back of his neck with his free hand when he asked Grace, "You can see them? The dead?"

Her throat seized. Outside of Noah, she'd never admitted that truth to anyone and doing it with the stranger who'd just tailed her ass out of work went against every instinct she had. Steeling herself, she rolled her hands in and out of fists and nodded.

"But you're un-Marked," he said more to himself, then to her, "Do you know who we are?"

She offered him a slow shake of her head.

He eyed her for several agonizingly long seconds before his mouth pressed into a hard line. "You're gonna have to come with us."

Her brows shot up. "That's a hard no."

"You don't really have a choice. We've got too many unanswered questions, and this isn't the place to finish this conversation."

"I'm not going anywhere with you." Where was everyone? Because she needed help with a capital H. Scrambling for any reason she could muster to buy herself time, she spat the first thing that came to mind. "I'm expected home."

His gaze darkened when he ground out, "Then I'd suggest you call your boyfriend and tell him you'll be late."

Her face twisted. Presumptuous conclusion to jump to. Either way, she wasn't about to correct him. Let him think some big, badass would be looking for her, and that trouble might come looking for him. She pulled back her lips and bared her teeth in what she hoped was an acidic smile.

He shifted his stance, the rise and fall of his chest controlled, not calm, but measured. Meticulous. "Just come with us, and we'll explain everything."

She blinked several times in rapid succession.

"You'll regret it if you don't," Trevor cut in, leaning toward her as he offered a feral grin.

Bad idea, jackass.

She was done with him. Done with the whole situation. She twisted and brought her knee up where it connected with Trevor's crotch. The hit was ruthless, and right on the money.

He cursed, cursed again, then retched as his hands cupped his man-parts like they could shield them. They couldn't. He dropped like a rock. Ben's hand snapped out to catch him, only half-managing. Trevor's bravado crumbled with him when he collapsed into a fragile heap on the ground...right on top of her damn keys.

Shit. Shit. Shit!

Ben glowered but whether it was for her or Trevor, she had no clue, and nor was she about to waste time figuring it out. She bolted and pushed her legs hard as she aimed for the staff entrance.

"Grace!" Ben called. The pounding of his footfalls drummed loud and fast behind her, but how close he was, she had no clue. "Grace, stop!"

Close. Too close.

"Help! Hellllllp!" she screamed, still fifteen feet from the door. She could make it. Once she got inside, she'd be safe. The hospital had security. They'd come. *Sweet lord above, please come!*

For the most infinitesimal of moments, hope had fluttered like a fledgling butterfly in her chest. There *were* others like her. She wasn't alone. But that hope had been shattered, crumbling to pieces like violently broken glass.

Ten feet. Nine.

"Grace, *stop*!"

"HELP!"

The staff door burst open, and her stomach dropped out from beneath her when Dr. Rodan Brookes stood backlit by the fluorescent lights within. *No, no, no.*

She skidded to a halt or tried to, but her feet lost their tenuous grip on the ice, and she crashed to the ground in a brutal heap. Her vision flashed white when she hit, knocking the wind out of her. She sucked in a ragged breath as she desperately sought air.

Ben stopped, his shadow eclipsing her while his chest rose and fell in rapid pants. His hair slipped forward, and he clasped his hands before him.

"You got this?" Rodan asked.

The nod Ben gave him was sharp. "You're finished?"

"Just wrapping up some paperwork."

"I'll text you where to meet us. Bring Jenna with you," he said.

Rodan inclined his head before slinking back inside.

Ben crouched by Grace's side. "Are you alright?"

She scowled. "What do you think?"

He showed her his palms before resting his elbows on his knees. His voice lowered, the command there easing. "I promise, I'm not gonna hurt you."

Her stare flicked to Trevor.

Ben's boots scuffed the ground when he leaned into her line of sight, pulling her attention back to him. "And neither is he." The tension around his eyes abated as he scanned her face, gauging, but it was different from before, less critical, more heat. The weight of it sent a confusing thrill chasing up her spine. "You've gotta want answers to what you are. We can give them to you, but to do that, you have to come with us."

Somewhere beyond him, Trevor groaned, then came into view again when he clambered unsteadily to his feet.

"Forget him. You and I will take your car. He can follow us," Ben said, shifting his weight as he extended his hand.

Her heart thrashed like a caged animal while she stared at his offering. She wanted answers. God, she wanted them so much it hurt. Trusting him was a risk—a big one. But it could also be a chance. If she said no, she'd forever wonder. If she said no, she'd forever regret. If she said yes…

"I drive," she told him.

He inclined his head. "You drive."

She breathed slow, steady, and it didn't do a damn thing to calm her frenzied emotions when she reached out and took his warm, strong hand.

CHAPTER 3
BEN

Ben leaned closer as he pulled Grace to her feet. His hand locked on her elbow, and he held her steady when she slipped on the ice again. He tried not to stare, which was pretty much impossible because she was hot as hell. Her face was perfect, her body tight. He'd thought Leah was beautiful, but Grace put the other woman to shame.

His nostrils flared, but he slammed the door on his rage at the thought of his ex and everything she'd put him through. Rolling his shoulders, he shook it off. Mostly.

He rubbed his chin then dragged his stare away from Grace when Trevor hobbled toward them looking pale as death and pissed as a bull. His friend deserved what he'd got, not that Ben wanted him to get hurt, but what'd he expect? Even a cornered mouse would fight for its life.

Trevor tossed Ben her keys and mumbled something unintelligible when he levelled a glare her way.

If Ben wanted her to trust him, he had to convince her she could. Things between them had started off bad and gone to shit from there, but her being unMarked had thrown him for a goddamn loop. He'd never heard of it before. He hadn't lied about getting her answers, but the other part…

"Here." He handed the key ring to her. A boon. Whether she liked it or not, she was coming with them. She had to, he didn't have a choice, not that he *wanted* to let her go. But he needed her to think it was her decision. Forcing her was a last resort.

Her gaze sliced between Ben and his offering, the blue of her eyes so pale it was like an icy dagger that cut through him. Piercing. Hypnotic. She bit her lip.

His pulse pounded in his throat. *Stop fucking staring, Ben.*

She took them, gripping so tight her knuckles whitened and tendons strained under the pressure. Tugging her coat, she straightened it.

He pivoted and set his shoulder against hers. Her warmth slid into him when he guided her toward her car. She smelled good, soft like vanilla, and his mouth watered, craving a taste.

Shaking, she reached for the driver's side handle. "I want it to be public."

He trained his stare on her and cocked his head.

"Wherever we're going. I want it to be public."

His mouth angled up at the corner. Smart. He couldn't guarantee her shit because what came next wasn't his call, but smart, nonetheless.

"Jesus," Trevor complained. "He told you we're not gonna hurt you."

She rolled her eyes. "Okay, random stranger who cornered me in a dark parking lot. I'll be sure to take your word on that."

He bared his teeth. "You're gonna have to."

Fuck. Ben's mouth thinned into a hard line. His idiot friend was fixing to shred the only iota of trust Ben had swayed Grace to accept, and there was no goddamn way he'd let that happen. He slammed the flat of his hand against the roof of Grace's car. "Enough!" She flinched. The glare Ben threw Trevor's way must've been menacing because his eyes widened, and he took a half-step back.

A clank filled the night when the side exit of the hospital popped open and a handful of people stepped out into the poorly lit lot, their chatter filling the void as they headed for their vehicles. Grace's gaze followed them.

His gut tightened. *Don't scream. Don't scream.* He needed to distract her, fast. But it'd mean taking a chance…a big one, not that he really had a choice. He cleared his throat. "It's cold out, Grace. Why don't you climb in?"

Letting her get in ahead of him when she had the keys was a risk. Yeah, if she fled, Rodan could find an employee record of where she lived, but it didn't mean she'd be there when they went looking.

Her hand flexed on the handle once. Twice. She glanced his way. He offered a tight smile and hoped like hell his expression relayed some semblance of calm. She opened the door and slipped inside. The exhale Ben loosed was ragged.

"Don't," Trevor ground out, voice low.

Ben stormed around the car to the passenger side. "Don't what?"

His friend followed, shaking his head as he went. "I've seen that look before. Don't start this shit again."

He stopped dead and wheeled on him. "What goddamn look?"

"That one," Trevor said when he stabbed a finger at Ben's face. "You can't get attached to her. We've got no clue how this is gonna play out."

Ben's brows slammed down, jaw clenching. "I know what I'm doing."

The laugh Trevor let loose was pure acid, and it stung as it burned Ben's ego. "You thought the same thing last time too." He shoved his hands in his pockets and looked away. "I don't wanna watch you go through that again."

Ben relaxed his balled fists. Trevor was wrong, Ben knew what he was doing. He'd lost too much the last time. He knew what to look for, and he wouldn't be played for a fool again. Besides, Grace wasn't like Leah. Sure, he'd just met her but there was something different about her—a blue fire in her eyes that hypnotized him.

He clapped his hand on Trevor's shoulder and repeated, "I know what I'm doing." When he peered into the car, Grace stared straight ahead. "I'll call Elijah on the way. Take my SUV and follow us."

Trevor grimaced and gave a slight shake of his head. "She's stubborn, man. There's no way she's gonna be cool with what's about to happen."

Ben dropped his arm and cracked his knuckles one by one. She was gonna have to be because there wasn't any other option.

"And she better have a good reason for being unMarked, 'cause shit knows what Elijah'll do if he thinks she's fucking with us."

He wanted to argue but Trevor had the unfortunate advantage of being right. Dragging his hand through his hair, Ben rubbed the length of his neck. He didn't want to bring Grace into anything, but too many people knew about her Sight, so that ship had sailed. All he could do was protect her. And there was one person he'd make damn sure to protect her from.

Trevor stroked his beard, and as if he'd read Ben's mind, he said, "Gideon's gonna need to be there. You think you can handle that?"

Grabbing the passenger door, Ben jerked it open. "I can handle it." The vehicle dipped under his weight when he slid inside, cutting Trevor off as he sealed himself in with Grace. He pushed his seat back while she started the car, cranked the heat, and blasted the fans, their white noise filling the void until he broke it. "Call him."

Her face twisted and she rubbed her hands together. "Call who?"

Trevor was rigid as he crossed the twenty feet to Ben's vehicle and climbed in.

"Whoever's waiting for you." Ben's teeth ground at the idea of another guy anywhere near her. "And put it on speaker."

She bit her cheek, worrying it between her teeth when she pulled her phone out and selected the contact. It rang and rang again.

"Hello," some guy answered, voice high.

Shit. She has someone. Of course, she does. He sank deeper into his seat.

Her gaze skipped from him back to the phone. "Hey, Noah. I'm gonna be late getting home tonight."

"Oookaayyy," Noah said. "You stuck at work?"

"No. I'm…headed out."

"Ooh! With a boy? Scandalous. Tell me everything."

Ben's mouth pulled into a grin, and he fought not to laugh. So, *not* the boyfriend. That didn't mean she didn't have one, but if she did, it would've made sense to call him first. He rolled his neck. There was something about her. Something powerful. Sexy. Something he wanted. He wouldn't lose it, not like he had with Leah.

Grace pursed her lips, words stiff when she said, "I've gotta go."

"Fine. Keep your secrets," Noah replied.

"I'll see you later."

"I'm spending the night at Kyle's. Remember?"

She pinched the bridge of her nose between her fingers. "Right."

He laughed. "You're being weird, weirdo. Have fun and I'll see you tomorrow."

"See you tomorrow," she grumbled. They said their goodbyes and she hung up, then plunked her hands on the steering wheel and twisted them.

Ben leaned his elbow on the ledge beside his window then offered her every bit of his attention. "Who was he?"

Her mouth twisted, her heavy blush clear in the dark of the car. "My roommate."

God, she was gorgeous. Even her frown looked good. His stomach torqued. He didn't want her to navigate what was coming alone, 'cause it would definitely be a lot. She'd need someone to help her through it. Him. She was gonna need him. He smirked and cocked a brow. "Anyone else that's gonna look for you?"

"The cops if I go missing!" she said, tone rising half a dozen octaves.

The laugh he'd held back broke free. "I'll get you home safe, Grace."

"I'm glad one of us finds this amusing," she mumbled as she put the car in gear. "So, where am I going?"

He sobered and his spine straightened when he took out his phone. It was his turn to make a call. "We're about to find out."

CHAPTER 4
GIDEON

The woman—whoever the fuck she was—rolled off Gideon and sprawled on the couch beside him, her languid legs spread, still panting. He pulled off his condom and lobbed it in the nearby trash bin.

Fastening his black dress pants, he pushed up from the couch. She'd been fun for all of five minutes, but there wasn't anything of substance there. Vapid didn't begin to describe her. Her eyes were vacant, and she'd made it clear with the way she flaunted that body she'd used it to get by—not that he minded seeing he'd spent the last while enjoying it. She was pretty in the conventional sense, but so were a thousand other women in the bar outside his office.

He tucked his shirt in. His belt clanked as he latched it and strode toward the massive television on the wall that displayed footage from the cameras overlooking his club. The strobe lights pulsed as people danced and drank.

"This was fun," the woman said.

"Indeed," he replied, the words dry.

She pulled her skimpy burgundy dress down over her body and shuffled closer. "We should do it again sometime."

Unlikely, considering he had his pick of women every night. His life was better left untethered.

His stare caught on his reflection and locked on the tattoos that rose above the collar of his shirt. There were a lot more beneath the surface, torquing around his torso, a constant reminder of what he was and the tainted blood that coursed through his veins. Of the power that bound him.

The woman splayed her palm across his back. "I'd like to give you my number."

His phone pinged, a distinctive tone set for one person, and one person alone.

Elijah? He cocked his head and strode across the office to his desk, happy to put distance between them as he took up his cell. The single text on the screen had his brows furrowing. He read it again to be sure.

Elijah: *We have something we must discuss.*

He never heard from the guy unless it was about disciplining one of Gideon's people or some official shit like a Marking. Elijah had always been upfront with whatever was going on. As the Agent, it was Elijah's job to dole out punishments and share information across sides, but the sides *never* shared information.

Gideon: *Where? When?*

The reply was instant.

Elijah: *We're coming to you. Now.*

Gideon straightened to his full height.

Gideon: *We?*

No response.

Whatever was up must've been big for Elijah to bring it to Bedlam. It wasn't the Agent's protocol. Gideon flexed his hands in and out of fists because he didn't like surprises.

"I was talking to you," the woman purred.

Time to handle shit. "Apologies. Business calls," he said, the same line he'd used a with a hundred women before.

"Want my number?"

His laugh was hard because he didn't do repeats. He angled his head down and offered her a dark smile. "No."

She stared at him, then blinked in rapid succession before snatching her purse from the arm of the couch. Stomping toward the exit, she yanked it open. "Go fuck yourself."

He shook his head. "That won't be necessary, you did a satisfactory job."

Her jaw dropped before she growled and repeated, "Go fuck yourself!" She stormed out into the club, then slammed the door—or at least tried to, but it was bulletproof, reinforced steel and weighed a fucking ton, so the slow-close hinges meant her exit was about as lackluster as it got.

He huffed a dry laugh.

Before the door closed completely, Davis Reardon, the Head of Security across Gideon's properties and oldest friend, sauntered in. He wore jeans and a navy t-shirt; casual and ready for whatever shit might fly their way. The guy's indigo stare was sharp, and he had an intimidating as fuck demeanor like he was ready to punch you at any moment whether you'd earned it or not.

"She seemed nice," Davis said through a crooked smirk. He stopped a few feet away and clasped his tan and tattooed arms before him. "Elijah's here."

That was fast. Gideon rapped his knuckle on the desk. "Who's with him?"

"He's alone."

His stare narrowed as he grabbed the controller secured to his desk and then pointed it at the television, switching to the surveillance cameras focused on the parking lot of the club's entrance.

Davis edged closer. "What's going on?"

"Fuck if I know." Gideon slid his phone over so the guy could see the Agent's texts for himself. "We have the catacombs for this kind of shit. Why the hell are they coming here?"

Davis lifted a shoulder in a shrug, tied his black hair back at the base of his neck, then scanned the messages, his expression flat. "Elijah's been escorted to the conference room."

Gideon took a seat and the chair's leather creaked under his weight as he made himself comfortable.

"You're waiting to see who else comes?" Davis asked.

Gideon offered a sharp nod. "I'm not about to get caught unaware." The club was his life—the only thing that was his. He'd worked too hard to have Shepherd bullshit threaten it. And whatever approached had the potential to be a big goddamn threat.

Ten minutes later, three vehicles pulled into his lot, following tight to one another. He crossed his arms over his chest as his jaw clenched. The SUVs he recognized, but the car...Whatever the fuck happened that would require *their* presence at his club, he had no damn clue. The last two vehicles emptied. Trevor, Rodan and Jenna moved into the night.

Davis shifted and his boots groaned as he cleared his throat.

The car's passenger side door swung wide, and Benjamin Jones stepped out.

"What the fuck is he doing here?" Davis growled.

Gideon's muscles locked down, his movements rigid as he shook his head because he couldn't come up with any logical reason for it, either. To say he and Ben disliked one another would've been an understatement. The fact that they sat on opposite sides of the longest war in history aside, the piece of shit had issues, and coming from Gideon, that said something.

When the driver's side popped open, a slender woman came into view. He leaned forward. She was dressed in sleek yoga pants and a form-fitting black coat. And that body. *Sweet Christ, that body.* Her dark brown hair hung around her shoulders and ended in the middle of her back, but those eyes...

"Well, well, well," he crooned. "What do we have here?"

CHAPTER 5
GRACE

Grace squinted against the club's massive neon sign, it's buzz faint over the whir of traffic and chattering voices. The bright fuchsias, cobalts, and aquas stood in stark contrast to the dark, cloud-covered night and left tracers in her vision when she looked away.

She swallowed around the knot in her throat, breath steaming on the frigid air as she tipped her head toward the building. "What does Bedlam have to do with any of this?"

Ben stared off into the distance, his movements jerky as he shifted side to side. "It's not what, it's who."

She scratched the long line of her throat. "Who?"

"Gideon," he said, the name harsh on his tongue.

"Wait," she took a half-step back and her gaze darted around, "I thought we were going to see Elijah?"

"We are. You asked for public, so Elijah instructed us to meet here *because* of Gideon."

She nodded slowly. "Alright. And who exactly is Gideon?"

Ben's brow lifted as he and Trevor exchanged a look. She was about to push for more but the warning in his answer derailed that train of thought. "He's on the opposing team."

Opposing team? Her stomach dropped as she chewed the inside of her cheek because not a thing about that boded well. Whatever secret they guarded, whatever sides they referenced, whoever Gideon and Elijah were, it was big.

Trevor stalked closer joined by a pretty woman with deep chestnut brown hair and fawn-toned highlights. Rodan brought up the rear, the sight of him setting Grace's blood on fire.

She stabbed her finger at him. "You!"

"Good evening, Nurse Crawford," he greeted, voice level.

"Shove it," she growled then dropped her arm with a snap. "This is all your big mouth's doing."

"I didn't make you what you are," he replied.

Her daggered glare pinned him to the spot while her emotions readied to spill over. These people—whoever they were—had thrust themselves into her life, violently. Sure, she wanted the information they had, but that didn't mean she was impressed with their tactics.

Ben shifted into her line of site, then gestured to the other woman. "Grace, this is Jenna Gonzalez."

"Nice to meet you," Jenna said brightly before she asked the group as a whole, "Now, can someone please explain to me what's going on?"

Trevor chucked his chin to Grace. "We've got a problem."

A *problem*? If Grace were a cat, her claws would've extended. Her stare snapped his way, and while he didn't wither the way she'd hoped, he did angle his hips away.

Ben rubbed the back of his neck. "We should go. Elijah's waiting." To Grace, he added, "Just be careful around Gideon. His kind are dangerous. It's ingrained in them to use you. They shouldn't be trusted."

Grace's lungs seized and her legs grew weak. Gideon's *kind*?

His palm against the small of her back was heavy. Warm. "I'll be there. You're safe with me."

What he offered to protect her from was lost on her. Considering he and Trevor had stolen her away in the first place, if *they* were warning her about Gideon, he had to be trouble. Oh, God, what the heck was she walking into?

Her gaze fell unfocused. She was moments away from answers, moments away from unlocking a secret she hadn't known existed. But no matter how many steadying breaths she gulped down, she couldn't seem to ready herself.

Trevor moved to Grace's other side, flanking her.

"Have you been here before?" Ben asked, a strange note in his voice as he guided them into the line to gain access.

Her voice caught in her throat, and it took her a few seconds to force the words out. "Once or twice."

"Only once or twice?" Trevor said, the edge in his tone an accusation.

Jackass. She crossed her arms over her chest. "Yeah, ya heard me. Not all of us have the luxury of a social life." Losing her mother had handed her way too much baggage to survive the party scene—baggage that'd cost her Hector, the only boyfriend she'd ever had. "It was nursing school or bust."

Jenna winced. "That had to be rough."

Grace nodded. Hector had needed more than she was capable of giving…in so many ways. As it turned out, he hadn't been amenable to that fact.

Ben pushed ahead and held the door. "Let me do the talking."

Her eyes pinched at the corners when she passed inside and took the place in. A heavy bass thumped, vibrating the building. It crawled across her skin and settled deep into her bones. The air hit her like a wall, thick with the scents of liquor and sweat. Rolling lights cut across the room while people in varying levels of dress writhed on the dance floor.

"Stay with me," Ben said, his shoulders tense.

The bouncer, whose name tag proclaimed him as Darren, veered in front of Grace. "ID"

"We're expected," Ben growled.

Darren widened his stance, his words hard when he repeated, "ID"

The heat of a blush rose to Grace's cheeks as she reached into her purse. Withdrawing her wallet, she fished out her driver's license and handed it over, to which Darren spent an inordinate amount of time examining it. She tapped her thigh, about to offer to read it for him when he lifted the radio clipped to his shoulder, and spoke into it, words low. He handed her license back and leisurely stepped aside.

Her eyes adjusted to the vibrant chaos as she advanced, and a colorful prism of lights painted the club in its vivid hues. The floors on both levels were reinforced glass, crystal clear and shined to a perfect reflection. The second level had wine-colored velvet couches and scarlet leather chairs. It was modern with sleek edges, yet oddly warm and inviting.

Bars lined the perimeter while the dancefloor overflowed with people in every state of inebriation. Seats everywhere were full, as were the standing tables scattered about but not haphazardly, because nothing about this place was by accident.

Ben eyed his phone before he headed into the throng and called over his shoulder, "Elijah says they're in a conference room on this level."

Grace fell in step behind him, or at least, tried to, but a broad, imposing form cut in front of her. His large hand hooked around her waist and dragged her back several feet before he released her then blocked her path. He stood close. *Very* close.

Her gaze followed the crisp lines of an expensive black dress shirt, lips parting when she found the most striking man she'd ever seen. He towered over her, and the devil-may-care grin he offered had a sheen of sweat slicking her skin–one that had not a damn thing to do with the temperature.

His amber stare was flecked with metallic crimsons and golds, and it burned like writhing fire when it locked on her. "Like what you see?" he asked, voice a deep baritone. It rolled over her like honey—thick and enticing.

Her heart stuttered.

The black-haired man who flanked him hunted the faces around them, skimming over Jenna and the others before it fixed on Ben.

"Move, Gideon," Ben said through his teeth as he faced the newcomers.

Gideon's eyes never left Grace's. "I think not." He raked a hand over his strong, hard jaw that was lined with a controlled, close-cropped growth of facial hair. "Who are you, beauty?"

She angled her head and let her hair slip forward like a curtain, using it as a barrier because she needed something to shield her from his heat. *Hot. So damn hot.* "I'm no one."

He shook his head. "Oh, you're someone." His stare raked her up and down, scorching every curve of her body it touched. "What's your name?"

Ben's nostrils flared. "Elijah's waiting."

"The lady and I are talking, Benjamin," Gideon said as his chest rose and fell in an easy rhythm.

She bit her lip and slowly raked it through her teeth. She should've pulled back, but her shameless legs refused to cooperate. The air around them grew thick with tension, and if she wanted to move along… whatever the hell was happening, she needed to answer him. "Grace. My name is Grace."

He cocked his head and his clean-cut, dark ash brown hair fell to the side. "No."

She frowned. "Pretty sure I know my own name."

"No," he repeated. "I think I prefer Crystal with eyes like that."

The laugh she released was completely without humor. *Cocky bastard.* "Has that line ever worked?"

He smirked. "You tell me."

Her pulse kicked up to an unhealthy level. There was no way she'd answer that. *No. Way. In. Hell.*

Shifting, he veered closer. "I haven't seen you around before."

Ben edged tighter to Grace's side. "She's new."

Her gaze flicked to Gideon's wrists, but like her own, they were covered by the sleeves of his shirt.

He followed her line of sight. "There's no such thing as new with our kind." He took Grace's hand in his calloused, tempestuous grasp. His hold was unrelenting, yet gentler than she'd have anticipated.

She stilled as somewhere in the far reaches of her mind, Ben's warning about him rang out, but she couldn't quite seem to heed it. Or think. Or breathe.

"Let her go," Ben warned through his teeth.

Gideon drew the sleeve of her coat up with slow purpose, and a shiver skated down her spine. When his attention locked on her unMarked skin, his brows rose. "Tsk, tsk, Benjamin. Breaking some very dangerous rules."

"We could say the same about you approaching us," Trevor cut in.

"You came here," Gideon said, the words level before his tone turned thick with implication. "Besides, I wanted to meet Crystal."

Grace looked away. "You're obnoxious." And she totally meant it. Sort of. Mostly.

Ben gripped her arm and pulled it from the other man's grasp—something she sensed only happened because Gideon allowed it. Maneuvering her tight to his back, Ben shielded her. Being passed over like some toy sent her blood pressure skyrocketing, nor did she think between them was a good place to be.

When Gideon spoke, his voice darkened. "We mustn't keep Elijah waiting. Davis and I will escort you."

"I've got you," Ben said at Grace's ear as he offered a reassuring squeeze.

Gideon cut a path through the crowd, who parted like the seas when he aimed for the back of the club. Stopping before a reflective silver door, he pushed it open and held it wide, then offered Grace a wicked grin. "After you, Crys."

Ben entered, glaring blood-stained daggers at him while Grace fought the blush that simmered across her flesh. Gideon's bravado made it clear he was accustomed to women fawning over him because that kind of swagger was learned. She wouldn't–*couldn't*–deny he blew attractive out of the water, and while he didn't put off the typical dangerous vibe, there was *something*.

The navy-blue room she entered had a bathroom on the far side with a gender-neutral sign on the door. A long window occupied the opposite wall, while several polished chrome tables with high-backed, gray leather chairs sat scattered across the space. A copper-haired man wearing a flat, bored expression was seated alone nearby. His stare lingered on her.

"Elijah," Ben greeted as he pulled back two seats, lowered himself, then gestured for Grace to take one.

The others spread themselves around the space, taking opposing sides. When the door closed over and sealed them in, it cut off all sound from the club beyond. She swallowed hard. No calling for help. So much for a public meeting.

Gideon strode across the room and propped a hip on the window ledge. He folded his arms over his chest, shirt straining against the dense muscles of his biceps and shoulders. "What causes you to darken my door?"

Grace stiffened. *His* door? There was no way he owned Bedlam, no way.

He must've read the thought from her expression because he offered her a brash nod, and mouthed, *Mine.*

She choked on the air in her lungs, then coughed to clear them of not a damn thing. The smirk he offered was nothing short of amused.

Elijah faced him. "Where are the rest of your people, Gideon?"

He shrugged. "I'll disseminate the information I acquire as necessary."

Inclining his head, Elijah turned his attention to Ben. "So this is the woman you claim has the Sight."

Ben nodded. "She does."

"The woman can speak for herself," Gideon said.

Grace rolled her eyes. "The woman has a name."

He winked. "Indeed, you do, Crystal."

On fire. She was actually on fire. She had to be. There was no other explanation for the sensations that scorched through her. Whether that heat was welcomed yet, she couldn't say. But it was very real, very present, and unequivocally dominating.

"Crystal," Elijah said.

She sighed and rubbed her temples with her thumb and forefinger. "My name is Grace. Grace Crawford."

Elijah's brown eyes flicked to Gideon, and his brow furrowed in a censure before he returned to her. "Grace, I'm Elijah Jacobs. Explain to me what it is you see."

Down to it, then. Her arm lowered as she cleared her throat. Please, God let the answers they held be what she wanted...and let her figure out exactly what that was. "I see the dead and their Marks." She gestured to Ben. "And I see his Mark too."

Gideon's head cocked, spine straightening with slow precision.

"And what about Gideon's Mark?" Elijah asked.

She scratched her scalp. "I—uh...haven't seen it."

Elijah paused for several seconds, then flicked a finger, summoning Gideon. "Tell me what you see with him."

Grace squirmed when Gideon rose from his perch and sauntered closer. Her breath quickened as her gaze dipped, lingering on the edge of the ornate tattoos that climbed from beneath his collar. He tugged the thighs of his well-tailored dress pants as he crouched before her. Drawing his sleeve up his densely muscled forearm, he exposed his wrist.

Ben balled his fists, his knuckles white. His stare snapped from Gideon to her. "Is this necessary—"

Elijah raised a hand, silencing him.

"She should trace it," Gideon said as Ben loosed a dark laugh. "If she's been told what it looks like, she'll recite the description. Tracing it on my skin should be sufficient to prove their claims."

Ben's chair creaked angrily when he leaned closer to Grace. The muscles of her throat tensed and her mouth ran dry.

Elijah patted his palm on the table. "Trace it, then."

The self-satisfied quirk of Gideon's mouth had her hand twitching to wipe it off. *Smug jackass.* She rolled her eyes, his torment an oddly welcome distraction from the storm of emotions that careened through her when she lifted her hand.

What secrets did they guard? What door was she about to throw open? And would she like what awaited her on the other side?

Extending a finger, she set it to his scorching skin. His temperature bordered on feverish but there was no sweat on his brow, no sign it affected him it at all. She trailed the outlines of his Mark, her soft flesh making a tsh sound as it moved. It was black as night and then blacker still. The wings were leathery with sharpened, talon-like spines that protruded between the hide and their ends. Similar to Ben's, it curved at the top and bottom, forming a circle.

With slow progress, she followed every edge and angle, passing over the thick, corded tendons of his forearm. It looked old as time itself, worn, and like it'd been put there thousands of years ago. Her heart pounded in her ears as she eyed it with a mix of emotions she couldn't quite pin down. Enthralled? Awe? Panic?

"What is it?" she asked, voice barely above a breath.

A complete and overwhelming silence permeated the room. She glanced up. The others stared wide eyed, save Gideon, whose brows furrowed, scrutinizing her like she was some specimen that intrigued him.

She drew her hand back.

Elijah bared his own wrist then set his arm on the table. "And now mine."

Doing the same, she outlined his gray wings, which were a mottled combination of feathered and leathered, also arcing to form a circular shape.

"Hmm." His lips pursed. "You have the Sight, a gift only those of our world possess. You see the things those blooded of this world cannot." He withdrew and folded his palms in his lap. "But before we go further, I'm required to clarify something. Everything you learn and everything you see regarding us is to remain secret. This is non-negotiable. I am the Agent who's tasked as the middleman. This," he indicated his symbol, "Marks me as such. What Ben bears is the Mark of the Nephilim." He tipped his head to Gideon. "And his is the Mark of the Lesser Daemonium."

Grace's heart thudded as it slammed against her ribs with its staccato beat. *Wait, what?*

He set his elbows on the table and when next he spoke, her world, the very fiber of her being tore to shreds, leaving tattered remnants strewn about. Pieces she could never reassemble because she would never be the same.

"The Nephilim are the children of Heaven, half-human, half-angel. And the Lesser Daemonium are the children of Hell, half-human, half-demon."

CHAPTER 6
GRACE

Grace's breath rasped as it burst from her. Sweet Jesus. Half-angel and half-*demon*. Her gaze darted to Gideon and away. She swallowed around the lump in her throat, then swallowed again. Answers. She'd wanted answers. *Why* had she wanted answers? She'd considered a lot of possibilities: a club, a weird cult, or something, but not that. Never that.

Some piece of her had always wondered about Heaven and Hell. How could she not? For her mother's sake, she wanted them to be real…well, wanted the former to be real. But having that reality smash her in the face was something else entirely.

She had two possibilities before her, either they told a terrifying truth, or they were more delusional than she was. Neither was good. She needed to get out of there. Fast. Five people were positioned between her and the exit. She was midway through calculating her chances of making it past them when Elijah pulled her back.

"We need to learn who you are, Miss Crawford."

Her head snapped back. "Who I am?" she asked, voice high while her hands clamped over her thighs. "I'm a nurse at Arillia Hospital. I'm Grace Crawford. I'm no one."

"You are most definitely not no one," Gideon rumbled, then narrowed his eyes. "Too many double negatives."

Davis gave a sharp nod.

"Go back to your perch, Gideon," Ben scoffed.

"I'll move if the lady wants me to move."

Grace tried to control her erratic heartbeat but failed miserably. Any thoughts of temptation, of his magnetism were obliterated. Dead and buried. All that was left was distrust. Fear. *'His kind are dangerous…They shouldn't be trusted.'* Ben's words rang like a death knell in her mind. Demons were dangerous. Demons shouldn't be trusted.

She offered Gideon the full weight of her feeble stare. "The lady wants you to move."

He smiled and his eyes lit with mirth as he rose then returned to his post by the window.

A frayed strand of tension released from the invisible noose around Grace's neck, but barely. Outnumbered as she was, her chances of escape were slim.

On her mental list of things to do, she scribbled:

- Figure a way out of this crap.
- Buy scary weapon…or mace. Or both. Definitely both.

Maybe if she answered their questions she could get out of Dodge and figure the rest out from there. That was a plan, and she desperately needed one of those. She faced Elijah. "What do you need from me?"

"An answer as to why you are not Marked to begin with."

Her stomach sank. Not a good start. "I don't have that answer."

His palm patted the table again. "Who are your parents?"

"My parents *were* Scott Morgan and Wyla Crawford."

"Those names are unfamiliar to me," he stated. "They're gone?"

Her gaze lowered as she fought, kicking, and screaming against the ache that rose in her chest at the reminder and at how alone she was in that moment. So crushingly alone. "They are."

"And they never discussed any of this with you?"

Was there a spotlight on her? She could've sworn there was because his questions sure sounded like an interrogation. She clasped her hands to hide their shake. "No. I didn't learn about it until I was eighteen, by then both of my parents were gone."

That got everyone's attention. Across the room, spines snapped straight, and eyes widened. Light from a passing car washed through the space, casting ghostly shadows along the walls from the bodies within.

Trevor's glare homed in on her. "Not possible. We're born with the ability."

The grimace she offered was so deeply embedded it would probably be permanent. "I wasn't. It started when I woke up after the accident."

"Accident?" Davis prompted.

Her eyes flicked to the Mark identical to Gideon's on the inside of his wrist. Her voice was even when she answered, "Accident. Don't ask me about it because I don't remember anything." For so many reasons, she didn't want them to ask.

Jenna pursed her lips before she questioned the room as a whole, "Could that have triggered the Sight?"

Elijah shook his head. "Our blood is our blood. I don't see how that's possible. Nevertheless, we'll need to check *The Chronicle* and obtain her Collection to learn who Miss Crawford is."

Learn who she was? Grace raked her hands through her hair as the words took on a whole new connotation. The walls closed in, constricting her ribs, and crushing her lungs, making it hard to breathe.

"I'll need access to see what I can unearth," Ben offered.

"Granted."

Grace's knee bounced wildly because she itched to run. To get as far from their madness as she could possibly get. "What will you be looking for in this *Chronicle*?"

"Your bloodline and parentage," Elijah answered.

"I just told you who my parents wer–"

"They suspect you could be adopted," Gideon said, then arched a brow. "Or kidnapped."

She grabbed the edge of the table when a wave of dizziness hit, and her world spun on its axis. If that was true, there was a chance her mother had lied to her. That her mother had lied about everything.

"Either would explain why she wasn't Marked," Rodan agreed.

"And her lack of knowledge," Ben said.

Davis shook his head. "But not her previous lack of Sight."

Ben glowered at the two half-demons.

Jenna tucked a stray strand of hair behind her ear. "It's a place to start."

Trevor laughed without humor before he mumbled under his breath, "She could still be lying."

The room fell deathly silent.

His attitude was seriously ticking Grace off…more so than before, which said something. The night had already gone well past sideways, and his mouth only made an untenable situation infinitely worse. He wasn't within kicking range, so her smartass sass it would be. "What's your problem, asshole?"

Gideon's lip tipped up at the corner.

"You're my problem. You're *all* of our problem." Trevor folded his arms over his chest and canted forward. "If you're lying and you're not a Shepherd like us, there'll be a price to pay."

The window ledge groaned under the force of Gideon's grip.

"Enough, Trevor," Ben ground through his teeth.

Grace's shoulders tightened, her elbows pinning so tight to her ribs it hurt. "What kind of price?"

"We have a duty to uphold, Grace," Elijah said. "If it's determined you've managed to deceive us, that you are not one of us, you will be killed."

When the words sank in, they sank in deep. Killed? *Run. Run. Run.* She had to get away. Sweat slicked her skin when she pushed as far back into her seat as she could go. "I just proved I can see."

"Regardless, the warning must be issued. No one outside the Shepherds can know of our existence. *The Chronicle* may take some time to retrieve. In the interim, you're to learn as much as possible before you're placed and sworn to a side."

Her phone was a lead weight in her pocket. If she could just send a message to Noah, he'd get help. His boyfriend, Kyle Garret, was a cop with the Arillia Police Department. He'd sic them on the Shepherds, get her the heck outta there. But they weren't likely to let her send an S.O.S.

Her gaze flicked around the room and landed on the bathroom door as an idea formed in her mind. She cleared her throat. "Sworn to a side?"

Gideon rolled his neck on his shoulders. "Once they figure out which of us you belong to," he raised his Mark for her to see, "you'll be branded like us."

Which one of them she belonged to. How was it possible things had just gotten worse? She could be like him. Heaven above, she could be like *him*.

Elijah rubbed his temples like his life depended on it. "Gideon." His stare slid from him to Ben. "I want both of you to teach Miss Crawford about your sides."

Gideon inclined his head. "And what if she's dual?"

"We'll cross that bridge when we get to it. Either way, she'll need to know these things. Show her a Calling."

"What's a Calling?" she asked as she scanned the room for alternate roads to freedom.

Ben rubbed his palms together and suggested, "It might be easier to show her."

Elijah's mouth pinched. His hand closed into a fist and gently knocked against the table while he considered her. He inclined his head. "Very well. Do it now. Nephilim first."

The smile Ben offered Grace when he rose might've been heartwarming if the threat of death hadn't hung like a slicy, stabby guillotine over her head.

Jenna, Rodan, and Trevor joined Ben, facing the far wall near the exit. He dragged up his sleeve and exposed his Marks, then tapped the wings closest to his wrist. "This is the Absolution Mark. Anyone who carries it is Nephilim. It lets us summon the Saved." At her narrowed gaze he added, "The dead bound for Heaven."

Her stomach roiled. Yes, of course. A summoning tool. Why hadn't she thought of that?

"Hey," he said, pulling her gaze. "You'll be alright, Grace."

Alright? She wasn't sure she'd ever be alright again, which meant she held not one ounce of his confidence when she nodded.

The Nephilim withdrew gold daggers hidden in their clothes. Oh, weapons...lovely. They brought the metal to their skin and sliced a thin line. Grace's pulse quickened when their blood seeped free and they used the knife's edge to spread it over the Absolution Mark.

The wings rippled, shimmering metallic and radiating like they were illuminated from within. The tissue of their wounds weaved together and stemmed the flow of their bleeding. She snapped to her feet.

"The blades are Heaven kissed. They heal any cut made into the Absolution Marks," Ben told her.

She swayed. The air around them quavered, glowing iridescent and surging like steam rising from the sea. Silhouettes began to appear, mist swirling as they took form throughout the room, too many to count. Souls of the Saved.

She edged back until she butted against the wall and gave it her weight. Her chest heaved as her palms splayed over its cool surface. God above, she didn't want to look, but she couldn't look away.

"The Absolution Marks call to the dead on this plane," Ben said. "Our mixed blood is what connects us to Heaven and Earth; the human part through this world, and the angel through the next." He indicated a symbol with three rings that nested inside one another halfway up his forearm. "This is the Gateway Mark. It opens the way." He swiped his blood-coated blade over it.

Frost dusted the room, creeping through every corner as it wrapped around her flesh. The cold oddly enticing. Clean. Pure.

Light sparked at the periphery of the souls then hovered above the ground when it flared to life, growing brighter and brighter. The air inside it rippled like a pebble dropped in a still pond, spreading wider before it spanned several feet across and grew transparent. A rift appeared at its center and fissured until a vast opening materialized. The archway was gilded, like the cuffs the Saved bore. And through it all was more light, endless, and calm. Like the gold of an evening dusk, but softer somehow. More inviting. It was the most beautiful thing she'd ever seen.

She hadn't expected it. Them. A "we help the dead resolve their issues" kind of thing, sure. But Heaven and Hell and opening portals to other freaking dimensions? Never.

Shapes materialized from the depths of the light, subtle outlines of beings that were unequivocally not human with white feathered wings that flared wide from their backs.

Ben pointed further up his arm. "This is the Passage Mark. It grants the dead access to the other side."

The Nephilim trailed their blood across it, and light burst to life in the center of the Saved soul's chests. It consumed, taking them in until they faded from the world. A breath later their silhouettes reappeared inside the Gate as they crossed over to eternity.

Grace's knees grew weak, and she started to slide down the wall before a warm hand gripped her elbow, catching her. Her head whipped to the side. Gideon's expression was impassive, but his amber stare blazed as it locked on her.

Demon.

What if she was like him? Did she even want to know? Could she handle it? The last two answers came easily. No and hell no. Things had gone so far off the rails she'd lost sight of the tracks. Between the threat of murder and her potential lineage, she was out. O-U-T. Out!

Her breathing was shallow, sharp. Its harshness clawed at her throat, slashing its way through her lungs. She couldn't get air. She couldn't —she…

Risky or no, she had to take a chance. She drew her arm from Gideon's grasp and glanced away. Her stomach rolled, then rolled again. She settled her palm there. "I think I'm gonna be sick."

His lip tipped up at the corner. "We can't have that now, can we?"

Ben's glare pierced him before it landed on her. "Shit, Grace. You're pale."

"I've got to—" She covered her mouth with her hands, pretending to gag like she was ready to heave. Which wasn't terribly far from the truth.

Gideon tipped his head toward the door in the corner, voice impassive. "There's a washroom there."

Ben made for Grace, but Elijah shook his head. "Close the Gate, Benjamin."

Trevor moved in. "I'll take her."

Wait, what? Take her? No. Her plan wouldn't work if she had a freaking escort. Especially a Trevor shaped one.

"Be sure to hold back her hair, Trevor," Gideon drawled.

"I can manage," Grace mumbled. *Please let me manage.*

Trevor opened his mouth to say something that would likely earn himself another junk kick, but Jenna scurried to Grace's side before he could get it out.

"I'll go," the other woman volunteered.

Crap. Not ideal, but workable. Sure, Jenna had a weapon, but Grace could overtake her if she needed to. Possibly. Maybe if she tripped her or knocked her out with something... She just had to buy enough time to type a text. That was all she needed.

The bark of laughter that escaped Trevor was dark. "Keep an eye on her," he warned Jenna. "She's trouble."

Grace's shoulders sagged. *Son of a–*

"Feel better, Crys," Gideon drawled, shifting his weight as her offered her a devastating wink.

Jenna stepped to her side then set a hand on Grace's shoulder as they crossed the room. "Hold on. You're almost there."

Had Jenna not been aligned with the people that threatened to kill her, Grace might've liked her. But she was, so...awkward. Trevor stayed tight to their backs, a shadow haunting her steps. He was so close, his rank cologne burned her nose.

"Don't do anything stupid," he told her.

Every fiber of her being wanted to lash out, tell him she'd already done something stupid when she'd decided to go with them, but that was counter to her goal. Instead, she angled his way and feigned a retch.

His bulging-eyed horror when he jumped back brought a minute sliver of joy to her frantic little heart.

"Leave her alone, Trevor." Jenna shoved the bathroom door wide, guided Grace inside and locked it behind them.

The room was open with only one toilet, no stalls, or dividers; nowhere to covertly send a message. Bad! A jolt of adrenaline exploded through Grace at the sight of the window on the far wall. It'd be a tight fit, but she could wiggle her ass out of it...she just needed to get to it.

Walking to the sink, she turned on the tap to cover any noise she might make, then steeled herself. She didn't want to hurt Jenna, but if it was the difference between living and dying, she'd do what she had to. Still, she'd need to catch her by surprise before Jenna could get to her dagger. Grace fisted her hands, readying.

"Give me your coat," Jenna whispered so low Grace had to strain to hear it.

It took several long seconds before her brain caught up to what was said, and her brows plunged in a furrow. "Huh?"

"I at least need to make it look like I *tried* to stop you."

Hope stumbled like a clumsy fawn in her chest. "Wait, you're gonna let me go?"

She nodded. "I get it. This," she gestured about them to their situation as a whole, "is a lot, and the way they're coming at you is wrong." Her eyes darted to the door. "But we do need to make this look real."

Grace froze, a new worry taking root, because if Jenna was aiding her escape… "Are you safe? You can come with me if you want."

A genuine smile took Jenna, one that reached her eyes. "I promise, I'm in good hands."

Grace had no clue what to make of that but nor did she have time to parse it out.

Jenna mussed her own hair, then undid the top button of her shirt and yanked the rest of it askew. Grace peeled off her jacket and passed it to the other woman. Stepping onto the toilet seat, she unlatched the window, and eased it open. The frigid night air struck her like a slap in the face, stinging her skin. She winced against it, but it was a small price to pay for freedom.

"Ready?" Jenna asked.

She took a slow inhale, then nodded.

"Grace, no! Stop! Ah!" Jenna yelled before she kicked the wall with the heel of her boot. "Don't!"

A heavy thump pounded against the door, startling Grace. Her footing slipped and she grabbed the window ledge, holding on for dear life.

"Open the door," Trevor's muffled voice commanded.

Ha! Like that was gonna happen. Glancing back, Grace mouthed *Thank you*.

"Stop!" Jenna screamed as she snapped Grace's coat in the air.

"Open the goddamn door!"

Time to move. She hauled herself up and clambered headfirst out the window where the snow and ice-crusted asphalt loomed five feet below. Letting go, she crumbled to the ground in an ungraceful heap of hair and limbs, grunting at the impact. She'd be decorated in a colorful array of bruises the next day, but at least she'd be alive.

Scrambling to her feet, she peered back as Davis burst into the bathroom. Shards of wood exploded inward followed by the door itself. Trevor staggered in behind him and cursed a string of epithets that might've made her blush if she hadn't been so occupied with keeping her feet while she fled.

"Grace!" Ben yelled, but she didn't stop. *Wouldn't* stop.

Her hands fumbled as she yanked her keys from her purse, dove inside, then disappeared into the night.

CHAPTER 7
THIRTY-SEVEN

Thirty-Seven's eyes skimmed the courtyard, seeking her. He stood under the astronomical clock tower as it ticked its count. It was somewhere after midnight, and each second that passed pounded like a drum in his chest.

Boom. Boom. Boom. It pulsed heavy against his ribs. Where the hell was she?

The scent of evergreens from a park across the street were sharp on the wind, and his breath torqued like a storm as it steamed in the cold air. Fitting for what was about to come.

His recruiter approached. Her heels clicked on the ice and salt-covered brick while she sashayed through the crowd. He let loose a heavy exhale. Her dress coat sat open, exposing the skirt that cut mid-thigh, and the crop top that bared her stomach. Not exactly weather appropriate, but she didn't seem to mind. Neither did he.

She flipped her platinum blonde hair over her shoulder while she offered anyone that looked a baiting smile. Always seeking her next objective. He crossed his arms over his chest. His jaw ached from the force of clenching it when every guy in the vicinity checked her out with a carnal hunger.

The things she did to him.

"Vicki," he said as she stopped in front of him.

The smile she offered was a warning and a promise.

She was a dangerous woman, the type his common sense told him to run from, because she had power, a seductive magnetism he'd never been able to turn away. She was trouble, the kind that made him slam the door on that logical part of his brain. The woman was a wild carnival ride he'd never been able to walk away from.

And he never would.

His stare pushed past her then slid from one shady character to the next. "I thought you said the historical district was the safest part of the city?"

She laughed, high and light. "Do you know anything about Trenton, my pet?"

He fixed his attention on her mouth. The things it could do... "Should we be so out in the open? I can't be seen in this territory without the proper permission."

She sidled closer and grazed her lips along his throat. "We could've done this in Arillia."

His laugh was dry. "No, this is a better testing ground. We'll move it there when the time comes. Gideon's hold on his people is too strong."

At the mention of the other man, her eager mouth curled up.

His blood ignited. Ryczek had everything; looks, money, power, and any woman he wanted to fuck at the snap of a finger. He was a hard guy to compete with. But Thirty-Seven had his own assets.

Clamping his hand around Vicki's waist, he jerked her close. If her languid smile was any indication, she didn't mind. "You can't have him."

She pouted. "What if I ask nicely?"

He crushed his mouth to hers, his tongue punishing as it broke past her lips and dominated her own. A small moan escaped her, one that begged for more, but he'd learned long ago that to hold her interest meant playing her games. Twisting a hand in her hair, he snapped her head back. Torture, push, pull. Just the way she liked it.

"Ryczek's busy tonight. He's out hunting," he said.

Her chest rose and fell in feverish pants while she studied him.

"We found an unMarked Shepherd."

"UnMarked?" she asked, voice rising. "That's possible?"

He nodded. "Apparently. She's on the run. Elijah ordered us to search the city."

"And you're not helping? Naughty, boy." She pressed in. "Do you like breaking the rules, my pet?"

For Vicki, always. The corner of his mouth lifted, part smirk, part affirmation. His hand roved to her ass and gripped it when he pushed the hard length of his cock into her stomach, showing her just how much he liked it. She shimmied against him, and he groaned.

"What about the woman?" she purred.

He really needed them to take things somewhere private. He cleared his throat. "She's being looked into."

"Good." She tapped his chest with the tip of her nail. "The Primary completed the brands."

His spine went rigid. Holy shit. Thirty-Seven had waited on those words so long, he wasn't sure they'd ever come. The Shepherds would finally learn what it was like to lose control.

"You have them?" he asked, working to restrain the anticipatory edge that crept into his tone.

The smile that took her when she raised her hand and wiggled her index finger was pure feline. "This one's mine." Opening her purse, she pulled a ring from its depths, displaying it for him. "And this is yours."

He leaned forward, attention never leaving the ring as she delicately placed it in the center of his palm. He examined the Latin script along its band that read "Claimed," admiring the intricacy of the small mark's design. The ring's cold metal felt good when he slid it on and rolled it around his finger. "When do we start?"

"Tonight." She nudged her head into his neck and raked her teeth along his flesh, grating them over his well-earned five o'clock shadow. "We're awaiting the Primary's instructions, but I suspect we'll be doing some hunting of our own."

He arched his back and drew his navy wool coat over the front of his pants to hide the effect she had on him.

The Shepards needed to be destroyed, just like they'd destroyed every member since the beginning of time. The Faction couldn't fail, because if they did, nothing would change and the Shepherds would own them for eternity. And if they were caught…

"I'm ready," he said.

Her hand slithered between them then grazed his hard length, her grin wide and saccharine. "Oh, I know you are."

His tongue licked out. "This is big."

"No, pet. This is *it*." She pulled back an inch. "I've given the Primary your contact information. He'll be in touch shortly."

"Will he be joining us?" He hoped so. It'd be an honor to meet the man who'd orchestrated this plan.

"That's not possible. Nothing changes. We hold to our protocols now more than ever. We can't risk the Faction being discovered."

"You and I meet," he replied.

Her lip curved in a wanton expression, and she trailed her palm down the front of his coat. "We've known each other a long time."

He rolled his shoulders as his phone vibrated in his pocket. His hand snapped inside, tearing it out. He wouldn't miss this call. "Hello?"

"Who are you?" the man on the other end commanded.

"The Thirty-Seventh member," he answered, using the Faction's order of joining confirmation.

"This is your Primary. I'm pleased to inform you the final holding location has been secured."

Thirty-Seven tried to cool his rising adrenaline. Until that moment, their plans had been just that, plans. Talk. But he was sick of talking. A malevolent smile took residence across his lips. He was ready for the Shepherds to fall, to burn, to reap what they'd goddamn sowed. "And the location works?"

"That's what you're about to find out. You and your recruiter are to test the brands tonight. Choose your targets carefully. Make contact when the task is complete. I'll have people in place to send the dead on." There was a rustling on the other end. "Get comfortable with using them, Thirty-seven. Your position will be pivotal when the true outfall begins."

He flexed his free hand into a fist to contain himself as he scanned the vagabonds around them. "How does the brand work?"

"Touch the Mark to skin."

His head cocked. "That's it?"

"That's it." There was a smile in the Primary's voice when he said, "Begin immediately."

There it was: the command he'd been waiting for. The Primary had come through on his promise to the Faction. The balance was about to be shifted, and it would be shifted in their favor.

He steadied his breathing and nodded. "Yes, Primary."

The click on the other end was the firing of a gun at the start of a race. He slipped his phone into his pocket then tipped his head toward a homeless couple that argued where they huddled together under a blanket nearby. "Time to go make some friends."

CHAPTER 8
GRACE

"Half-angel and half-demon?" Noah harsh whispered.

"Yes," Grace hissed as she tucked her phone between her shoulder and ear, then scurried from the main office of the motel she'd looked up. It backed onto Trenton's historical center, the safest section of the city. Being there put her far enough away from Arillia she shouldn't be found, but close enough to get back if she ever figured her craptastic situation out. Her gut told her it was right, or as right as anything could be in that moment.

Making a beeline for her room, she dodged the windblown trash and an exceedingly intoxicated man who staggered by, the scents of alcohol and urine wafting off him on the cold night air.

"I have one suggestion. Run! Run far, run fast, and run long because these people are delusional."

She frowned. "I *am* running! Have you listened to nothing I've said so far?"

"Sorry, I was probably distracted by all the talk of demons! I can't believe Gideon Ryczek is one of them."

"*I'm* one of them." She swallowed hard. "Wait…how do you know who Gideon is?" Her hands shook when she slipped the key into the lock of her door, and it rattled against the metal. When the door opened, she burst inside, slammed it closed and twisted the deadbolt into place. She was about to secure the chain, but the screws that should have held it in place were either loose or nonexistent.

"How do you not?" Noah said. "Never mind that he's in the society pages of the Arillia Times every week, but he's one of the wealthiest people in the city, and I'm in *finance*."

"Thanks for the input, Grandpa." Grabbing the rickety chair with a worn-out wicker seat from the small desk in the corner, she jammed its back under the door handle.

"Did anyone follow you?"

She snapped the curtains closed, then peered through a small crack between their musty panels. The burned-out bulbs in the lampposts surrounding the parking lot did nothing to help her see. The only thing that offered any illumination was the muted yellow light from the motel's front office.

"I don't think so. I've been driving for hours. I took a ridiculous route to get here."

She'd have ditched and headed for the hills if her entire life wasn't centered around Arillia. Tears stung the backs of her eyes. She'd have to get a new job, find somewhere else to live. She'd lose the house. Even splitting expenses with Noah, there was no way she could afford the mortgage *and* another place at the same time. All because those Shepherd asshats had forced her to bolt. No, she couldn't go there, not yet. Those were later problems.

She sniffed. "Mom had to know something."

"You didn't find anything in her papers?"

Her shoulders sagged. "It was all legal stuff."

"And what about her old laptop?"

"It just had a bunch of files labeled for taxes." She sighed. "Where's Kyle?"

"Sleeping."

Good. It wouldn't help to have him aware of anything. "What am I gonna do?"

"Where are you? What's the name of the motel? I'll come to you."

"I'm in Trenton. But I won't ask you to do tha–"

"You don't have to ask, Gracie. Let me tell Kyle and the others. We'll get the APD involved and come get you."

And that's why she loved him because he was there, no matter what. He'd always been there. That didn't change the facts though. "And tell them what? The truth? They won't believe me." Sure, she'd been ready to call them for help earlier to get herself out of Bedlam, but the truth had *never* been on the table. Sharing that would put her right where she'd feared all along, in the crosshairs of crazy–hers and the Shepherds. "I'll lose everything."

"If you go through with this plan, you've lost everything anyway."

The words struck like a punch to the gut, and she raked a hand through her hair. If she ran, there was no way she could use her real name again. The Shepherds would easily hunt her down. But without her name, her nursing license was useless. She'd lose her career, her income. There'd be nothing left.

Her lungs burned, each breath like a trail of acid as it rolled through her. When Ben and Trevor cornered her, they'd said something about Sects and territories. Which meant there were more of their kind out there.

"You can't just vanish," Noah said, voice strained. "Your graduation lunch is tomorrow."

She pulled her phone away from her ear, frowned at it as if it were him, then replaced it. "I think there are more important things than a graduation lunch, Noah."

"Yeah, but did you forget that literally everyone else in attendance at said graduation lunch will be a cop? You don't think Kyle, Tara, Ivan, Charlotte, or *Jake* will ask questions about where the heck you are? I'm a terrible liar. They'll figure out something's wrong. Whether you want it or not, either these Shepherds or your friends are going to come looking for you. You can't hide."

Rubbing her forehead with the heel of her palm, she worked to alleviate the headache that'd set in behind her eyes. She couldn't run forever, not that she even knew how. But would the Shepherds ever stop coming for her? Would they circulate her image through their twisted network? So many questions with not a single answer.

She had to carry their blood. There was no other explanation for her Sight. No matter how hard she worked to convince herself of that fact, she wouldn't get confirmation of it until *The Chronicle* was retrieved. A wave of anxiety crested, constricting her chest because the reality of that answer terrified her to the far reaches of her soul. Yet what if...what if she *wasn't* one of them?

She didn't want to walk away from everything she knew, everyone she loved. Everything she'd worked for. But was it worth the risk to stay?

"God, Gracie. Just let me help."

"I—" She stepped away from the window and threw herself down on the bed. A cloud of dust rose around her like a miniature sandstorm, and she loosed a raucous string of coughs. When she finally regained herself, she continued, "I don't know what I'm gonna do, Noah. I need to think. Just...go to lunch with the others tomorrow. Carry on as normal until I figure things out."

The exhale he released was frustration and exasperation rolled into one.

"I'll text you in the morning."

"No. You'll tell me the name of your motel now and call the second you wake up. If I don't hear from you by eight, I'm telling Kyle."

She snapped into a seated position. "What the heck, Noah?"

"Someone needs to know where you are. I promise I won't come to you, but those are my terms."

Her mouth hung open, catching the dust particles that continued to swirl. She swiped at her tongue and coughed again. "If you were here, I'd hurt you."

"Why do you think I'm brave enough to make this threat?"

In spite of the situation, a small smile tugged at the corner of her mouth. It ebbed a smidgeon of her spiralling emotions. Her best friend didn't make threats–he made promises. And while that promise only added to the layer of troubles she faced, it felt good to have someone in her corner—someone who cared what happened to her.

She sighed and filled him in as her body slumped in on itself, then said goodbye, praying whatever she decided to do didn't destroy everything she cared for. That it didn't destroy her.

GRACE GROANED as she fought to ignore the voices threatening to pull her from sleep. They were muffled but annoying. When consciousness filtered in, she bolted to her feet, tripped on the blankets, then crumpled to the floor in a painful heap.

"Ow," she moaned as her head slid around and she took in the room. She was alone, but the voices still carried, coming from outside. Disentangling herself from her cloak of mediocre warmth, she dashed to the window.

She peeked out and frowned at the couple who clutched each other as they shuffled across the parking lot. Their gate was unsteady. Jerky. Not from intoxication, more like neurological impairment.

"What's wrong, Cor?" the woman complained, the words muted by the window and broken as if there was a cognitive gap in forming them.

He pushed her away, then swung a fist, aiming for something or someone that wasn't there. "Go away."

"Who you talking to?"

"Get back, Elise!" he said, or at least, that's what it sounded like. "Go away!" He struck out at his invisible enemy again. His fist's momentum torqued his body and twisted his leg. He lost his footing and collapsed, landing on his side, body going stiff as a board before he broke into a violent fit of convulsions.

The spit and vomit that slipped from his mouth reflected the lobby's dim light. *Not good.* Grace bolted across the room, threw on her pants and shirt, then shoved her feet into her shoes and snatched up her phone.

As she passed the window heading for the door, her stomach dropped, and her spine went rigid. She stopped. A soul materialized over the downed man's deathly still body, like mist it crawled, taking form above him. Three gold cuffs encircled his right arm, with two snakes on the left. Her eyes narrowed, and she pushed her sight when a new symbol came into view at the center of his chest—one she'd never seen before. It was red and circular bearing a cross and several other symbols too far away to recognize, along with writing at the center in a language she couldn't understand.

"Cor?" Elise nudged his side with her boot. "Get up, Cor! Corey, get up!"

A blinding flash of lights cut through the gap between the curtains, followed by the distinct crunch of tires against ice and asphalt. Grace blinked several times until the streaks that painted her vision were gone. The last thing she wanted was to end up in the middle of *more* trouble or worse, get in the way if it was an ambulance—not that it mattered anymore.

The vehicle was pointed directly toward her. Two people climbed out, their forms backlit by the headlights. It cast their faces in shadow and rim lit them in a whitish glow. They advanced but made no move to help.

"You?" Elise stumbled then crouched at Corey's side. "What are you doing here?"

"Following you," a woman replied. Her shrewd voice was thick with an implication that chilled Grace to her bones.

"I don't see the Mark," a man said, standing closer to the vehicle, his words muffled against its engine.

"You're not supposed to. It'll let us to go unnoticed. Protect us in the long run." She set her hand on his shoulder. "We must trust the process, pet."

Wait...did they mean the red Mark? The one Grace *could* see? What the hell did that mean? If that was true, if they had the Sight, could see the dead, then they had to be Shepherds. Her mouth watered when a wave of nausea crested. She pointed her phone down so the screen's glow didn't draw attention.

"Let's get this done," the man said. "I don't want to linger."

"Hey, what the heck did you give us?" Elise asked.

"What you need." The menace in the woman's tone sent a shiver down Grace's spine she wasn't sure could ever be warmed. The woman ran her silhouetted finger down the length of her compatriot's coat.

"Now for the real test." She maneuvered around Corey's body, her steps silent as she came to stand over Elise. Gently, she rested a hand on the other woman's head before her fist locked around Elise's hair. "Thank you for your contribution."

Grace clutched her arms to her chest when an ominous pit took root in her stomach, one that set her teeth on edge.

The woman shoved Elise, and she careened into Corey's soul. The instant they touched, Elise bucked, gasping before she collapsed on top of his body. Her mouth hung open like she was trying to call for help or beg for mercy. Corey's soul grew thicker, less transparent, as if it was getting...stronger.

Elise's breathing grew agonal before it stopped altogether. She fell still and the strangers pushed back to give a wide berth. Elise's soul appeared, and Grace's throat seized around the scream she held back.

Sweet lord. It was as if...as if Corey's soul had *taken* Elise's strength. No, not just taken it, drained her until she was dead. *Dead*!

"Holy shit," the man said. "This is going to work. This is going to fucking work!"

The reverence in his tone opened an immeasurable chasm of fear in Grace's chest. Because his words were confirmation that whatever had just happened, whatever they'd done, it'd been intentional. And the only context under which that made sense was if they referenced a plan. And whatever that plan was, whatever its end game, it was bad, craptastically bad.

The woman brandished a phone, and Grace peered deep into the night, trying to catch her features, to catch something. *Anything*. But with the glare from the car's lights, it was impossible. "This is Twelve. It's done. Send them through."

Less than a minute later the souls vanished. Grace flinched as she choked on the air in her lungs, biting her tongue to hold back her horror-stricken whimper. They could see the dead. They were Shepherds. Very dangerous Shepherds who were only steps away. Close. Entirely too freaking close. *Shit. Shit. Shit.*

The two peered around the lot. Grace dropped to the floor and drew her knees to her chest, trying to offer herself the comfort she sought and failing miserably.

Her mind careened in a thousand directions at once. What had she just seen? The only thing different was the new Mark. It had to have something to do with it.

"Take me home," the woman said as she let loose a tinkling laugh. "You should get back to Arillia before you're missed."

He was from Arillia. God above. Had Grace met him? His voice was too obscured to gauge. God, she'd been running from the Shepherds and instead, stumbled into an even deeper cesspool. Was this some sick joke? Some bizarre twist of fate? A punishment?

The car doors closed, and the lights moved away, leaving her alone with the shadows of her room, and doubt, and terror, and...

Gideon. Her sights honed in. Sharp. Ben said she couldn't trust his kind. He was half-demon, born of hell. Poison ran through his veins. She rejected the possibility of that poison claiming her because that was all kinds of inconvenient. But if it wasn't him, he knew who it was. He was darkness, evil. It was the only explanation. It had to be.

The idea of facing the Shepherds, of learning who and what she was, made her sick. Literally. She scrambled to her feet, retched, and bolted for the bathroom. Dropping to her knees before the toilet, she upchucked the contents of her stomach, violently.

No matter which way she turned, the choices before her sucked. While running was still on the table, it no longer felt viable. If what the strangers said was true, if there was some plot to use souls to suck life from the living, then Noah and everyone else she loved was in danger.

She raked her hands through her hair. She couldn't just stand by. She wouldn't be able to live with herself if she walked away and something irrevocable happened. But who did she tell? Who could she trust? She had no damn clue but sitting on the bathroom floor of a motel room in Trenton, she wasn't about to find out.

Leaning over one final time, she vomited, swiped her mouth with the back of her arm, rose on unsteady legs, and left.

CHAPTER 9
GRACE

Grace sat alone at a large restaurant table, the scents of fried meats and peppered spices thick on the air. Her mouth watered and her stomach growled, loudly. She hadn't eaten since…when *was* the last time she'd eaten? She had no clue. A fact that partially explained how her terror had morphed into a dogged anger. *Or hanger? Definitely hanger*. Maybe if she ate something she wouldn't feel so vengeful and stabby. Less stabby was good.

Placing her butter knife down, she swapped it for her phone and stroked her thumb across its screen. Her chair creaked as she shifted, eyeing the door while she waited for—

"Noah!" She flapped an over-eager hand to get his attention.

His face was ashen like he hadn't slept. That made two of them. When he spotted her, he dashed in her direction, his snow-dusted coat cold when he threw his arms around her.

"Thank God," he breathed. "I was so scared."

"We talked this morning," she wheezed through his crushing hug. "Where's Kyle?"

He exhaled slow and long when he pulled back. "Parking, but he'll probably be a few minutes. They're plowing the lot."

That worked. Dropping into her seat, she got comfortable. Or as comfortable as the wooden monstrosity would allow. "I need to get in contact with the Shepherds."

"Just call the hospital and get that doctor's number."

"Rodan?" She shook her head. "If I call asking for his personal information while I'm off duty, it'll start rumors with the staff. I'm gonna need my job, so I can't afford issues."

He shrugged. "Then that only leaves one other option."

She crossed her arms over her chest like a sullen child. "But I don't like that option."

"Well, it's your only option."

"We've already established the options I have."

He grinned. "We have, haven't we?"

For so many reasons, the idea of contacting Gideon scared her. But if she really intended to do this, to hunt for answers, then she might as well dive in headfirst. She brought up her web browser and searched Bedlam's contact info.

Noah's hand rested over hers. "Once you open this door, there's no going back. I'm not gonna tell you what to do, but whatever you choose, just make sure you think it through."

Her face twisted. "Why the heck do you think I talked to you?"

He laughed and pulled back his arm. "I do offer sage advice."

"The sagest!"

He cocked his head. "Is that even a word?"

"It doesn't feel weird when I say it."

"That's our language standard now?"

"Did we have one before?"

"I think the better question is, do we have any standards?"

Laughing, she crossed her legs and smoothed the creases in her navy pencil skirt. There wasn't a shadow of doubt she could trust Noah with her secrets, nonetheless, she needed to warn him. To protect him. "You can't tell anyone about this. *Anyone*. If they're willing to kill me for not being one of them, I can only assume the same would apply to you. I don't want to drag you into this anymore than I already have. From here on out, I'm on my own. I can't—"

He shook his head. "You have to talk to me, Gracie. You're my no-matter-what."

The warm smile that spread across her lips reached so far it touched her heart. "We're here for each other, no-matter-wha–"

"No. You have to tell me everything, no matter what!"

She frowned. "That's not what that means."

He stabbed a finger on the table. "It most certainly is for the convenience of this conversation. This world you're stepping into is dangerous. I want you to talk to me. You don't know these people. Someone outside should be aware of what's going on with you, just in case."

She wanted to argue, but the level glare he wore told her he would accept no less. He wasn't about to leave her to the Shepherds, a lamb for the slaughter. He loved her too much. She was his family, and he was hers. She meant what she'd said, the last thing she wanted was to put him at risk, but he had a point. The idea of cutting him out sounded smart in principle, while in reality...

The single nod she offered him was slow. She took a steadying breath, tapped Bedlam's number, and tried to fight the sudden rise of heat that enveloped her as it rang.

"You've reached Bedlam, this is Lisa speaking. How may I be of assistance to you?" the woman answered, voice lilting and pleasant.

"Can I speak with Gideon Ryczek, please," Grace replied.

"May I ask who's calling?"

Time to sink or swim. She swallowed hard and pushed past the clamp that'd tightened around her vocal cords. "Grace Crawford."

Noah released a heavy breath.

"Please hold," Lisa said, and the line clicked. A second later, it rang again. Noah grabbed her arm and pulled her closer, forcing her to share the phone so he could eavesdrop.

"Hello, Crys," Gideon's deep voice crooned. A loud hum whirred in the background—one that sounded like tires on pavement.

Noah drew back and mouthed *Crys?*

Straightening in her seat, she brushed her hair back from her shoulder and threw her palm over the receiver. "Crystal. For my eyes." She removed her moist hand. "Hello, Gideon."

Noah did a mini dance of delight when he jerked her closer again.

"I thought we'd lost you," Gideon said. "Are you safe?"

Was that really what he cared about? "I'm at lunch with friends. Surrounded by many, many people."

He huffed a laugh. "I'm glad to hear it. To what do I owe the pleasure?"

She cleared her throat, then cleared it again...and again. "I want to come back."

The tick-*tick,* tick-*tick,* tick-*tick* of a signal light tolled. "You're welcome at Bedlam anytime, beauty."

She sighed and stared at the ceiling for patience. The man was infuriating. *Infuriating*. "Not to your bar, Gideon. I want to come back to the Shepherds."

He laughed, low and rich. There was a shuffling, the creak of leather, then the heavy, distinctive thunk of a door closing. "I'm pleased to hear it."

"What's going to happen to me when I do?"

"Nothing."

HA! "That's not how it felt last night."

"Nothing will happen, Crys. I promise."

Trust the promise of a half-demon? She'd done many dumb things in her life, but that would never be one of them. She didn't need to touch Gideon's fire to know it would burn. "Don't do me any favors." She glanced toward her lap. "Elijah said something about me learning from both of you..."

"Indeed, he did. Why don't I come get you now? I'll gladly teach you everything I know." The words were so thick with implication it was a wonder they'd slipped from his tongue.

Was it hot in the restaurant? It sure felt hot in the restaurant. It must've been because Noah fanned himself too. *Don't let him get to you, Grace. You've got a job to do.* "I'm sure you would," she mumbled. "I need to get a message to Elijah."

"Your wish is my command."

Noah's tongue flicked out like he might lick the phone. She scowled and shoved him away, then added another silent memo to her to do list:

- *Give bestie a serious talking to.*

Before she could even start to understand the depth of her situation, she had questions to ask and many, many things to learn. Having Gideon be her first—scratch that—*starting* with him didn't seem productive. She needed to clear her head. Discover what she could about him so she might better gauge exactly what kind of trouble he was and whether her suspicions over his involvement with the new Mark were warranted. For that, she knew exactly where to begin. "I'd like to arrange a meeting with Ben this evening."

"And what about our meeting, Crys?"

"Um. I'm not sure." She bit her lip. Smooth, Grace. Real smooth.

"What's your work schedule?"

She could lie, tell him she had shifts, give herself more time to get her head right. Yet somehow with him, she doubted there'd ever be enough. "I'm five days on, four days off with alternating day and night shifts."

It was his turn to pause. "Then I'd like to reserve you for tomorrow at noon."

How did he figure that—

Crap.

Noah grinned from ear to ear. Judging the way his hands twitched, she was sure it took every ounce of strength he had not to clap.

She flicked her nail before tearing at its loose cuticle. "Tomorrow. Please have Elijah call me. I have to go."

"Have a wonderful lunch, Crys."

"Goodbye, Gideon." She hung up, set her phone on the table, and turned her glower on Noah. "There's something wrong with you."

He rubbed his hands together. "Demon-boy sounds just as good as he looks."

She had to fight the bark of laughter that threatened to escape at the nickname before she scoffed, "You can't talk like that. He's trouble and you're taken."

"First, you don't know that and second, I may be taken but I'm not dead." He steepled his fingers. "I look forward to meeting these men."

Her head canted. "What makes you think you get to?"

"Listen, I have rights. At this point, I'm as invested in what's happening as you are."

She clamped his lips shut with her fingers.

He leaned back in his seat and broke free of her miniature prison. "Kyle's coming."

She cocked a taunting brow. "Yes, we should definitely be quiet. We wouldn't want him to think we're strange."

"He already thinks it. I'm trying to make sure he doesn't *know* it." His stare drifted toward Kyle, a smile in his eyes. "I bet he parked close."

"Of course, he did. You complain about walking through the snow to no end."

Noah grinned. "Yeah, I do."

Kyle shrugged off his black winter coat as he pushed through the main entrance. His keen, cop's stare scanned everyone and everything before he headed their way. Claiming the seat beside Noah, he placed his jacket over the back of his chair and set himself down. The dark gray suit he wore complimented his ebony skin and fit his tall, toned frame well as he commanded the space he occupied. "The others just pulled up."

"Wonderful. The sooner they sit, the sooner we eat," Grace proclaimed as she steepled her fingers in glee. *Hungry. So freaking hungry.*

"I don't know why you're so excited. You're only gonna get chicken fingers," Noah grumbled.

"She's excited because she loves chicken fingers," Kyle said, voice even.

Grace offered a fervent nod. At least *someone* understood her.

Noah waved a flippant hand. "You should be ashamed of yourself, Gracie. We're here to celebrate you graduating and joining the adult world, and here you are ordering off the kids' menu."

"Chicken fingers again?" Charlotte cut in. She swiped the melting snow from her spritely auburn hair as she and her wife, Tara, took their seats.

"Has she ever ordered anything else?" Ivan taunted when he dropped into his chair and smoothed the strands of his dense black beard.

"Watch it, Singh," Grace said, using his last name as she mock scowled.

The last one to take his place on Grace's other side, was Jake. He must have come straight from the detachment because he was still in uniform, complete with his nameplate that read "Constable Owen." She cringed at the weight of the stares that darted their way. Cops were an undesirable presence at the best of times, least of all in a pub.

"Did you have to wear that?" Tara scolded, the militant cut of her sandy brown hair shifting forward as she bowed her head.

"I'm on break. This was the only way I could make it," he said and offered Grace a lopsided smile.

Inclining her head, she glanced away, the weight of his attention too much, as it usually was. Not that she felt unsafe, but the things they wanted from one another did *not* align.

Kyle's tawny stare found Jake. "How's the shift?"

"Busy, as usual. I'm not sure how long I'll be able to stay," he said, apologetically. He leaned closer to Grace. His ash-gray eyes held hers and she squirmed under the weight of them. "Congratulations on graduating. Sorry I couldn't make it to the ceremony."

Her movements were jerky when she waved off the apology. "It's fine. The rest of this lot were loud enough to make up for your absence."

"Yeah, we were!" Tara chimed in, and a raucous wave of laughter rolled around the table.

Grace grinned. "You guys are something."

Noah raised his chin. "Don't give us that sass, Gracie, or I'll be forced to take back your graduation present!"

Her face twisted. "You didn't give me a present."

"My presence is your present."

"We live together. Your presence is compulsory," she said as a waitress placed glasses of water around the table.

Jake reached into his pocket and pulled out a small, rectangular box. His shoulder brushed hers when he set it on the table beside her. Her stomach twisted into a deep knot before he informed her, "It's from all of us."

Oh, thank God! Her heart tripped and stuttered its way back to a normal rhythm. The last thing she needed was to turn him down in front of their friends. Nothing dampened the mood like public rejection.

Noah nudged her foot under the table. She casually drifted her attention his way. She knew her best friend better than she knew herself, so when their eyes met, his message was clear. *He wants you baaaaaaad.*

Her lips pinched. Returning to the task at hand, she tore open the present like the savage she was. When she lifted the box's lid, a fancy schmancy pen with the words "Nurse Crawford" engraved on the clip sat inside. She traced her finger over the letters, admiring its sleek beauty. It was such a simple, thoughtful gift that her chest warmed. "Thanks, guys."

Humble as ever, Tara patted herself on the back. "It was my idea."

Kyle picked up his menu. Unfastening the buttons on his dress coat, he set his free arm over the back of Noah's seat. The movement casual, yet tender and caring.

Charlotte snickered, pulling Grace back to the conversation. "None of us are dressed well enough to go to Prime."

Ivan barked a laugh. "None of us are *rich* enough to go to Prime."

Grace cocked her head. "What's Prime?"

"The swankiest restaurant in town," Jake said as he thunked his elbows on the table's edge.

"That's probably why I've never heard of it," she replied, only half-joking.

Noah's hand skimmed over Kyle's short, jet-black hair while the two sat locked in quiet conversation. Grace inwardly sighed. What would it be like to have someone look at her the way they looked at each other?

When she turned back, Tara's narrowed gaze was trained on her. "Jealous, Grace."

Maybe. Not of them, but of what they had. She laughed, trying to shrug it off. "Something tells me I'm not their type."

But Tara was the "dog with a bone" kinda cop, so that wasn't about to fly. She threaded her fingers together and linked her hands before her. "Have you ever dated?"

A heavy blush seared Grace's cheeks. Oh, sweet Lord. Not that conversation. Anything but *that* conversation. Least of all in front of Jake. She was mortified. Absolutely mortified.

Charlotte elbowed her wife.

"What?" Tara said.

"I've dated," Grace replied, indignant on her own behalf. It would've been easier if she had some kind of high ground, or a track record, but on those fronts, she fell woefully short.

"Not since you've known us," Ivan noted. "When was the last time you saw someone?"

Her chin dipped and she grimaced. "It's been a while."

Noah raised a hand, interjecting. "His name was Hector. They broke up in her second year of nursing school."

Grace's mouth dropped open. She considered stripping him of his best friend title right then and there while she offered him a glare. *Traitor*. The grin she received in answer implied he felt no such treachery.

"That's quite the dry spell," Charlotte said through a wince before she took a long swig of her water.

Grace looked away, wanting to be anywhere but under the microscope of the five cops at the table. "I had my reasons."

"So, you broke up with him?" Ivan said.

Her hands scrunched her skirt. By the time most people started their careers, they had some semblance of a romantic life. Or at the very least had one on the horizon. Hers was well past DOA. She had no doubt her friends meant well, but they were police through and through. They weren't about to quit until they got an answer that satisfied them, so she gave the only one she could manage. "I don't like losing people." Her voice was colder than she'd intended but it didn't make the words any less true.

Silence fell long and drawn. Jake's hands flexed so tight, his skin creaked and turned white from the strain while Charlotte pinned her wife with a glare.

"Shit, Grace." Tara's eyes pinched at the corners. "Sorry."

Grace shook her head and fought the sting of tears that burned the backs of her eyes. Tara was a good person, she just didn't realize the floodgates she'd pressed on.

After Hector walked out, Grace hadn't had the strength to try with anyone else. She'd meant to...at some point. Maybe. But her friends hadn't come into her life until after—she swallowed around the lump in her throat—losing her mother. They didn't get who she'd been before. What she'd become after. The chasm of pain she'd sealed shut started to crack. Thinking about her mother was too damn much.

Please let it go. Please, *let it go,* she silently begged them.

Kyle flipped the page on his menu with far more vigor than necessary. "Everyone figured out what they want to order?"

Grace shot him a grateful smile before he tipped his oval-shaped face down to read. Or pretended to. Who knew? Either way, she welcomed the break in tension with open arms as everyone fell back into easy banter.

Orders were placed and when everything arrived, Jake raised his glass. "To Arillia Hospital's newest ER nurse."

The others joined in, thrusting their drinks high.

"And to the best friend a man could ask for," Noah said before he added in a shaky voice, "Your mom would have been proud."

Grace's breath shuddered while she gripped the stem of her wine glass like it could keep her grounded. It couldn't, but the weight of Noah's hand when it clutched hers under the table did the trick.

Jake's radio chimed, and he cursed under his breath. "Time's up." Leaning in, he slipped his arms around Grace's waist. "Sorry to cut and run."

She tensed and her eyes widened. It took her a second to reciprocate his hug before he pulled away and she offered him a tight smile. "Duty calls."

His mouth curved at the corners before he grabbed his things, said his goodbyes, and left. The heavy thump of his service boots pounded as he headed to the front counter to pay his bill.

"That was awkward," Noah said through an over-dramatic grimace.

Grace let loose a heavy exhale that blew several strands of hair from her face. "I have no doubt he'll make someone happy someday, but that someone's not me. He's a great guy. I like him, just not that way."

Tara sucked in a sharp hiss. "*Ouch*."

"She's entitled to feel how she feels," Charlotte said.

A pang of guilt twisted Grace's stomach while the trickle of cool condensation rolled from her glass down over her fingers. "I'm not trying to hurt him."

Ivan shook his head. "You're not sending the wrong signals. He's just hoping you'll change your mind."

Jake chucked his chin and flicked his dark brown hair from his face as he handed the hostess some cash. He was a decent-looking man with the capable, strong presence cops usually had. She meant what she'd said, he was a good guy. She couldn't explain why she didn't feel anything for him, but it was what it was.

"Forget about it, Gracie. We've got other things at hand," Noah said. "'Cause we're gonna celebrate all…night…long."

"Not too late." A grin slipped across her lips, and she shimmied her shoulders. "I'm a working girl now."

Ivan furrowed his brow. "You know that doesn't mean what you think it means, right?"

CHAPTER 10
BEN

Ben parked his SUV outside the Home Brew coffee shop Grace had suggested in Arillia's city square. It was about as public as public got. He'd been jacked about her reaching out to join the Shepherds, until he learned Gideon had been her first point of contact.

Why the hell she'd called that piece of shit… He unclenched his jaw and let the thought drop. The last thing he needed was to show up in a rage and scare her away again. Besides, she might've called Ryczek, but she'd wanted to meet with *Ben* first. That win was his.

He jammed his vehicle into park and shut it off. The sun was nearly down, so the clear glass windows of the café were easy to see through. Grace sat in the far corner, her hair was down, hands wrapped around a steaming mug. Those icy-blue eyes scanned everyone in the place. She was looking for him.

A smirk spread across his face. Popping his door open, he climbed out.

A bell buzzed when he crossed inside. She glanced his way as he approached, and a small smile took her when she spotted him. His chest tightened. Jesus, she was beautiful. She was like the damn sun, her presence lit the room and it was almost painful to look at her.

"Grace." He pulled out his chair, took a seat and angled closer as he set his forearms on the table. *Don't overdo it, Ben.* He relaxed the set of his shoulders. "Let's try this again, shall we?"

She laughed. It wasn't much, but it was better than her diving out another window. He wasn't about to say it, but that shit had stung bad.

She leaned back in her seat and clasped her hands in her lap. "Thanks for meeting me. Did you want something to drink?"

"I'm not here for the coffee," he said, putting as much insinuation in the words as he could manage.

She blushed. Deep. That was good. He liked knowing he could affect her like that. He raised his chin. What else could he make her do? "I was surprised when Elijah contacted me."

Brushing her hair back over her shoulder, she exposed the long lines of her neck. He followed the v of her shirt collar down and tried not to stare at the curve of her breasts, but sweet Christ they were perfect.

"I'm surprised Gideon passed the message along."

His stare snapped up and he went rigid. The sound of the guy's name from her mouth had his anger spike. *Keep cool, Ben. Keep fucking cool. You'll shut her down if you lose it.* He flattened his sweat-slicked palms to the cold table. "He's compelled to," he replied, because like hell he'd ever give the guy credit. He wanted her thoughts as far from Ryczek as possible. Peering at her from the corner of his eye, he forced the edge of his mouth up. Forced it hard. The hum of voices around them drowned out any potential bleed of their conversation, regardless, he kept his words low. "Time for an education."

Her head tilted. That hair slipped forward and the visual of her straddling him while it curtained his face flashed across his mind.

"An education?" she asked.

He cleared his throat. "There's a lot you need to know. First thing's first, I'm Benjamin Jones, Head of the Arillia Territory Sect of Nephilim." He extended a hand.

She moved slowly and her gaze narrowed as she shifted in her seat. Leaning forward, she took it. Her skin was warm and soft, and he had to fight the urge to hold her there, especially when she blushed. Again.

He gave her hand a slight squeeze, then released her. "Let's start with the basics. Do you have other family?"

She shook her head. "Noah, but he's not blood."

A twinge of irritation twisted his gut. The idea of her living with another man, whether he was gay or not, grated on him.

"What about you? Do you have family?" Her palms wrapped around her mug, nails tinking against it before she took a long drink.

"If I do, I don't remember them."

"What do you mean?"

He shook his head. "Our kind are handed over by our mothers at birth, raised by the Shepherds, then educated and trained until we begin our service."

The wince she wore was cute as hell. "Given over by your *mothers*?"

He inclined his head. "Only the female Cherubim and Dark Seraphim are permitted to conceive."

Her grip tensed on the cup. "And what are they?"

You idiot, Ben. He'd backed himself into a corner because he didn't have a single fucking answer that wouldn't freak her out. His mouth ran dry. "Angels and demons."

She rubbed the back of her neck and her eyes darted to the exit. "And why..." She cleared her throat. "Why are they the only ones permitted to conceive?"

He hadn't thought about that stuff for a long-ass time. Being discarded by your mother wasn't something he enjoyed looking at too closely, but if it'd get that "I wanna bolt" look from her wide eyes, he'd say whatever the fuck he needed to. He shrugged and let loose a dark laugh. "Ripping infants from human mothers would draw too much attention to our world."

Her shoulders dropped, and when she spoke, her words were soothing. "I'm so sorry."

Back on track. His heartbeat kicked up a notch. *Oof.* That attention. He fucking loved it. He wanted more. "It's all I've known."

"It's just wrong. You were only children." Her mouth turned down at the corners. "What about your father?"

"I never met him." *The piece of shit*. "What about your parents? You said your mom died a few years ago."

Grace looked away. "She was killed in a car crash."

"I'm sorry," he said as he echoed her sentiment, hoping to draw her gaze. He didn't like her attention anywhere but on him. Wanting it back, he opened his mouth to change the subject but was cut off before he could.

"Grace?" a familiar voice called.

Her face lit up, then fell immediately. Her eyes landed on Ben before they flicked back to the other woman.

His hand twitched when Jenna stopped beside their table. Her voice was thick with tension when she said, "You came back."

He supposed the unease made sense considering Grace had man-handled her just the night before. And who knew what'd been said between the two when they were in that bathroom alone?

Grace nodded. "I, ugh…I should probably apologize for what happened. I just–"

"It's fine," Jenna said, tone rising as she set a hand on Grace's shoulder. "I would've been freaked if it were me."

When Grace squeezed that hand, white spots flashed in Ben's vision, and he infused as much *time to leave now* into the stare he gave Jenna as he could. And she might've gotten the hint if she'd been looking.

"What are you doing here?" Grace asked her.

Jenna reached inside her navy-blue winter coat and pulled out a lanyard with her work pass on the end. "I'm an archivist for the city. I work across from that high-end hardware store around the corner. I just finished up for the day."

His blood burned a path through his veins. It was his time with Grace. *Mine. Move. The. Fuck. Along, Jenna.*

"You should join us." Grace offered.

Shit.

Jenna glanced his way. Stuff with Grace was still too tenuous. He didn't need to ruin things by tearing Jenna a new asshole. Plastering on a fake-as-shit smile, he nodded and used his foot to nudge a chair back for her.

She opened her coat and sat. "How are you doing, Grace?"

Why hadn't he thought to ask that? *Dammit.* She might think he didn't care. He'd need to work on that. Leaning forward, he gave Grace every bit of his attention.

Picking at a loose thread on her sleeve, she said, "I'm alright, I think. Who knows? I'm still wrapping my head around everything. I have so many questions."

"What do you want to know?" Ben cut in. "Ask anything." There, that'd show her he was open, that he gave a shit.

She tipped her head down and pointed at his forearm. "About the Marks…"

He rolled up his sleeve and exposed them.

Reaching out, she set her finger to his skin and bit her lip. His cock twitched. Christ, he *had* to chill. An erection straining his pants wasn't what he needed. *Want, yeah. Need, no.*

Jenna peered around, but Ben didn't care. No one outside of them had the Sight. They'd likely think Grace was being handsy, or that they were together. He was good with that. Would he have done it if Elijah was there? Abso-fucking-lutely not. But the Agent wasn't, which meant Ben was in charge.

"So, this is the Absolution Mark," she said as she traced it. Her touch trailed from his wrist to the center of his forearm. "This is the Passage." She moved higher and stopped just under his elbow. "And this is the Gateway?"

He swallowed hard, trying to get his damn throat to work. His voice was rough when he said, "Yes."

"Are you the only one who has it?"

His pulse kicked up. "Only Sect Leaders are granted access to the Gateways. Not everyone can be trusted with what sits on the other side." He smirked inside. *See, you can trust me, Grace.*

Her eyes flared wide, and he had to fight from stopping her when she drew back her hand. "And what about the Marks on the dead? What do they mean?"

A woman and her child walked by, passing too close to their table. He followed them in his peripheral vision until they were gone. "The ones on the right arm belong to us. They're the *Remissibilia Peccata*."

The laugh that escaped her was high, and she vigorously rubbed the back of her neck. "And what are those?"

"It's Latin for forgivable sins." Jenna elaborated. "Bad, but not *bad,* bad."

"And the ones on the left arm?"

If Jenna hadn't been there, he'd have said more, but her presence was a complication. "Elijah's ordered me just to share the Nephilim side of things. I'm capped with what I can say, so that's on Gideon to answer." Just the mention of the guy had his heart pounding in his ears.

Grace worried her lip between her teeth, and her eyes fixed on something across the room like she was thinking. Hard. "Am I in danger with him?"

"Yes," Ben said, the answer swift. Forceful.

Jenna pursed her lips. "He's not going to *hurt* you."

Grace's gaze bounced between them. "What am I missing?"

"Lesser Demons are manipulative," he finished. "You saw how Gideon was the other night. He's always looking for a way to reap the benefits of his situation."

Twisting the sleeve of her shirt between her fingers, she bit the inside of her cheek. "And what benefit would I present?"

"His kind seek any advantage they can find. That and he likes women. A lot. You'd just be added to his collection."

She glanced down.

"The guy's got a reputation for screwing anything that moves." Ben slid his hands into his pockets to hide his clenched fists. "You can't trust him, or any Lesser Demons for that matter."

"Careful, Ben," Jenna warned. "Elijah's rules."

His jaw locked down so hard he thought his teeth would break and he had to stifle the growl that wanted to rip from his throat. He took a beat to consider his words before he offered Grace the full weight of his attention. "Let's try this this then; the Nephilim fight for Heaven and the virtue of mankind."

Her voice hitched when she uttered, "And Gideon fights for Hell." Her piercing eyes rose to his. "I get the sense your distaste for him is personal?"

Jenna's hair jolted when she looked away.

Why was Grace so interested in the guy? He thought he'd been clear about everything, but apparently not clear enough. He'd fix that. Angling back, he gave the chair the rest of his weight. "Hard not to be when he slept with my fiancé."

Her lips parted, and she sucked in a shallow breath.

Hold up. Had that made it sound like he was still engaged? "I ended things with Leah as soon as I found out what happened." The smile he offered her was empty. "Gideon likes taking what isn't his."

"Is Leah still a part of your Sect?"

"She's not a Shepherd," Jenna answered.

Grace's head cocked. "I was under the impression all of this," she gestured between the three of them, "was supposed to be kept quiet."

"It is," Ben said. "I told Leah I worked for the church." He lifted a shoulder in a shrug. "Just not in what capacity. People can't know the truth of our world."

"But why?" A line creased between Grace's brows when she frowned. "Wouldn't it serve them better if the truth was out there?"

Jenna shrugged. "If they knew Heaven and Hell were real, would their choices be from want or necessity?"

Grace pursed her lips but nodded. She blew out a heavy exhale and tipped her head toward Jenna's name badge. "So how does that work? You having a job *and* being a Shepherd?"

"Because I live off-compound—"

"Wait." Grace stuck her hands out, palm up, then dropped them. "Off-compound? What compound?"

Ben clutched the inside of his pockets so he didn't cross his arms over his chest. The last thing he needed was Jenna saying too much and ruining his progress. If he wanted control of the conversation, he was gonna have to take it.

"It's where the majority of the Nephilim live," he said. "Anyone who doesn't have a traditional job usually helps out with the Hall of Shepherds where our kind are schooled."

Grace's eyes slid his way. "And how do you afford to pay bills? Survive?"

Jenna shifted like she was about to add more but that wasn't her call. *He* was the Sect Leader. Elijah had instructed him to talk to Grace, so he decided what was shared and what Grace was ready for.

"They pay us." He shifted and levelled a savage glare Jenna's way.

Taking the hint, she grabbed her purse and pushed back from her seat. "I should probably get going, Grace. But listen, my job gives me access to information. If you ever decide you want to, I can help you research your parents."

Grace paled like she'd been punched in the gut then nodded and offered a tight smile. "Thank you."

Jenna walked away, *finally*.

Ben slipped his hands from his pockets. "Everything alright, Grace?"

She set her chin in her palm. "All this talk of my parents just has me..." She sighed. "Either the mother and father I grew up believing in weren't actually my family, or mom kept a pretty dark secret from me. No matter which way I slice it, she hid the truth. I've gotta find out why."

He wrapped his palm around her dainty forearm, enjoying every goddamn second of it. "Don't worry about that yet. We'll need to go to *The Chronicle* before you can get those answers anyway."

Eyes narrowing, she asked, "Why?"

He winced. *Not good.* "To make sure their names match what you've been told."

Her shoulders sagged, and she twisted her drink, staring at it for several seconds. "What did you mean before when you said the Nephilim *fight* for Heaven?"

His fingers flexed against her. "This is a war." She pulled herself from his grasp. *Shit. Fix it, Ben. Fix it!* "The majority of it's perpetrated through influence, so the Nephilim try to lead people towards salvation."

"So your purpose is to sway people to your side."

"That's part of it." He angled closer. "But at the end of days, it's our job to fight and protect Heaven and its souls."

Her laugh edged on hysteria as she peered toward the ceiling.

Too far. You went too far, Ben. Walk her back. "It's alright, Grace. I'm here to guide you through this. I promise, you can trust me."

The tension around her eyes eased, but barely. Not enough for him to relax. He stilled when an idea hit. Maybe scaring could work in his favor, as long as she was scared was of the right thing. He needed to make sure if she ever ran again, it was towards him. He smiled inside. "When *The Chronicle* arrives, we'll figure out which side your blood belongs to. But someday, Heaven and Hell will face off in the war to end all wars. If Heaven wins, it means deliverance. If it's Hell, then it's the end of days."

Her hand dropped to her stomach, and her throat bobbed as she swallowed.

There it was. Time to move in for the strike because he wouldn't lose to Gideon. Not again. Sitting up straight, he squared his shoulders and put as much confidence into his next words as he could. "Our blood makes us who and what we are. It determines *everything*, Grace. Never forget that."

CHAPTER 11
GRACE

Grace paced the living room as she peered at her watch. 11:43 am. She hadn't heard from Gideon. She'd waited for a call or text or *something* to confirm, but there'd been nada. And no chance in hell was she about to call him. She'd agreed to meet, if he missed it, that was on him. There was no way he'd show though, considering he didn't have her address. Maybe he'd forgotten. Her spine straightened. *Rude, but possible.*

Withdrawing her phone, she checked the screen.

"Waiting for someone?" Noah teased from the entrance of the room.

She rolled her eyes, glanced back at her watch, then ran her fingers through her hair to smooth it for the thousandth time.

"It'll be alright, Grace," he said. "You wanted answers, you're getting them."

She threw her hands in the air. "Yes, but now I need the right answers." The new Mark had devastating potential. While she'd learned a lot from Ben the previous day—things that'd left her world weary and tired—it wasn't nearly enough. What he'd shared about his mother had struck the deep, shattered pieces of her heart. They'd both lost so much. It was a crappy thing to have in common, but there was a bizarre solace in it too. Facing Gideon after she'd confronted all of that, it weighed so heavy she feared it might crush her.

The crunch of tires in her ice and snow-covered driveway caught her ear and her stomach clenched. She and Noah scuttled to the blinds and peered out, eyeing a fancy car as it parked. It was matte-black, and the windows were tinted so dark, they obscured the interior and whoever was inside. The driver's side door flipped up, wing-style.

"Show off!" she scoffed when Gideon climbed out.

He wore head to toe black. His dress pants and shirt were tailored to his well-honed body to perfection. His black leather coat was bomber style and accented the cut of his broad chest and shoulders.

Noah nudged her, then exaggeratedly mouthed, *demon-boy's hot*. His finger traced a line from the corner of his mouth as he mimed drool dripping down his chin.

"He's obnoxious," she said.

"He can be whatever he wants when he looks like that."

Her face twisted. "Since when are you so superficial?"

It looked as if it took great effort for Noah to tear his eyes from Gideon when he peered her way. "Since now. Since right now."

She ducked and crawled across the floor so demon-boy wouldn't see her, then clambered onto the couch and plucked several clumps of lint from her clothes. Her heart rate spiked, the tension in her chest ratcheting up to an unsustainable level. *Breathe, Grace. Breathe.* Her attention settled on Noah. "You should hide now."

"Unequivocally not! I need to know what he looks like if I have to identify him to the cops."

Her gaze narrowed so deep it was a wonder she could still see. "You already know what he looks like."

"I need the finer details."

She scowled. "Finer details?"

"The depth of color in his eyes. How many hands I can set against his broad chest. The exact curvature of his ass. It's best to be precise, Gracie."

She opened her mouth to remind him exactly who Gideon was but was cut off when the doorbell rang. Shooting to her feet, she smoothed her jeans and tugged down the hem of her ivory, V-neck sweater. A sheen of sweat slicked her skin and she fanned herself. "Fine. Answer the door." She glared daggers at her best friend. "And act normal."

He arched a brow. "You might wanna try that yourself."

"Just don't act like you know anything."

"And how does one act like they don't know anything?" He grinned. Too wide. Too eager.

Pulling out that invisible notebook, she added:

- *Find new best friend.*

Noah disappeared around the corner. *Oh, God. Oh, God. Oh, God.* What had she gotten herself into? She didn't know the first thing about investigating. Her eyes darted side-to-side as she looked for an escape. Not finding one, she bolted down the hallway as the creak of the front door filled the void.

The muffled rumble of male voices carried toward her as she crashed her back against the wall to steady herself. Noah laughed a little too heartily at something Gideon said. *Don't befriend him, Noah!* She leaned forward. When her roommate came into view, her mouth dropped because he was practically swooning. *Swooning*!

He glanced her way. *Demon-boy* she reminded because his senses had straight up quit. When he offered her no acknowledgement and continued his shameless banter, she pushed off the wall. She was going to have to save him from himself. When she rounded the corner, Gideon stood there, dominating her entryway.

His hair was styled to the side, the dusting of his beard trimmed shorter than when she'd seen him days before. His amber stare roved her body as he rasped, "Looking good, Crys."

Her skin burned from the wildfire in his heated gaze. She pressed her mouth together in a hard line and crossed her arms over her chest. "How did you know where I lived?"

He clasped his hand over his opposite wrist. The movement made the edge of his tattoos push up from beneath his collar. "It was on your driver's license."

Darren. The bouncer from Bedlam. She frowned.

"I'm aware of everything that happens in my club," he said, confirming her suspicion.

She snatched her coat from the closet, stuffed her phone into her purse, and pointed to the door. "We should go."

"Text me," Noah said. The instant Gideon's back was turned he mouthed *Everything*!

She blinked rapidly, and she stumbled before she closed the door behind her. Following demon-boy, he led them to the passenger side of his car.

"I can get my own door," she said.

He stopped. "Can you?"

"I'm not inept." She approached it, paused, then stared. Extending her hand, she ran it along the smooth body of the car as she tried to figure it out. And tried. And *tried*. It was just a door, for God's sake.

"Whenever you're ready," he taunted.

Retracting her arm, she glanced toward him. "Would you please open this?"

He advanced. "My pleasure, Crys." His shoulder brushed hers when he leaned past, and she caught the scent of expensive oak, and musk. His palm skimmed a sensor, and something beeped. The door popped open and glided up.

Needing to distance herself from him, she scrambled into the belly of the beast. Gideon pushed the door closed and sealed her in, then strode around the front of the vehicle. His movements were sharp, fluid, and that of an entirely too self-assured man. His confidence dripped off him, ruling the space as he climbed into the car. It was clear he knew what he offered, how enticing he was. She looked away, at anything but him.

The car was warm and smelled of cleaner, like it'd been detailed. The dash was all carbon fiber and leather with a series of screens and metallic accents. It was as lavish as lavish got.

"Not the most practical vehicle for winter," she said over the creak of his coat when he settled himself further into the cockpit-style seat.

He pushed the ignition and the engine roared to life. "You don't like it?"

She didn't answer.

"I promise, Crys, I can handle it." Hitting another button, they reversed out the driveway. His stare lingered on the house before he raised a hand and waved to her best friend, who gawked shamelessly at them through the window.

Speechless. She was speechless.

"So Noah knows," Gideon said.

Her head whipped toward him, and she fumbled over her words. "I—I didn't say that." *Not good. Not good. Not good!*

"You didn't have to." He peered at her from the corner of his eye and promised in a coy tone, "Don't worry, I won't tell."

If Ben was right about Gideon, then lord only knew how he might use that knowledge to his advantage. If Noah hadn't been the tip off, doubtless her awkward response was. Gideon wasn't a fool, so treating him like one wasn't about to help. She rang her hands in her lap and admitted without admitting, "He's my best friend."

"I can see that," his brow lifted. "I like him."

"That's because he likes you."

"He has good taste," Gideon said before his voice lowered, going even. "You should talk to him."

That wasn't suspicious at all. Her eyes narrowed as she pinned him to the spot. "Why, so I can be killed for it?"

"That won't happen." The words were dark. A promise. "Besides, you're one of us."

"You sound confident about that."

"I am." He stretched and rolled his shoulders before he adjusted his position. "You don't know us, which means you should question everything you're told by everyone you meet."

Ha! If only he knew. Scanning the car again, she took it in with new eyes as she looked for something that could link him to the new Mark or what happened the other night. She cleared her throat. "Everything and everyone? Even you?"

He smirked. "Especially me."

"Pretty sure the blood running through your veins tells me all I need to know."

His head canted. "And what of the blood running through your veins?"

Her heart shuddered an uncomfortable beat when the panic she'd thrust aside earlier came flooding back in. What if she was a Lesser Demon? Did that mean *she* was tainted? That she was inherently evil?

She released an explosive exhale and forced the dark thoughts from her mind before eyeing him askance. "My inclination is not to trust you."

He shook his head and veered them onto the highway. "Don't trust your inclinations. Trust your instincts."

The words were a trigger that jolted her memory back to a time she'd long thought lost.

"Trust your instincts, Grace. If you see someone, anyone that makes you nervous, get away from them. Do you hear me?" her mother said, car revving as she accelerated.

"I hear you." Her voice shook while her pulse pounded in her ears like a drum. "You're scaring me, Mom."

"I know, and I'm sorry, but you need to understand how serious this is. Decisions will have to be made. You need to figure out who you can turn to. Don't let your mind trick you. It'll try to explain things away and cloud your judgement, but your instincts never lie. So, trust them, Grace. Always."

She snapped back to the present, the haze of the flashback's edges fogging her thoughts. She stared off into space while she tried to right her mind. What the heck was that? Why had her mother been so terrified? It had to have happened around the accident since she had no recollection of it otherwise.

Gideon's stare was trained on her, his body still. The weight of his attention dragged her from her tumultuous reverie. She didn't know what emotion played across her features, so she schooled them. The last thing she wanted was to give him more leverage.

Swallowing around the lump in her throat, she returned to their conversation. "If that's the case, should I really be in a car alone with you?"

There was a short pause where he considered her. "You tell me."

She was *not* about to answer that. "Who are you, Gideon?"

To say his smirk was impish would've been an understatement. "Who do you want me to be, Crys?"

God, he got under her skin. Rolling her eyes, she tugged her pant legs, then crossed her arms over her chest. "Don't you want to know about me?"

"I'm learning about you as we speak."

That had to be bad, didn't it? Deflect, deflect, deflect. "So you studied with the others."

His mouth drew up at the corner. "As youths we were encouraged to know our opponent."

Interesting. "And what else were you encouraged to know?"

"Religious history, human behavior and tendency, influence, and sway tactics. We're Marked, educated, taught about the Callings, the function of our purpose, how to deal with the dead, to counter our enemy's efforts, and fight, among other things."

Her brows rose. *Oh, no. No, no, no no no.* She couldn't have heard correctly. "To fight?"

His amber stare locked on hers. "This is a war, is it not?"

Other than the occasional slap-fight with Noah, she'd not fought a day in her life. She was a nurse, for God's sake. It was her job to help, not hurt. If there was anything in the world she was *not*, it was a fighter.

She pushed her head back into the seat. What had she done? She should've run. God above, why hadn't she run? But it was entirely too late for that. Biting her lip, she pulled it through her teeth. "Ben said the Shepherds are taken at birth."

His attention roved forward as he scanned the road. "We are, but I still see my unSighted father." He offered her a slow smile. "And now we're even."

"Even?"

"Even," he repeated. "Now you know one of my secrets."

She scratched her temple. "The fact that you see your unSighted father is a secret?"

He cocked a brow.

Why would him seeing his father need to be a secret? While she wanted to dive further down that rabbit hole, Ben's voice whispered in the back of her mind that the fewer secrets she and Gideon shared, the better. She wasn't daft. He'd only told her—if it was even true—to assuage her fears. To lull her into some semblance of comfort or trust. To manipulate her.

His low, rasping voice pulled her from her thoughts a moment later when he prompted, "So, Crys, why is there no Mr. Crawford?"

She flicked her nail. "How do you know there isn't?"

"Because there isn't."

"You seem fairly confident about that." Too confident. Frustratingly so. Did she have a stamp on her forehead in all caps that read "DESPERATE AND ALONE?"

"That's because I am."

If the car had room, she would've plunked her hands on her hips. "You shouldn't be. That information isn't on my driver's license."

He huffed a single laugh. "No, but it is on your social media."

Lovely. She mentally slapped herself. "You were *creeping* me?"

Inclining his head, he said, "Indeed. You should really change your privacy settings."

"I'll get on that," she mumbled under her breath. What the heck else had she posted on there? She wasn't the kind to overshare but when someone was trained in manipulation—when they were *born* of it—who knew what they could find of use.

She sighed and took in their surroundings. They were headed deeper into the city center where the skyscrapers that made up the downtown core towered so high it was like they skimmed the clouds. Their sleek glass exteriors reflected the midday light with a blinding glare. She squinted against it but welcomed the sun's warmth on her skin.

"Where are we going?" she asked.

"For a walk."

"But we're driving."

"Smart girl." He winked. "I knew I liked you for a reason."

She shook her head and angled her chin up. He'd been pushing her the whole drive. Time to put him back on his heels. "I heard you like lots of women."

He released a dry, sardonic laugh. "Did you now?"

"I did." She inwardly preened as she shimmied her shoulders. *How do you like the heat, demon-boy?* "I also heard you like them often."

"Hmm," he said, the sound more a growl. The steering wheel creaked beneath his grip. "I'm experienced."

Push, push, push. "You're modest."

"What about you?"

Her smile fell and her stomach sank. "What about me?"

"Are you experienced, Crys?" A sly grin took residence across his lips.

No. They were *not* going there. There was no way in hell she was about to discuss her sex life—or lack thereof—with him. "That's unequivocally none of your business."

"And yet you're curious about mine."

"I'm not curious. I'm merely repeating what I've been told."

"Yes. And I find it interesting that you were told, at all." He turned them down Clarington Avenue toward the city's most expensive food and shopping district. A district she'd never bothered with since it was so far beyond her financial reach it was virtually nonexistent.

Heads snapped their way as the car moved, and she eyed the reflection of it in the glass buildings. It had to be some sort of concept car, a very sharp one. But she'd die a slow death before she'd ever tell him that.

She squirmed in her seat. "Do you actually like this kind of attention?"

"Why do you think the windows are tinted?"

He pulled them into the entrance of a private underground parking lot. A motor whirred as its door rose, inviting them in. The strong scent of tar assaulted her when they passed inside. Its new asphalt was black as coal with barely a speck of dirt on it. There were stainless-steel guardrails, glass dividers, and a ridiculous number of the most expensive vehicles she'd ever seen, like it was some kind of showroom. An underground one. Shifty.

She pursed her lips. "Why does this place feel familiar?"

"It's Bedlam. We entered through the back," he said, thick with innuendo.

She barked an unimpressed laugh. He parked and tapped some button on the car's center console that unlatched the doors. They floated open, and she and Gideon climbed out. Pressing something on his key fob, they sealed back over.

Her frown was deep. "You can control them with a button?"

"Of course."

"Why didn't you use it back at my house?"

He raised his hand to his chest. "I'm nothing if not a gentleman, Crys."

She fought the growl that threatened to escape the deepest recesses of her throat. If she'd been weaker willed, he'd have gotten to her... more. But she'd spent the last four years constructing strategically placed walls around her emotions. Walls she wasn't about to take down anytime soon. She needed them in place. For so many, she needed them in place.

He guided her to a door that brought them out to street level. People surveyed them, their stares wide.

She smoothed her top, then smoothed it again. "I presume you don't come out of your cave often."

He smirked but made no reply as they headed farther and farther away until he eventually aimed them for a park bench that lined the sidewalk. "Take a seat," he told her then did so himself.

Her eyes pinched at the corners as she set herself down beside him. The outside of her thigh grazed his leg. She glided to the opposite end to put as much space between them as possible, which, with his broad, imposing form, wasn't much.

He chucked his chin, indicating the road before her.

She followed his line of sight to a soul in the center of the street. "Sweet Lord," she uttered, and a cold shiver slithered across her skin at the reality of what stood before her. Snakes coiled around the soul's left arm, their bodies so thick, there was barely space between them.

"He was hit by a car this morning," Gideon said.

"How did you know he'd be one of yours?"

"Because I knew him."

Despite her suspicions, she couldn't help the small pang of remorse that took her. "I'm sorry."

He offered an almost imperceptible nod. "Don't be."

His expression was schooled, unreadable. But his eyes were creased at the corners. It was subtle, but it was there. Was it the man's death that bothered him? Did he have something to do with it? The soul didn't carry the new Mark, but maybe the man had learned something? Was that how Gideon knew where the soul would be?

She slid further back onto the bench, giving it her weight. "At Bedlam the other night, Ben said you *summon* the dead..."

Gideon leaned forward and set his elbows on his knees. "Their Marks are drawn to our connection with the other side when we call them."

"Why the Marks?"

He drew his left sleeve up and his large, calloused hand made a tsh as it skimmed over it. "They designate the Forsaken's destination, and we Shepherds are the conduit to that eternal end."

Grace's stomach clenched. "Who are the Forsaken?"

He tipped his head in the soul's direction. "The damned. Those bound for Hell."

She suppressed the shudder that threatened to slip down her spine while the fear that clamped around her chest pressed tight, crushing her. "Why are you called Shepherds?"

Angling his face her way, he offered her the full force of his smile. A smile that didn't touch his eyes. "Because we, Agents, and the others in our world work in tandem to corral the flock."

She cleared her throat and returned her attention back to the soul. "And how do the Agent's fit into all of this?"

"They're blooded both angel and demon. They're the facilitators. They don't take sides, only act to control the Nephilim and Lesser Demons, and draw in resources when needed." He flicked his hand toward the Forsaken's left arm. "Their Marks represent the *Irremissibile Peccata*. The unforgivable sins."

She had no doubt the answer to her next question would make things so, so much worse, but that didn't change the fact that it had to be asked. Her voice grew strained when she spoke. "What constitutes forgivable versus unforgivable?"

"Intent." He stared down at his hands. "It's the difference between ignorance and malice."

"So then," she rubbed the back of her neck, "whatever the Forsaken did, they did knowingly?"

"They did intentionally." The distinction was minute, but powerful. Terrifying. "A single unforgivable sin will earn you a one-way ticket to Hell."

Heaven above. How many times had she seen those Marks? All souls bound for Hell—actual, literal Hell. She bounced her foot. "W-why can we only see the Marks on the dead? Why not the living?"

"Because they aren't on the body, they're on the soul." He tapped the leathered wings at his wrist that designated him what he was. "This is the Scourge."

She eyed his Passage and Gateway Marks, but there was another, one that sat above his elbow. Its rounded edge protruded from under his coat. Unlike the others, it rolled red and orange with a writhing fire that moved like a living thing. When she set her finger to the exposed portion of the Mark, heat permeated her skin, embedding in her bones. "What's this?"

His unfathomable gaze locked on hers. "A weapon."

She withdrew her hand, shoulders so tight they ached when she gestured to the soul in the road. "Are you going to help him?"

His stare grew hollow when it focused on something—or nothing—in the distance. "What I have to do won't help."

Her pulse thrashed in her ears as she focused on the soul. The level of torture, of suffering that he'd endure for the rest of—

"Don't feel bad for him," Gideon said. "He's reaping what he sowed in this life."

She peered at him through her lashes. "Says the man who's giving him time."

His lip tipped up at the corner. "He has an eternity to pay, and I wouldn't wish what's coming for him on anyone."

The way he said it, the evenness in his tone, caught her. It wasn't pity but something else. Something deeper, an awareness… "You sound like you know from experience."

His devil-may-care expression returned as he rose, and it sparked a new dread in her heart. "Welcome to the dark side."

THE WALK back to Bedlam was quiet as Grace tried and failed to absorb…everything. It was all so dark and unimaginably heavy. The one —and only—positive; it'd opened the door for questions.

"You should probably text Noah," Gideon said as he broke her from her wildly churning thoughts. "I'm sure he's dying to know how things are going between us."

"He'll live," she assured him. Never mind that there was entirely too much to put in a text. She was gonna need a letter or a book. Maybe an encyclopedia. Did those things still exist?

He slid his hands into his pockets. "How did you two meet?"

She swallowed hard and glanced toward the ground. "We've been best friends since we were six. He moved in with me after my mother died and his family disowned him."

"And why would they do that?"

Wait, had she said too much? She side-eyed him, attempting to gauge his angle. Like her own, Noah's social media was wide open, so none of it was secret. Gideon could've easily found those answers. For all she knew, he already had them.

"They refused to accept that he was gay. We were all the other had for the longest time until his boyfriend Kyle came along."

He arched a single brow. "And we like Kyle, do we?"

"We love him. Noah was in a dark place for a long time. Kyle helped turn that around." She wheeled about and stabbed a finger Gideon's way. "And Kyle's a cop, so I suggest you watch yourself." *There. Good and threatened.*

A lone laugh escaped him before his smooth voice proclaimed, "I'll consider myself warned." He turned them left onto a different street. "How did Kyle and Noah meet?"

"Noah's an accountant. He offers discounts for First Responders. Kyle hired him to do his taxes, and the rest is history."

"And what about you?"

"What about me?"

"You said your parents passed." He let the words stand.

Worrying her cheek between her teeth, she contemplated changing the subject, but for some ridiculous reason she couldn't explain, she didn't. "I don't know much about my father. He died before I was born. My mother didn't like to talk about him." Or anything from her past.

"Too hard?"

She shook her head. "I got the impression it was a bad relationship. She seemed more relieved than disappointed that he wasn't around. I don't think I missed anything by not having him in my life."

"No stepfather?"

"No. She never dated. Ever. Never really did anything. She rarely left our house actually. Whatever happened before I was born really put her off people."

His leather coat groaned as he grazed a hand over his facial hair. "And you didn't get your Sight until you were eighteen, after an accident."

Was he always so…attentive? Aware? Everything? "The one that killed my mother." She cleared her throat and turned away. "The shock of seeing the them—the dead—terrified me, at first. Until the other night, I thought I might be losing my mind. I'd always hoped there was more, but I didn't quite expect this." When next she spoke, her voice was even. "You're asking a lot of questions."

"I'm trying to get to know you, Crys."

She trailed her tongue along her teeth. She needed to change the subject because he was interested in a lot of stuff she didn't know the motive behind. She'd let things get too personal. *Stupid, foolish, rookie mistake.*

"So, what's next?" she asked.

"Food." At her narrowed gaze, he shrugged. "I don't know about you, but I need to eat."

She *was* starved. "I could eat."

"What would you like?"

She rubbed her palms together. She didn't have to think long. "Chicken fingers!"

Gideon fell silent, but an amused expression creasing his eyes.

"What?" Her brows lowered in a frown. If he was about to mock her for her love of chic–

"Nothing. Chicken fingers it is." He withdrew his phone, punched several buttons, and sent a message.

She flicked her hand toward him. "What are you doing?"

"Sending our food orders to one of my chefs," he replied as he slid the device away again.

"You have a *chef*?" Of course, he did. Why wouldn't he? The man was in a whole other class of wealth. Even the way people looked at him was different, like he was some idol to be worshipped.

His stride was even, gait steady, when he said, "I have several."

She rolled her eyes. "Can't cook your own meals?"

The grin he wore was the definition of proud. "I own two-thirds of Clarington Avenue, which encompasses a few restaurants."

"So that's a no," she mumbled.

He laughed, the sound a thick, rich rasp.

They rounded the final corner, passing the Casino before Bedlam came into view. The music inside thumped a heavy base that rattled the windows. Gideon held the door, and she blinked hard trying to ignore his heady, musk scent as she slipped under his arm and headed in. An employee tweaked the speaker system across the way. When he spotted them, the sound dropped out so suddenly the beat still echoed in her ears.

Every eye in the place followed them as Gideon led her across the bar and aimed upstairs for the second floor—or at least, he started to before they were intercepted.

"Gideon," a high-pitched, feminine voice called, one Grace vaguely recognized.

He stopped, his towering form less than an inch from hers. The heat he kicked off brushed every exposed section of her flesh. She took a half-step back.

"Lisa," he acknowledged.

Lisa's big, brown doe-eyes scanned Grace before they returned to demon-boy. She made idle banter, twisted her hair around a finger, and arched her back so her breasts pushed forward before she asked him a series of questions concerning things to be done across his properties.

He was patient and polite, but the flat, all-business answers he offered made his thoughts on her advances clear before he said his goodbyes and continued on. Grace didn't miss the glower Lisa offered her before she turned away.

"One of your admirers?" Grace asked as they reached the top step.

"I hadn't noticed." He reached out and opened a heavy, steel door for her.

Oh, he'd noticed. He'd have to be dead not to. She crossed over. "Mmhmm."

"How about this." He moved tight to her back. "I don't shit where I eat. My employees are off limits, and so is my home." He tipped his head to indicate an indiscriminate black door at the back of the room.

Her eyes widened. "You *live* in this place?"

"I do, and it's my sanctuary. I don't let people in there."

She'd suffice to say he didn't let people in, at all. Not that she could judge. She wasn't exactly what one might call "open." "You make a distinction between here," she pointed to the door ten feet away, "and there?"

"That I do." He cocked an overconfident brow. "Do *you* want to see it?"

"Ha! I'm not one of those girls." Ab-so-lute-ly not.

He linked a hand over the opposite wrist. "And what kind of girl would you be, Crys?"

She crossed her arms tightly over her chest, noticed how it thrust her breasts up, and dropped them back to her sides. "One with boundaries."

A knock sounded at the door.

Gideon's heated stare lingered on her for several long seconds before he approached the desk. Taking up a remote, he shut off the television that had multiple split screens from security cameras around Bedlam, then pressed a button for the intercom on its center. "Come in."

Davis entered and offered Grace a nod which she returned. He made his way to Gideon and the two spoke low. A younger male employee carrying fancy food containers appeared, and her her stomach growled.

Gideon huffed a laugh. "Tell Frank he'll be compensated, and if he doesn't like that tell him he's replaceable."

Davis smirked. "I look forward to it."

The two left and Gideon set to opening the boxes. The rich aroma of fried meats and savory spices that filled the room had Grace's mouth watering, and she scurried closer. He'd ordered himself some kind of fancy beef. It looked good, but she was on the hunt for another treasure as she pivoted toward the other box.

"Would you like a fork—"

She snatched up a chicken finger then bit into it like the uncivilized peasant she was. "This is finger food. You don't eat finger food with a fork, demon-boy."

His expression turned impish, and his body relaxed when he eased himself down at the desk. "For someone who purports to be unnerved by us, you sure don't act like it."

"Shh. I'm busy judging." She took another bite. Was she scared? It was a complicated question. Too complicated to parse out at that moment. She had eating to do.

"And what is it you've judged so far?"

"That these chicken fingers are pretty good."

His head cocked. "Just pretty good?"

She picked up her container and sauntered to the couch across the way, settling down in the far-right corner. *Far away. So far. Not far enough.*

He used his fancy fork to impale a piece of steak before he raised it. "You've had better?" When he set the meat to his tongue, he bit down with a slow, seductive expertise.

She looked away. "Once, on a rare outing with my mother. It was a small food truck somewhere south of the city called Mr. Cock's Chicken."

He coughed as he choked through a laugh. When he finally regained himself, he noted, "That's quite the name."

"Why do you think I remembered it?" She chomped another

mouthful of her chicken and took in his office. The black-stained mahogany desk he sat behind was obnoxiously big and oddly suited him. It held two large screens and a machine with a series of indecipherable buttons on it. A massive TV at least eighty inches in size occupied one of the gray walls. The couch she used was black leather, as were the chairs opposite her. A large, tinted window that overlooked Clarington Avenue lined the back, while elevator doors stood closed to her right.

His level of wealth was staggering. It would offer him a lot, like say the ability to create his own Faction. She peered around the room again. There wasn't anything obvious, but then he wasn't a fool. Not that she even knew what to look for. If she could just search it without him there. Her gaze narrowed as an idea took root in the back of her mind. She tapped her chicken finger on the food container. In the meantime, she needed to get him on a useful topic. "Ben tells me the Nephilim are paid through the church."

"As are we."

Her head snapped back. "You are paid through the... *You*?"

He grinned. "Well, I would be if I didn't have my own enterprises. It's all about equality, Crys. An advantage cannot be offered to one side that isn't offered to the other."

She threw her hands out, palms forward. "Wait! You're not paid by them *because* of your businesses?"

"None of the Shepherds who work are." His eyes narrowed, and he leaned forward. "We're required to give a percentage of our earnings back to them as penance for our lesser availability."

The knot in her stomach twisted painfully, and she set a hand over it, fighting to keep her food down. "No." She shook her head, and the longer she did, the more aggressive the shaking became. "I'm not handing over a red cent of my paycheck to them."

She might've sworn he winced, but the expression was gone before she could be sure. "It's compulsory."

"I can't, Gideon." She did well with her career, but if her income took a cut, she didn't know what would happen.

She rubbed her thighs as she sought a solution, but without knowing how much would be taken, it was impossible. She wasn't about to ask Gideon. Confirming just how vulnerable she was—financially or otherwise—was a hard no.

He leaned forward, rested his forearms on the edge of the desk, then gave her the full brunt of his attention. "Crys?"

Going there with him was a bad idea. She shook her head.

Clearing his throat, he sat up straighter, and she was oddly thankful when he changed the subject, but that thankfulness faded to nothing at the subject he selected. "Are you ready for what's coming next?"

Her heart froze in her chest. "Do you mean the Calling?"

"That I do."

She'd been distracted enough through the day she hadn't had time to think about it. Neither did she want to. "You tell me."

His level answer sent a shiver down her spine. "No."

CHAPTER 12
GRACE

Grace's brows locked down as she studied the indiscriminate warehouse Gideon had taken her to on the outskirts of Arillia's industrial district. It was large, had one level, silver metal siding, and no windows. There was unequivocally nothing special about it.

"Is this where you take your victims?" she asked, tone dry.

He offered her a tempter's smile. "I've informed everyone in my territory to meet us here for a Calling so I can show you off."

"You're introducing me to the people you don't trust?"

He tapped his key fob to his thigh as his stare homed in on her. "What makes you think I don't trust them?"

"When Elijah asked where the rest of your people were in that first meeting, you told him you'd 'disseminate the information you acquired as necessary,' which tells me you didn't feel comfortable with them having it."

"Keen little thing, aren't you?" he uttered more to himself. "When it comes to matters of the Sect, I'm careful with what I share."

"With everyone except Davis."

His smirk built slowly as he inclined his head. "With everyone except Davis."

That's right, you're not the only one who pays attention, demon-boy. She shrugged. "First, he was in the meeting that night. Second, if he's your Head of Security, you should probably trust him."

"I should, shouldn't I?" He approached the entrance and punched a code into a security box off to the side. It made a loud buzz before the door unlatched and he pulled it open. He held it wide, swept his arm out and offered a gallant bow.

The heat of a blush burned her cheeks when she crossed over. Her boots tapped on the concrete floors, echoing through the open space. The tin walls were a matte, gunmetal gray, while wide beams crossed the ceiling. To her right was a short hallway where several doors sat closed, one in particular that looked like it belonged to an industrial freezer.

Her lips pursed when she scented the air and found the odor of... wait, was that *chlorine*? She could've asked but really, how much did she want to know? "Where is everyone?"

"They'll be here soon. I just wanted more time alone with you." He pushed his coat back from his hips as he slipped his hands into his pockets. It exposed the two black handled, wicked-looking daggers that rested in sheaths at the small of his back. The weapons made him look every bit the man she'd been warned about. Brutal. Sexual. Dangerous.

She bit her lip.

He must've caught her looking because he explained, "They're on me just in case."

That didn't sound good, like, at all. Her rib cage constricted around her lungs making it harder to breathe. "Just in case of what?"

He smirked, but there wasn't anything pleasant about it. "You'll see."

"Am I gonna I need something?"

His stare pinned her, assessing. He reached back and withdrew one of the blades, then handed it to her hilt first. She breathed slow as she braced herself. Her trembling fingers wrapped around its cold grip and grazed the rough skin of his hand. She retreated.

The dagger was heavy in her grasp, awkward. "What am I supposed to do when your people arrive?"

He straightened to his full height. When he answered, all signs of humor were gone. "Stay with me."

Her body was wound so tight, she worried her muscles would tear under the strain. She slipped the knife into her coat pocket as the door popped open and people started filing in, most dressed in everyday clothes. She wasn't sure what she'd expected, but normal hadn't been it, and save for their Scourge Marks, she never would've known what they were.

Only one met her expectations; a man she pegged as a few years older than herself with a solid frame. He wore tattered jeans and a navy blue, threadbare t-shirt. A sinister skull tattoo covered the entirety of his face. His forehead, the hollow of his eyes, temples, cheeks, and jaw were all shaded in black, while the sharper planes of his face were done in yellowish tans, mimicking the color of bone. His lips were overlaid by jagged, angry teeth that staggered in uneven layers like a shark's.

His hair was shoulder-length, unkempt, and done with a God-awful dye-job. She assumed it was meant to be blue, but the coloring had faded so much it held more of a yellow-ish tint. Sweet Lord. He was like something straight out of a horror movie. *Or Hell. Yep. Straight out of Hell.*

Grace took a half-step back when skull-face smiled, baring his real teeth. The others eyed her like prey, as if she was their meal, and they were very, very hungry. She swallowed hard, the lingering aftertaste of partially digested chicken fingers heavy on her tongue.

She edged closer to Gideon where he stood at the head of the room. His hands hung loose by his sides as he scanned his Sect with a threatening promise. Davis flanked her right, caging her between the two. She wasn't about to complain.

"We have a visitor this evening," Gideon said to the room, voice deeper, harsh. It projected across the warehouse with a heavy resonance that was impossible to ignore. Not a trace of the roguish demeanor he'd had with her remained. Exactly how many sides did he have?

"Why?" a black-haired woman asked, the lone word an accusation.

"She's here at Elijah's direction. Beyond that, it's not your concern." His hands rolled into fists at his sides. "We do the Calling now, and if a single goddamn one of you lets something through again, I'll send you back with it my-fucking-self."

An almost violent fear twisted in Grace's gut as she angled toward him. "Let something through?"

He gave a sharp nod. "Like I said, Crys, stay with me," he replied before ordering the others, "Do it!" He withdrew his vicious black dagger and pulled up the sleeve of his coat. Metal glinted as it bit into their skin. Blood poured from his wound when he swiped his blade through it, then over his Scourge. His wound slowly stitched together and his Mark flared from within, its bat-like wings surging at the contact. Gliding the knife up, he spread the blood across his Gateway Mark.

The air in the room rippled. She pressed tighter to his side, trembling as her shoulder brushed his. He was hard as stone when he shifted, set his stance, and held his blade at the ready.

What had she done? *Sweet lord, I shouldn't have come!*

The dead answered the call, materializing across the warehouse and before long the place was full of Forsaken with varying tallies of unforgivable sins. The energy in the room grew heavier, darker. It made the air thick and cloying, harder to breathe. Another wave surged, deeper than the last, and an intense heat pulsed out. It radiated through her, down to the very fiber of her being. It screamed a warning. *Danger. Malevolence. Pain.* And her instincts screamed an answer. *Run.*

Grace's legs weakened as she scanned the dead, seeking the new Mark but it was nowhere to be found. Was that good? She had no freaking clue. All she knew was the horror so complete consuming her.

Her hair shook in the corner of her vision, and she raked it back while something that resembled a black, circular archway coalesced. It came clearer and clearer until it was fully manifested in all its terrifying glory.

The portal to Hell. *God above, it's the portal to Hell.*

Her legs twitched, begging to run, but she stayed rooted to the spot because somehow, she knew she couldn't outrun what was about to come.

The archway oozed a viscous fluid that was some horrid combination of black tar and blood. It ran in thick, lazy rivulets down the sides while smoke billowed from the entrance, carrying a scent unlike anything she'd ever encountered. It was death, it was rot, it was melted flesh and all things putrid. It made her eyes water, and she swallowed hard against the nausea that threatened to take her as the coppery taste of blood flooded her tongue.

Gideon tipped his head. "Look at the Gateway."

Her chest heaved. She pushed her sight, and her gaze flew wide at the black wall of snakes that formed the mouth of the portal. They slithered, torquing, and coiling over and around one another. They were so thick, she had no clue where one ended and the next began.

Fire rose and enveloped everything inside the Gate. Grace sucked in a sharp hiss, the heat staggering to the point of pain, yet her skin did not burn. She raised a hand like it could shield her against it. It couldn't.

"It's hellfire," Gideon said over the booming crackle of the blaze. The flames flared in his eyes and lit the strong planes of his face, making him look every bit the–

Screams filled the world, the voices of Hell's Forsaken begging for help. For release. For mercy. They spoke other things, but the words were lost as they drowned in the savage sea of writhing bodies.

Grace's adrenaline spiked, ratcheting up to a perilous level. Her foot ground against the concrete as she eased away.

"Stay where you are," Gideon warned.

Something from inside the portal stalked through the flame toward them. Burned and blackened wings attached to a burned and blackened body, both ringed in an orange glow like embers that crawled across a charred log. Snakes wound around its human-esque form, binding it. A Mark that matched the one Gideon called his "weapon" sat on its upper arm.

Another of the beasts appeared to its right, then another and another —a pack who'd scented their prey. Her hand edged toward the pocket with the knife.

"Now!" Gideon roared.

The Lesser Demons smeared blood onto their Passage Marks. The dead began to waver and undulate. A red flare ignited at the center of their chests, emanating out before the hellfire engulfed them. One by one, they were consumed before they were pulled through the Gate where the dark creatures awaited, but they did not burn. The beasts closed in on the Forsaken and dragged them deeper, their ravenous screams a blood-curdling shriek.

"Demons come to collect Hell's due," Gideon said, grip tightening around the hilt of his dagger while his tendons strained from the force.

A larger demon drifted through Hell's blackened sky aiming for the portal. Each flap of its great wings sent the smoke whirling high. Commotion erupted across the warehouse as the Lesser Demon's scrambled back–all except Gideon, Davis, and the skull-faced guy.

"Absinthe, Hennessy, HOLD THE GATE!" Gideon roared, glare fixing on two of his people closest to it before he angled toward Davis. "Stay with Crys."

"Where are you going?" Grace demanded as her arms locked tight to her sides. *He couldn't leave her.*

He cocked a brow. "Worried about me? I'm flattered." In the next breath, he was gone, making for the Gate.

A sheen of sweat slicked her skin, feeling exposed without him at her side.

His leather coat strained across his shoulders before he pulled it off, then stalked the space, readying. Absinthe and Hennessy dove from the demon's path before the thing crossed the portal unchecked.

Grace's heart strained against her ribs when it threatened to break free...or explode. Either way, there was no getting control of it or her anarchic emotions.

The second the beast touched down inside the warehouse, steam rose from it, and a loud popping, sizzle filled the space. It let loose a shriek that pierced Grace's ears, and she winced.

Skull-face edged in, taking Gideon's place at her side. His yellow contact-covered stare slid to hers. He looked her up and down, sizing her up. "Where are your Marks?"

She glanced down at her partially exposed wrists, and her mouth dropped open.

"If you don't already know," Davis cut in, "it's because Gideon decided you don't need to, Bernard."

Bernard's lip arced up at the corner, but whether it was a smile or sneer, she couldn't tell.

Grace's attention snapped back as the demon unfurled and came to its full height. It spread its bat-like leathered wings wide and bared its teeth in a wolfish snarl.

"Son of Azazel," its gravel-filled, inhuman voice greeted Gideon. The sound was caught somewhere between a growl and a hiss, as if it rattled around the chambers of its chest before being released.

Gideon rolled the blade in his grasp. "Turn back, Dark Seraphim."

The beast's eyes snapped to Grace.

Her chest rose and fell in aggressive pants as she struggled to get air, but there'd never be enough to soothe the burn that took root in her lungs. Her hand plunged toward the dagger, fumbling around the material of her pocket. When she clutched the hilt, it offered no comfort. Safe. She needed to be safe. And there was only one way that would happen.

She back pedalled, something she'd gotten pretty good at in recent days.

Davis cursed.

The Dark Seraphim snapped its wings back, making itself sleeker as it lowered into a crouch.

"Crys, no," Gideon roared.

The beast's head angled back, and its nostrils flared as it scented the air. Could it smell fear? It smiled a hungry, predatory smile.

Ohhhhh, she'd made things worse. She wanted out. She wanted out. *She wanted out.* She fled and drove her legs hard, or at least tried to, but Davis' arm clamped around her waist, locking her and her knife in place. She kicked and struggled, feet going airborne, but he didn't let go.

"It's alright," he said.

Their definitions of *alright* weren't even close. She wasn't sure she'd ever be alright again. Regardless, her muscles were on fire from her pathetic grappling effort and his hold was just too strong. Conserving what was left of her strength, she stopped fighting.

Gideon exploded forward and closed the distance to the demon. It lunged and extended its taloned claws so quick, they whistled in the air. But Gideon was fast too—unnaturally so. He sidestepped the attack and swung out with his dagger. When the metal grazed the demon's shoulder, it howled, and steam rose from the wound.

"The blades are Hell-forged," Davis explained as he slowly released her.

Black-tar blood slipped from the demon's gash as it reset its position. "You disappoint, Son of Azazel."

Gideon's tone took on a deceptively pleasant lilt when he said, "There are rules."

"Rules." It tsked before it spoke in another language, one foreign to Grace's ears, but its savage, snarling tone was clear enough.

Gideon responded in kind, using the same tongue, and despite the blazing heat that permeated the warehouse, a cold shiver slithered down Grace's spine.

The demon circled, but Gideon cut it off, keeping it near the portal—cornering it. And like any cornered animal would, it attacked. It struck out and Gideon twisted away as the talons whipped past. The demon swung again, slicing across the Sect Leader's right forearm. Grace's heart skipped a beat when Gideon advanced then drove his dagger up and into the beast's chest. It jerked to a stop before its body dried, splitting like desiccated wood. Its shrill, piercing screech rang out while a rolling wave of vapor blasted from the wound.

Grace's mouth ran dry while the knot of dread in her chest unfurled, but barely. He'd killed it. Gideon had killed it. She thanked everything that was holy and would've thanked him too if he'd been close enough.

The Dark Seraphim broke apart piece by piece, segment by segment, as it crumbled to ash. Gideon's dagger clanked to the concrete floor below. The demon's soul burned up, vanishing from earth's plane, and reappearing inside Hell as a reformed beast a moment later.

Sweet lord. Her gaze snapped between it and its remnants. "It—" Grace asked. "It passed over on its own. H—how?"

"Demons aren't tethered to this world like the Forsaken. An open Gateway is all they need to cross over."

Gideon sheathed his black sludge-stained daggers and pivoted toward Absinthe and Hennessey. To say he stalked them would've been an understatement. She ventured the word hunted would've been more appropriate.

The two pushed back as he neared, while the other Lesser Demons pushed in, blocking their path. The group's eager smiles bore no sense of justice, just a simple, greedy desire to see their comrades suffer. It was mob mentality at its finest—a dangerous, demon-blooded mob.

The hairs on the back of Grace's neck stood on end.

Gideon grabbed the two by the throat. "You were warned." As he dragged them, they clawed and kicked and spit and snarled their way across the warehouse. His menacing expression looked every bit the man she'd feared when he stopped before the flaming portal and shoved them in.

Grace lost feeling in her limbs, going numb.

When Absinthe and Hennessey passed the boundary, they dropped to the ground. Their mouths opened on wordless screams as wings tore from their backs and spread wide. Serpents slithered up from the depths of Hell, encircling their torsos.

Gideon stripped the blood from his Gateway Mark and severed the connection. The portal vanished.

"He left them there," Grace breathed before finding her voice. "Sweet Jesus, he actually *left* them there!"

"They need to know his threats are real," Davis said. "Don't worry, they've earned the second strata."

Her gaze flicked toward the exit. His last words meant nothing to her, and neither was she about to ask him to elaborate. She didn't care about anything but leaving.

"Get the fuck out of here!" Gideon snarled to his remaining people then made his way back to Grace's side.

The color in his amber eyes practically flowed as they rolled crimson and gold. Fire. *Hellfire.* Those eyes locked with hers, but his words were for Davis when he spoke. "How long should we leave them?"

"Elijah didn't tell you?"

"He said it was at my discretion."

She edged away because Gideon was dangerous with a capital D, and more than capable of the plot behind the new Mark.

Davis lifted a shoulder. "A few more minutes. Let the point sink in."

Gideon inclined his head and his lip tipped up at the corner. "So, what does the beauty think of our side?"

Her gaze fell, fixing on a divot in the concrete, on *anything* but him. Black demon blood dripped from his sheath, sizzling against the ground. Her fingers ached while she returned his dagger and tried to control her shake. "She thinks she's had enough."

He huffed a single, cynical laugh when he accepted it. To Davis, he instructed, "Take her to my car. I'll finish up here."

She didn't have to be told twice.

THE SUN WAS WELL and down when Grace all but fled from the warehouse. Davis stood outside Gideon's car like a hovering gargoyle. She'd told him to go, but his response had been simple, "No."

Gideon exited the building a short while later…alone. Her gaze widened. He strode to Davis and a portion of their muffled conversation carried through the vehicle.

"They're out?" Davis asked.

He gave a sharp nod. "They're out. They'll need to recover a while longer."

"I'll come back and check on them later."

"Much appreciated," Gideon said before the men parted ways and he climbed inside the car.

The weight of his stare seared Grace's flesh, but she didn't look back. *Wouldn't* look back. Demon blood. That's what he was made of. It was one thing to conceptualize the beasts. Another entirely to see one coming for her.

He eased them out of the lot and his hands flexed over the wheel as he maneuvered them through the city. When he finally spoke, the words were level. "I won't comfort you with a lie."

She angled his way, caught somewhere between dazed and exhausted as the adrenaline slowly ebbed from her system. "Hmm?"

"You need to know who you're dealing with and what it entails, because if it turns out you're on our side, you'll be forced to face it regardless. So, like I said, I won't comfort you with a lie."

Her shoulders dropped, and the car fell quiet again. She side-eyed him, but his mask of indifference made reading him impossible. Shaken as she was, it didn't change that he was right. If she was one of his kind, he'd be her Sect Leader and she be compelled to deal with him—to deal with all of it. The idea was grim.

Her finger traced an absentminded line in her pants. The gashes the demon left across his forearm were darkened by a thick, tar-like substance that soiled their edges. She worried her cheek between her teeth. "Your wound needs to be treated."

And just like that, his devil-may-care expression returned. "Would you like to take care of me, Crys?"

She pursed her lips.

He laughed. "Don't worry. It looks worse than it is."

Frowning, she said, "It looks terrible."

"I'm part demon, remember?" His mouth quirked up. "This poison runs through my veins."

She shook her head. Incorrigible. He was nothing short of incorrigible. Her nose wrinkled, words rising when she asked, "Why didn't the demon die when you stabbed him?"

He stared toward the road. "Because Hell-forged steel just sends them home."

So they could make a break for it again the next time a Gateway opened? Wonderful. "And if it was Heaven-kissed?"

His expression fell even, unreadable. "Then say goodbye."

She swallowed hard as they neared her neighborhood. Desperate to veer from that topic, she glanced at her purse. Reaching inside, she withdrew some cash, and pushed it at him.

His brows furrowed.

The money flapped when she shook it. "It's for dinner."

He barked a rough laugh. "No."

"I don't want to owe you."

"You don't."

She pushed the cash at him again.

"I'll tell you what, how about you take me out for chicken fingers sometime and we'll call it even."

"No." She withdrew her hand. That wasn't happening. *Nope. Not. Ever. Happening.*

"Yes."

Her arms crossed over her chest. "That's blackmail."

"Not even close," he replied.

Her driveway came into sight, and she strained to place the SUV parked there, but the darkness didn't help. Its lights were on while exhaust pumped from the tailpipe.

"Oh, look. Benjamin's here to greet us," Gideon said with feigned glee.

"Ben?" Was something wrong? Her stomach tightened. Why would he be there if something wasn't wrong?

"Don't worry, Crys. He's just making sure I haven't stolen you away."

Gideon veered them into the driveway, and the door to Ben's vehicle popped open. His body was coiled as he climbed out and waited for them to park.

"I thoroughly enjoyed our time together today," Gideon told her.

Had that been genuine? Or was he just trying to goad her? Before she could speak a retort, he pressed a button and the winged doors rose. She climbed out and came around the car as he exited then rose to his full height. The two men offered each other sharp, wildly unpleasant glares as Grace closed the distance to them.

"What's going on?" she asked Ben.

His stare lingered on Gideon momentarily before it slid to her. "I got worried when you didn't answer my texts."

He'd been texting? Her face warmed, and her heart fluttered in her chest.

"She was busy, Benjamin," Gideon said as he leaned against his vehicle and crossed his arms over his chest.

Ben's brows slammed down when he spotted the Lesser Demon's wound. "There was a Dark fucking Seraphim there."

Gideon raised his slashed-up arm, inspecting it as if it were a scratch. "Indeed. A hazard of the job."

Grace winced as a pang of guilt twisted her chest. It really did look bad.

He dropped the limb back to his side. "Should you be here, Benjamin?"

Ben's jaw ticked, and his nostrils flared.

Not good. She didn't need to know their history to get having the two of them together was a crap idea. Like, the crappiest. She twisted the hem of her sleeve. "I'm tired," she cut in, hoping to diffuse the bomb that was set to explode. "I should probably head inside."

Ben nodded. "Come on. I'll take you." He rested his palm on the small of her back and led her away.

Gideon's gaze flicked to that touch before it rose again and he offered her a lascivious smile. "You have a nice evening, Crys."

She glanced away as she and Ben crossed into her foyer. Rolling her neck, she tried to release the knots that'd formed there. It didn't work and she gave the wall her weight because she'd meant what she'd said, she was dog tired.

"What happened?" Ben asked.

The low rumble of Gideon's engine faded as he pulled out of her driveway.

"He showed me the Forsaken, explained what the unforgivable sins meant, introduced me to his Sect, and did a Calling."

He rubbed the back of his neck. "And there was a demon."

An involuntary shiver slithered down her spine. The scent of death and rot clung on her clothes, her hair, her skin. She needed to shower. Badly. "There was a demon."

The strain around his eyes eased. "I can't believe he put you through that."

"He ordered his people not to let it pass," she said, because, well, he had.

Gideon had left her way past confused. He'd flirted endlessly, bought her dinner, controlled his Sect with an unyielding strength, then topped it all off by tossing Absinthe and Hennessey through the portal. She shuddered. Sure, they'd let the Dark Seraphim through after he'd explicitly ordered them not to and said Dark Seraphim *had* tried to come for Grace, but was the punishment he'd doled out proportional? Would she even be asking that if the beast had gotten to her?

Ben laughed without humor. "He's a Lesser Demon, Grace. Everything they do has motive."

She rubbed the backs of her arms as she tried to chase away the chill that took her. "He said I should know the truth of things."

"He wants you to know the truth that benefits him." He took a step closer and rested a warm, reassuring hand on her shoulder. He was so close she was forced to look up. His head canted down, and his blond hair slipped forward. "I'm here for you, Grace. I'll help you navigate this."

Grace sagged, letting those words sink into her soul. She had help. She had someone. She had *him*. She wasn't alone. "Thank you."

He shrugged, his smile shy. "There's something else." A cool shiver chased his touch as it skimmed down her arm and lingered on her hand before falling away. "*The Chronicle* is ready. I've been granted access to it tomorrow afternoon if you're available."

It was a good thing the wall held her up because a faint spell swept over her. She stared past him unseeing as the guillotine suspended over her neck edged closer. She'd learn who she was, who she belonged to, or whether she belonged at all. She'd learn if her mother was who she'd claimed to be. And if she survived all that, she'd be able to look into her mom—a terrifying prospect on its own.

In spite of her anarchic emotions, she forced herself to respond. "I'm available."

"Good. I look forward to it." He turned back to the door. "You'll be alright, Grace. I'll call in the morning."

"I look forward to it," she said, using his words back at him as she worked to hide the tremors that wracked her.

The answering smile he offered as he left was so beautiful it could've stopped traffic, and the way it touched his eyes transformed his face.

Ben was Nephilim. He was safe. He'd been honest with her. He'd been chosen as his Sect's Leader and entrusted with the Gateway Mark. That meant something. She ignored the voice inside that told her Gideon had been too because that truth was entirely too inconvenient. But then, someone had to do it. Maybe he was just the best of the worst.

She could trust Ben. She *would* trust him. And she needed someone to trust. Desperately. She wasn't ready to share about the new Mark... not yet. But when she did, he'd be the one she went to.

She moved in a haze as she took off her coat and boots then pulled out her cell phone, finding four messages from Ben.

Ben: *How are you?*

Ben: *It's been a while. Everything alright?*

Ben: *Starting to worry.*

Ben: *I'm coming to check on you.*

From Noah, there were three.

Noah: *Soooooooo?*

Noah: *Not checking your phone...I'm impressed.*

Noah: *That good, huh? Have you given it to him yet?*

Her mouth dropped open while her roommate scampered down the hall toward her. "Have I *given* it to him yet?"

"What? Demon-boy is hot. If your first time is gonna be with anyone, I vote him." He waggled his brows. "I bet he's a devil between the sheets."

She rolled her eyes, headed for the living room, and dropped herself on the couch. "I doubt you'd be saying that if you saw what happened today." She ran a hand through her hair. "You could have invited Ben inside to wait instead of making him sit out in his vehicle in the middle of winter, you know."

He frowned. "I did."

"Oh." Her brow furrowed.

He plunked down beside her. "So, what'd you learn?"

"So much and yet not nearly enough." She flattened her palms against her lap, offering him the entirety of her attention. "But I might have a plan."

CHAPTER 13
GRACE

Grace's yoga class was *intense*. She'd hoped it'd help extricate the stress that'd taken root. Turned out that feat was harder than anticipated, the impossible kind of hard. She'd peered into the shadows of Hell, and some things once seen couldn't be unseen.

When class was done, she headed for the showers, dressed, and made her way out into the cool winter's day. Her phone buzzed, and she glanced at it expecting to see Ben's name, but instead found a text plastered across the screen.

Unknown: *Good morning, beauty.*

She didn't recognize the number, so her response was simple.

Grace: *Who's this?*

Unknown: *My heart breaks that you've forgotten me so soon.*

Her toes curled deep in her boots. How? How had he found her number?

Grace: *Gideon?*

Gideon: *I'm glad to see I've left an impression.*

She shook her head, vehemently.

Grace: *Doesn't a fancy-pants businessman have better things to do besides pestering me?*

Gideon: *I have minions for such things. When you hire people who are good at what they do, it affords you time. What are you up to?*

Grace: *Walking to my car after yoga.*

Gideon: *Ooh. I like a bendy woman. I hope you're wearing another pair of those lovely yoga pants.*

She blushed. Hard. So hard a sheen of sweat rose across her skin.

Grace: *There's something wrong with you.*

Gideon: *Indeed. In an effort to make my day, you should send a photo of you in said pants.*

Holding up the phone, she contorted her face, snapped a quick selfie that offered him a decidedly rude gesture, then clicked send.

Gideon: *Stunning. Is that your favorite finger? P.S. You missed the pants.*

Her knees weakened, and she stumbled. Her hand shot out and she caught herself on the car before she glanced around to make sure there weren't any witnesses. *How does he affect me like this? How?* She shook herself.

Grace: *I'm in the pants whether you can see them or not.*

Gideon: *Sneaky girl. Just for that, I'm making that your contact photo.*

Grace: *Don't you dare!*

Gideon: *If you'd prefer I use a different image then I suggest you send one.*

Grace: *Now that's black mail!*

Gideon: *Most definitely.*

She worried her lip between her teeth. It really was a terrible picture. Raising her phone high, she adjusted her hair, set her position, smiled, took another photo, and sent it.

Gideon: *Stunning. Would you like to see what I'm wearing?*

For so many reasons, that was a hard no.

Grace: *I think not.*

Gideon: *Are you free today?*

Grace: *I'm headed to see* The Chronicle *with Ben.*

Gideon: *Lovely. I eagerly await the answers to who you are.*

Her throat ran dry as she rocked back and forth on her heels.

Grace: *Goodbye, Gideon.*

Gideon: *Good luck, Crys. Be sure to tell Noah I said "Hello."*

GRACE'S MIND churned over the possibilities before her because if it turned out she wasn't a Shepherd, she needed to be ready...to run...again.

She scanned the vast parking lot of the secluded building Ben had taken them to. There wasn't anything special about its brick facade. No markings or signs, nothing to indicate what lay inside held any significance. It was like something straight out of every true crime show ever. The perfect place to hide a body—

"You look great, by the way," Ben said, interrupting her thoughts as they climbed from his vehicle.

Her heart fluttered as she smoothed her jeans and adjusted the form-fitting ivory wool coat she'd changed into. It was practical, and the fact that it was also cute played no part in her decision to wear it. *No part at all.*

Ben made for the door, unlocked it, and held it wide. Grace clasped her hands before her as she passed into the small foyer. He stepped in tight behind her—so tight, his chest pressed into her back. Reaching past her, he hit the call button for the elevator. His heat pulsed against her, seeping into her bones, and she welcomed the distraction.

The doors slid wide, and they crossed inside. Ben hit the button to go down to which the elevator jolted and clanked then descended and descended and descended. It rocked before it ground to a halt, and Grace loosed a heavy exhale.

The metal doors parted, and she was greeted by stagnant, musty air that sat heavy and stale in her lungs. Carved stone covered every surface and bore frescos so intricate the figures depicted in them could've walked straight out of the paintings. As she advanced deeper, rectangular indents appeared, filling the walls that lined their path. Each was overlaid with marble and stacked one on top of the other until they reached the ceiling at least thirty feet above.

"What are they?" she asked

"The tombs of our dead." He edged closer and swiped a hand over the unfamiliar script etched beneath one. "This is Latin. It gives the name, birth, and death dates. Our people rest to the right." He pointed across the catacomb. "The Lesser Demons to the left."

"Even in death you're separated," she breathed, her arms heavy as she ran her fingers over the chiseled Latin words. It was beyond sad.

"We're eternal enemies, and death is when eternity begins." His stare pinned hers when he added, "Their blood decides who they are just like ours does for us. It's why you can't trust them. They're born of the depths of Hell. Their darkness *makes* them. That taint runs through their souls. Their path is already determined."

Wait...what? Pump the brakes. She couldn't have heard that right. "What do you mean their path is already determined? I thought we were offered repentance to determine our own end?"

"That's for mankind, not our kind. Our end is set, which is why Gideon and his people are dangerous. Their seats in Hell are reserved regardless of what they do in this life. But the more havoc they wreak, the higher that seat might be on the other side."

That hit like a punch to the gut. What if that was her fate? A suffering beyond imagining while she burned for eternity. The tension in her chest reached a fever pitch and her voice quavered when she said, "That's awful."

His eyes narrowed. "Don't pity them. I promise, they've earned their end."

Her hand trembled wildly as she tucked several stray hairs behind her ear and uttered, "What if I'm one of them, Ben? Do you think I've earned that end?"

He clasped her forearm and offered a gentle squeeze. The hard planes of his face were staunch when he gave a decisive nod. "You're Nephilim."

"You can't know that." Her head swam. *Dizzy.* She was so dizzy. She swayed.

Ben's hold locked down and kept her upright. "But I do, because *nothing* about you is like them."

She wanted to believe him, but it hadn't escaped her notice he wasn't rushing to *The Chronicle*. She needed that truth, to know her destiny, but fear of her dark potential kept her rooted in place.

He stepped closer. "I get all this is a shock, but I'm not gonna let anything bad happen to you, Grace. I promise."

The earnestness in his stare was so intense, so believable, a small knot in her stomach unwound. He wouldn't hurt her. It wasn't in his blood. She was safe. She'd be alright. *Please, God, let me be alright.*

His palm slid to her elbow, and he held tight when he led her deeper into the Catacombs. Time slowed, each step like trudging through hip-high snow, and she concentrated on that alone because if her thoughts strayed anywhere else, she didn't think she'd make it.

Before long, Ben stopped them in front something that resembled a pulpit. A golden book with Latin symbols, a circular, bronze-ish inlay, and a wrought iron-like texture sat atop its stone surface. He flipped it open, and Grace was hit by the heavy, dank scent of metal. The parchment was yellowed and looked every bit as old as she suspected it was.

She cocked her head. Her mouth opened and closed, then opened again. "The pages are empty." Helpful. Very helpful.

He released a throaty laugh. "This is *The Chronicle*." His grip glided down her arm, to her wrist as he withdrew a gold dagger from inside of his coat.

The hairs on the back of her neck stood on end when her gaze jumped between him and his jabby weapon. "What are you doing?"

"The book reads your lineage through your blood."

"Oh." That wasn't disturbing at all. What was it with these people and blood? They really wanted to take everything; her finances, her blood…her life. She swallowed back the bile that climbed her throat.

He set the tip of the blade to her index finger and winced. "Sorry for this."

Ben broke skin, and she flinched at the pain, sucking in a sharp hiss. He guided her hand over the book while her blood trickled free. It fell in thick rivulets and made a tap-tap-tap when it landed, rolling across the parchment before it absorbed and vanished into the page.

Like air rising in water, words ascended from the book's depths. The Latin lettering shimmered, its colors a mixture of black and gold that reflected iridescent against the light. When Grace shifted, the transition between colors was so seamless, she couldn't tell where one ended and the next began. Several seconds later, it stopped.

Her voice matched the frantic beat of her heart when she asked, "What does it say?"

His brows furrowed as he stared at it. Silence reigned.

That expression…it couldn't be good. A paralyzing fear gripped her. It constricted her throat, her lungs, her chest. She couldn't breathe. Couldn't think past anything but the panic. She planted her foot, readying to bolt. "What is it?"

He dropped her hand and shook his head, the movement slow at first before it steadily gained strength. "Nothing," he replied, voice even. "Sorry, it's just been a while since I've done this."

A smidgeon of her tension ebbed.

Setting a finger under the symbols, he followed them as he spoke. "This is your father's name: Scott Morgan, and your mother, Wyla Crawford." He offered her a tight smile. "The color of the writing means you're Nephilim."

"Nephilim." Her hand rose to her chest, and she took a step back, then inhaled a free breath. "Nephilim." Just the feel of it on her tongue was a salve to her soul.

That smile of his widened. "I told you."

Her heart trembled, then tripped, and sputtered its way back to a normal rhythm as her terror waned, drifting from her body like dust on the wind. Nephilim, not a Lesser Demon. "Does it say more about my parents?"

"No. *The Chronicle* only gives your affiliation." He squared himself to her. "You're shaking."

"I'm alright," she said, and meant it. Kind of. Her head canted when a truth hit her. "Wait...I thought only the female Cherubim or Dark Seraphim were supposed to carry the children?"

"They are."

"But my mother wasn't—"

"If they carry the right Marks, they can be seen and appear as human to the unSighted."

Her mind flitted from thought to thought, lost in a hurricane of its own creation. "Is—is that the only option?"

He shook his head. "The chances of a pregnant Cherubim slipping past unnoticed is slim to none considering their movements are tracked." He shrugged. "Both of your parents could've been Nephilim, or your mom might have been Nephilim, and your father human, or vice versa."

She stared into space, trying to comprehend the enormity of that information, but nothing came clear. Her mother *was* her mother, but she'd lied about everything else, literally. And that truth hurt almost more than she could bear. Her shoulders sagged. "I think I'm gonna need to take Jenna up on that offer to research my parents."

Ben's eyes narrowed. "What?"

"This gave me one answer, but I still need a thousand more."

He took her hand and stroked his thumb across her skin, leaving a warm trail in his wake. "Don't worry about that now. You've been through a lot, try not to overwhelm yourself."

I bowed my head. *He's right, Grace. Just chill. You can only do—or handle —one thing at a time. One. Thing. At. A. Time.* She offered him a nod, mentally shoving the business of who she was aside while letting the issue of the new Mark shimmy into its place.

"I'll let Elijah know our findings and he'll schedule your Marking Ceremony."

She raised a finger, putting a pin in his suggestion. "Before that, I think I'd like to meet with him," she said, initiating the beginnings of that plan she'd mentioned to Noah. "I just, I have some questions. Stuff I'd like to clarify."

His Adam's apple dropped low as he swallowed. He closed the book with a thump, gave her the full weight of his attention and stepped closer. "Is something wrong? Anything I can help with?"

Her face heated under a blush. God, he was sweet, but she really needed this meeting to come through. "No, it's nothing. I appreciate the offer, but I'd really like to talk to him." She braced for the next part because she was infinitely confident Ben wasn't about to like it. "And could…could we do it at Bedlam?"

His jaw clenched, chest caving like she'd punched him. *Crap.* She hadn't meant to hurt him, but if her idea was gonna work it *had* to happen there.

She gestured around them. "This place creeps me out. I think it'll just be easier there," she said, the words not necessarily a lie, but that didn't stop the pang of guilt that swept through her.

He watched her, stare calculating. Slowly, and with a predatory flare, he grinned. "Fine. I'll make that request as long as you do something for me in return."

A trade? She could make a trade...probably...maybe. Depending. "Okay?"

He dusted his hands. "Go out with me."

Her mind froze like a block of ice. It wouldn't move, wouldn't work. Nothing. She was blank. "Like…for a walk or something?"

He laughed. Thick and heavy. The sound of it sent soft tingles chasing over her body. "For a date."

He was good looking, gave a shit about protecting her, and was literally a descendent of angels. They shared a heavy, similar, and painful past. Yet a date meant opening doors to her heart she'd held shut for so long, she wasn't sure they'd open, not properly, or fully. But if there was ever a guy she should try for, who made better sense than him?

Her voice was light when she said, "Alright."

Angling in, he tipped his head. "I'm glad. And now that we know we're on the same team, the rules won't be an issue."

She blinked rapidly. "What rules?"

His hands made a ssh sound as he rubbed them together. "After your Marked, consorting with the other side is off the table."

Her brow furrowed, and her stomach plummeted. "Why?"

The smile he offered was well beyond satisfied. "Because the Nephilim and Lesser Demons are forbidden from personal associations."

CHAPTER 14
GRACE

Grace strode into her patient, Laura's, room. The woman's color was good, a hell of a lot better than it'd been hours before. "Here are your discharge forms and the scripts for your medications. Remember what the doctor told you, if you start to feel another gallbladder attack coming on, take the meds right away. You're better to get ahead of the pain than to try and catch up with it."

Laura nodded. "I'm on it."

"There's a pharmacy near the main entrance." Grace smiled and handed the papers over. "You take care." She left and paused in the corridor when her phone pinged with an incoming text.

Noah: *Kyle's invited the gang to dinner at his place Friday night.*

Grace: *Are you just rubbing it in my face? Or am I invited too?*

Noah: *Jake would be ever so disappointed if you didn't show.*

She flicked the phone with her finger, pretending it was his face. But when an idea hit, she smiled.

Grace: *Can I invite Ben?*

Noah: *I'd prefer Gideon, but…*

He was obsessed. She scoffed, flicked the phone again, and was half a millisecond from hitting send on the wittiest of witty retorts when his next message appeared.

Noah: *Of course, you can invite him. I'll let Kyle know.*

Clicking off their conversation, she selected Ben.

Grace: *Kyle's hosting a dinner Friday evening. Just a few friends. Wanna join me?*

She was about to set her phone aside, but his reply was quick.

Ben: *Kyle's Noah's boyfriend?*

Grace: *Good memory.*

A brief pause.

Ben: *I've got some things to do.*

Her frown morphed into a pout. It would've been nice to introduce him to everyone. She sighed. Some other time.

Ben: *Elijah's available to meet at 9:00 am tomorrow.*

She worried her cheek between her teeth and tamped down the anxiety that followed the message. Her plan had fallen into place easier than expected and she'd take every victory she could get.

Grace: *I'll be there.*

Ben: *Are you ready for our date?*

She did a squirmy dance. A date. God, did she even know what she was doing anymore? Things couldn't have changed that much…could they? She smoothed the front of her scrubs and smiled.

Grace: *Very.*

Ben: *Good. I look forward to seeing you.*

Lifting her head, she eyed Rodan as he headed down the hall toward her, attention buried in a chart. It was the first time their shifts had coincided since the night he'd outed her. If she hadn't been wearing her mask of professionalism, she would've offered him the vibrant string of epithets that hovered on the tip of her tongue.

He stopped and glanced up. "Grace."

"Doctor," she acknowledged, tone sharp.

"I'm headed for a quick break. Care to join me?"

She pursed her lips. As much as the idea rankled her, they *would* be working together on two fronts. It'd probably be beneficial to sort stuff out. She was due for her lunch anyway, and her stomach picked that opportunity to growl. She shoved her phone away and fell in line beside him. "Fine."

"I didn't get the chance to apologize before." He shrugged. "I'm required to notify my Sect Leader of any unlisted Shepherds in our territory."

She huffed and released her irritation—somewhat. Mad as she'd been at how it'd all gone down, at least she'd gotten some answers. Sure, she had a million more questions in their place, but it was a start. When they arrived in the kitchen, they grabbed their meals from the fridge then took a table off to the side for privacy.

"I hear you're one of us now." He stuck his fork into his food.

"So I've been told."

He raised his water in salute. "Welcome to the team."

"I'd thank you, but I'm unsure if I'm thankful yet."

His lip tipped up. "Ben seems thankful."

The heat of a blush burned her cheeks, and she fidgeted with her sandwich when that wave of anxiety hit again. It rolled in her chest, end over end. Tumbling into the abyss of her tumultuous emotions.

"I'm glad he's taking you out. He could use someone."

Interesting. "What do you mean?"

He leaned back in his seat. "You heard about Leah?" At her nod, he continued, "From the start it was obvious she wasn't right for him. He wanted to settle down, but she wasn't ready. He's a serious guy. Once he commits, that's it. He's all in and then some."

Serious was good. The last thing she needed was to have her heart stomped on by someone looking for a fling. Her emotions were fragile enough in that regard. The fact that he was Nephilim was a bonus.

"Leah knew who Gideon was. Knew Ben disliked the guy, so that whole situation left a deep mark on him. It'll be good for him to move on with someone else."

She winced. "So they got together to hurt Ben on purpose?"

"Her, yes. Gideon…" He shook his head.

Her brows climbed so high she thought they might slip from her face because Gideon was just so…cocky. "Really?"

"I don't think he knew who she was. The guy can be accused of a lot of things, but he's meticulous about his businesses. He doesn't bring trouble there."

Combing her fingers through the end of her ponytail, she said, "I'm surprised you're defending the enemy. Scandalous."

He smirked. "Facts are facts. Besides, you've seen him. He doesn't need someone else's leftovers." The words weren't bitter, just a simple statement of fact from a self-assured man.

"Ben doesn't seem as forgiving."

He lifted a shoulder in a half-shrug. "He refuses to acknowledge that Gideon didn't know but the guy's hands are full enough with his own people. He doesn't give a shit about the goings on of the Nephilim."

The image of the Lesser Demons at their Calling flashed across her mind. "They are something."

His brows ticked up as he laughed.

"How did Leah end up getting caught?"

"She left a picture on her phone. I didn't see it, but Ben nearly lost his mind when he did."

She sucked in a sharp hiss as she winced, because she could only imagine how that must've felt. "They took a *photo*?"

"Well, she did," he corrected. "Gideon's pretty cautious about his public persona. I doubt he knew, but who can say for sure?"

Gideon liked to flirt. *A lot.* His provocative air dripped from him like liquid sex, so the possibility that he hadn't been party to any of it struck her hard. She rubbed her temples. "Why would Leah even take a picture like that?"

"To get caught."

Her jaw plummeted so fast it was a wonder it didn't hit the table.

"Like I said, she wasn't ready for the kind of commitment Ben wanted."

Awful didn't even begin to describe it. No wonder Ben had baggage. Who wouldn't when they'd been ravaged like that? "She's entitled to what she feels, but there are a lot of other ways to tell a guy you want out."

"Yes, but one would need a spine for that." He twisted his drink and the light caught on the distinctive, bronze ring on his right index finger. It highlighted the Roman numerals etched into its surface. Grace read a three and the beginnings of some other number but was distracted when Rodan's jaw clenched. She followed his attention to the lunchroom entrance.

Dixie Morranis, a Palliative Care nurse, stepped inside. The coquettish smile she offered Rodan fell when her gaze landed on Grace and turned all sharp and stabby. *Wow. Harsh.* It was a wonder Dixie hadn't walked over and challenged her to a duel.

Grace's stomach hardened. "I think you have an admirer."

"More like a stalker." He lowered his head and harsh whispered, "She's everywhere I go lately. I keep expecting to see her skulking outside the compound."

She awkward laughed, but he'd handed her a thread, so she grabbed it and ran. "Why do you live there if you have the freedom not to?"

"Freedom is a relative term." He rolled his neck. "Living there makes it easier with what's required of us. Besides, I've got mounds of debt from medical school, so it's cheaper. I'll leave some day, just need to get my affairs in order." He took a bite of his food and dropped his fork with a clank. "Will you be moving in?"

"No," she said to squash that idea before it could gain traction because that would not be happening. Ever. "What was it like being a child in this system?"

"The Hall of Shepherds was an interesting place to grow up," he said by way of answer, not answering at all.

His use of "interesting" implied many things, none of which sounded good. "Why?"

He finished chewing, then swallowed. "It was tough. Strict, corporal punishment, no nonsense. No negotiation. Us and the Lesser Demons, we grow up and train together to make sure the training is equal, but in the end, we're torn apart and pitted against one another. Some find it hard since this life was chosen for us and we don't get a say. A lot of our kind would rather have been born normal."

That wasn't an unreasonable position considering she'd been with them for a matter of days and already felt constrained. She couldn't fathom having her entire life taken from her. "And how do you feel about it?"

"In the end, what I want is irrelevant. It is what it is, and I am what I am. All I can do is make the most of what's in my control."

A page came over the P.A. system, calling a Code Blue.

"That's us." She jumped to her feet. Setting their things aside, they headed out, but stopped at the door when they spotted the Charge Nurse, Angie. "What are we dealing with?" Grace asked.

"A patient collapsed in the parking lot. When paramedics approached, they collapsed too. Could be airborne."

Every hair on Grace's body stood on end. That's exactly what happened the night she'd bolted from the Shepherd's and landed in Trenton. The night she'd stumbled across the new Mark. Could it be? Was it possible? If it was, everyone was about to be in some big ass danger. Grace had to know.

"Idiopathic collapse," Rodan murmured, thoughts churning in his eyes. "Alright. We move them into quarantine along with anyone else who's come in contact with them. We follow protocol, full protective gear. Shut the hospital doors and get rid of all unnecessary people," he said, then he was on the move.

If there were any problematic souls in the parking lot, Grace'd be able to see them from the E.R. windows. But on the off chance she was wrong… She headed to the supply room, readied, then emerged. When she arrived people fled, screaming as they shoved past or careened into one another. She took a breath to tamp down on the terror that threatened to consume her.

Near the entrance, a paramedic fought to maneuver a gurney carrying a patient through the pandemonium. Thoughts of the Mark were paused as she rushed to help him. She made it all of five steps before someone slammed into her side and knocked her to the floor. She tried to stand but legs and feet pummeled her, holding her down. Her heart pounded a staccato rhythm while spots painted her vision. She grunted when a boot caught her in the ribs as a man stumbled passed.

Someone gripped the collar at the back of her neck and hauled her to her feet. Wheeling around, she found Rodan. His chest heaved, his face was scratched like a wildcat had gotten at it.

"Thanks," she said, breathless.

He nodded.

Shaking herself off, she made for the paramedic again and gripped the gurney's railings like her life depended on it—because it did. Rodan appeared on the other side and latched on too.

Grace's stare narrowed when it landed on the pale and unconscious patient. "She was in here earlier with gallstones."

"Was it confirmed?" Rodan yelled over the cacophony.

She inclined her head. "By an ultrasound. She was discharged with a surgical referral."

"Let's get her into isolation. Remove her clothes in case they're contaminated, then start a line. We run blood work; CBC, Lytes, B.U.N., Creatinine, blood gases, toxicology screen, blood sugars, drug screen, and white blood cell count. Do it all and rush it."

"We've got six more," Angie called as she pointed in the general direction of the exit.

Damn it! Grace peered over her shoulder, straining to see past the crowd toward the parking lot, with no luck. There wasn't time to linger, and without any confirmation it was the Mark, she had to treat it otherwise.

"Her vitals and ECG were normal," the paramedic said.

Grace's spine went rigid. Normal? Angling toward Rodan, she asked, "What's the interim treatment?"

His expression fell and when he spoke, his voice so low, she had to strain to hear. "I don't know."

CHAPTER 15
GRACE

Grace tapped Ben's name on her phone's screen and dialed his number. Her arms were heavy, burnt out after the night's events. It rang twice before he picked up.

"Hey there," he said, a smile in his voice.

She tugged a loose strand of her hair then tucked it behind her ear. "I have some bad news."

"Oh?"

"I'm not gonna make the meeting with Elijah tomorrow," she winced as a pang of guilt twinged in her chest, "or our date. I'm in quarantine at the hospital."

There was a long pause. "What?"

"I can't say too much, but we have an issue with a potential contagion." Potential being the operative word. What would she have told him if she knew for sure?

"Whatever it is, you're safe, Grace. Our blood makes us impervious to illness."

Good to know but, unfortunately, it didn't change another fact. "I can't leave, it's mandatory. I'm under a two-day observation."

"Rodan can probably get you out."

The laugh she released was so dry it scratched her throat. That same stubborn hair slipped forward, and she shoved it back again. "That's unlikely since he's locked down too. Besides, it'd throw up some major red flags here."

He was silent a moment before he released a long, slow breath. "Alright. I'll talk to Elijah, see what I can do to move things."

"Thank you." Saying their goodbyes, their call ended.

Grace counted the ceiling tiles, then counted them again to be sure. Fifty-eight. Yep. There were fifty-eight tiles. She tapped her phone with her nail before clicking on her social media. The green tally of a notification appeared, and she sat up with a snap. "Gideon Ryczek has requested to be your friend."

"HA!" Friends? Did he even know what the word meant?

A text came in.

Gideon: *I've heard there's quite the ruckus at the hospital.*

What the Hell? He either had eyes everywhere or knew the Mark had been used. A small pang of doubt nagged at the back of her mind, one that had her scratching her head. And one she forcefully shoved aside. Gideon was a master of manipulation, had literally been trained in it. Letting him get to her was the epitome of stupid. But that didn't mean she wasn't about to ask.

Grace: *How did you hear that???*

Gideon: *I have sources.*

Her theory *had* to be right because there was no way in the depths of Hell he'd learned it from Ben.

Grace: *Your source is good. I'm in isolation.*

Gideon: *Not playing nice with others?*

She snorted.

Grace: *Obviously.*

Gideon: *How long do you have left in there?*

Pulling her phone from her face, she checked the time.

Grace: *Forty-four hours and seventeen minutes.*

Gideon: *Would you like me to come down and get myself locked up with you? I'm sure we could find some way to pass the time.*

Her body heated to an uncomfortable level. Shaking her head, she laid back on the bed. He had no quit in him. None. And it bewildered her for so many reasons.

Grace: *There's something wrong with you.*

Gideon: *That's interesting coming from the woman stuck in quarantine.*

The laugh that broke from her was deep and heavy. It eased some of the tightness that'd taken root in her chest. She couldn't remember the last time she'd laughed. Like, really laughed. Her life had been flipped around by the Shepherds. At times, she barely kept her head above water, so it was nice to shake some of that heaviness off. Not that she'd tell him that.

Grace: *You haven't asked who I belong to yet.*

Gideon: *You don't belong to anyone, but I don't have to ask.*

Grace: *That source must be pretty good.*

Gideon: *I don't need a source for this one, Crys.*

She smirked.

Grace: *You figured it out all by yourself?*

Gideon: *I'm going to ignore the implication of surprise in that question.*

Her head tottered back and forth. *Ignore it all you want, demon-boy.*

Grace: *You think you're something, don't you?*

Gideon: *What I think is of no consequence. All that matters is what you do.*

Fluffing her pillow, she sighed.

Grace: *I think this is going to be a long two days.*

Gideon: *My offer stands.*

The confusion swirling through her mind made her head spin. Whether he intended to or not, he was big time messing with her head. Was he actually capable of the new Mark? Could he kill people for his own gain? *Would* he?

Grace: *I'm not accepting your friend request.*

Gideon: *We can keep our relationship secret if that's what you prefer.*

She could practically see his smirk, and she released a garbled, scoffing sound.

Grace: *You're hopeless.*

Her lips parted, pulse pounding in her throat when his reply arrived.

Gideon: *I'm whatever you want me to be, Crys.*

EVERY INCH of Grace's body throbbed because her hospital bed left a lot to be desired. Rubbing her head, she tried to chase away the headache that chipped at her skull. *Thump. Thump. Thump.* It pulsed with the beat of her heart.

She jumped when her phone buzzed as a call came in. Squinting, she peered at it when Noah's name flashed across the screen.

"Hey," she answered, voice thick and groggy.

"Where's your room?" he asked, breathing heavily.

Considering she hadn't texted him about being quarantined yet… "How do you know I'm in a room?"

"Never mind that. We have more important issues at hand. Now, where is it?"

"You can't visit me, Noah. I'm in isola—"

"Hush. What direction does your window face?"

He was being weird. Why was he being so weird? She probably should have questioned it past that but really, he was who he was, and who was she to judge? "Ground floor toward the back parking lot."

"Okay. Go to your window."

She yanked her phone from her head and stared at it, but like the bestest of friends, did as he asked. Returning it to her ear, she drew the curtains aside and fought a hiss as she winced against the blinding light of day. "I'm here."

"Hold on." More panting.

A minute later he appeared, trudging through the knee-high snow and straight up to the glass. Her heart soared, the sight of him like a balm to the soul. While being alone had given her lots of time to think, it'd also given her lots of time to *think*. Seeing his face—a trusted face—was all she'd needed to center herself again.

She beamed and wrapped her arms around herself in a hug, swaying side to side. "You came to see me!"

"We come for each other, Gracie. No matter what."

"No matter what. I love you, Noah."

"Of course, you do," he replied and waved her off as if there was any other option. "You look exhausted. You okay?"

She grimaced and ignored the growing ache in her neck. "This is a great place to work, but not so much to sleep. It's loud in here."

He raised her bag. "Will some clean clothes and anti-stink products make you feel better?"

She set her palm over her heart and meant her next words from the deepest caverns of her heaven-bound soul. "My hero."

Flourishing a hand, he bowed. "So, what's the deal with your meeting?"

"Ben helped me get it moved. It's tomorrow morning."

He shifted, and the sound of the snow crunching under his feet carried through the phone. "Are you sure you wanna go through with this plan?"

"I have to."

"No, you don't. You owe nothing to anyone, Gracie. Nothing."

"Would you want me to stop if it was Kyle who got hurt?"

He flinched. "I'm just...I'm worried about you."

"I know, but I have to do this, Noah. I have to try." She helped people. It was who she was. Walking away or turning a blind eye, she couldn't do it, least of all when her friends could be hurt. Between the Shepherds and her shift, she was exhausted. Everything was just so out of control. Her heart shuddered a dismal beat. "I'd never forgive myself if there was something I could do, something I could learn, and I didn't."

His nod was slow, heavy. "What's the plan if you find something?"

"Then I'll have my answer," she said. "And I tell Ben."

He glanced away, the movement stiff, choppy.

The small hairs along the base of her skull stood on end. "He's Nephilim, Noah."

"And?"

Had he heard *anything* she'd said about the Shepherds? "Annnd, Gideon is a Lesser Demon." His silence drove her crazy, so she pushed on. "I know he's hot as all get out but—"

When Noah's eyes came back to hers, they were sharp, and deathly serious. "The devil was once an angel."

She blinked. When the weight of those words hit her, she staggered back. She tried to speak, but her voice seized in her throat. Trying again she managed, but it was soft, barely audible. "What are you saying?"

"I'm saying you should expect anything from anyone."

Sure, but Gideon had a reputation, one he hadn't earned by accident. He knew things, had access to things. It couldn't be a coincidence, could it? She plunked her hip on the window ledge and set her forehead against the cold glass. Dismal was an understatement for how she felt.

There was one thing she kept circling back to, the one thing she couldn't seem to move past... "Regardless of what he does in this life, Gideon's bound for Hell. That's makes him—his *kind*—dangerous. I can't ignore that."

There was a strained pause before he cocked his head. "What?"

"Ben told me our blood guarantees our place in the afterlife."

Noah's brows drew together so hard they formed a crease. "And you don't think the same could be said of the Nephilim?"

"What do you mean?"

He shrugged. "If they're guaranteed a seat in Heaven, why does it matter what they do in this life?"

A nagging sensation crawled up the base of her spine—one that felt suspiciously like a warning. The more she thought on it, the more it rang true, because if the Nephilim were so pure, why was it necessary to limit who had access to the Gateway Mark?

But Grace had to trust someone, and Ben *was* the Nephilim Elijah gave that Mark to. That meant something. It had to. He'd been vulnerable with her, shared about his family—or lack thereof. He'd been good to her. His actions spoke for themselves, end of story.

"I'm not trying to scare you, Gracie. I just want you to think. Don't go into this with blinders on. You need to be safe in *every* way. If you're serious about giving Ben a shot, you should protect yourself from, you know, stuff happening."

She threw her hands up pumping the brakes on *that* conversation.

"We're not even close to there yet, but either way, it's fine. I'm already protected."

"Really? Why didn't you tell me?"

"I didn't think I had to. I've been storing it in the fridge for years." At his blank expression, she continued. "It's the birth control ring. The pink box on the door."

His hand flew to his chest, and he gasped in horror. "I thought that was some weird kind of tea."

He had to be kidding. "It literally says contraception on the label."

With the wave of his hand, he swatted her comment away.

Letting loose a heavy breath, Grace blew the hair that'd fallen free of her ponytail back from her face. There were so many questions. So many unknowns. Too many. "I wish mom was here."

His eyes creased at the corners. "Me too."

"I had a flashback," she confessed. "Mom said something. Sh-she was frantic, told me to trust my instincts. Something had her spooked." She shook her head. "None of it makes sense. She was always protective but whatever this was must've been bad because I'd never seen her like that." She pursed her lips and sighed. "I'm gonna look into her, but I've gotta go through with this, Noah. All of it." She couldn't tell if the words were more to convince him, or herself.

"You're a smart woman, Gracie. You'll figure it all out." Reaching into his pocket, he withdrew something. "Now, onto our second order of business." Unfolding the paper, he stepped up to her window and pressed it against the glass. "I've put together a spreadsheet covering the ranges of what the Shepherds could take from your pay. As long as it isn't over the fifty percent mark, it'll be tight, but with us sharing expenses, you can manage."

She inspected his meticulously detailed and very "Noah" accounting handiwork. The numbers were nothing short of depressing, and if her home hadn't been her mother's she'd have opted for the compound. But it was what it was. "Where would I be without you?"

"Destitute," he said with a grin that fell a second later. "Handing over your income, being forced to comply, this is all moving so fast."

"It is." *Very fast. Too fast*. Seeing as that topic daunted her to no end, she changed it. "How did you even know I was in here?"

He shimmied his shoulders. "A little demon-boy told me."

Her mouth gaped, and her eyes darted around the parking lot. "You have his number?"

His nod was fast and furious. "He added me on social media and gave it to me."

She glanced up at the ceiling for patience. "You didn't tell him you were coming here, did you?"

"Why, Gracie?" he taunted. "Were you hoping to see him?"

She was not answering that. Lifting her shoulder in a shrug, she said, "It won't matter soon enough."

"How come?"

She traced a random curlicue pattern into the steam her breath created on the window then trailed a bead of condensation as it slithered down to the sill. "Because we're on opposite sides of the war, and I'll be forbidden to see him once I'm Marked."

Noah paled, his gaunt, wide-eyed expression nothing short of devastated. "And how do you feel about that?"

The exhale she released did nothing to ease the pressure that closed in around her. "Tired. I feel tired."

CHAPTER 16
GRACE

The next day and a half of Grace's quarantine passed at a glacial pace. When she was finally permitted to leave, she showered and changed into soft plum colored yoga pants and a white form-fitting shirt, put on her makeup, coat and boots, then fled.

The crisp air cleared her lungs of the stagnant hospital scent. A chill slithered deep into her sleep-weary bones, one she didn't think would ever be warmed.

Rush hour was in full swing, so she veered her car onto Elshirl Rd. to avoid the traffic. She thumped along avoiding the potholes, if possible, which was hardly ever, but it'd get her to Bedlam faster and she needed that extra time.

When she arrived, she parked in the vacant lot, then waited, struggling to keep her eyes open. The hospital bed hadn't gotten any more comfortable, and with the commotion going on, sleep had been virtually non-existent.

Her phone *pinged*. She reached into her purse and took it out.

Gideon: *Go inside and wait in my office. I'll be there in a few.*

Yes! She'd prayed this would happen—had counted on it, actually. But letting him in on that fact was counter to her purpose.

Grace: *Are your spy cameras facing the parking lot too? How do you know where I am?*

Gideon: *Magic. Now go inside.*

Grace: *I'm fine in my car.*

Gideon: *It's winter. Get. Inside.*

Good and scolded, her plan was in place. Tucking her phone away, she climbed out and headed for the entrance. Midway through reaching for the door it swung open, and Davis appeared.

"Grace," he greeted. "You're early."

"After I left the hospital, I had just enough time to do nothing," she said, the words mostly true.

He pointed to Gideon's office. "It's unlocked."

"Thanks." Sweet warmth enveloped her as she passed inside and made her way up and into the room. Closing the obnoxiously heavy door, she set her purse down, removed her coat, walked to his desk, and stood there, staring. That wave of guilt rushed over her…again. What she was about to do was a huge breach of privacy. And probably illegal.

She tapped her finger on the edge of his desk, kneaded the back of her neck, and took a deep breath. She'd was stalling…or trying to work up the courage. *Both. Definitely both.* She thought she'd had herself under control, but that control was tenuous, and fleeting. Regardless, time was ticking. If she didn't move, she'd lose her chance, and if he was behind everything, it was worth it. She had to know.

Taking up the remote whose brand matched the TV, she turned it on. When said TV flared to life, it showed camera views of the parking lot, throughout the club, over the underground parking. *Perfect.* She'd have tons of heads up if anyone came.

Her gaze flicked toward the door to his home. Maybe if she had time, she'd scope out his lair too.

She perused the papers on his desk for anything of note while her heart pounded in her ears. When she flipped through, she found a series of financial documents far beyond her level of comprehension. She threw the drawers open. More remotes, general office supplies, other documents related to his businesses. Dropping to her knees she climbed beneath the desk and scanned its underside for secret cubbies. She ran her hands along its edges and found nothing. No latches or false bottoms. *Nada. Pfft.* If he was a villain, he wasn't a particularly stealthy one.

A pen fell and clacked onto the floor. She jumped and smacked her head off the corner of the desk.

"Ow!" she whined. That was gonna leave a welt. An ugly one she deserved. Touching her palm to the back of her head, she checked for blood, then thanked all that was holy when it came away clean. She hissed as she rubbed it, then crawled into his chair.

She checked the cameras on the TV. Still no sign of anyone.

When her finger skimmed the keyboard, the dual computer screens burst to life. A password bar popped up before there was a strange beep and it vanished, opening to the desktop. Her eyes narrowed. Not the smartest security feature, demon-boy.

She went through the icons. Nothing obvious, but that was to be expected, so she brought up the computer's history. Clicking on his email, she opened each one, then scanned his sent and trash sections. *Nothing. Nothing. Nothing.*

Biting her lip, she fought the well of emotions that threatened to overtake her before her attention flicked to the TV again. A sharp, gun-metal colored SUV pulled into the underground parking lot beneath her. Before it disappeared, she spotted the driver.

Her stomach dropped hard. As fast as she could, she closed window after window as the sound of the elevator to her right climbed higher. *Oh, God. Oh, God.* What would he do if he caught her? Open a Gateway and chuck her into Hell?

Her hands vibrated as she clicked the last window, shut the computer down, turned off the TV then bolted for the actual window that overlooked Clarington Avenue. She worked to control her frantic breathing as she brushed her hair back over her shoulder and wiped the incrimination from her face. She hoped.

The elevator *dinged* and the doors slid wide.

Gideon stepped out wearing a knee length, black wool coat that hung open and exposed the dark gray suit he'd paired with a lighter gray dress shirt. His hair was tousled, but in an intentional kind of way. His short, controlled beard was freshly trimmed, while his tattoos protruded above his collar. And not for the first time, she wondered what they were.

He held a box in one hand and a tray of coffees in the other. "Crys," he greeted, tone smooth. His stare landed on her backside before it slid back up. He offered her a slow, appreciative smile.

"Gideon," she breathed as she released the tension that'd gripped her. He didn't know. She hadn't been caught. Turning, she made her way to the couch and fought the sigh that threatened to escape when she settled into it. It was the first comfortable thing she'd occupied in days and her body welcomed it. She scratched her cheek. She didn't deserve that comfort, not after what she'd just done.

He stepped around and set the tray of drinks onto the coffee table, then crouched before her and opened the box he held. "Pick."

Her tongue trailed across the back of her teeth. What was done was done. She'd have to live with her decision. But the last thing she needed was him becoming suspicious, so she shoved aside her torrid thoughts and focused on what lay before her. Food.

Steepling her fingers, she studied the assortment of gourmet muffins and her mouth watered like the hungry savage she was. Her lips pursed, torn between a chocolate chip and fruity looking one. She chose the latter. Gideon removed the chocolate chip and handed it to her as well before he closed the box. Taking one of the drinks, he left the tray on the coffee table along with several creams and sugars, then aimed for his desk. Placing everything he carried on it, he took off his coat and set himself down.

"Thanks," she said around a mouthful of the chocolate chip, then swallowed. "Will any of your other cohorts be joining us today?"

"Just Davis."

She was glad to hear it—exceptionally so.

Her hair was still damp, so a chill raked her spine, and she eyed the throw across the back of the couch. Sure, it was decoration, but that didn't mean it couldn't also be functional. She threw it over her legs, took up her coffee, and drank deep.

Gideon's amber stare skimmed the blanket, and he cocked a brow. "Making yourself comfortable?"

"I'm already comfortable. I'm making myself warm."

An ear-splitting grin took him. "If it's heat you're looking for, I could assist you in making some."

She choked, then cleared her throat, then cleared her throat again. "The coffee's doing a good enough job."

"The offer stands if you change your mind."

Biting into the muffin again, a creamy, liquidy-chocolate flowed from its center into her mouth, and she moaned. Her gaze slid to Gideon who straight-up stared.

"Don't let me stop you."

She didn't, but when she took her next bite, she kept her pleasure silent.

"The Arillia Evening News is reporting there's an outbreak happening," he said.

She swallowed her mouthful, kicked off her boots, and lifted her feet onto the couch. What should she tell him? There were only a few things she knew for sure. "I'm not confident enough to call it an outbreak yet, but it's not far off."

"Are they close to figuring it out?"

She creased her eyes. "Honestly, no. There's one dead and nine affected so far, the survivors are all offering the same story. They were fine one moment and collapsed the next, completely drained and too weak to function. We've had eighteen more unaffected but kept in isolation due to potential contact or carry. All their blood work has come back clean. None of the symptomatic patients are connected to anything that would explain what's happening. And the only thing we've found that helps is IV fluids.

"We're in close contact with the CDC and other national and international agencies, but so far, nothing. Whatever's going on, we're ground zero."

"Shit."

She bobbed her head. "Shit, indeed." She took a final bite and finished off the muffin before she picked up the second one and inhaled it as well. Between the food hitting bottom, her last few days at the hospital, and her self-induced snooping stress, an oppressive wave of fatigue crashed over her. She picked up her coffee and took a long drink before asking a question that had surfaced during her alone time in the hospital. "So, what's the deal with Purgatory? Is it real?"

"Mmhmm," he replied through his closed mouthful of muffin, his manners far superior to her own. When he was finished, he continued, "It's where the improperly Marked end up."

She shifted to better face him. "And how does one become improperly Marked?"

"Once in a while the death happens faster than the Marks can take, or when someone is midway through repenting, which might create a state of limbo for the soul. When that happens, they can end up caught in-between."

Her eyes grew heavy again. She set her coffee down and offered it a pointed glare since it wasn't doing a damn thing to help. "And who sorts that out?"

Linking his hands, he set them over his abdomen. "The Delphi regulate Purgatory."

She yawned. "And who are the Delphi?"

"Part-human, part-angel, part-demon."

"Like the Agents?"

"The Agents and Marksman."

Her ears perked up. "What's a Marksman?"

"They make the Marks. Without them none of this would work. No Gateways, no passage."

The Marks were *made*? She worked to control her reaction because she needed to get her head right. It made sense, they had to come from somewhere, but somehow that possibility had never occurred to her. Like, not at all. She'd ultimately concocted the meeting with Elijah to gain access to Gideon's office, but maybe she could use it for another purpose.

"Is that what you meant when you said I could be dual to Elijah?"

"It was."

"What would've happened if I had been?"

"Then you'd have gone down a very different path," he replied.

Like the path of an Agent, Delphi, or Marskman? She was too tired to push that topic further, so instead she asked, "Have you seen it? Purgatory, I mean."

"I have."

She shimmied further down onto the couch and stretched herself out. "What's it like?"

"It's nothing. A void. Like walking through an endless fog." He turned and faced his desk. "How's your head?"

Some nagging sensation grew in the pit of her stomach, but why that was, she couldn't be sure. "My head?"

He took up the remote, turned on the TV, and flicked it to another screen—one that displayed the interior of his office. His chair creaked when he leaned back and offered her the full weight of his amber stare.

Not good. Not. Good. Shame so all-encompassing crested like a storm on her horizon. He *knew*! How had she not considered his office had cameras? How? It was like she'd *wanted* him to catch her.

"How's your head?" he repeated when he placed the remote down with such precision, it made no sound. His tone hadn't changed. There was no angry inflection, no sense of betrayal. His eyes were heavy on her, but his expression was flat—unreadable. And it all made her feel so, so much worse.

She couldn't deny what she'd done. He had the evidence in front of him, he'd caught her red handed. The reddest of reds. An invisible vice punched into her chest and crushed her lungs, making it hard to breathe. "Gideon—"

"What did I tell you, Crys?"

She clenched her hands to hide their shake. He'd told her many things. Her heart stuttered a beat while she braced.

"I told you to question everyone and everything, including me."

She froze. Wait, he was fine with her rifling through his life? He hadn't even pushed to learn what she'd been rifling for and the only reasonable explanation she could come up with was that he didn't care because he had nothing to hide. It wasn't possible for her to feel any worse. It just wasn't. "Did you know what I was doing that whole time?"

The smirk he offered held not one ounce of malice.

Of course, he had. Like he'd said, he knew everything that happened in his club. "And you gave me access to your computer."

He winked.

She shook her head, unable to help the anxious burst of laughter that escaped. "I can't believe you let me finish."

"Oh, Crys," his shoulders drew back, "you'll always finish with me."

Her stomach torqued, and the heat that consumed her had not a damn thing to do with the blanket.

Angling forward, he set his elbows on the desk and tipped his head toward the door to his home. "Do you want to look in there?"

She swallowed hard. There'd been no innuendo, no implication of more. It was a serious offer, and beyond any shadow of a doubt she had her answer. "I don't need to."

His gaze held hers, sharp, weighing. After several long seconds, he spoke, "You didn't answer before. How's your head?"

"Sore, but I'm not concussed, if that's what you mean."

"Good. Now go to sleep."

"I'm fine, Gideo—"

"We've got an hour before the meeting. Close your eyes," he ordered. She was ready to protest again, but he cocked a brow in challenge.

"You're pushy," she said as she slid herself down until she lay on her side, because in truth, she had zero confidence she could keep her eyes open even if she wanted to.

He offered her a devil-may-care grin. "Would you like to see just how hard I can push?"

She ignored that, which had him laughing to himself as he turned to his computer, logged in, and started working. Her body sank further and further into the couch as she settled, then drifted.

CHAPTER 17

GRACE

Grace struggled to ignore the voices. They were arguing. Well, one was; the other just offered calm and quiet retorts—the kind of calm that accompanied controlled anger. She was too out of it to discern what they talked about, but whatever it was, there was a dangerous edge to it.

Someone touched her arm. "Grace."

She released a whimpering whine. She didn't want to wake up yet. *Sleep*. She needed it. *Want more*.

The person nudged her again. "Grace."

Her eyes opened to a slit but only because she forced them to. The figure before her was blurry, and she blinked several times to clear her sight. "Ben," she said, voice groggy.

He was on his knees before her. "Wake up."

Where was she? She peered around. Gideon's office. Why was she there? There was a reason, but it was out of reach. Ben's brows were furrowed, his eyes creased at the corners. Had something happened? "What's wrong?"

"Nothing." His tone was rough and totally unconvincing. "The meeting's about to start."

The meeting! She tried to sit up, but the blanket was like a weight that pinned her in place. She tried again, and a dizzy spell took her, so she stayed where she was for a moment. She scanned the room and landed on Davis where he leaned against the frame of the open door. Gideon was still seated at his desk, arms crossed over his broad chest, his stare on Ben. He looked tired, like he'd been close to sleep himself.

The air was thick with tension. It coated her thoughts and made them slow to surface.

Gideon turned to his Head of Security. "Tell the others we'll have the meeting here."

Davis nodded and left.

Ben leaned closer to her. "Are you alright?"

Of course, she was. Why wouldn't she be? Her gaze slid between the two men again and realization dawned, but with her brain still coming online, it took a second to form an answer. "I didn't have enough time to go home after I was discharged, so I just came here," she looked around again, "and passed out." She omitted a few things, but it wasn't exactly a sharing circle. Sitting all the way up, she took the blanket with her and tucked her legs tight to her chest.

Ben's movements were stiff as he rose. He set himself down on the arm of the couch to her right then rested his hand behind her when the others filed in the room.

Jenna followed behind Davis before she propped herself on Grace's other side. "Fancy meeting you here."

Grace inclined her head. "It's almost like it was planned."

Trevor dropped into the space to Jenna's left with a thunk, shifting the couch back several inches. Elijah and Rodan took the two chairs across from them, the former crossing his legs, while Davis set himself on the edge of Gideon's desk.

Gideon pushed up, strode across the room, and set the box of muffins on the coffee table between everyone, then returned to his seat.

No one made a move for them, but Grace was still ravenous and not about to let a good thing go to waste. Snatching up another one of the delectable treats, she caught Jenna's eye as she leaned back. "Try the chocolate."

Without hesitation, the other woman plucked one up herself, took a bite and sighed.

Elijah's gaze narrowed on the two before his attention flicked to the muffins, then back up. "Grace, you requested this meeting. The floor is yours."

Straight to it then. She cleared her throat. "I have a few points of contention," she said. Ben stiffened. She broke off a piece of her muffin and popped it in her mouth. "What if I don't give you my paycheck?"

Elijah folded his palms in his lap. "Offering half of your income is compulsory if you work or live off compound."

Half. Her world tilted on its axis. It was the first time she'd gotten an official number—the worst number. That couldn't stand. She had to fight it. "That seems a bit unreasonable given the circumstances, don't you think?"

"The circumstance is that you're a Shepherd."

"But that's not all I am. I came into this situation at a disadvantage. I have financial responsibilities that were accrued long before I learned about any of this. The other Shepherds knew what they were getting into when they accepted their debts. I didn't. I would hope a reasonable concession could be made."

"There are no concessions for either side. I do not make the rules, Grace, but I will enforce them." The words weren't a threat, but warning dripped off them like blood from a blade.

A headache thrummed in her ears while she did everything in her power to tamp down on the surge of emotions that threatened to erupt. She hated it so much. The Shepherds hadn't done anything to help her, hadn't done anything to earn that income. They'd just reached out to take it. Yeah, she'd ultimately be okay, not the best, but okay. Her hand twitched, begging to chuck the remainder of her muffin at him, but she threw her words instead. "Blind obedience never served anyone."

"Those are the rules."

She placed her muffin down. "What if I don't like them?"

"You do not have a choice," he said, his tone brokering no room for negotiation.

Fire coursed through her veins. "Is this why we're meant to be taken as children? Easier to mold? Easier to control?"

He didn't answer but offered her a pointed stare. His mannerisms were so muted, she couldn't tell if he was angry or surprised, and in that moment, she didn't care.

"Grace," Ben cautioned.

"I'm still allowed to ask questions. I'm not under anyone's jurisdiction yet." The words hadn't been unkind, more matter of fact. She glanced back to Elijah, waiting.

"You're meant to be taken as children so you can be trained and readied for the war that will eventually come."

"And what if I don't want to be trained? What if I don't want any part of your war?" She crossed her arms over her chest. "What if I don't want to be Marked?"

"You do not have a choice," he repeated.

"What would you do if I said no?"

His spine straightened while his jaw angled up. "We would rend your soul from your body."

Everyone in the room shifted—everyone save Gideon, who sat unmoving. When her gaze found his, he offered her a subtle shake of his head. She treaded close to some imaginary line of disobedience. And while she wanted to fight more, if *he* suggested against it, it was probably a bad idea, monumentally bad.

She glanced at her lap. She loathed being forced into anything. Yes, if she'd have been given a choice between Heaven and Hell, the choice would've been easy. But she *hadn't* been given that choice, and something about it was wrong.

Her shoulders fell. "Tell me about the Marking."

Elijah inclined his head. "The Arillia Nephilim and Lesser Demons will gather at the catacombs to bear witness as I set the brands to your skin."

God, she'd be *branded* like she was some piece of chattel. She scanned the others and their Marks. She supposed that's what they were, property of one side or the other, at the Shepherd's beck and call, required to submit to a will that wasn't their own. Freedom was an illusion. Have a career, have a home, have as many dreams as you want, but at a cost. Believe it's yours, but make no mistake, it was only a belief.

She flicked her nail. "Will it hurt?"

"It will sting."

"Like the prick of a needle," Ben added. His warm hand settled on her back and his thumb stroked a rigid line across her shoulder blade.

She nodded, the movement tight. Her gaze flicked to Gideon again. "Can they ever be removed?"

"No," Elijah said. "The Shepherd Marks are permanent. Once they're in place, there's no going back."

Irreversible. The Marks were *irreversible*. She'd be branded forever. No, not her, her *soul*. She swallowed around the lump in her throat, violently forcing that thought aside. She'd have to dwell on that horrifying truth later because the Agent had just offered her a half-assed opening she couldn't miss. "Will a Marksman be the one to do it?"

"No. They do not come to us. Their identities are hidden to protect their charge."

Well, that wasn't helpful. How was she supposed to talk to one if they weren't there? She'd have to see what she could do about that. "And what exactly is their charge?'

"They're the gatekeepers. They've created all Marks from the beginning of time. They formed the link between our blood and the afterlife, all of it is their doing."

If that was true, then a Marksman *had* to be involved with the new Mark on some level. That didn't mean they were behind it, someone could've forced them or stolen their knowledge somehow. But the Mark had been made.

"Does anyone speak to them?" she asked.

Gideon's head cocked infinitesimally.

"We have our methods of communication," Elijah replied.

What kind of a nothing answer was that? *Ugh! These people and their vague, half-replies.*

"When is your next round of shifts?" the Agent asked.

Crap. How was she supposed to bring up the Marksman again

without looking like she had an agenda? "I'm off the next four days, then start a stretch of five-day shifts."

"That's complicated," Trevor complained.

"Maybe if you have the intelligence of a rock," she mumbled.

Ben's hand stilled while Davis choked on a laugh and looked down at his folded arms to hide his smirk.

Elijah uncrossed his legs. "I'll set the Marking ceremony for ten days from now."

A knot twisted in the depths of her stomach as she nodded then exhaled slowly. Ten days until she was branded forever.

"Did you have any further questions?"

She bit her lip, hard. Pain zinged across her mouth, which was good, because she needed to hold back the words that teetered on the edge of her tongue. She adjusted the blanket. "Am I supposed to dress a certain way? Wear anything specific?"

"I vote yoga pants," Gideon drawled.

Her eyes flew wide as her head snapped his way.

"Back off, Gideon," Ben said through his teeth.

The Head of the Lesser Demon Sect grinned, all confidence and secrets.

Elijah shook his head and looked to the ceiling like it might hold answers…or an escape. Probably an escape. "I would suggest loose or shorter sleeves to expose your forearms." He offered the others pointed looks. "This meeting is adjourned." Rising, he stepped forward, took a muffin from the box, and left.

Gideon tipped his head toward Grace when he proclaimed to the room as a whole, "She shouldn't drive."

She scowled as she folded the throw blanket, replaced it, and stood. Well, she tried to stand but instead, she stumbled and fell back onto the couch. Her scowl dropped, transforming into a grimace. *Damn him for paying attention.*

"You don't need to concern yourself, demon." Ben spat the last word like it was acid on his tongue. Taking Grace's elbow, he helped her to her feet. "I'll drive you."

She hated to concede Gideon was right about anything, but her being behind the wheel *was* a crappy idea. "Alright."

Ben grabbed her coat and purse then guided her across the room to the door.

When she glanced over her shoulder, Gideon's gaze was fixed on her body. It roved up to her stare, and she raised her finger, offering him the rudest of gestures. The last thing she heard before his office door closed behind them was the thick, rich sound of his laughter.

GRACE SLIPPED her coat on as she ambled forward and kept her eyes on the devious icy patches of Bedlam's parking lot. They threatened to take her down, but her dignity wouldn't allow it. When she passed Ben her keys, their fingers brushed. "Thanks for this."

His smile was blinding. "My pleasure."

She turned to Jenna. "I've been thinking about your offer. If you're still up for it, I'd love your help looking into my parents."

A huge grin split Jenna's face as she linked her arm through Grace's. "Absolutely. I'm free Tuesday."

"Tuesday works!"

"I'm so happy to have another girl in the Sect," Jenna said, a bounce in her step.

Grace choked on a laugh. "There aren't any others?"

She lifted her shoulder in a half-shrug. "There are back at the compound. I just...don't feel like I have much in common with any of them." Her voice pitched low. "They tend to stick their noses where they don't belong."

Interesting. And where exactly did their noses not belong? She would've asked if it hadn't meant sticking her nose where it didn't belong.

"I've never seen anyone challenge Elijah like that. It was great," Jenna said. "I thought Trevor was gonna high five you."

Grace's face twisted. "Like, in the face, with his fist?"

Jenna snickered.

The other woman's mood was catching, which meant Grace couldn't hold back her smile. "I don't know how well Elijah took it. I can't read him."

"He must've taken it well enough," she said, voice firm. "I promise, you'd know if he didn't. I think he likes you. You amuse him. I've never seen him accommodate anyone's schedule before."

That's what she considered accommodation? Grace's face contorted. "I'm glad, I think."

Jenna gave her a squeeze before she released her. "You've been a very interesting mix-up to our circumstance."

Ben edged closer, set his hand on the small of Grace's back and guided her away. His shoulders were stiff when he tossed Trevor his fob. "You, Jenna, and Rodan can follow us."

Trevor nodded.

Ben popped open the passenger side door for Grace. When he climbed into the driver's seat, he grinned. "Alone at last."

Her stomach did a happy little flip.

His posture was rigid when he faced her. "Did Ryczek hurt you?"

Her mouth dropped open. Her silence must've sent the wrong message because his hands fisted on the steering wheel, turning white as the bones strained against his skin. Reaching across the space between them, she rested her palm on his forearm.

"No. He didn't." He wouldn't hurt her. That wasn't Gideon, but Ben couldn't see that. After what he'd been through with Leah, Grace couldn't expect any less.

He offered a stiff nod. "I got us a reservation at Prime for our date. The earliest available was in three days."

Prime? Wow. Her heartrate quickened. He'd pulled out all the stops. Not that she knew anything about the place other than it was fancy-schmancy and expensive.

"I suppose that means I'll have to make myself pretty then," she teased.

He started the vehicle, put it in gear, and pulled out. "Pretty would be a downgrade for you."

The heat that warmed her cheeks was so intense it was a wonder she didn't burn. They drove for a few minutes before the car slowed with the heavy traffic. She glanced at the clock—too heavy for the time of day. "What's with this gridlock right now? We're past rush hour."

"I have no idea." He shifted as he tried to see around the vehicle in front of them. "Looks like an accident up ahead."

The flashing lights of emergency vehicles came into view. Police, fire, and ambulance were all on scene. The cop's tape quartered off the area and narrowed the flow down to one lane.

Her instinct was to jump out and help, but there were already plenty of hands on deck. The tires crunched as they rolled past, and it gave Grace a clear line of sight to the havoc that'd been wreaked. Her heart sank.

Several people sat on the sidewalk crying while an officer stood above them, notepad in hand. Skid marks tracked across the road leading to a car whose hood had a body-sized dent and a fractured windshield. A bicycle with thick tires for winter riding sat mangled on the ground nearby. About thirty feet ahead, a black tarp covered the cadaver outlined beneath it.

At the trunk of the car stood a soul—the cyclist. It had to be. The woman was somewhere in her forties with short hair done in a pixie-cut. Two forgivable sins sat emblazoned on her forearm. Grace's gaze lifted then froze when it landed on the new Mark. Cold, liquid dread streamed through her, rushing to every corner of her body until it was consumed.

Grace had learned virtually nothing in her hunt for answers. If she wanted to make progress, it meant speaking up to either get help or dump it in someone else's infinitely more capable lap. Still, she had to be smart. Telling the Shepherds she knew what the Mark did was a bad idea. Super bad. But nothing could be done about the damn thing unless it was confronted.

If the rogue Shepherds in Trenton were right, the others wouldn't see the Mark, but she had to try. She crushed the strap of her purse in her grasp to steel herself.

It's now or never.

She trembled slightly when she pointed, and her head swivelled back to Ben. "What's that?"

He glanced past her toward the accident, eyes pinched at the corners. "What's what?"

"On the soul's chest." She lowered her arm, settling it in her lap and wringing her hands. "I've never seen that Mark before."

His brow furrowed. "I don't see anything."

Traffic stopped, so he leaned over, and his shoulder skimmed hers when he looked. He shook his head. "Sorry, Grace."

Her lips pursed. She couldn't let the opportunity pass. She needed to know, to gauge. "Can we call the others? Ask them?"

He rubbed his chin. "Grace—"

"Please, Ben."

He sighed, sat up, pulled his phone from his pocket then handed it to her. "Call Rodan. Put it on speaker."

The terror she'd kept at bay reignited with a fury as it burst to life like an accelerant-fueled fire. Her fingers shook, which made hard work of the buttons. When the phone finally connected, its ringing pulled her focus.

"What's up?" Rodan answered.

"Hey, it's Grace. Have you guys reached the accident yet?"

"We're coming up on it. Why?"

"It was a fatal." She cleared her throat. "The cyclist's soul is there. She has a Mark on her sternum. I'm wondering if you can see it?"

There was a pause. "What?"

"It's circular and red with a crucifix, something that looks like a fox, a tree, overlapping rings, several other symbols I don't recognize and Latin script at the center. Do any of you see it?"

He was quiet another moment before he relayed her words to Trevor and Jenna.

"What's going on?" Ben rolled them forward as traffic started to move.

Rodan must've heard him because he answered, "Hold on. We're just passing it now."

Trevor's muffled voice carried from the other end. "What the hell is she talking about? There's nothing there. Christ. She's fucking crazy."

"Don't be an ass," Jenna snapped.

Grace's teeth ground together. She doubted he'd be so brave if she was within crotch-shot range. The image of him doubled over in pain brought the ghost of a smile to her lips.

"I'm sorry, Grace," Rodan said. "We're not seeing anything."

That smile fell. They pulled far enough ahead that the soul disappeared from sight, and she faced forward again. Dammit. "You need to do a Calling," she told Ben, because she did *not* want to leave the soul there. Just in case. She couldn't take that chance.

Ben eyed her askance. "Why?"

Shit. "It's just…if we don't know what it is—"

Trevor scoffed. "What's this *we* shit? There's nothing there."

Channeling her inner Zen, she caged the violence that fought to overcome her. Well, mostly caged it. It still struggled to break free as it rattled that enclosure.

"Enough, Trev," Ben growled then glanced her way.

Her eyes creased at the corners. "Please, Ben. I don't like leaving it there."

He loosed a heavy exhale, then inclined his head. "Get in touch with one of the others at the compound, Rodan. Tell them to do a Calling. I'll send it through as soon as I get there," he ordered, and retrieved his phone from her, ending the call.

At least it'd be away from the public, and while she wanted it immediately, if she pushed it might mean putting herself at risk. She was out of options.

When they pulled into her driveway a short time later, they climbed out. Ben raised a finger to the others, instructing them to wait while he followed her inside then closed them in.

She peeled her coat off. "You guys think I'm insane."

He shook his head as he slipped the jacket from her grip. "No, never." He set it aside. "It's just, without seeing the Mark myself, I can't say anything for sure."

"I saw it, Ben."

Edging forward, he set a hand on her hip. "I believe you saw something." The words were firm, yet there was something missing, something he wasn't saying.

"But?" She tensed. *Don't say I'm crazy. Don't say I'm crazy!*

He rubbed the back of his neck and looked away. "There are a million things it could've been. A trick of the light, something through the soul's form, a visual disturbance. Anything."

Her brows rose as she aggressively adjusted her clothes and stared past him. Anywhere but at him. "A visual disturbance?"

"You're running on close to three days with next to no sleep," he said, voice apologetic.

Grace pulled away, butting up against the wall as she painfully ground her jaw. "I didn't hallucinate."

He raised his hands in surrender. "That's not what I mean. I'm just trying to approach this logically. I've done this my entire life, and I've never heard of anything like what you described."

She released a breath and shook the tension from her shoulders—or as much of it as she could manage. She had kind of ambushed him. If the new Mark had jarred her, she could only imagine what it was like for him. That didn't mean she'd let it go. "Then we should ask Elijah."

"Elijah doesn't like having his time wasted." He advanced and his arm snaked around her waist, ensnaring her as he crushed forward. His eyes met hers, his face filling her sight. "I'm protecting you, Grace. I promise, you wanna deal with him as little as possible."

She hated the idea. *Hated* it. But the others took the Agent seriously. There was obviously a reason for it. She pursed her lips. "Jenna says he likes me."

He rolled his neck. "Elijah doesn't like anyone. He won't show you any additional kindness, so I wouldn't expect it."

"Fine," she said on a sigh. She'd hit wall after wall, which meant she'd run out of places to turn. Why hadn't she learned anything? Well, anything of use, anyway.

"You're cute when you pout." He angled forward, drawing closer and closer. His heat pulsed into her when he pressed his lips to hers. His mouth slanted open while his tongue sought entry. She released a small gasp as he plunged inside. He moaned low as his grip locked down. Pulling her tight to him, he deepened the kiss.

She clutched his elbows as she leaned into him. His hands dipped over her ribs and abdomen to the band of her pants where his fingers edged below. He shifted to give himself better access and something hard pressed into her stomach.

Panic rose like a fast-moving tide and her eyes flew wide. She broke the kiss, chest heaving as she sucked in air. "Ben, I—"

"We can do this quick, Grace."

OHGODOHGODHOGOD. She tensed and swallowed around the dry lump in her throat. She had no clue how far he meant for *this* to go, regardless, she chickened out.

He must've realized something was up because he froze. "What's wrong?"

Her face heated a thousand degrees. It was probably melting. "I just..."

His tongue stabbed into his cheek as he drew back a fraction. Only enough to see her. "You just what?"

Shifting, she let out a ragged breath. "I'm not really...experienced." *Please let that be vague enough. Please!*

He blinked in rapid succession and shook his head. "Wait. You've never—" He cleared his throat. "You've never been with anyone?"

Definitely not vague enough. She thumped the back of her head against the wall as she prayed for it to break open and swallow her whole.

That must've confirmed it for him because his brows snapped up his forehead. "Holy fucking hell. You're a virgin!"

She winced. She wasn't a fan of the term but was entirely too humiliated to address it. She should've just kept her mouth shut. *Why* hadn't she kept her mouth shut?

"How are you a virgin?"

"It's a long story." Was it though? "Oh, God." She'd been willing to try a relationship with him, but the idea of diving into her emotional baggage was not something she was ready for. Her hands came up and she scrubbed her face. "I just—I just wanna take things slow."

"Hey," he said as he took her wrists and pulled her arms down, "whatever you need." He inhaled long and easy before he set his forehead to hers. A small smile curved his lips. "Does anyone else know?"

She buried her face in his chest to hide. "Noah. Why?"

"Gideon looks at you like a toy. He'll want you because he can't have you. If he knew this, he'd want you even more." He brushed her hair back from her face. "Especially now that we're together."

He had nothing to worry about on that front because the idea of telling Gideon had never crossed her mind. *Never*.

"If he's ever bothering you, tell me. I'll make sure it stops."

She was pretty sure Gideon was the kind of man who stopped when he wanted to, but nonetheless, she uttered, "I will."

Ben set his lips to hers again, but this time the kiss was heavy with a feverish edge. His tongue stroked hers, easy. Hungry. Her body heated.

A horn blared outside, and Ben growled.

The front door pushed open, and Noah stepped in. "Good evening, Gracie. Benjamin."

"Evening," she said, breathless.

"Noah," Ben returned. He untangled himself from her and took a step back.

Her best friend removed his outerwear, set his things on a nearby chair, then headed for the kitchen.

Ben ran a hand through his hair roughly while his chest rose and fell in rapid bursts. He chucked his chin toward the door. "I should go. What are you doing tomorrow?"

"I have that dinner at Kyle's."

He gave a sharp nod, then reached for the handle. "I'll text you later." Bending down, he gave her one final kiss before he slipped out.

She offered the wall her weight and set her fingers to her lips. Sweet baby Jesus, that was intense.

"You hungry?" Noah called.

"Starving." Feeling any number of emotions she couldn't pin down, she strode to kitchen, where Noah had himself half buried inside the freezer.

"Did I interrupt something?" he asked, voice muffled. "I feel like I interrupted something."

"No. Well, kind of. I just told him I'm uninitiated in the art of making love."

He climbed out and his face twisted while he worked that out. "Uninitiated in the art of–*OH!*" He climbed back into the freezer. "You mean that you are unsexed."

Unsexed? Sure, it was true but when he put it that way… She shook her head. "Yes, that, Mr. Wordsmith."

He laughed. "You just became his prize horse."

Her mouth hung open before she wagged her finger at him. A finger he could not see, but heedless, it made her feel better to wag it. "First and foremost, I resent being compared to a horse."

There was a crunch and crackle when he shuffled the frost-covered products. "Horses are noble creatures."

There was that. "Fine."

"And second?" He withdrew and held out the rectangular lump of whatever he'd been searching for.

She furrowed her brows. "Second what?"

"You said 'First and foremost,' I naturally assumed there was a second."

She shrugged. If there had been, she'd lost it in the labyrinth that was her mind. "What are you making us for dinner?"

The frozen casserole banged when he tossed it onto the counter. "Disappointment."

CHAPTER 18
GRACE

Grace was dying, she was sure of it. She pulled the hair back from her shoulders to expose the skin of her neck as she tried to cool herself. The fact that Kyle's oven was on, coupled with the number of people crammed around his dining room table meant his place was downright sweltering.

She'd worn deep burgundy dress pants paired with an ivory camisole and cardigan, and she practically tore off the latter to help. It didn't.

"We should open the window," Tara complained.

"Yes," Charlotte seconded.

Grace threw her hand in the air. "I third that motion."

Jake rose, crossed the room, and popped open said window. There was a collective sigh as the wintry air hit them. A chill chased across Grace's sweat-slicked skin, one she welcomed because it cooled her quickly. Too quickly. She replaced her cardigan.

Ivan took a swig of his drink. "Is that a thing? To third a motion?"

She was assaulted by the savory scent of meat and spices as she chomped down on a piece of broccoli. Its buttered flavor made her mouth water as she pointed the remainder of its gnawed stem at him. "Of course, it is."

"You can't make it a thing just because you proclaim it's a thing."

"I certainly can, Singh!" God, it was nice to be surrounded by people she knew. People she didn't have to question. To be distracted from the chaos happening in the rest of her lif—

"How are things at the hospital?" Jake asked as he strode back to his seat.

Well, crap.

"The outbreak's gotta be making it difficult there," Charlotte said.

Grace twisted her face in answer. How the hell else was she supposed to address that?

Tara leaned back in her chair. "The media are turning it into a firestorm."

"They have a tendency to do that," Grace grumbled as she twisted the rim of her drink. The condensation rolled down its side where it pooled against the wooden top of Kyle's live edge table.

"Gracie was quarantined herself," Noah put in. Everyone's forks froze mid-way to their mouths. The silence that followed was deafening.

She scowled at him before releasing an awkward-as-all-get-out laugh. The last thing she wanted was her friends running for the hills. She needed everyone she had. "It was just a precaution. I've been cleared." Not that she was even confident there'd been anything to clear her of.

They resumed eating.

"I'm surprised the hospital's not calling all hands-on deck," Ivan said.

She rolled her fork between her fingers and was about to answer, but Jake beat her to it.

"The staff need their rest, too, otherwise, mistakes are made, and this gets a whole lot worse."

Seeing as her mouth was full, she raised her glass in agreement.

"Marshall has whatever it is," Tara stated. "He dropped when we were on scene at a fatal cycling accident yesterday."

"Shit," Ivan replied.

Grace's stomach rolled, and she leaned back in her seat. *Please, don't let it be the one I saw.* "I think I drove by that," she said, testing the waters. "Was it a woman?"

Tara nodded. "That's the one."

No. No. No! She'd asked Ben to do a Calling. Had he not done it? Had they been too late?

"It's happened to three of our uniforms now," Kyle added.

Ivan twisted several strands of his beard. "I've heard the number is up to twelve people in total."

Grace's stare grew vacant as she set her fork on the table. "Nineteen affected with three fatalities."

The group turned to her in unison.

"I called my Charge Nurse before coming here to get an update," she explained. "It's hitting First Responders in the field hardest." She wanted to protect her friends, needed to. She didn't have much information, but she would give them what she had, or at the very least, what she could. "Wear masks and gloves, put a barrier between you and the public."

Kyle's thumb stroked the handle of his knife. "Headquarters hasn't sent out the order on that yet."

"Do it anyway."

Ivan leaned back in his seat. "That'll make the public nervous."

"They should be." No matter which way things shook out, either it was a dangerous contagion or a Mark on the dead. Neither of which they would see coming.

Charlotte cursed under her breath.

"They really don't know what's causing it?" Tara asked, voice high.

Grace shook her head. "We're trying to figure out the mode of transmission." She sat up straighter and set her forearms on the table. "Do yourselves a favor and keep food on you at all times. And please, take this seriously, guys."

Charlotte's gaze pinched. "Food?"

"Food," Grace said. "Orange juice, sugar cubes, anything that gives you quick energy."

"Why?" Kyle asked, his tone level.

"So far, it's the only thing we know of that combats it. So, do it, and tell the others at the detachment to do the same."

Slow nods of ascension went around the table and a small relief slithered over her. It wasn't much, but it was better than nothing.

Kyle ran a hand over his hair. "Since it's the point of origin, will the hospital be doing an internal investigation?"

She shrugged. "That knowledge is way above my pay grade." But God, she hoped not because that was the last thing she—or any of the staff there—needed.

"Well, this is depressing," Noah said, then gasped. "Oh! Has Gracie told everyone about her new beau?"

Oh, no.

The hand on Jake's beer stilled while the others grinned.

Tara raised her drink in salute. "The dry spell is over."

"And what do we think of him?" Ivan asked Noah in that protective, big brother fashion. As much as she wanted to reach across the table and swat her best friend like the pest he was, it was nice to have people care.

Kyle cut in as he mumbled to himself, "We think he would've preferred Gideon."

Heaven above. 'Cause that wouldn't pique their interest. Grace plunked her face in her palms to hide but peeked between her fingers so she wasn't left out.

Noah raised his hands in a conciliatory manner. "We think that if Gracie likes Ben, that's all that matters."

Charlotte rubbed her hands together. "And who's Gideon?"

A boyish grin spread across Noah's mouth. "Gideon Ryczek."

There it was. He'd gone and done it. The heat that flooded Grace's entire body was all consuming. Maybe she should climb out the window? Just curl up in the snowbank? It'd be a less painful death than the one she faced.

Ivan lifted a coy brow at her. "The guy who owns Bedlam?"

Her best friend's head bobbed enthusiastically.

"I like that place. Rarely gives us trouble on shift. It's well run, no bullshit," Tara said.

"Either that or he's good at hiding the bullshit," Charlotte countered before she lifted her beer to her lips.

Grace was *not* going there.

Ivan shook his head. "I'm pretty sure he's above board. I don't think he wants the heat."

"Having cops all over your establishments does have a way of attracting unwanted attention," Charlotte said.

"I was under the impression cops were the unwanted attention," Grace grumbled. As one, all said cops at the table offered her the same rude finger, and she snickered. Served them right for nosing around in her romantic life.

"He's a decent guy. I've never had an issue with him," Tara relayed.

Ivan nodded. "And a good looking one."

"Good looking?" Noah's hands clasped his chest as if he were offended on Gideon's behalf. "He's spectacular!" *Totally offended.*

"It's a good thing I have a healthy self-esteem," Kyle said under his breath.

Charlotte's lip tipped up. "And that Ryczek's not gay."

Self-assured as ever, Kyle tipped his glass to that, and the table laughed.

"And what about the one you're actually dating?" Jake asked.

"Thank you. At least *someone* here cares," Grace replied as she glowered at the others as if that could shame them. It didn't. "His name is Ben Jones."

"What does he do?" Ivan asked.

Dang it! How had she not thought that through? "He, um. He works for the church." *Smooth, Grace. Real smooth.* Picking up her drink, she took a long swig to hide the guilty expression fighting to paint her face.

Charlotte's brows rose. "A literal choir boy."

"You should've invited him," Ivan told her.

She lowered her cup. "I did. He couldn't make it." Noah's face twisted, and she eyed him, but he averted his gaze.

Tara set the edge of her forearms on the table and threaded her fingers together as she circled back. "And how do you know Ryczek?"

And back to Gideon they went. "I met him through Ben," Grace said, because it wasn't a lie.

"They're friends?"

Gulp. "They know one another."

Tara laughed. "So that's a no."

"They know one another," Grace repeated, refusing to elaborate because there was no way in hell she'd wade into the dumpster fire of a history between those two men.

Ivan pulled up his sleeves. "How do they know one another?"

Her eyes met Noah's and implored him to interject, but instead, he shrugged and offered her a *What the heck do you expect me to say?* face. She pinned him with her stare and sent a message of her own. *I am so scrubbing the toilet with your fancy loofah tonight!* His hands flew to his mouth.

She returned her attention to the table. "Also through the church."

"So, they're religious?" Charlotte asked.

Sweet Lord. That's what she got for having cops as friends. "Ben more so."

Charlotte waved a hand in her direction. "You're being weird."

"I'm being interrogated."

"That's what you get for having cops as friends," Ivan retorted.

Laughter filled the room, and they fell into easy banter as they finished their meal and broke out the poker chips. She had absolutely no clue how to play, so she sat out the game and watched, picking up not one single thing.

"Has Corporal Harris been transferred to the Detachment yet?" Kyle asked, tone sharp as he tapped his finger on the table, awaiting his cards.

Charlotte's jaw clenched. "She starts Monday."

Grace's attention jumped between the two, then around the table to the others, finding their sentiments mirrored. *Ooh, intriguing. Their turn to explore an uncomfortable topic.* "Who's Corporal Harris?"

"She's our new C.O.," Jake said. When Grace scratched her temple, he elaborated, "Commanding Officer."

"They call her the Bulldog," Ivan interjected.

Noah set his hand on the back of Kyle's chair. "Why?"

"Because once she's decided on a suspect, she doesn't let go."

Grace's nose scrunched. "That can't be a compliment."

Jake shook his head. "It's not. She's relentless. She's got a high conviction rate but has a reputation for bulling over her suspects and subordinates. There are plenty of rumors behind closed doors."

"She sounds lovely," Grace added, sorry she'd asked. "On that note, I should get going." She rose and glanced at Noah. "You coming?"

"I think I'll stay here tonight. Text me when you get home?"

Leaning over, she kissed him on the cheek. "Of course. See you tomorrow, house husband." She carried her dishes to the kitchen, wished the others goodnight, and aimed for the door.

"Grace," Jake called, following her.

A small wave of panic crested as he closed the distance between them. His posture was stiff, had been since he'd learned about Ben. And she prayed to all things holy he was not about to bring it up.

He cleared his throat. "If things down at the hospital get bad, let me know."

Oh. If the new Mark was behind what was happening, things would definitely get bad. But he couldn't know that, so she tilted her head in question. Her heart sank at his reply.

"When the public realizes the scope of what's happening," he lowered his voice, "these things have the potential to turn ugly fast. If you think you need help, if you're in danger, you call me."

GRACE'S BODY was one giant knot. The tension coiled in her muscles was painful, and her forearms ached from her grip on the steering wheel. The temperature outside hovered at freezing, and the misty drizzle that coated the air meant her drive home from Kyle's was treacherous. It was the kind of moisture that froze the instant it touched the windshield—or more concerning, the road.

The wipers snapped back and forth, doing their best to clear her view. The lesser traffic outside the city limits meant the pavement didn't heat from the constant friction of tires, so black-ice coated the black-top. Easing her foot off the gas, she slowed.

The clouds lay low, the night well and dark. Her headlights struggled to penetrate the dim night while her eyes strained against the fog as she tracked the lines on the road.

Like her own, Kyle's house was further out of town at the opposite end of Arillia, which meant crossing the city to get home. Some of her anxiety ebbed when she reentered it and the streetlights brightened the way—kind of.

Her mind spun. Between Jake's parting words and the weather, she couldn't quiet her torrential thoughts. The traffic light ahead turned red, and she slowed to a stop. She swivelled around, peering into the dark corners for trouble. When her gaze settled on the alley to her left, her spine snapped straight.

Her attention darted to her rear-view mirror. There was no one behind her, so she shoved the car in reverse and—when her tires stopped slipping from her aggressive shot of gas—she backed alongside the curb and parked.

Grabbing her purse, she threw her door open and climbed out. The skunky scent of cheap weed lingered in the frost-dampened air, but there was no one attached to it. She moved with slow progress and kept her feet. She crept like a cat that stalked its prey as she approached the head of the alley. A man lay dead in its depths, his body sprawled prone on the ground. As bad as it was, he hadn't been the reason she'd stopped—at least, not the flesh version of him.

She scanned the street for strangers, shoulders sagging in tentative relief when she found herself alone. Controlling the tremor in her hand, she pulled out a pen and paper from her purse and then sketched the new Mark on the dead man's soul.

The fact that the others couldn't see it was so far past unnerving it headed into creepy territory. But a weird hope blossomed in her chest because this was a way to show them.

Voices bounced off the brick walls nearby, and her heart rate jumped from frantic to explosive in a single beat. Careful not to touch the soul, she scurried around it and tucked behind a dumpster, hoping whoever it was kept on trucking. Her safety aside, if anyone saw her hanging out with a dead guy it was sure to look mildly suspicious.

She peeked through a small gap between the garbage and the wall at her back. Her lungs seized. The silhouettes of two men backlit by the streetlights came into view where they paused at the head of the alley.

"Gimme your lighter," the shorter of the two said.

There was a quick rustling. "Here."

The distinctive clank of a Zippo top being opened echoed through the night, followed by the grind of the flint, and the faint light of its small fire as it flashed to life. Short guy's cigarette accepted the flame, and it sizzled when he took a deep draw. The end glowed bright, highlighting the plains of his face.

For all she knew, they were well adjusted, decent citizens, but the hysteria that threatened to take her over said otherwise, because alone in the shadows, everyone and everything was trouble. *Move on. Please, just move on.*

The scent of the smoke hit her, and she held her breath, fighting the cough that tried to break free of her chest. Short guy took another draw before he and his friend turned away and disappeared into the night. She released a violent exhale.

Climbing from her hiding spot, she finished the sketch, and offered the dead man a silent apology, because there was no way she was calling it in to be questioned by the cops. Not that anyone could save him anyway.

Scurrying from the alley, she beelined back to her car, then jammed it in gear and fled into the night.

CHAPTER 19
GRACE

Grace's living room looked like a tornado had torn through it. The *Arillia Times* newspapers she'd fished from their recycling were spread across every available surface. Each opened to the obituaries, starting with the day she'd seen Elise and Corey die in Trenton. *Correction. Killed.* She'd seen them killed.

She looked for faces, patterns, then highlighted anyone who'd died from the "outbreak" in pink, jotting down the basics of who they were to consolidate the information. She would've searched for the guy from the alley, but he wouldn't have made the news, not yet anyway. A rolling wave of guilt torqued her stomach. Had he even been found?

She didn't have the cyclist's name, so the woman's appearance was the only thing she could go by. The papers rustled when she opened them. Flipping the pages, she circled all the death announcements for women first, then backtracked to take a better look.

Opening her laptop, she selected a few news articles and rolled her eyes when she skimmed passed the society pages and business articles that gushed over Gideon. She cycled through the internet tabs, cross-referencing her respective results until she narrowed the selections down to one. That was her! It had to be—the woman's facial structure, skin tone, hair color, and eyes were all familiar. She was thirty-five and survived by her parents, husband, two children, and three siblings.

"Alright, Sarah Stern." She brought up a search engine and punched in the name. Multiple options surfaced and she scrolled through until she found an image of the woman associated with a social media profile. She held her breath when she clicked it, then released it in a burst. Thank you, Sarah, for absolutely no privacy settings!

They had that much in common.

She scrolled and scrolled and scrolled, heart sinking at the posted condolences. When she passed them, she found a picture of Sarah seated on her bike surrounded by several other smiling cyclists captioned *"Arillia Triathlon, here we come!."* That was followed by a status from a few days before that tagged her location as Arillia Hospital. *"In for a minor procedure. So stupid. Can't wait until this is done."* The comments were all of the *"hope you feel better soon"* variety and too vague to figure out what that procedure might've been.

Grace's bottom lip pushed out and she shoved the papers away. There weren't any glaring religious references of note. She'd figured out who Sarah was but had no idea what good that did her.

She jumped when her phone rang and scowled at Noah's face as it flashed across her screen. Snapping it up, she answered. "Hello."

"Have you made it home yet? I got worried when you didn't message."

"I'm home." Her shoulders sagged. "Sorry, I got sidetracked trying to research anyone that died and could've had the Mark."

"Oh." Silence, long and drawn, then, "The Nephilim really couldn't see it?"

"They really couldn't."

"What about demon-boy?"

She chucked her highlighter onto the coffee table and thumped her head against the couch's back. God, she was just so bone weary and tired. "I don't know."

His voice brightened. "You haven't asked him yet?"

"I have not."

"What if he *can* see it?" He gasped. "Oh! You should invite him over to discuss it in the name of research." There was a proud, mischievous grin in his voice, and it made her want to reach through the phone and smack him.

"How many times do I have to remind you, I'm dating Ben."

"First of all, you might be, but I'm not."

She threw an arm up. "You're dating Kyle!"

He continued as if she hadn't spoken. "Second, you're not Marked yet, which means you're still allowed to ask him questions."

"You just want me to see him again," she scoffed.

"That's beside the point."

She stared up at the ceiling for patience. "That *is* the point."

"I forget my point."

"The point is finding out whatever I can about all of this."

"By inviting demon-boy over?" He snickered and that urge to smack him again had her hand twitching. "Speaking of learning things, are you and this Jenna woman still planning on researching your mom?"

A rolling wave of anxiety hovered like a storm on the horizon of her heart. Because the potential truths that research might reveal was suffocating. She swallowed hard. "Yeah, tomorrow."

AN HOUR LATER, Grace lay on her back in bed, holding the picture of the Mark. She stared up at it like answers might magically appear. And stared. And *stared*.

The paper rattled as she rotated it in every conceivable direction and tried to unlock its mystery, to no avail. Her gaze flicked to her phone, back to the drawing, then back to her phone. Releasing a loud huff, she picked up the device, snapped a picture of the Mark, and texted it to Gideon accompanied by a message.

Grace: *Does this mean anything to you?*

She eyed the screen, awaiting a response. It rang and she flinched then fumbled until she dropped it on her face. *Ow!* Taking it firmly in hand, she answered, "Hello?"

"Good evening, Crys," Gideon crooned.

"Good evening, Gideon."

He rasped, smooth and low when next he spoke. "Before we begin, I'll need you to do something for me."

Heat flared across her body. "What's that?"

"Get rid of that photo."

Not what she'd expected.

"You don't want Elijah finding out you sent it, so before this conversation goes any further, commit the drawing to memory, then destroy it and any evidence of the picture you texted."

The level, deathly somber tone he used had every muscle in her chest snap taught, making it hard to breathe. She pulled the phone from her ear, deleted that portion of their text conversation along with the picture from her images and tore up the drawing.

"Done. Would he really be that upset?"

"Yes. Having it leaves it at risk for being discovered."

"Would anyone even know what they were looking at?"

"It doesn't matter. The chance exists. Elijah may seem flat, but he takes the rules seriously. Don't ever let him catch you breaking them."

She pulled her hair from the messy bun she'd styled it into. "And what happens if he does?"

"The punishments with our kind are severe. So, don't let him."

"You've had experience with this?"

"It's something you only have to learn once."

With the tips of her fingers, she massaged her forehead and temples. Her eyes pinched as she pushed back the headache that threatened to creep in. "Why do I get the feeling you required it more?"

He huffed a laugh. "Once, I promise you."

She fell still, voice softening, "That bad?"

"Strange as it may be, Heaven and Hell make an effort to keep their people in line. Seeing as our blood determines our end, harsh discipline is their only recourse on this plane."

A sheen of sweat rose across her skin. She put him on speaker and then scrolled through her previous text conversations with him, Ben, and Noah, ensuring there wasn't anything problematic.

"What does that discipline entail?" she asked.

"There are three strata of punishment. The first for you as a Nephilim would be the soul-sword."

The strata term was familiar. She was pretty sure Davis had used it when Gideon threw Absinthe and Hennessey through Hell's Gate. But before she could dwell on that the weight of his words sank in... "Wait," her head tilted, "*soul*-sword?"

"Indeed, because the sword does not strike the body, it strikes the soul."

She really should've run when she'd had the chance. Words escaped her, but Gideon saved her the trouble of a response when he pushed on.

"Both the Nephilim and Elijah carry the Mark for it, them as their weapon in the end, he as a form of punishment for them."

No wonder the others were so afraid of the Agent. She swallowed hard and forced her next words out from a throat that didn't want to work. "I've never seen it before."

"It's above the elbow, away from the other Marks to prevent it from accidentally being triggered."

His words hit her like a bolt of lightning and jolted her to her core. "Noah knows, Gideon. Is he in danger?"

"Who else have you told that he knows?"

"No one."

"Keep it that way, make sure he does, too, and it'll be fine."

She released the tight grip of her muscles and let the bed take her weight. "He'd never betray that confidence. He's my no-matter-what."

There was a brief silence. "Your no-matter-what?"

"We're there for each other, no-matter-what," she replied as if the answer was obvious, because, frankly, it was.

His voice lowered and its deep rumble rolled across the phone. "Then you don't have a problem."

She flailed her hand in the air. "I do have a problem, Gideon. I have you."

"I'm not a problem for you, Crys. And you don't have me yet but say the word and I'm yours anytime you want," he said, a smirk in his voice.

Her lips pressed into a thin line. She hated having to trust anyone with such a thing, but she was already beholden to him on that account, which meant whether she liked it or not, she had to. "So what are the other two strata of punishment?"

"Are you sure you want that answer, beauty?"

Not at all. While a morbid part of her was curious, the rest understood anything that followed the soul-sword had to be horrible. She shook her head. "No." Steering the conversation back to the issue at hand, she said, "Did you recognize the Mark?"

"No."

Dammit! She tapped her palm against her thigh. *All that for nothing.* "What about the Latin script?"

"It reads 'Claimed.'"

"Does that mean anything to you?"

"It doesn't, but if you'd like, I can come over and we can discuss it more thoroughly."

"Ha! No." Had he and Noah shared notes? They must've, otherwise they'd read out of the same playbook.

He laughed, rich and heavy. "Where did you find it?"

Twisting her hair around a finger, she considered her options on how best to answer that, then opted for the truth. "I saw it on four different people."

"Their souls?"

"What magical powers of deduction you have, Mr. Ryczek."

He coughed, then coughed again. When he regained himself, he said, "That tongue of yours is quite sharp."

Damn her sass. Why couldn't she control it around him? Mocking him while asking for his help likely wasn't her best tactic. She shook her head. "Sorry, I—"

"Don't apologize, Crys. I quite like to taste its sting."

Her lip slowly tipped up. "How do you make everything inappropriate?"

"It's a skill." The sound of leather creaking passed through the phone. "Where did you find these souls?"

Fluffing the pillow under her head, she tried to get comfortable. It didn't work, so she beat it into submission. "The first two were in

Trenton the night we met. The next was a woman at an accident scene I passed."

"And the fourth?"

She rolled onto her side. "I spotted him down an alley I went into tonight."

"As one does," he quipped about said alley expedition.

"It was dark and there was no one around. I wasn't seen."

"Wonderful," he said, tone dry. Before she could add anything, he continued, "Have you brought this to the others?"

"They were with me for the woman but couldn't see it." She released a frustrated exhale. "They don't believe me."

"They said that?" His voice hardened and if that anger had been directed at her, she might've cringed.

"They think I'm seeing something other than what I say I'm seeing." Until the words were out, she hadn't realized how much it'd bothered her. Actually, ticked her off was more accurate.

"The drawing you sent is pretty specific." There was a shuffling, then another creak. "If we told anyone outside the Shepherds about our Sight, do you think they'd believe us?"

That'd been her fear since Jump Street. "No."

"Indeed. Just because they can't see it, doesn't make it any less real. We have access to something they don't. It's possible you have access to something the others don't. You didn't develop the Sight until later in life, so you're already different. That aside, I've known my fair share of dramatic women and you're not one of them, Crys. So, if you say you see it, I believe you."

She closed her eyes. At least someone did. The clamp that'd locked around her chest loosened a notch. "So, what should I do about it?"

"Fucked if I know."

She coughed, trying to hide her laugh, and failed, which meant it came out as more of a choked-cackle.

"The Marks have power. Each portion, every line or symbol, has meaning. They can command, bind, control, anything. Whatever the Marksmen imagines, they can create it."

Her face twisted. *Whose crappy idea had that been?* "Is there a way we can speak to one of them? Or research the symbols?"

"First, I'm quite fond of your use of 'we' in that sentence, but alas, there isn't. They and their craft are too heavily guarded. Elijah would be the only facilitator for that access. Since you've been blooded Nephilim, Benjamin would have to make the request on your behalf."

She reopened her eyes. "And if he doesn't believe me?"

"Then he's unlikely to help. Either way, leave it with me. I'll see if I can learn anything."

"I don't want trouble, Gideon."

"Oh, but, Crys, you are trouble in its greatest form. Don't worry. Discretion is my middle name."

"I can think of others I might use," she mumbled, her fingers tingling where they held the phone.

"Would you like to hear my names for you?"

She sighed. "Doubtless they have something to do with yoga pants."

"It's like you can see into my soul."

Shaking her head, she set it on her arm because the pillow was doing a terrible job. "I've been told a lot about you, Gideon. I worry about your motives. I'm just trying to take this all in. I still don't know that I can trust you."

"Have I lied to you so far?"

Her brow furrowed as her voice rose ridiculously high. "How would I know?"

"What did I tell you the first time we went out, Crys?"

God, he loved getting under her skin. "We didn't 'go *out*,' Gideon."

The laugh he released was low before he pushed on. "I told you to trust your instincts, and your instincts are something no one else can or should influence. Only you have the answer to how you feel. You just need to be willing to accept it, either way."

She stabbed a finger in the air and pointed at nothing in particular. "See, that right there. *That's* what worries me. The subtle influencing, the flattery and whispering sweet nothings in my ear to sway me."

"If I whisper sweet nothings in your ear, you'll know it. Besides, would you prefer my influencing be more overt?"

She ran her hand through her hair roughly. Yes, he'd said the right things, but at the end of the day, he was born of Hell. That blood ran through his veins. That had to change a man. It had to. Didn't it?

"I'd prefer it if I could take everything at face value."

"Not even among the unSighted can you do that."

She made a garbled sound of agreement.

"I'd like to note, for someone who isn't sure she trusts me, you did seek me out for these answers."

She squirmed. Regardless of whether it was true, there was unequivocally no way she'd cop to that. No way in hell. "I'm just trying to figure you out."

"I'm an enigma."

"You're something." When it came to him, she didn't know what to think. Regardless, he had her secrets in the palm of his hand, secrets that could destroy her in more ways than one. She stared down at the torn scraps of her drawing, and uttered, "Please don't betray me, Gideon."

"I would never," he said, tone even before he finished in true Gideon fashion, "I swear on your yoga pants."

She barked a laugh and sighed. "You never told me yours."

"My what?"

"Your first strata of punishment." His level answer made her blood run cold.

"Hellfire." He cleared his throat. "And, Crys, next time you consider wandering down a dark alley by yourself at night, don't."

CHAPTER 20
THIRTY-SEVEN

The sidewalk Thirty-Seven occupied was packed with people. He fought the crowd as he went, like wading up-river against a strong current.

The roaring of chainsaws drowned out practically everything as the sculptors carved their ice blocks for a competition. Chunks of its debris filled the air and threw a cloud of snow downwind from him. When he passed through it, the frost stung his skin while its metallic flavor coated his tongue.

People gathered to watch, enthralled by the process.

He kept moving.

Pulling the phone from his pocket, he dialed the number he'd been ordered to memorize. He wasn't happy about making the call, but everything could hinge on it. The coming conversation was one most might keep private, but he'd learned the best kept secrets were ones you didn't scurry off into the shadows like a rat to protect. Not that he wasn't careful—just the opposite—but people started asking questions when every conversation required privacy, and questions were a problem.

"You shouldn't be calling me," the Primary said, voice cold.

"It won't be traced," Thirty-Seven assured.

"Contact should only be made if it's imperative, and for no other reason. The rules are clear."

"It's necessary, Primary." He paused to await censure. When none came, he continued, "We have an issue. The Claimed Mark has been seen."

Silence reigned for several long, torturous seconds. He rolled his neck on his shoulders to loosen the vice that'd locked around him and closed in.

"Who has seen it?"

"Her name is Grace Crawford. She's new. UnMarked. Purports to have acquired the Sight at eighteen after an accident."

"That's not possible."

"It shouldn't be," he said. No one else had commented on the Mark because no one else had noticed—exactly how it was supposed to be. How Grace had was beyond his comprehension. "Is it conceivable that it could be seen?"

"I will not speak to that now," the Primary said.

Thirty-Seven's stomach hardened and inclined his head. He glanced toward a group of women who'd taken seats on the bench about ten feet way. Leaning against a light stand, he offered one of the blondes a salacious smile to distract her annoyingly direct attention. She blushed and turned away. "So far, she isn't believed, but her description is accurate."

The Primary cursed. "What is her background? Who does she belong to?"

"She's been named Nephilim and claims her parents, Scott Morgan and Wyla Crawford, are deceased."

"You're skeptical?"

"The Head of the Nephilim Sect accessed *The Chronicle* with her. He didn't counter those facts. I just have trouble understanding how her assertions can be real."

"Do you suspect she's a plant? That there's a chance we've been discovered?"

A plant? Shit. He'd not even considered that. His gut knotted and he stared down at his feet as he tried to concentrate. Had Grace been sent to investigate them? If she was, someone had to have sent her, which would mean dissension in their ranks. Her reaction had come across genuine, but the timing of her arrival was suspect.

"I don't know," he said. Still, there was another potential… "Could she be a rogue from inside the Faction?"

"I'll find out. In the meantime, keep watch on her. We do not move against her until we know what we're dealing with. It would be imprudent to cut off the head of the snake without first discovering how deep it's burrowed. Contact me when you have something. Discover what you can."

CHAPTER 21
GIDEON

Gideon hated the drive to Trenton, and it wasn't just the traffic–which was always utter shit. The place was a dive.

"So, what'd Malcolm's text say?" Davis asked when he glanced up from whatever string of emails he answered on his phone.

"Absinthe was found in his territory unwarranted," he said as he fought the pissed-off growl that wanted to rip from his throat. She'd torn at his nerves ever since he'd taken over as Sect Leader, so they were good and frayed.

"He didn't mention what she did?"

"No." Which meant he didn't want to put it in writing. *Always a good sign.*

Davis set his elbow on the ledge of the passenger side window. "What the absolute fuck is wrong with her? Infringing on a Lesser Demon's turf and messing with their gets is a good way to end up dead."

"She's a problem on a good day, but now she's a goddamn issue." She was used to her body getting her into or out of everything. Not that Gideon could judge since he'd accrued his own trail of women, but Absinthe's sometimes took her out of her lane and right into another's jurisdiction—queue Malcolm. He gripped the steering wheel, and the leather groaned under the strain as he pulled off the highway and into Trenton proper. "She's got a lot to learn."

"Or unlearn." Davis tugged the chest strap of his seatbelt. "So, what's Malcolm like?"

"He's not the worst to deal with, but he's not easy, either. He's only been the Head of his Sect for a year, so he's still figuring shit out."

"Their Agent couldn't have had much to pick from then."

His laugh was sardonic. "Just be thankful our kind aren't left to make that call."

"We'd be good and fucked."

And that was the truth. You needed some semblance of rationale to run their side, otherwise it was chaos on chaos. There had to be practicality in the darkness.

"Do you figure you'll have to make a concession?" Davis asked.

Gideon stared at him through his brow. "What do you think?"

He inclined his head. "You gonna let Elijah deal with Absinthe?"

"It's not off the table."

Davis' phone rang. He pulled it from his coat and answered. "Hey," he said. "Alright. Yours?" he paused. "Just with Gideon. We're headed to deal with Absinthe." Silence for a second, then in an exasperated tone, "Yep, again." He laughed and the buzz from his device vibrated through the vehicle. Pulling it back, he glanced at the screen. "Sorry, another call's coming in from Bedlam." Pause. "I'll see you later." He clicked over. "Hello," he answered, all business. There was a long pause while whoever it was spoke. "Where exactly?" he asked. "Shit. Alright. I'll let him know and text you his instructions." He hung up and told Gideon, "Three people just dropped on Clarington Avenue from the outbreak. One's dead, two not. The cops have the street quartered off. It's blocking access to six of your businesses, including the Casino."

Gideon cursed. Could the day get anymore fucked up?

"What do you wanna do?"

The area being turned into a closed scene was *bad* optics. "Have Lisa send out a press release saying we'll be closed for the day so we can protect the public and not impede the police, or some shit like that."

"Use it as a P.R. move?"

He nodded. If done right, that stuff built a reputation, and reputation was the majority of success. His businesses were the only thing he had. He wouldn't let anything affect them, which meant mitigating the damage.

Davis fired off the text to Lisa.

Gideon's phone rang through the truck's Bluetooth system. The screen on his dash showed "*Arillia Times*." Fuck. He glared at it like it was a face that required punching. She was the last thing he needed. He hit the button to accept the call. "Ryczek."

"Hello, Gideon," a familiar, unwanted woman's voice purred.

"Allison," he said, doing what he could to keep his tone neutral.

"How are you?"

"Busy. What can I do for you?" He already knew the answer, 'cause she wanted whatever she could damn well get.

"I hoped you might have a comment for me concerning the outbreak around your properties," she said, emphasis on "me" like she was a goddamn priority.

"I'm sorry to hear about these tragic events. My condolences go out to the families of the victims. I hope the survivors stay safe and recover quickly. Whatever the APD need, I'll be happy to provide." *To the point. Done. If only she'd figure that out.*

"That's so kind of you."

"Is there anything else?"

"Yes. Would you be available for a sit-down interview sometime soon?"

Again, with that. Christ. The woman wouldn't take a hint. "I have a lot on my plate."

Davis smirked, so Gideon balled a fist and snapped it down, punching the guy in the thigh. He grunted, then laughed some more.

"Are you still planning to attend the Help the Homeless gala when they release their date?"

His teeth ground together. "Probably," he admitted, 'cause saying anything to the contrary would just end up as fodder in the gossip column.

"Maybe I'll see you there." He was pretty sure her high-pitched reply aimed for sweet, but instead it bordered on desperate.

"I'm in the middle of something right now."

"Of course. I won't keep you. We'll talk again soon."

He hung up.

Davis guffawed.

"She forgets that my willingness to talk is based on getting good press."

"Considering how much you spend on them, you'd think it wouldn't be necessary. Besides, she doesn't forget, Gid. She wants the access her job grants to you."

Gideon rolled his shoulders to shake off his agitation.

"So, does anyone understand what this outbreak is?" Davis asked, bringing the conversation around.

"Crys says they don't."

"Hm." He set his elbow against the door. "She's interesting, that one." There wasn't any hidden context. He'd meant the words.

"That she is." Gideon'd told her he was the enigma, but he didn't have a goddamn thing on her.

Davis peered out the window. "How she wasn't found for so long is baffling."

"Trevor thinks her backstory's a lie. It's written all over his face." A face Gideon wouldn't mind rearranging. When he'd heard how Crys's crotch shot had dropped the guy like a rock, it'd lessened that urge…somewhat.

"Do you believe her?"

He laughed. "Considering the shit we're surrounded by, I know a liar when I see one. She's telling the truth. The thing I can't figure out is why she gained the Sight so late." And why she could see the Claimed Mark, or why hadn't he met her sooner.

"You didn't seem too shocked when you learned she was Nephilim."

He shook his head. "Ben wouldn't have rushed to schedule her Marking if she was one of ours."

Davis's lip tipped up, the expression more animal than humor. "He's trying to cut the two of you away from each other."

"Not that anything's happened."

"That's not the point for Jones. This is payback."

Gideon contained the snarl that threatened to loose itself when he replied through his teeth, "It's payback."

The wind wasn't in their favor, 'cause it carried the rank, sulphur stench of the neighboring town's pulp mill. It filled his airway, and he coughed to force it back out. He had a vague recollection of the area. He'd been there just enough to recognize everything, but not enough to remember it, hence the GPS.

"Ben's got his eye on you," Davis said.

"I'm aware." He even understood it to some extent. But possessive wasn't a strong enough word to describe that particular Nephilim. The dude had issues, and then some.

"Do you think he'll be a problem for Grace?"

In fifty feet, your destination is on the right, the vehicle announced.

Gideon cut the wheel to pull into the parking lot of the auto body shop Malcolm owned, then veered around the back of the building. "Yeah, but I don't think he knows what he's in for with her."

Dismantled cars and their scattered parts littered the edge of the area, and even from inside his truck the mix of paint fumes and soldered metal carried. It was bright, so the sun bounced off every reflective surface, and there were a lot. Pulling his shades from the visor, he threw them on.

The Head of Trenton's Sect already stood outside, his long, blond hair tied back in a ponytail. He wasn't a tall guy, but what he lacked in height he made up for in his stocky build.

When Gideon and Davis opened their doors and climbed out, Malcolm walked toward them. His dark brown eyes tracked their approach, his hand clamped around Absinthe's upper arm as he dragged her behind him.

She grinned when she spotted Gideon, but it fell just as fast at the expression of wrath he wore.

"What'd she do?" Gideon growled.

Malcolm threw her forward and she stumbled, falling onto her hands and knees on the ice-covered gravel. "She's trafficking in my territory."

He was brought up short because that was some bullshit. *Drugs?* Didn't make sense. That wasn't her scene. He crossed his arms over his chest and gave Davis a nod.

His Head of Security advanced and grabbed her by the collar. He jerked her up and launched her toward Gideon's vehicle. "Shut your mouth and get in the fucking truck," he said as he stalked her like the shadow of death.

"She's out on bail," Malcolm informed him.

Gideon's brow locked down. "She got arrested?"

"Hard not to when the cops catch you red-handed with the kids yourself."

His fists clenched so hard they creaked, and he worked to control himself when he clarified, "*Human* trafficking?"

"Yep. You get why I might be put out that it happened here."

He offered a sharp incline of his head. She was lucky she'd called Malcolm to bail her out because Gideon would have left her sorry ass to rot. "How much do I owe you?"

Davis's boots crunched on the ground when he rejoined them.

Malcolm rubbed his thumb and forefinger together. "Six grand."

Gideon worked to control his pissed off tone when he said, "The money will be transferred today."

"Good to know." Malcolm chucked his chin in Absinthe's direction. "What are you gonna do about her?"

"Let her fucking sink. I'm tired of her shit."

"Good man." Malcolm cleared his throat and his smirk fell. His stare flicked passed his shoulder as he scuffed his boot over the ground and then shoved his hands in his pockets.

Gideon braced for the boon he'd be forced to grant. *Just spit it out, man.*

"Have you had any weird shit happen at your Callings lately?"

Gideon's head drew back. *Interesting.* His attention was good and piqued. "That's a pretty broad question for our kind. You're gonna have to narrow it down."

"One of our dead didn't go through after we granted Passage. It disappeared but didn't show up again inside the Gateway."

Davis shifted, settling his weight onto his back leg while he linked his hands in front of him. "Are you sure you didn't just lose sight of it?"

Arillia was a big city, so that might've tracked there, but Trenton wasn't. The numbers of dead in their Callings should've been traceable, and the idea that they'd lost track of one was off.

Malcolm's eyes narrowed, and he lifted his shoulder in a half-shrug. "I don't know, but I swear to fuck it looked like it just vanished."

Gideon's mind turned over everything he and Crys had talked about with the Claimed Mark the night before. He didn't know if the two were connected, but it was worth a shot. He kept his voice even when he asked, "Was there anything off? Something different about the soul?"

"Not that I or any of mine saw. Why? Do you know something?"

He shook his head, 'cause like fuck he was about to share that information.

"Shit. Let me know if you learn anything."

"Will do. Have you told your Agent?"

"Not yet. I want to search the Revenant Archives and check that the soul actually made it to Hell, but I'd need its name for that. I'm not about to waste her time requesting that permission until I'm sure this is a thing."

He understood that sentiment all too well. "Was there anything else?"

"I don't need anything *yet*."

There it was. "Let me know when you figure it out." He hated open ended favors, but it was what it was. Pivoting on his heel, he left.

When he and Davis climbed into the vehicle they shared a look that said, *What the fuck?* He would've talked more about Malcolm's Calling, but Absinthe was there so he shut his mouth.

Seeing Crys wasn't one of his, he couldn't go to Elijah with her issue, and the same applied to Malcolm's. Doing that would only put the guy at risk of backlash from his own Agent. He didn't like him, but he wasn't about to fuck with him like that.

He'd memorized the Claimed Mark after Crys's text then took his own advice and deleted it. He'd looked up everything he could—which wasn't much—and found not a damn thing.

Crys wasn't stupid. There wasn't much that slipped past her notice. Ben had to know that, which was why Gideon didn't get the guy's choice not to look into her claims. For the time being, there was fuck all he could do about it, so he returned to the problem at hand.

"You're trafficking kids?" he said through his clenched jaw. His glare landed on the rear-view mirror, locking on Absinthe.

"It's not for sex," she huffed, then crossed her arms over her chest.

"Then what the fuck is it for?"

She snapped the gum she chewed and looked out the window. "It doesn't concern you."

He gripped the wheel like he might tear it from the dash. "Then why the fuck am I here?"

"I'm not at liberty to say." She flipped her hair over her shoulder.

Gideon turned to Davis. "Call Elijah."

Her eyes flew wide, and she flailed her arms. "No, no, no. Don't do that."

"I'm done with your shit, Absinthe. So, you've got three seconds to start talking or I'm pointing this goddamn truck toward the Agent's house, and then you'll have a whole other world of problems."

"Fine! I was paid to deliver them. It was good money."

Christ. What the hell was wrong with her? Never mind. There wasn't enough time in eternity to get to the bottom of that issue. When he spoke, he enunciated every word. "Deliver them for what?"

She released an exasperated huff. "The guy said something about trials."

"What kind of trials?"

"I don't know. For real. He told me the less I knew, the better."

"Then who's the guy?"

She shrugged. "He wanted someone from outside Trenton. Someone unknown to the cops in his area who could handle things for him. We haven't even met. I got the inside track from a friend."

"What *friend?*"

"He's not a Lesser Demon. You don't know him."

"When we get back, you're giving Davis his info." It wasn't even close to a request.

"Where did they come from?" Davis cut in.

She stared at him, expression blank.

Davis shook his head, his hollow stare telling Gideon he'd lost brain cells for each second he dealt with her. That made two of them. "The kids, Absinthe. Where did you get the kids?"

"Oh. Them. They're homeless. I found them on the streets, sleeping in parks and shit. That's what the guy wanted, 'cause then no one would miss them."

"Where are they now?" Gideon growled.

"Probably headed to "better homes,'" she said, using air quotes before she smacked her gum again.

Beating his head off the window would've been less painful than talking to her. "And how'd you manage to get caught?"

"The cops pulled me over for speeding."

Davis shook his head and said under his breath, "Could you be any stupider?"

"Fuck you." She crossed her arms over her chest and leaned back in her seat. "Where are we going?"

Gideon's answer was flat. "The warehouse."

Her eyes widened. "No, Gideon! Don't put me in there again!"

"We're past apologies or negotiation. When we get back, you're transferring me the money to repay Malcolm."

"What the hell? Why can't you pay him?" she whined. "You're rich enough that you won't feel it."

He glanced back and offered her a wolfish grin. "You're right, but you're not worth a red cent of my money, sweetheart." He faced forward again. Besides, if he paid, she wouldn't learn a goddamn thing, which meant she'd pull the same shit again or worse.

"I can work it off," she offered, voice sultry, the insinuation making his skin crawl.

Davis laughed, the empty sound of it caustic. "Pretty sure he'd rather cut his cock off then stick it in you."

Gideon nodded.

She cursed under her breath. "Please, not the warehouse, Gideon."

"Too late. Be thankful it's not worse." *Be thankful it isn't the Agent.*

"What can I do?" she said, voice frantic as she linked her hands in prayer.

Crys had looked at him like he was a fucking savage after he'd issued the second strata of punishment and thrown Absinthe and Hennessy into the Gateway during the Calling. And he supposed he was. But they'd earned it after they'd let that demon through. Elijah had given him permission to escalate at his own discretion when it came to his people, and sometimes that shit was necessary. Like the Agent's, his reactions had to be swift and un-fucking-yielding. Anything short of that and he wouldn't be taken seriously.

His voice was cold when he told her, "Nothing, Absinthe. You can do nothing."

CHAPTER 22
GRACE

Grace's arms and back burned as she hefted the boxes from her trunk, pretending she was stronger than she was. It was dumb. *So dumb.*

Jenna winced. "Are you sure you don't need a hand?"

"Nope. I've got it," she said, voice strained as she stumbled across the snow-covered parking lot of the city library. The sun broke through the clouds, and its bright rays reflected off the wet ground, making it harder to know where to put her feet.

The other woman scurried ahead. "Here, let me get the door."

When they crossed inside, Grace was hit with the scent of leather and pine-based cleaners. Jenna led her to a semi-secluded table near the back. Two agonizing, breath-stealing minutes later, Grace dropped the boxes on their table where they made an obnoxious thump. Dusting off her hands, she threw herself down into a chair and did her best to hide her heaving chest.

Jenna scrubbed the backs of her arms. "It's cold in here."

Grabbing a stack of yellowed papers, Grace plunked them down. "My ex, Hector, once said they do it on purpose to keep people from falling asleep."

"Well, it's working." Jenna's phone buzzed and she glanced at it. A broad smile touched her eyes before she reached out and closed the screen fast. *Too* fast.

Grace's head cocked. She desperately wanted to ask but if the other woman had wanted to share, she'd have said something. Chucking her chin toward the stack, Grace said, "These are my mother's personal documents. If there's anything of use, it should be here."

Jenna rubbed her palms together before she hauled a bunch toward herself. "Let's get to it, then."

"So, what are we looking for?"

"Whatever we can find. I'd suggest we start with associations, though. Don't just look for documents that might explain things. Look for people that could, too."

"And how do we do that?"

"We write down names that are linked to your mother, then research who they are. Who knows if we'll find anything, but if it's a private investigator, or a lawyer who specializes in something relevant, it'll give us a path to follow."

That sounded…anxiety inducing. "What's considered relevant?"

Jenna's voice softened, the words gentle when she answered, "Name changes, adoptions. Sometimes it's the small things that lead to big revelations."

"But my parents' names matched *The Chronicle*." It wasn't supposed to be a question, but with the way her words rose at the end, even she wasn't convinced.

"True, but are we sure those identities weren't overtaken?"

Overtaken? As in her mother had assumed someone else's life? Kidnapped Grace and done God only knew what to her real parents? Her body went cold. She was hurt and angry and betrayed and every emotion in between. Why hadn't her mother just told her? Been honest? God, she'd never have thought her capable of it, but it was the only explanation. Wasn't it? Had her father been a part of it? Or was that why he'd never been around? Were either of them even connected to the Shepherds?

Her breathing turned frantic, shallow. She couldn't get enough air.

Jenna settled a hand on her forearm. “We’re only ruling it in or out. It doesn’t mean we’ll find anything.”

She released a slow exhale to gather herself then nodded. Taking the remainder of the documents, she flipped through them with vigilant eyes. “How did you become an archivist?”

The other woman grinned. “I fell in love with history at the Hall of Shepherds.”

“Well, I appreciate your help on this.” Grace shifted in her seat to get more comfortable—or as comfortable as the uncomfortable wooden chair allowed. “I went through all of this after mom died, but I’d just been looking for the will and other legal documents. I didn’t have any questions back then, but now…”

“I can’t imagine how this must feel for you, or your parents, for that matter. They took huge a risk having you.”

She blinked. “What do you mean?”

“Oh. I, um, thought you knew.” Jenna fidgeted with the pen she held. “We’re forbidden from having children.”

“*What?*” she said louder than she’d intended. Every face in the vicinity turned their way.

A shadow crossed Jenna’s eyes. “They say it’s to prevent a numbers advantage on either side.”

Grace’s heart stuttered. She wasn’t ready for kids, not even close. Regardless, she’d envisioned them on the horizon, a someday kind of thing. But *never*? She tamped down on the riptide of emotions that threatened to drag her down and drown her in the sea of her parents’s making.

She wanted to rage and scream and cry, but those were later problems because she had a task at hand. One that required her focus. She shook out her shoulders and dove in. She didn’t know how long they searched but her eyes eventually turned dry and started to cross.

“Everything looks legit,” Jenna said through a frown, then sat up straighter. “There’s always a chance she didn’t keep any of it around for fear of you finding it.”

That dismal thought had crossed Grace’s mind, as well. She plunked her head in her hand. Why had her mother lied to her? And what else had she lied about?

"Have you ever looked into your father?"

She shook her head. "Not in any serious way. I was curious a few years ago and searched for an article about his accident online but didn't find anything."

"Do you have contact with his family?"

Her mother had been so affected by whatever happened with Grace's father, even that miniscule search had felt like a betrayal, so finding his family had never been on the table. The idea of learning about him or seeing his face was so unappealing it made her stomach roll. "No."

"Alright. I'm not sure if the *Arillia Times* would have online records that far back, so let's check the microfiche for the newspaper, see if we can find his death announcement. It might list next of kin. They could have some answers."

They walked the ten feet to the machine and started their search, the strange tick and whir of the motor hypnotic. It was a tedious process as they scrolled the archives for accidents and obituaries, one that ultimately came up empty.

Jenna frowned. "Are you sure your father's accident happened in Arillia?"

"That's what mom said."

"A fatal accident would have been reported," Jenna said, more to herself. She pushed back and came to her feet. "That's alright. We'll try another route." Returning to their table, she pulled out the documents, then opened her laptop. "This time we'll do a Civil Registrations search. It's the government's general database for birth, marriage, and death records."

Pulling several of the documents they'd gathered, Jenna entered the necessary information. She read and read and read. Her head jerked back before her gaze darted between the screen and the papers. "You said your father's name was *Scott*?"

Grace's stomach twisted. "Yes."

"That's not the name on file for this Social Security Number."

"What?"

"That S.S.N. belongs to a thirty-five-year-old woman named Marina Morallez, who is very much alive."

Grace's heart fluttered like the wings of a demonic hummingbird. Her gaze fell unfocused. "So, my mother lied about him, too?" she asked, the words scarce above a whisper.

"There could be a few explanations."

Grace eyed her, hoping beyond hope that those explanations wouldn't cut any deeper because she was already bleeding out, slowly.

"He could've lied to your mother about his information."

She snapped straighter. That was a thread she could hold onto—the thread she *wanted* to hold onto. "What if he was protecting *his* identity?"

"That would definitely make sense."

While it was better than the alternative, nothing about it was appealing. Sweet lord, her emotional baggage just kept piling up and she was sick of dragging it around. "What if his death was a lie, too?"

"We'll need Ben to request access to the Revenant Archives from Elijah," Jenna said as an excited fervor crept into her words.

"What are the Revenant Archives?"

Jenna's gaze narrowed. "It's the history of the dead, where all information about souls is contained."

Taking a strand of hair, Grace twisted it around a finger so tight it cut off circulation. "What kind of information?"

"Who they were, manner of death, relevant dates of existence, sins committed, penance, and where they're spending eternity. There's only one of them in use, so it can take a while to access." She tapped her pink painted nail on the table. "Do you have anything personal of your mom's? Diaries? Journals? Anything she might've written in or shared those kinds of secrets?"

Grace's spine went rigid. She snapped up, gathered the documents, and shoved them back into the boxes. She'd never felt compelled to do a deep search of her mother's laptop—the one sitting on the shelf of her bedroom closet. But if her mom had hidden anything… It was worth a shot.

Her eyes jumped to Jenna's as a stitch of hope sutured the edge of her emotional wound. "I just might."

GRACE CHECKED the time on her dash, annoyed at the unnecessarily thick traffic. Heading south toward Arillia's rural outskirts, she bypassed the worst of it. When they exited the city proper, the trees edged tight to the winding roads. It was a familiar route, one that was always beautiful in winter. The snow-covered branches arched to create a white canopy and framed the drive like a wild tunnel.

"How are things going with you and Ben?" Jenna asked.

A small smile crept across her face. "Good."

Jenna looked out the passenger window, voice formal, "I'm glad."

Her head canted, and a small twinge of some emotion she couldn't pin down twisted in her gut. She was about to dive deeper on the other woman's response but when they rounded a narrow turn, they came face-to-face with someone standing in the middle of the road.

They screamed.

Grace cut the wheel sharp and slammed on the brakes. Her ABS kicked in and her tires locked up as they caught on a slick pile of slush. The car slid, and the screech of rubber on road pierced the world.

Her gaze caught on the man in the road, and her heart stopped when she found a Forsaken soul with the Claimed Mark on its chest. The car's hood passed through him, and an instant later, so did she.

The second they touched, an overpowering wave of exhaustion hit and drained her. She slumped forward then lost her grip on the wheel. The weight of her foot was too much, and it dropped onto the gas pedal. The car accelerated.

Jenna screamed again as they careened straight for the ditch and a second later, found it.

CHAPTER 23
GRACE

"Grace?" Jenna called sounding distant, like she was underwater. "Grace? Are you alright?"

"Huh?" she mumbled, her voice thick and groggy. When she opened her eyes, Jenna was there, several small cuts across her face, a white powder coating her.

The other woman mashed down the airbags while papers fluttered around them like some bizarre snowfall. Cubes of glass were everywhere. The car engine still ran and revved higher than it should while the scent of burnt rubber, talcum powder, and gasoline filled the air.

Grace's body was heavy. *Too* heavy. Like a lead weight pressed down on her. Something about the moment was familiar, and a memory tweaked then flashed bright and hot as it tore across her mind.

Grace was trapped, her legs pinned between the dash and her seat. Her face was angled out the passenger side window, too weak to turn.

"Mom?" she called, feeble. "Mom? Are you alright?"

She snapped back to the present and the carnage. She tried to lift her head and failed, which meant it thunked against the steering wheel. The windshield was shattered, the hood a crumpled mess of metal. The world was off. Its angle messed with her because the steam from the engine wasn't going the right direction. She peered around to orient herself. The car was propped on its side in the ditch, the driver's door tipped skyward.

"Are you hurt?" Jenna repeated. "Do you need an ambulance?"

"No," Grace mumbled. "Weak."

Jenna turned, face paling more—which said something under the circumstances. "Holy mother of God."

Grace's gaze flicked to the passenger side mirror. The Forsaken stood in the road. His position hadn't changed, but everything else about him had. He was more solid, less transparent. So much so, she could barely see through him. Her heart raced, thrashing in her ears. Countless thoughts tried to surface but were beaten back by a fear-laced stick.

Jenna pulled out her phone and dialed a number. "Hey. I need your help. Grace and I had an accident." She paused. "A car accident." Another pause. "I'm alright, just a few cuts and bruises." Pause. "Yes, I'm sure I'm okay." Pause. "I think she is. She says she's weak. Something happened with one of the dead. He's one of yours." Pause. "I can't explain it now, just come please. And whatever you do, don't touch it when you get here." Pause. "We're on Weston Road near the Terrace Drive intersection." Pause. "Okay, please hurry." She glanced at Grace, then away again. "You, too." She hung up, leaned over, and turned off the engine. "I don't think it's safe to stay in the car."

Grace tried to nod but had no clue if she'd managed.

"Can you move?" Jenna asked.

"Not without falling."

Jenna pulled the latch on the passenger door. It groaned as it fell open and jostled the vehicle. She unbuckled her seatbelt and dropped like a lead weight into the snow-filled ditch below.

"Ooph," she grunted as she landed.

"You okay?"

"Yep." She looked up at Grace. "I don't think I can get you out without hurting you, so we're gonna have to wait."

Waiting was good, if only she knew who she waited for. Gravity pulled her down, the belt cutting deeper into her side the more time ticked by. It hurt—a lot—but it was better than the alternative, kind of.

Jenna worried her lip between her teeth, attention fixed on the road. It didn't take long before a loud engine roared. Its tires screeched when it accelerated, getting closer. Fast.

"I think they're here," the other woman said. Her eyes darted to Grace's before she stood and dusted herself off. Ducking into the car, she grabbed both of their purses and slipped free.

Less than a minute later, their help pulled up. The vehicle rumbled as the sound of two doors snapped open.

"Holy fucking shit," a familiar voice cursed.

Davis? What the heck is he doing—

"Over here," Jenna called.

Heavy, fast approaching footfalls pounded out before Gideon appeared. He took Jenna's place and filled the opening on the passenger side. His chest heaved from the harshness of his breaths as he took Grace in. The sight of him had her shoulders sag, relief flooding her like a dam breaking its walls.

"I couldn't get her out," Jenna apologized from further away.

"I thought you said she didn't need help?" Gideon growled as his arm wrapped around Grace. "Take hold of me."

She did and slipped her ineffective grasp about his neck while his other hand unfastened her seatbelt. Her weight dropped toward him, but his grip was unyielding.

He maneuvered them out of the vehicle. "Are you okay?"

"Mmhmm."

"Getting a little desperate for my attention, aren't you?" he said, but the words were off, and the devil-may-care smirk he offered didn't touch his eyes.

She smiled as best she could, but it was a wholly pathetic attempt.

He trudged through the thigh-high snow, carrying her like she weighed nothing. Davis took Jenna's hand and pulled her from the ditch. A quiet conversation passed between the two, one Grace only caught portions of.

"Didn't know what else to...panicked..." Jenna stopped as she reached the asphalt then bent forward and set her hands on her knees.

Davis shook his head. "It's alright...at the warehouse... finished...Absinthe."

"I think I can walk," Grace uttered.

Gideon loosed a low laugh that held no humor. He didn't put her down. Repositioning his grip, his hand slid to her backside as he carried her up to the road. "You're shivering."

"That's because I'm cold."

His eyes narrowed on her but there was no anger there.

"What happened?" Davis asked.

Jenna pointed to the Forsaken. "Him. When he touched Grace, she collapsed, but he grew...stronger." The words were tight and mirrored Grace's emotions. This was bad—very bad.

Davis paced around the soul while Gideon maneuvered behind it and made for the black truck across the road. Its doors stood open, and she was more than happy to be distanced from it.

Jenna wrapped her arms around herself. "What's wrong with it?"

Gideon's heat brushed Grace's cheek when she leaned into him. "It has the Mark we talked about."

"What Mark?" Davis asked.

Gideon opened his mouth to answer as he closed in on the truck when the soul's head snapped their way. He went rigid.

Jenna screamed and jumped back several feet.

"What the fuck?" Davis said as he set himself in front of her.

Time slowed. The soul moved. That shouldn't have been possible. *God. How?*

Her heart pounded in her ears. "Gideon, what do we do?"

His stare was locked on the Forsaken when he set her onto the front passenger seat. "Stay here." He closed the door over and stalked back into the road. Reaching behind his back, he withdrew his sleek, black dagger.

Off in the distance, a car approached, aiming straight for the intersection and the soul. She put her window down as bile burned the back of her throat. "Someone's coming."

Davis eyed Gideon. "Should we send it through?"

"We can't leave it here." He widened his stance, planted his feet, and cut into his arm. "Keep your eyes peeled for Dark Seraphim. We're gonna have to do this fast."

"Get in the truck," Davis told Jenna while he edged to Gideon's side.

She didn't hesitate and scrambled into the back seat behind Grace.

Gideon cut into his Scourge then spread his blood over the Gateway Mark. The air rippled and the portal appeared. Heat billowed out as fire and smoke filled the way. Demons took flight and made for the Gate when he used the other side of his bloodied blade to trigger his Passage Mark.

The Forsaken ignited and the hellfire licked over it until it was engulfed. It vanished but didn't reappear inside the Gateway.

Grace's hands flew to her mouth.

Davis's head snapped around. "Where the fuck did it go?"

The demons were close—only three heartbeats away. She needed a weapon. Not that she was in the shape to use it, but the illusion of safety would've been nice. *Two.* Jenna whimpered and Gideon stripped the blood from his Marks. *One.* The connection severed. The portal disappeared.

The two men stared into the void for several long seconds before they exchanged a "what the fuck" look. Pivoting, they made their way back to the truck where Davis climbed into the back with Jenna just as the other vehicle passed.

Gideon strode to Grace's side and popped open her door. His amber stare roved her face. "You're bleeding."

"Flesh wounds. I'm just exhausted." She scrubbed a hand over her face. "It's the same thing, Gideon."

"What is?"

Their eyes met, fire on ice. "The illness that's going around. What just happened to me is exactly what's been happening to the others." She released a steadying breath and braced for the truth that came next. "I've seen it before, the night I fled, I headed to Trenton. Two Shepherds were there. They didn't see me. One was from Arillia—a guy. I don't know who. They tested the Mark. Someone from our city's involved in whatever this is." She winced. "And that day in your office..."

His expression was flat. Unreadable. "You thought it was me."

Guilt consumed her and gnawed at the frayed edges of her heart. She wouldn't blame him if he ditched her right there. It was no less than she deserved. "I tried to convince myself it was."

His mouth tipped up at the corner while his gaze hooded. He leaned in and his shoulder brushed her chest. "I'm glad you failed." The heady scent of musk and wood skimmed her senses when he turned on her seat warmer. Pulling back, he stripped off his coat and set it over her.

She raked her lip through her teeth. Her gaze flicked to Davis and Jenna who spoke in hushed tones before it returned to him. "I have to be careful who I tel–"

"You're safe with everyone here," he promised, the words even as he put up her window and closed her door.

Everyone here. Everyone. She peered at Jenna again.

The truck dipped when Gideon climbed into the driver's seat. "Jenna, Call Elijah. Tell him we're headed to Crys's place. If Rodan's available, make sure he comes to look you two over. We can discuss the rest of this shit then."

"What about Ben?" Jenna asked.

"Bypass him."

Grace did a double take because there was no way in hell that would go over well.

"Okay," Jenna said, the word tremulous.

Gideon pulled out his phone and dialed. "It's Ryczek," he said. "Yep. I'm gonna need you to tow a vehicle for me." Pause. "No, it's not mine." He recited the details of Grace's car without looking—including her license plate. *Interesting.* Next, he gave the location and its precarious position in the ditch, then hung up.

Slipping off her boots, she tucked her jittery legs under his coat, his warmth still lingering in it. "I need to call the police before it's towed so I can go through my insurance."

"Don't worry about that now. We've got bigger things to deal with." He stuffed his phone back into his pocket, put the truck in gear and pulled away. "Do you need anything?"

She needed to replenish herself, badly, and there was only one way to do that. "Food. Something with sugar. Ooh! Ice cream!"

He cocked an inquisitive brow. "You're already freezing, woman."

She narrowed her eyes in a pathetic challenge. "Ice cream!"

A heart-stopping smile slid across his face when he gave a single, slow incline of his head. "The lady has spoken."

He took them through the back roads as he aimed in the general direction of her home. The ride was smooth, and regardless of whether that credit was owed to the truck or his ability, she welcomed it. Not that she'd tell him that.

Her muscles clenched, her body wound tight. The adrenaline faded, leaving her aching bones and frazzled mind in its wake. Not great since she was pretty sure they were the only things that kept her going. She jolted when a series of images tore across her mind, and for the second time that day, she was taken back.

The night was dismal. It made the road hard to see while heavy rains whipped against the windshield, matching Grace's crappy mood.

She sat, lips thinned, arms folded over her chest in the passenger seat of her mother's car. "What's going on, mom? You've been acting weird since yesterday."

Her mother took a slow breath, then rang the steering wheel in her grip. "There are some things you need to know, Grace. Some things I didn't tell you." She opened her mouth to continue but her spine went rigid as she stared at something off in the distance. "Oh, God."

Cold terror gripped Grace's chest. Ominous. Sinister. She followed her mother's line of sight, but there was nothing there.

Gideon's hand brushed her leg, and she snapped back to the present. His stare lingered, a question in his eyes.

Her answer was barely above a whisper. "A flashback." Her head fell back against the seat as she fought the tears that attempted to slip free. "The night I lost my mother." She shook herself to chase away the memory, but it wasn't easy with the agony that clawed open her chest. Her mother had the Sight. She *was* a Shepherd. "I—I think we were running from someone."

"Shit," he said as they crossed back into the city limits.

"Shit," she agreed.

She was frayed, her emotional strands unravelling. Wanting—*needing*—to change the subject, she glanced around the vehicle and took it in. It had every bell and whistle imaginable; screens, buttons galore, everything and anything one might need. It was more practical than the concept car, but still the swankiest truck she'd ever been in—or seen. "How many cars do you have?"

His eyes narrowed, and his thumb drummed a slow rhythm against the wheel.

"You have to *think* about that?" She rolled her eyes. "Ridiculous."

He huffed a laugh. "I haven't even given you a number yet."

"A number of what?" Davis cut in.

"Of how many vehicles I own."

"Oh. That." Davis fell into contemplative silence and started ticking off fingers.

Grace shook her head. "You've got to be kidding me."

Gideon turned them into a small plaza and up to a fast-food joint's drive thru. "It would seem Crys thinks I'm ostentatious."

"Wow! Big word, lots of syllables," she uttered.

The widening of his eyes gave her the distinct impression not many people spoke to him that way. A proud smirk slipped across her lips, and she wiggled in her seat. *Take that, demon-boy!*

Davis guffawed as he slapped Gideon on the shoulder. "I didn't know there was a mouth out there smarter than yours, Gid, but I think you've met your match."

A low rumble of laughter emanated from the deep recesses of Gideon's chest while he pulled up and placed their orders. Straddling the fine line between starved and ravenous, Grace snatched the ice cream from his hands and scarfed it down like the animal she was. She ate it so fast, he handed his own over and looped back for more.

When he passed her the third, he said, "If you try and repay me for any of this, I'll throw you back into the snowbank."

She scrunched her face but—too grateful and weak to be proud—accepted as someone's phone began pinging incessantly.

"Ben says he's trying to text you," Jenna informed her. "He's worried you haven't responded."

Dammit. In the pandemonium, she'd not thought to message him. Her phone was buried in her purse in the backseat with Jenna, but she still hadn't recovered enough to manage. "Can you tell him we're on our way?"

"Of course."

Gideon's seat groaned as he rested his elbow on the center console between them, leaning closer. "Feeling better?"

Grace ducked her head. "Starting to."

When he turned them onto her road, the tenor in the vehicle changed. Drastically. The air grew thick with unease. There was a strain in Jenna and Davis's silence—not between them, but about *something*.

When her home came into view, an army of vehicles filled her driveway. Ben stalked toward them as they parked, his expression hard. He tore the passenger-side door open and when he spotted Gideon's coat, the glare he offered the other man was sheer hatred. He tossed it onto the truck's floor before he scooped Grace into his arms and carried her away, kicking the door shut as he left.

"Easy," she told him.

"What took so long?" he asked, voice, and everything else about him stiff.

Wait, is he pissed at me? Gideon she got, because, well, it was Gideon. But her? "I had to eat." She wriggled in his grasp, wanting to be put down, but her feet were bare so that wasn't an option.

"You had to *eat?*"

Definitely pissed. She scratched her cheek. "I'll explain when we're inside."

Gideon, Jenna, and Davis climbed out, the former with Grace's boots in hand. Jenna ran and caught up to them. Ben pivoted to her, and his nostrils flared.

"Why are you with *them*?" Trevor said.

"Indeed, Miss Gonzalez." Elijah stare was pointed as he closed in. "Fraternization between sides is forbidden. You know this." His tone was level, disconcertingly so.

"I apologize, Agent. I asked Davis for help, but it was necessary," Jenna said, words shaky and kinder than either man deserved.

"How do you even have his number?" Trevor accused.

God, he's such an ass. Was he *trying* to get Jenna punished? The pointed glare Grace offered him was so sharp it was a wonder he wasn't skewered. Jenna's chest rose and fell in rapid bursts, her eyes wide. Davis edged closer, his body coiling.

A warning pricked in the back of Grace's mind, one telling her to do something before things got ugly. "Jenna doesn't have Davis' number," she said. "I called Gideon but made her take the phone when I got too weak. For whatever reason, Davis answered." Elijah's mouth opened to speak, but she cut him off at the pass. "Don't you dare give me crap for having Gideon's information. I'm not Marked yet."

Ben tensed, and his hold tightened. Davis's intense stare landed on Grace, but what thoughts lay behind it, she had no clue.

The Agent grimaced and asked Gideon, "Why didn't you answer?"

He shrugged and rode the lie with her. "I was taking a piss."

These people and their rules. They were ruled to a fault. Never mind logic, never mind safety, the rules were all that mattered—compliance was all that mattered. *Control.*

Elijah straightened. "And what was it that required their immediate assistance?"

Grace met his gaze head on. "We should probably go inside. You might want to sit down for this."

CHAPTER 24
GRACE

Grace slid from Ben's arms when they crossed inside.

He stayed tight on her heels. "Are you alright?"

She nodded, beelined for the couch and plunked down in a less than graceful heap. She felt better, the sugar from her ice cream binge-fest finally hit her bloodstream, but that didn't mean she was good to go.

Ben crouched before her. "You should've called me."

A nagging sensation pricked her spine because his priorities were way off-track, and it grated on her already-frayed nerves. She batted off some of the airbag dust that clung to her hair. "It was a Forsaken soul. You couldn't have helped."

His words were pained when he took her hand in his. "I could've helped *you*."

Oof. She winced. Heedless of the fact she hadn't placed the call for help, her guilt struck her like a punch. He cared for her. Wanted to be there. It wasn't fair to dismiss that. His loathing for Gideon was an issue, one she shouldn't ignore, but they had a significantly bigger problem at hand, so she filed that thought away for later and smoothed the turbulent skies between them the only way she knew how. "I'm sorry."

The Agent took position in the middle of the room while the others filtered in. Ben set himself down beside her while Jenna and Trevor occupied chairs. The two Lesser Demons stayed standing, and their large imposing forms made the room feel smaller. Gideon leaned a shoulder against the wall, his arms crossed over his chest, eyes wolfish as they took in the room.

There was a light knock at the door and a second later, Rodan pushed inside. When he crossed into the living room, Gideon said something to him too low for Grace to discern. Rodan changed direction and aimed for her. Grace offered Gideon a frown, but he remained impassive.

Rodan checked her over then moved on to Jenna and gave them both the all clear.

"I want answers," Elijah declared. "So start talking. Quickly."

She cleared her throat. "Jenna helped me go through some boxes of my mother's documents at the library. We came back here to get an old laptop she owned, but the accident happened first." She relayed about the Forsaken soul and the Mark on its chest. What had happened when it touched her; that she grew weak, and it grew strong. That it moved.

Elijah raised his hands to stop her. "You saw a new Mark?"

She nodded, and Ben shifted. His Adam's apple dipped low as he swallowed hard.

"And the soul *took* your strength?" Rodan said.

"Yes. I think it's what's behind the outbreak."

"Grace—" Ben started, and while she was sure he meant to protect her from any potential Elijah-based backlash, there was too much at stake to hold back.

"Ask Rodan. None of the hospital's tests show any evidence for a cause or contagion and my symptoms were identical to what our patients experienced. But they were all unSighted, so they couldn't see what was coming. The data shows First Responders are the most affected by it—people who consistently deal with death. This all fits."

Rodan's eyes narrowed. "You're not as sick as the others."

"We were driving, so I passed through it fast. I didn't linger in the same place after I collapsed like a lot of them."

"And you say it…moved?" Elijah added.

"It moved." It was no wonder the outbreak spread so fast.

Trevor scoffed. "This is ridiculous. They probably both hit their heads."

The fire of rage that crackled to life burned through Grace's veins and lit every corner of her being. Her hand twitched, itching to introduce itself to his face.

"Gideon and I saw it too," Davis said, his tone dark. Level. And she got the distinct impression they were on the same wavelength.

Trevor looked him up and down. "And you think we should take a Lesser Demon's word on that?"

The guy must've had a death wish because Davis's "don't mess with me" air oozed off him like liquid menace. And Trevor was about half a step from wading into that deadly swamp and never resurfacing.

"No, but I expect you to believe your own," Davis said through his teeth.

Elijah cleared his throat then faced Gideon. "This is true?"

He inclined his head. "It's true."

The Agent stroked his jaw as he stared off into the distance, considering or absorbing, Grace couldn't say. "Four Shepherds claiming to witness the same thing should give us pause. Regardless, I will need to see this for myself."

"I'm the only one who's seen the Mark, so far," Grace told him.

"What do you mean, 'so far'?" the Agent prompted.

Ben paled and swallowed hard. "She claimed to see it a few days ago."

Elijah's mouth thinned into a hard line as he wheeled on the Head of the Nephilim Sect. "And you did not feel it pertinent to share this information?" His voice boomed through the house and Grace flinched.

"It only happened once," Ben said.

She bit her tongue to stop from correcting him since only Gideon knew about her other run-ins. Seeing as she couldn't read Latin, calling it the Claimed Mark would come across suspect and likely cause a whole other firestorm of issues between Ben, Gideon, and presumably Elijah. She'd have to watch her words…closely.

The Agent's eyes were hard. "Once should've been enough. In the future, you are to come to me with such things immediately."

Ben lowered his head. "My apologies, Agent."

"The Forsaken didn't go through," Gideon said.

Elijah pinched the bridge of his nose, released a slow exhale, and lowered his arm. "What do you mean it didn't go through?"

Davis shifted. "It vanished but didn't reappear on the inside of the gate."

"Then where the fuck did it go?" Trevor said.

"The vanished part implies we don't know. Maybe buy a dictionary, asshole." The glare Davis levelled at him would've wilted her. She wanted to high five him for it because he was her kind of people.

Elijah clasped his hands before him like he prayed for strength.

Grace worried her lip between her teeth. The only way they'd believe them was if they saw it for themselves. Her stomach dropped. The idea of touching one of the Claimed again utterly terrified her, but it didn't change the fact that—in the name of progress—it needed to be done. "Let's do the Callings then. If one is there, I can prove it."

Ben's hand settled on the small of her back. "Like hell you're risking yourself again."

Gideon offered her an almost imperceptible nod. Was the sky falling? It had to be because he and Ben had just agreed on something.

The Agent raised a hand to silence everyone. "Grace is right. If there are others like this, then further investigation is required. We do the Calling, and she will show me if a soul with this new Mark appears."

"If she finds one, I'll test it," Gideon volunteered.

She whipped around to face him. His stare was already on her, which meant he got a full view when she mouthed the word *IDIOT*. His lip quirked up and he offered her a wink. Rolling her eyes, she folded her arms over her chest.

The Agent shook his head. "No. You'll be needed to close the Gateway. *I* will test it and allow both sides to bear witness."

Trevor eyed Davis and when next he spoke, his words grated Grace to the depths of her core. "I suppose we'll find out the truth soon enough, won't we?"

ELIJAH ORDERED everyone to meet at Gideon's warehouse, so they filed out of Grace's home and headed for their respective vehicles, save her and Jenna, who were to ride with Ben.

"A word, Benjamin," Elijah said.

"See you there, Crys," Gideon said, voice a smooth smoke as he climbed into his truck. He turned it over and it roared to life before he backed out.

Grace's body heated while she tucked the orange juice she'd taken from her fridge into her pocked and followed Jenna to Ben's SUV. When they closed their doors, sealing themselves inside, she spun to face the other woman. "So...you and Davis?" she said, letting her implication hang in the air.

Jenna's eyes were wide, and a pure terror hovered there.

She shimmied her shoulders. "I like it."

Releasing a heavy breath, Jenna smiled. "Thanks for covering for me."

"Don't worry about it. It's a stupid rule anyway," she said and meant it with every fiber of her being. "How long have you two been a thing?"

Jenna blushed. "Two years."

"That's gotta be a tough secret to keep." She laughed when so many little things fell into place. "I'm guessing that's why you don't live at the compound."

She offered a vehement nod. "It's just easier this way. Ben's got an attentive eye, and with Gideon being the Head of his Sect, Davis has more leeway." She tipped her head toward the windshield. "He's coming."

Grace winked. "Your secret's safe with me."

Ben popped the door open and slid inside. His silence was notable as he rubbed the back of his neck, clenched his jaw, and continued to peer her way the whole drive. What had Elijah said to him? Was he still upset with her? She'd never meant to hurt him. Her heart twisted. She really did feel awful about it. Reaching over, she took his hand and gave him a small, tentative smile.

His shoulders fell, and his mouth pulled up at the corners. He raised her hand to his lips and pressed a gentle kiss to it. She didn't know if she should be complimented or concerned that his mood had revolved around her—that she could affect him that way. No, she wouldn't think her way into doubting him. He'd been worried. Having someone who gave a crap about her well-being was a good thing.

The others waited as they arrived at the warehouse. Gideon led their group inside where Grace was hit with that distinct chlorine scent again as everyone assembled in a semi-circle facing Elijah.

"I want you to tell me what you see, Grace." To the others the Agent said, "One side at a time. The Nephilim will go first."

Ben, Trevor, Rodan, and Jenna stepped forward as Gideon and Davis moved in to flank Grace. They didn't speak, but the latter offered her a slow nod before his attention swivelled back and fixed on Jenna.

The Calling began, and the Saved appeared along with the Gateway. There were too many to search from her position, so she swallowed hard and fought the cold that threatened to freeze her tongue when she said, "I need to get closer."

Ben half-turned toward them.

"Keep your distance," Gideon warned, his low rumble rolling over her. He didn't have to tell her twice.

She advanced, and Elijah moved to her side. Stepping into the throng of souls, she maneuvered between them, eyes wide, body tight, too tight. She was so scared it hurt. Her muscles strained beneath her skin and compressed her ribs making it hard to breathe.

She scanned their chests as she checked row after row until they'd covered their entirety. *Dammit!* "None of them have it."

"Send them home," Ben instructed.

Grace returned to the front of the room but came to an abrupt halt. She'd been so fixed on finding the Mark, she hadn't actually looked at the souls themselves. But there was one in particular who looked familiar. Her eyes narrowed and she took a half-step forward. Too late. Light burst to life in its chest, obscuring it.

"What is it?" Gideon asked.

"Nothing. I just thought…" She shook her head. "Nothing."

Elijah gestured toward the room, an instruction for the Lesser Demons to begin.

Gideon edged forward, pulled a dagger, cut into his Scourge Mark, and drew blood. "Stay with her, Benjamin."

Ben stalked to Grace's side. "Watch yourself, Ryczek."

He smirked and cocked a brow. "If you'd prefer, I can take care of her."

The returning glare Ben threw his way was nothing short of disturbing.

Squaring himself to the Agent, Gideon warned, "We might not have much time depending on what tries to come through."

Grace took a steadying breath.

Elijah nodded. "As fast as we can." But whether it was an instruction or a mantra, she didn't know.

They Called to the Forsaken, and Gideon opened the Gateway. The air rippled and the portal appeared, filling the warehouse with its heat and the roar of the hellfire. The instant the Forsaken appeared, Grace bolted. She scanned them at a feverish pace while Ben and the Agent stayed hot on her heels.

The Forsaken stared off into nothing. Their expressions hung with a hollowness, like they knew what awaited them. It was a sinister kind of graveyard.

Her eyes locked on something three rows over—something red. "There's one!" Her next step took every ounce of will she had because her instincts were like an air raid siren blaring at her to run the other way. She fought not to recoil when she stopped before it. "It's her. She has it."

"We've got one inbound," Davis called when a demon emerged from the recesses of Hell.

"I see him," Gideon said, entirely too calm.

The two readied their daggers as they stalked to the Gateway then set themselves on either side of it.

Elijah took a sharp inhale and guided his hand toward the Claimed soul.

Grace grabbed his wrist. "Move through it quickly, don't linger."

Because if her theory was correct, the longer he had contact, the worse off he'd be. *Much* worse off. Like, the dead kind. She released him.

He inclined his head, pulled back his arm and swung. The second he connected, his knees buckled, and he dropped. He canted forward and into the soul. And like any leach would, it fed from him, growing more solid.

Ben cursed while shouts of horror rained from behind her.

"We need to move him!" She grabbed his leg and pulled for all she was worth, gaining only inches before Ben took over and hauled him clear. The Agent's pallor was gray, but his chest still rose and fell. The soul didn't take everything from him, but it'd taken enough.

The soul's head snapped their way, and it reached for her. Grace froze. Ben grabbed her collar, yanking her back. It stopped when its attention landed on Elijah. Changing course, it aimed for the Agent.

Grace lunged forward to do *something*, but Ben threw her back again, and she stumbled.

"We have to help him," she said, righting herself.

"Go!" he told her, then took hold of Elijah and dragged him with them.

A sliver of relief slowed her thrashing heart until she spotted Gideon on the move. He barrelled full tilt toward them, coated in demon blood, his amber stare fixed on something above her. An immense shadow swooped past before leathered wings whipped down. A blast of air hit her and sent her hair flying. The demon's taloned claws reached for Ben.

"No!" she screamed.

Gideon loosed a dagger. It caught the beast in the wing, torquing it and sending it off its trajectory. It clipped her, and she winced when she was knocked aside, then did the same for Ben, tearing him from Elijah. The demon howled as it crashed to the ground, painting black-tarred streaks across the concrete while steam filled the air. Gideon was on it before it could stop rolling.

Ben hurdled to his feet and pulled Grace with him. Her eyes darted between the advancing soul and the demon, unsure which was the bigger threat. The beast's black, hollow pits for eyes fixed on her. It bared its fanged teeth in a promise.

Gideon loomed over its downed form when he grabbed it by its mangy hair and snapped its head back. "You're not welcome here, Dark Seraphim." He ripped his blade across its throat, and the demon's eyes flew wide. It opened its mouth on a scream, but only a garbled, gurgling hiss came out.

Grace's stomach turned and bile kissed the back of her throat when its body split then crumbled to ash. Its soul vanished, then reappeared inside the Gate.

Gideon flew past them, seized Elijah's crumpled form, and threw him over his shoulder. Falling in behind her, he shielded her back. His glare met Ben's. "Go!"

Ben ran, aiming hard and fast for the edge of the Forsaken while Grace followed, Gideon tight on her heels.

"We've got three more incoming!" Davis called.

"Send the souls on!" Gideon roared.

Something red on a soul up ahead caught her eye and her heart stopped. "There's another one, Ben. Go right!" She thanked everything holy when he listened. His stare flicked back to her as the hellfire burst to life within the Forsaken.

"Don't let it touch you," Gideon told her.

Grace cried out, the heat so intense, she was sure her flesh melted. Ben hissed and angled sideways as the blaze rose to a crescendo and the dead were engulfed. She winced as she peered back. The Claimed trailed behind them, flaming like some predatory nightmare come to life as it stalked its prey.

An orange glow lit Trevor's wide eyes before he swallowed hard. "Holy fuck."

The demons inside the portal closed in. The fire was agony and stole Grace's breath, slowing her advance. They needed to get out. Out, out, *out*!

Ben exploded from the edge of the souls and joined the others, then doubled over while he tried to catch his breath. Grace burst free next, legs giving out as she collapsed to the ground and Gideon emerged. The Forsaken burned away, reappearing inside the Gate—save the two Claimed who simply vanished.

The demons were almost free.

She scrambled back, spine going rigid. “Gideon!”

He dropped Elijah’s still form, then wiped the blood from his Gateway Mark and sealed the portal.

CHAPTER 25
BEN

Ben had fucked up. Bad. He'd legit thought Grace imagined that Mark, a fact that'd inadvertently sent her that piece of shit Gideon's way. And the guy had been all too eager to take his turn. Knowing him, he'd let that demon come for Ben on purpose.

"Where the fuck did they go?" Trevor asked, mouth open as he stared at the spot the Gateway had been.

"Believe us now, asshole?" Davis said, body coiled. Demon blood dripped from his clenched fists, smacking against the concrete when it fell.

Ben's mind spun. He had to get himself right because that run through the Forsaken and hellfire had rocked him. It'd been a close call on so many damn levels. And seeing that soul come for them…shit. That was fucked.

He peered past Jenna and Rodan who were pale as hell before he spotted Grace. She was on all fours, gaze fixed on the ground, chest heaving. Gideon's stare was on her as he tugged his overpriced pant legs up and started to crouch by her side.

"Are you alright, Grace?" Ben cut in to pull her attention his way, because like fuck he'd let that asshole play hero again.

Ryczek stopped. His glare flicked up as he slowly rose back to his full height.

Grace nodded and glanced around. "I'll be fine."

Ben tucked his elbows tight to his sides when he approached her. He'd win in the end. She'd be coming with him. Soon enough, Gideon wouldn't see her again. Ben had ensured that future was set. He smiled inwardly. Couldn't hurt to remind the guy.

He took a knee at Grace's side and ran a hand over her hair, brushing it back from her face before he set his mouth to hers. It wasn't much of a kiss, but that wasn't the point.

She pulled back, eyes falling as she blushed. "Seriously, I'll be alright. I just—that was a lot. I need to check on Elijah."

When he pushed to stand, he took her with him then slipped an arm around her waist to support her. She trembled but was steady on her feet, so the contact was more for his own benefit, which was fine by him. *Touch her and get under Ryczek's skin? Win-win.* Leading her to the Agent, he offered Ryczek a *"she's mine"* grin.

Gideon's lip pulled up in a humorless smirk.

"Elijah?" Grace set two fingers against his wrist and checked his pulse.

His eyes opened, and he let loose a weak groan.

She pulled a bottle of orange juice from her pocket, held his head, and set it to his mouth. "Drink." As he did, she told him, "Once this hits your system, you'll start regaining your strength. Just take it easy for a few minutes."

He nodded his feeble thanks.

Rodan scanned the group. "So, what's next?"

"The Revenant Archives," Davis said. "See where the dead have gone."

Trevor raked a hand down his beard. "We'd need to know who they were for that."

Ben's chest constricted, and he glared at his friend to shut the hell up. The Revenant Archives were bad for him. Very fucking bad.

"I know one of them," Grace said, pulling every eye her way. "The female cyclist."

His jaw clenched, and he rolled his shoulders. She hadn't told him that. *Why* hadn't she told him that? What else had she left out?

"I'll make the necessary requests tomorrow," Elijah said, voice weak. He sat up but fumbled. Grace gripped his upper arm, and he groaned as she helped him to his feet.

"Jenna and I had some questions about my father, so we were hoping for access for that, as well."

Ben's throat tightened, and he tried to clear it. It didn't do shit to help, which meant his words were stiff when he spoke. "I can oversee that with her when it's available, Agent."

Trevor's stare narrowed when he eyed him.

Elijah inclined his head. "From here on in, you're all to tell me immediately if anything strange happens. Until the Archives arrive, catalog every name from every death in Arillia. When the time comes, Benjamin and Grace will review what we have and find out where they've gone."

Bullet dodged. Ben exhaled, long and slow.

Gideon folded his arms over his chest. "Do we notify the other Sects?"

"I'll contact their Agents so they can disseminate the information." The Agent winced. "We've learned what we can for now. You're dismissed."

Good. The faster Ben got Grace away from Gideon the better. He still had work to do. Yeah, she'd apologized for not including him sooner with her accident, but he needed more. He needed her eyes only on him. He needed Gideon out of her goddamn head. Nothing else would stand.

Everyone filed out. Ben instructed Rodan to take Jenna home, his stare on Grace as she walked beside Elijah, hand on his elbow.

"Are you sure you're alright to drive?" she asked the Agent.

"I am. Thank you." When he stopped by his vehicle, there was a wildness in his eyes, like he was shaken. They had that in common.

"Her home needs to be consecrated." Gideon chucked his chin Grace's way before he climbed into his truck and closed the door. Her eyes narrowed on him, and Ben's gut torqued when Gideon's lip quirked up. The truck rumbled when he turned it on and got even louder as he put it in gear and drove away.

Consecrated. *Shit.* Ben's anger spiked and his breath clouded the air. Why hadn't he thought of that? *God dammit.* He was slipping. Gideon made him see red, which meant he wasn't thinking straight.

"What's that mean?" Grace asked.

"It's a protection," Jenna answered.

Ben's dark stare followed Gideon's truck as it faded into the distance. "Holy water can be used to make your house hallowed ground so the dead can't enter."

Her head bobbed when she nodded. "Consecrated is good." She peered down at her feet and chewed her lip like she was thinking before she returned her attention to Elijah. "We should go public with this."

"That's not possible," the Agent said, bowing his head in apology.

She lowered her brows. "People are being killed. If we don't do something, more will."

Ben set his hand on the small of her back. "We'll figure out what's happening."

"The problem is from the inside." Her hands dropped to her hips. "Someone *made* that Mark. We need to think outside the Shepherds right now, give people a warning."

Trevor scoffed and rolled his eyes. "And what do you think happens when we tell them the outbreak is caused by the dead who carry Marks even we don't understand?"

"I have friends I care about out there. People I'd prefer *didn't* die!" she growled, and Ben was pretty sure if she'd been within kicking distance, Trevor's balls would've been relocated to his throat.

The Agent opened his vehicle's door and gave it his weight. "There are many reasons we cannot disclose this information. Most important among them that it would incite distrust or panic, which would only kill more people. We'd be offering a problem without a solution."

Ben nodded. "Even if we told them, there's nothing they can do. It's on us to figure this out."

Grace's eyes pinched at the corners. "If we can consecrate—"

"We cannot consecrate the world," Elijah said, voice gentle.

Her shoulders slumped.

"Go home and rest, Grace. I promise, I will do what I can to seek those responsible from my end," the Agent said before he practically fell into his car and closed the door.

"Let's get you out of here." Ben gave her his best smile. Her frown was tight, regardless, she nodded and aimed for his SUV. Sure, she was upset, but he'd give her what she needed to feel better.

Trevor took him by the elbow and stopped him dead. When he spoke, the words were low. "What's going on, dude? You're acting weird again."

Ben's stomach dropped to his fucking feet, and he matched his friend's volume. "What are you talking about?"

"You know exactly what I'm talking about. Be careful. Don't do anything stupid this time. She's not worth it."

His brows locked down. The guy didn't know what he was saying. He didn't know her. She *was* worth it. "Back off, Trev. I know what I'm doing."

Trevor dropped his arm, his words hard when he replied, "Do you?"

CHAPTER 26
GRACE

The passenger seat of Ben's SUV wasn't the best place for Grace's emotional tsunami to hit—it receded then crashed ashore—but it was what it was. It was a relief the others knew about the Mark, but she'd assumed they could do…more. Something. *Anything*. Just when it looked like things were about to move forward, there was a roadblock.

By the time they reached her house, it was good and late, the night dark and ominous, matching her mood.

"You knew a lot more than you told me," Ben said as he walked her to her front door, the words tense.

She couldn't figure out if it was a frustrated question or an accusation, but it didn't matter because either way, she wasn't having it. "Why would I tell you? It's not like you believed me when I mentioned the Mark in the first place."

He stared at the ground and exhaled a heavy breath like he'd thought through some great problem. "I suppose I deserved that."

She nodded because he did.

Setting a hand on her shoulder, he slid it down and back up again. "If anything else happens, can you just call me first next time?"

Considering they were together, it wasn't an unreasonable ask. The tightness in her chest ebbed as she withdrew her keys. "I wasn't trying to hurt you today, Ben. I thought I did the right thing. It was a Forsaken soul."

He pulled her to him, then locked his arms around her waist. "As your Sect Leader, it's my responsibility to go through official channels to request the Lesser Demons assistance."

Gah! The Shepherds and their *rules*! But being angry at him for that wasn't fair considering he hadn't made them. She placed her palms against his chest and pressed her face into him, muffling her voice. "I know, but we couldn't leave it there for someone else to get hurt."

"I get that." He set his chin on her head. "I'm just worried you'll end up putting yourself in a situation that gives Gideon leverage."

Her face twisted. "Leverage?" What leverage could he have possibly gained?

"He's half-demon," Ben replied, as if that was answer enough. It wasn't.

She leaned back to offer him the full weight of her glower. "Yes, and that half-demon believed me."

He flinched, eyes pinching at the corners like she'd slapped him. "He told you what you wanted to hear. It's who he is. What *they* are."

Her mental brakes pumped so hard it was a wonder they didn't squeal. Gideon had accepted her word without question. But had it been too easy? Was Ben right? Had he told her what she'd wanted to hear? Was it some weird game to make Ben look bad? She and Ben *were* fighting. Was that his intention?

She dragged a hand through her hair. She didn't know what to believe. Ben had experience with Gideon, experience she didn't, and she shouldn't overlook that. Her gut told her things she didn't want to ignore but then it wasn't like Gideon's influence would matter much longer. She hung her head.

Ben's finger hooked under her chin and angled her to face him. The warmth of his words brushed her lips when he said, "I did what I thought was safest for you. I'm sorry I didn't act quicker. I promise, it won't happen again."

GRACE WAS SO sore it was hard to move, which made showering and changing into her nightgown ridiculously more difficult than they should've been. It was like someone had taken a baseball bat to her. No, a baseball bat would've been kinder—maybe a bulldozer?

She lay in bed then winced and whimpered as she slithered under the covers. Her eyes were halfway through closing when a thought catapulted to the forefront of her mind, one she needed the answer to ASAP. An answer only Gideon could give.

She raked her lip through her teeth as she eyed her phone. Plucking it up, she punched his number.

"To what do I owe this pleasure, beauty?" he drawled.

She rolled her eyes. *Owww. Even that hurt.* "Did your tow guy happen to take pictures of the accident?"

"No, but it doesn't matter."

Crap. She needed those photos. Rubbing her temples with the tips of her fingers, she said, "It matters for an insurance claim."

"There weren't any skid marks on the road because you didn't hit your brakes. They'd have called it careless driving. All reporting it would do is hike your rates."

That was a giant problem. She crushed her eyes closed as her head fell against the pillow. With the Shepherds about to take a chunk of her income, paying out of pocket to repair or replace her vehicle was flat out impossible, but without it getting to work was an issue. She rubbed the back of her neck. "I need that car fixed."

"It'll get fixed."

She moaned as she rolled onto her side and curled in on herself. Something about his response nagged at her, and her gaze flew wide when she figured out why. "You are *not* fixing my car, Gideon."

"Of course not. That's what the body shop is for."

"No!" She was still trying to figure the Shepherds out. He already held her secrets. The last thing she needed on top of everything else between them was to be indebted to him too.

"What are you gonna do about it, Crys?"

Her brows furrowed. "Stop speaking to you."

His voice was even when he said, "You'll be forced to soon enough."

She would, and she hadn't let the gravity of that truth sink in, nor was she about to. Pressing the heel of her hand to her forehead, she sighed. The fact that their blood positioned them as mortal enemies was ridiculous. She didn't even have regular enemies, least of all the mortal kind. What did she even call him? Were they friends? It didn't seem to fit but then nothing did.

"Mmhmm." She picked a piece of lint from her top and rolled it between her fingertips.

"Don't worry, Crys. It won't be me covering it."

She blinked in rapid succession. *Huh?*

There was a shuffling on the other end of the line before Davis said, "It'll be me."

She shook her head. "No."

"Yes. I owe you."

"You don't owe me anyth—"

"It's done," he told her. "The repair company's been paid."

What? How the hell? He was nearly as stubborn as Gideon, a trait she was well acquainted with since she saw it in the mirror every-damn-day. "I'm paying you back!" She didn't know how, but she would.

"No," Davis repeated, his even tone brokering no room for argument.

Well, he clearly didn't know her. She opened her mouth to retort but was interrupted when the line shuffled again.

Gideon cleared his throat. "Now that that's settled."

She stared up at the ceiling for patience. The two men were made for each other. Yes, she was grateful. How could she not be? But Ben's words kept echoing in the back of her mind. "This isn't necessary."

"We've been informed the car will be ready in three days. A replacement vehicle will be in your driveway in the morning."

She huffed and turned her petulance on him. "Stop sounding so pleased with yourself."

His self-satisfied tone practically oozed through the phone. "If you'd prefer, I can cover it, and you could repay me however we deem fit."

Her mouth dropped open. “Gideon!”

He laughed. “You are a different sort of woman, Crys.”

“Considering the ones you usually consort with, I’ll take that as a compliment.”

There wasn’t an ounce of humor when he replied, “You should.”

CHAPTER 27
GRACE

The rental car in Grace's driveway the next morning was just as ostentatious as Gideon. But as much as she wanted to hate it, she couldn't. The thing handled like a dream and its sleek black exterior was, quite frankly, beautiful.

With the chaos of the previous day, she'd completely forgotten about the boxes with her mother's documents, so she was surprised to see them sitting neatly in the backseat. Her battered body complained as she transferred them to her house. She barely made it to the table before she dropped them onto it with a thunk. She froze when she spotted the *Arillia Times* newspaper there. It was opened to an article that showed several black body bags in an alley. An alley she recognized.

She stared at the small photo identifying the dead man with the Claimed Mark as Lorne Vance. Releasing a heavy sigh, she walked to the living room and grabbed her purse to leave for her yoga class. Her phone buzzed. She pulled it free, and her brows pinched when she found three missed calls from Noah.

Her heartbeat quickened as she dialed his number.

His hoarse voice answered on the first ring. "Gracie." His pain was so thick when it permeated the phone it made it hard to breathe. In all the years they'd been in each other's lives, she'd only heard him that way once; the day he'd come out to his family. The day they'd disowned him.

Tucking the device between her shoulder and ear, she shoved on her boots. "What happened?"

"Can you come to Kyle's?"

Oh, God. "Please tell me he's alright?"

"He's okay," he said and repeated, "Just come to Kyle's, please."

She was already on the move because not even Hell itself could stop her. "I'm coming. What happened, Noah?"

A sob broke from him, and there was a scuffling on his end of the line.

"Grace?" Kyle said.

"Kyle?" she replied, his name a question. Her stomach rolled, and her breakfast climbed higher and higher, kissing the back of her throat. She swallowed it back.

"We'll tell you when you get here. He needs you," he said, the words thick, like he worked hard to keep his control. He was the most even-keeled person she'd ever met, so a crack in his façade terrified her to the depths of her being.

"I'm on my way." No matter what.

They hung up.

The drive to Kyle's was nothing short of agony. If she'd thought her mind had raced before, she'd been sorely mistaken. She was aware she drove, stopped when she should, checked her blind spots, used her signal light, but it was like she watched herself through a fogged-over lens. There, but not.

When she pulled into his driveway, her shoulders tensed at the number of vehicles parked there, the majority of them cop cars.

"Please, God," she begged, but what she begged for, she had no clue.

She jumped out and ran, legs weak as she stumbled across the threshold. The house was warm, the air dense from the horde of people inside. The scent of sorrow hung in the air—a distinct metallic odor she'd grown accustomed to from work. The windows were lined with condensation, and every seat in the living room was taken. No one looked up, save Kyle and Noah. Her best friend rushed to her, his eyes red-rimmed and bloodshot. If his swollen face was any indication, he'd been crying for a while.

"Noah?" She held her breath, bracing.

"Charlotte," was all he could manage.

Her heart stopped as her eyes flew wide. That couldn't mean what she thought? *No. No. No.* Her gaze rolled in an out of focus as she looked past him to Kyle.

"Charlotte's dead," he confirmed.

To anyone else, the words might've sounded cruel. But their jobs required clear, concise language. Saying someone was "gone" might beg the question: Gone where? Dead was unmistakable, final. It ripped the bandage off to expose the raw truth. And raw was exactly how she felt.

"When?" she uttered.

"Sometime last evening. We just got word."

Her exhale left her in a rush. Time ground to a halt. The soul at the Nephilim Calling, the one she thought she recognized but hadn't gotten a good enough look at. *Charlotte.*

She tightened her grip around Noah and took Kyle's hand. His returning grip almost crushed her, and she welcomed it because it kept her grounded. When she drew back, Noah swiped at the moisture that streaked his face. Kyle slid an arm around his shoulder, and her best friend leaned into him.

Her tears slipped free, their warm rivulets trailing her cheeks. *Dead. Charlotte is dead.* The words rang like a bell that reverberated inside her mind.

Jake approached. He was in uniform, as were half the others in the room. Her gaze met his. He hadn't been crying, but the dark circles that painted the undersides of his eyes were somber.

She closed the rest of the distance between them and used every bit of control she had to steady herself when she hugged him. "I'm so sorry."

He nodded against her as his arms wrapped around her waist and he pulled her to him. "Are you alright?"

She shook her head. "You?"

He let out a heavy, strangled breath in answer.

She released him as Ivan strode toward them and threw herself around him next. When she let go, she sniffed. "Where's Tara?"

"With family," he said.

"Good. That's good."

"Let me take your coat, Grace," Kyle told her.

A stabbing pain shot through her back as she slipped it off, and she fought the wince that tried to escape.

Jake's stare flared wide when it locked on her collarbone, and he stiffened. "What the hell happened?"

She bit her lip. The seatbelt strap had left an ugly scratched up bruise, one she'd clean forgotten about. "I was in a car accident yesterday." She raised her palms before they could say anything. "I'm fine."

Under normal circumstances they'd have probed for details, but the circumstances weren't normal, so they returned to the issue at hand.

"Come on," Kyle said and guided them to the kitchen.

Grace reached for Noah as they went and threaded her fingers through his. They pulled out chairs next to each other and held tight. Kyle went to the fridge and grabbed a beer, then offered one to everyone in the vicinity who wasn't on duty.

"Gladly," Ivan said as he took one in hand, his knuckles white as he clenched it. But he didn't drink.

Grace declined. "How did it happen?"

"The outbreak," Jake said. "She was dispatched to an accident during her shift last night. She dropped when she was surveying a scene." He cleared his throat, then looked away, the void in the conversation hollow.

"She didn't get up," Ivan finished for him.

Kyle took a long drink.

Charlotte was her friend. *Had* been her friend. And her death had been a nightmare come to life—taken by a danger she couldn't see, one that haunted her steps. How scared had she been?

Dead. She's dead.

A strangled sound escaped Grace as her hand clamped over her stomach. She hadn't even had the chance to try and help. Her chest rose and fell in frantic pants as the tears poured free. An idea burst to life in her mind as she tried to hold herself together. She stood.

Kyle, Noah, Ivan, and Jake eyed her.

It was too late for Charlotte, but there might be something she could do. Something that could help everyone else. "I need…" She searched for the words. "I need a minute." Then she bolted from the kitchen and out of the house.

"Grace?" Jake called as he caught up to her.

"I just—there's somewhere I have to go. I'll be back," she told him and didn't wait for a reply before she scrambled into the rental car and left.

GRACE'S PHONE was at her ear as she flew up the steps of the church and burst through its large wooden doors. "Pick up, pick up, pick up," she begged as it rang. The distinctive void when it was answered filled her world, but she didn't give Gideon the chance to speak. "Is it still holy water if it's been stolen?"

A brief pause, then, "There've been very few moments in my life I've been left speechless."

"Is it?" she pleaded, desperate. She needed to know now. She needed to act.

His level answer came fast. "Yes, people take holy water all the time. What's going on, Crys?"

She untwisted the cap on her water bottle as she peered around and scurried toward the font. No one was there, so she dunked it in. Water sloshed over the sides of the basin and onto the floor. When her bottle was filled, she replaced the lid, and fled.

"How do I consecrate a house?"

"Use the water to make a cross on all the windows and doors that line the outer perimeter of the home and say a prayer of blessing while you do it," he said, then again more forceful, "What's going on?"

Climbing into the rental car, she set her purse and water bottle on the passenger seat. "Charlotte," she uttered, voice breaking at the end.

"Someone you knew."

"She was at the Nephilim Calling. I didn't realize…I didn't…" She started to hyperventilate, so she gulped in air to keep from losing control and spinning her world off its axis. "Will it work on a car?"

He paused for several seconds. "I don't know." There was a creak as if he rose from whatever expensive chair he occupied. "Do you want my help?"

"I have to go."

Another pause. "Call me if you need anything else." An instruction, not an offer.

WHEN GRACE ARRIVED BACK at Kyle's she grabbed Noah's hand and steered him out to the driveway under the pretence she needed air. He squirmed the entire way, but she refused to let him go. He needed to know. She needed to protect him.

"Where did you go?" he asked, eyes pinched at the corners looking wounded.

"I'm sorry, but I had to get this." She showed him the water bottle.

His face twisted. "I think you need to check your priorities, Gracie."

"It's holy water," she said as if that explained everything.

His mouth opened like he might say something, but no words came out.

"I was right about the dead causing the outbreak."

His gaze widened.

She offered his hand a reassuring squeeze before she released him and removed the lid of her bottle. Dipping her finger inside, she strode to the window of his car. "The world won't find a cause or a cure because they can't perceive what it is."

"How long have you known?"

She shook her head. "I only learned for sure last night."

"Do you know who's behind it?"

Regret pierced her heart like a poison arrow. "No."

He took a steadying breath and indicated her bottle. "What does holy water have to do with it?"

"It'll keep the dead out. Well, it will for the house. It's a theory for the car. We need to work fast so keep an eye peeled for anyone coming." Turning away, she used the water to draw small crosses on each of his windows and spoke her prayer. The instant she'd finished, the air rippled then circled out and encompassed the vehicle.

She jumped back. "Holy crap!"

"What?" He glanced over his shoulder toward her.

"I think it worked."

"That's what we want, isn't it?" he said, voice high.

"It sure is." In spite of the circumstance, a teensy glimmer of hope blossomed in her chest. It could work. Her plan could work. It was a small scale, but it was action, so she'd take it.

They continued around the driveway until they'd consecrated every vehicle there, then headed back inside. Pretending they searched for something, they trekked from room to room where she touched each window. They were just about to reenter the living area when Noah took her wrist and stopped her.

"What about people? Can it work for them, too?"

She shrugged and pulled out her phone. There were several messages from Ben that detailed what time he'd pick her up for their date, but she'd have to reply later. Clicking Gideon's name, she kept her message specific enough he would understand, but vague enough no one else would.

Grace: *And people?*

The reply was immediate.

Gideon: *Yes, but it's temporary.*

Her earlier hope morphed to optimism because it was better than nothing. She shoved her phone away.

"Who was that?" Noah asked.

"Your favorite person." She dipped her finger into the water. "He says this one doesn't last, so you'll need to keep some of this stuff on you. Now give me your hand." He extended it, and she set her finger to his palm. "Here goes nothing."

"Wait. Try doing it silently."

Her stare narrowed.

"If we're out there mumbling prayers, it's gonna draw attention."

Fair point. She repeated the process and offered her silent benediction. When the air rolled around him, her body sagged. He was safe. Praise everything that was holy, he was safe.

His brows were raised in question.

Tears fell as she nodded and set her forehead against his.

He shuddered, words ragged when he said, "Thank God."

"I'm the only one who can see the Claimed, Noah. I've gotta do what I can to stop them. I can't have that kind of blood on my hands."

He gave a slow incline of his head. "I hate that you're a part of this, that you'll be Marked like them. I know I was caught up before, but it scares me now."

She twisted her hands. She'd barely had time to think about being irreversibly branded to a side, and the reality of what that meant, of what it would cost her. The permanency of it weighed heavy on her shoulders. Eight days. Eight days until it was official.

"Just be careful, Gracie. Please."

"I will," she promised, then kissed his cheek. With their new plan in place, they split the water into two cups and reentered the living room. She feigned distraction as she traced over the condensation on the glass to finish safeguarding the house. With that done, she and Noah worked their way through the room, hugging people as they offered condolences and—discretely—their protection.

Kyle, Ivan, and Jake stayed close like ever-present shadows. She welcomed it. Welcomed the known. Welcomed their safety, their friendship.

The radio on Jake's hip went off, and he cursed under his breath. "I have to get back to the shift. When Tara's feeling up to it, I plan on getting her out for a drink."

Seizing her chance, Grace took his hand, gave it a gentle squeeze, and traced the cross over it. "Let me know when you do. I'd like to be there."

His grip tightened and he cleared his throat. "I will."

CHAPTER 28

THIRTY-SEVEN

Thirty-Seven slipped through the woods. There wasn't a footpath, so he broke his own trail, and the evergreens dropped their heavy, crystallized snow onto him as he moved. It was cold and miserable, but it needed to be done.

The time was somewhere around 3:00 a.m. The snowfall made it too dark to read his watch, and he wasn't about to risk the light his phone would render. He'd hidden his vehicle out of sight so there'd be no chance of connecting him to what was about to happen. He'd driven past Grace's house and clocked the distance on his odometer from where he'd parked, then counted his paces as he trekked so he'd know when to start working his way back toward the road.

She wasn't home because of her dead friend. Fine by him. It gave him the opportunity he needed.

His adrenaline was through the roof when he exited the forest across from her home. No one was coming, so he aimed for her driveway. His footprints weren't an issue. The falling snow would cover them within the hour.

The Faction had intended to roll out their plan in increments. While that was still the case, those increments had increased exponentially since the other sides were in the know. Well, partially. They didn't know everything, just enough to be an issue.

He crept around the back of the house and headed for the bathroom window he'd left unlatched when they'd gathered to hear Grace spill her guts about the Claimed. Pushing it open, he hoisted himself up, and dropped inside, landing in the tub.

He took his boots off and left them there so he didn't track prints through the house. There weren't any security cameras, something he'd already ensured. He was good to go.

The place was silent to the point of disturbing. The only sounds the creaking floor, the thump of his feet, and his breathing. Each set an eery soundtrack to his task. Stepping into the hall, he flicked on the light and moved deeper inside. To a passerby, a house light being on wouldn't draw suspicion, but the flickering beam of a flashlight might.

The place was clean, which meant it'd be obvious if things were disturbed, so he needed to be careful.

He maneuvered around the living room and studied the pictures on the walls. There were several with a younger Grace and a woman he assumed to be her mother. He didn't recognize her, but maybe someone in the Faction would. Taking out his cell phone, he snapped several photos.

Scanning the bookcase, he found textbooks on nursing and accounting along with fantasy and romance novels. Nothing of note. He moved to the kitchen and stopped dead when his stare lit on the boxes on the table.

"Be what I think you are. Be what I think you are," he chanted, and a dark smile crawled across his lips as he pulled back the cardboard flaps.

Grace had practically gift-wrapped the information for him. He flipped through the pages finding legal documents, tax forms, her mother's last Will and Testament—pretty much everything he needed to confirm an identity or research one. He photographed them all before he replaced them.

The laptop she'd mentioned wasn't anywhere in sight, so he headed for the bedrooms. The first was her roommate's. As expected, there wasn't anything of note there, so he aimed for Grace's. He opened drawers, lifted panties and papers.

His burner phone buzzed with an incoming text, and he jumped. "Christ." Vicki's recruitment number flashed across the screen with her message.

Eight: *Hello, pet.*

He smirked as he headed to the closet. No doubt she was fishing for information, but her hunger would have to wait a while. Sliding the closet door aside, he peered into the shadows. Tucked on a shelf at the back sat a laptop. The model was older, and it was covered with a heavy layer of dust. Everything in his gut told him he'd just hit pay dirt.

"Let this be it."

Grabbing it and the accompanying power cord, he plugged it in then took a seat on the edge of the bed as he waited for it to power up. When it did, he clicked around, opening file after file, until he landed on one titled "taxes."

"Jackpot." He grinned as he punched a response into his phone.

Thirty-Seven: *I found that toy we wanted.*

There were logs of encounters with Arillia Shepherds. Sightings of Marks and the people who had them. Areas of the city where they were seen. Places to avoid. Where the compounds were. Whether they were Lesser Demon, Nephilim, or Agents. She'd researched everything; who they were, what they did, and where they lived. A map was highlighted with sections crossed off as "high frequency" locations.

To spot Markings, she had to be able to see them in the first place. "Oh, tsk, tsk, Wyla, keeping secrets." The only question left was—who did she belong to?

His stare dropped to the dust that covered his pants and the fingerprints that pockmarked the computer. Shit. He'd gotten overeager. Rookie mistake. No matter what he did, there'd be evidence it was tampered with. What constituted the greater risk? That Grace realized it was missing? Or that she found what was on it?

"Fuck it." He strode across the room, unplugged it, then tucked it under his arm before he pushed her closet door closed. Doing a final sweep of the house, he left, retraced his steps back to his vehicle, set the laptop in the passenger seat and grinned.

His phone buzzed again.

Eight: *And? Is it worth it?*

Thirty-Seven: *I'm about to take it home and find out.*

Eight: *Ooh. Naughty boy. Why don't you bring it here? We can play with it together.*

His cock pulsed.

The Primary would be pleased, and sure as shit, Vicki was about to please him for it. Thoroughly.

CHAPTER 29
GRACE

Police lined the sidewalks as far as Grace could see. They marched the streets to the funeral home in formation. Only four days had passed since Charlotte's death, and the pain was still as raw as the first. There wasn't enough room inside for everyone, and the spillover outside created a blue sea of mourning.

Grace and Noah walked in the procession with Kyle and Ivan, who looked sharp in their parade uniforms. Jake wanted to join, but he was on duty, so whether that would happen was anybody's guess.

She edged to the front of the receiving line, and her heart cleaved at the sight of Tara, whose red-rimmed eyes and pale, tear-stained face were the picture of devastation.

Taking Tara into her arms, Grace stroked the other woman's hair. "I am so sorry."

Tara's chest shook through her sobs. "Promise me they'll contain this fucking outbreak."

Grace's chest seized when a tidal wave of guilt dragged her under. Making a promise she had no right to make, she murmured, "They'll contain it." She wanted to linger, to hold her friend until her pain was gone, but she couldn't be selfish. She wasn't the only one hurting. Grace drew back. "If you need anything…"

"Thank you," Tara murmured as they pulled away.

When she passed outside, their small group reconvened, eyes creased, faces downcast.

"Anyone wanna grab something to eat?" Ivan asked.

She'd have loved nothing more than to drown her sorrows in a greasy plate of chicken fingers, but it wasn't in the cards. She'd already swapped shifts and pushed back her date with Ben. *Again*. She sighed. "Sorry. I've gotta work."

Noah shook his head. "Don't be sorry. You've already switched shifts to be here. You had to go back eventually."

Wrapping her arms around her best friend, she offered him a crushing hug, her throat tight when she moved on to Kyle. "Take care of him," she whispered at his ear because Noah couldn't fall back into that dark place. Not again.

"I will," he promised, then he kissed her hair and pushed back.

She offered them a weak smile and left. Next, she climbed into her car, which she'd finally gotten back, and headed for home. She was happy for it—albeit, sad to see the rental go.

When she arrived at her place, she went to the kitchen and set her purse beside the flowers Ben had sent. Taking them to the sink, she replaced their water. He'd visited during the brief period she'd swung by to grab everything she needed and was less than enthused when a delivery of chocolate-filled muffins arrived from Gideon. Hiding her excitement had been hard. Not eating one in front of him even harder. Her mouth watered as she pulled one out and crammed it into her face.

The boxes with her mother's papers sat right where Grace had left them, staring her straight in her depressed face. She wanted answers, but that subject had been forced aside for the time being. A large part of her was terrified of what she might learn, but worse than that, she didn't know how much more she could take.

GRACE'S STOMACH was about to eat her alive. The day had been long, and her nightshift wasn't helping. When her break hit, she hurried to the staffroom, eager to rest her legs and bite into one of the three chocolate muffins she'd brought.

As she stepped inside, her gaze was pulled to the newly setup TV in the far corner that showed the Arillia Late Night News. "What's this?"

Angela's glower was so deep it was like a fixture. "The Hospital Board wants us to be kept informed."

Grace's jaw clenched. Just what the staff needed, a constant reminder of the public pressure that closed in on them. As if their jobs weren't stressful enough. Grabbing her food, she took a seat and started eating.

A cute blue house showed on the screen. It sat in a small cul-de-sac surrounded by a horde police cruisers and ambulances with flashing lights that painted everything in their staccato reds and blues.

"Two are dead and three more hospitalized after another outbreak struck a family gathering in the city's Roseville District," the male reporter said. "Eve Stannis, wife of one of the deceased victims, Clive Stannis, was visibly upset when she spoke to reporters."

The shot cut to a red-headed woman whose hair was so vibrant, it was like living fire. Her chestnut eyes were wild and bloodshot. "My husband's dead. The rest of our friends were taken to the hospital, but that's where all of this started in the first place," she said through a cascade of tears, as her voice broke.

The shot returned to the reporter. "Stannis's husband died on scene. Three of the victims are still being treated, while the second passed in transit."

The news anchor picked up the papers before him then tapped them on the desk. "Many are beginning to question whether protocols should be implemented to protect the public. To discuss this further, we've brought in Head of the Board at Arillia Hospital, and former Epidemiologist and Infectious Disease expert, Yolanda Summers. Good evening, Mrs. Summers."

The camera switched to her. She wore a crisp white blazer that looked striking against her deep ebony skin. Her sable eyes were sharp when they locked on the anchor. "Good evening, Roger."

"What do you believe should be done to safeguard the people of Arillia at this point?"

She folded her hands in her lap. “That question is difficult to answer. The problem is that the outbreak’s mode of transmission is yet to be determined. Without that information, it’s next to impossible to set parameters.”

Grace released a long sigh. All she’d wanted was a few minutes of peace. No such luck. She pushed up and made her way back to the nurse’s station. An alarm for one of the patient’s went off, so she headed that way. She stopped dead in the doorway and her heart thrashed in her ears at the sight of the Claimed soul that hovered beside the elderly woman it belonged to.

Her gaze darted up and down the hall. If anyone else showed up to help, things would get bad. Her hands shook as she clung tight to the wall and edged around the soul until she reached the machines to shut them off. She retraced her steps, made sure she was alone, then pulled out her phone and dialed.

“Hey,” Ben answered, voice thick with sleep, which stood to reason considering it was early as all get out.

“I need your help. Can you do a Calling? There’s a Saved soul here with that Mark, and if it’s not taken care of…”

“I’m on it.”

She stayed on the line while he worked, and less than a minute later, the soul vanished. Her body sagged. “Thank you.”

“You can always count on me, Grace.”

That’d been close. God, everyone was just so vulnerable. She hated it. What would’ve happened if she hadn’t—

She froze as an idea tumbled around in the recesses of her mind. There *was* a way she could help the hospital. It’d already worked for her once.

“I really appreciate it,” she said, then with more urgency, “I’ve gotta to go.”

“Oh—okay. I, uh, rescheduled Prime. The quickest reservation I could get was in two days.”

She didn’t want him to misinterpret her quick exit, so she thrust as much enthusiasm into her exhausted voice as she could manage. “I can’t wait." She ended the call then bolted for her locker and snatched what was left of the holy water from her purse.

It was quiet, the patients slept, and she'd already completed her rounds. A doctor needed to officially proclaim time of death for the elderly woman before her body could be moved, and one would be coming in for change of shift at 7:00 am.

She checked her watch. 6:03 am.

There weren't any windows on the basement level, only the morgue and a few doors for emergency exits. If she worked quickly, she could get it done without being missed. Darting into the elevator, she hit the down button.

When she arrived, she ran from door to door and checked them off, cursing her less than adequate fitness level. When she pushed inside the morgue, she cringed. The cold stole her breath and nipped at the exposed portions of her skin with its icy teeth. Heading for the transport door, she did the cross, said her prayer, then faced the room.

Gideon said Marks were on the souls, yet the others couldn't see this one, so it was already different. But what if there was something visible on the bodies? Something they could be on the lookout for with the living? Sure, there'd be autopsies, but Grace wasn't privy to that information, so the only way she'd know was if she looked herself. It felt wrong on so many levels, like she'd disturb the dead, but it was better than them disturbing her.

She scrubbed the back of her neck. It was a good thing her blood secured her seat in Heaven, otherwise, what she was about to do would've earned her a direct flight to Hell.

Heading to the first locker, she unlatched the handle and pulled out the tray. Its rollers echoed around the empty space. She winced. Unzipping the body bag, she was hit with the putrid scent of death, its fruity undertone unmistakable. That and chemical cleaners—ridiculously pungent ones.

She went through corpse after corpse. She lifted limbs, rolled torsos, and checked nooks and crannies that would forever traumatize her, but there was nothing to find. Dammit! Why couldn't she catch a damn break?

Stomping to the exit like the petulant grown-ass adult she was, she threw it open and jumped-squeaked when tense voices carried from farther down the hall. She tucked back inside, leaving the door open a crack to see.

"I hope you understand what a royal pain in the ass this is," the familiar voice of her Charge Nurse said, her gaze angled down at whatever papers she held.

An older man with gray hair set his weathered palm flat against the wall beside him as the fluorescent, headache-inducing lights buzzed overhead. "I understand, Mrs. Logan. But this is necessary for the investigation."

Grace's stomach torqued, and she fought not to gasp. *Investigation?* There was an investigation? She should've expected it. Her friends had mentioned as much, even still…

Angie pinned the man with her glare. "And *I* understand why the board has hired you, Mr. Redford, but your presence is going to make my job exceedingly difficult."

He fixed a firm smile on his face. "I recognize that, so the quicker I can get the information I need, the quicker I can learn the origin of the outbreak and be out of your hair."

"Indeed. I just hope this doesn't turn into a witch hunt."

"I'm an independent investigator—"

Angie lifted a sharp brow. "An independent investigator paid for *by the hospital*."

His nostrils flared and he bristled. "I assure you, I hold no allegiance. I follow evidence, not the money."

Grace's heart hammered like a kick drum in her chest. She hadn't done anything wrong…well, her gaze flicked to the morgue momentarily, anything *illegal* anyway. But the twinge in the depths of her gut couldn't be quieted.

The Charge Nurse crossed her arms over her chest and the papers crinkled under her elbow. "And what even qualifies you for this job?"

"I'm a retired police officer."

"But do you understand the inner workings of a hospital, Mr.

Redford? Can you interpret the information you acquire and apply it using the proper context to our jobs?"

He shook his head. "I made it very clear to the Board that investigations are my specialty, not the goings on of this building. I've been given a budget to hire a team of experts." He tipped his head toward the forms she held. "I'll be requiring a copy of the nurses' schedules and access to all their patient records from the date indicated until present."

Grace's mind raced. It was like when a cop drove behind her in traffic, and she felt like a criminal for absolutely no reason.

Angie scowled. "I expect you're looking at more than just the nursing staff."

"Of course. I'm looking into everyone and everything. My purpose here is not to assign blame."

"No, it's to dispel public pressure and protect the hospital by deflecting *their* liability," she said. "I don't want one of my people to go down with the ship."

Thank all that's holy she's in our corner.

"I assure you, I'm simply trying to confirm protocols were followed. The only way one of your people will be implicated is if the evidence guides me there. I go only where the findings lead me."

Unfolding her arms, Angie stabbed a finger toward the floor before she spoke with that mother bear "don't mess with my cubs" quality. "I'd vouch for every one of my nurses."

He gave a crisp nod. "I'm glad to hear it."

The Charge Nurse held his stare. "I know I have no authority to block you, so I will ask that you remember we're still in the middle of a crisis and require as many hands on deck as possible."

"I'm not here to waste anyone's time."

The papers buckled when she lifted them. "When will you be needing these things?"

He raised his chin. "Before days end would be preferable."

She rolled the documents into a tube. "I'm needed back on the floor. Is there anything else?"

Investigator Redford offered her a tight smile. "For now, no, but that will depend on my findings."

Angie strode the ten steps to the stairwell door, set her hand on the push bar, and stopped. "I need my people ready to do their jobs, not terrified into inaction because a guillotine hangs over their heads."

He arched his brows. "If they've done nothing wrong, they have nothing to fear."

The Charge Nurse left, and Mr. Redford retreated into the room to his right, then sealed himself in.

Grace's head fell against the morgue's cold door as she exhaled a ragged breath. Why was everything such a mess? She sighed, then pulled the exit wide, so caught in her own panic that the ding of the elevator doors opening took several seconds to register.

"What are you doing here?" Dixie demanded.

Grace gasped, hand flying to her chest. "God, you scared me half to death." She scrambled to explain, but her brain was too busy chirping like a cricket, which meant she came up completely empty. Time to deflect. "What are, uh, *you* doing here?" *Smooth, Grace. Real smooth.*

Dixie frowned as her gaze slid between Grace and the morgue. "I have an interview with that investigator, Horace."

"Pretty early for an interview." Grace aimed for casual but instead managed awkwardly jovial. *Emphasis on awkward.*

"He's accommodating my schedule so it doesn't interfere with my work," she said, voice stiff before she repeated, "Why are you down here?"

A sheen of sweat slicked Grace's skin as her heart rate skyrocketed into dangerous territory. "Things—uh. Things have been hectic on the floor. I was looking for a quiet place to take my break." She slow clapped inside her mind. *Good one, Grace. Not suspicious at allllll.*

Dixie's face twisted. "In the morgue?"

She offered a floundering laugh as she chucked her thumb toward the door. "I don't have to worry about anyone bothering me in there."

Ugh. She was totally screwed.

Dixie crossed her arms over her chest, then flicked a finger Grace's way. "What's the deal with you and Dr. Brookes? You two talk all the time."

Grace had whiplash from the abrupt change of subject, but anything was better than her less than mediocre excuses, so she'd take it. "Rodan?"

Dixie bristled like the use of his first name from Grace's lips was offensive. *Oooookay.*

She wrung her hands. "We share a circle of friends. I'm seeing one of his roommates."

The stick jammed up Dixie's ass loosened a bit. "Oh. That's good. So, what's his deal? Is he with anyone?"

Grace edged closer to the elevator. Rodan's disinterest in Dixie had been made good and clear, but she was in a bind. The last thing she needed was the other woman sticking her nose where it didn't belong. Besides, Rodan had dragged Grace into the Shepherds in the first place, so he kind of owed her.

She smiled. "No, he's not. You should definitely approach him."

Dixie's answering smile was a threat. "I think you should approach him for me."

Her eyes flew wide.

"Do that and I won't tell anyone you were down here being weird."

Grace's mouth dropped. If Dixie said anything, it could cause a world of trouble she couldn't afford. Swallowing hard, she nodded, because really, what other choice did she have? "Fair enough." The rest of the consecration would have to wait. She waved a pathetic goodbye, then scurried away, post haste. Pulling out her phone, she cringed as she pinged a heads-up text to Rodan about the wild cat she'd just sent his way.

CHAPTER 30
GRACE

Ben held the door for Grace as she entered Prime, and the only word she could use to describe the place was posh. It was open concept and surrounded by glass walls edge-lit with soft, white lighting. Black-topped marble tables with crisp, polished, silver accents decorated the room. The staff were dressed in impeccable charcoal-colored uniforms and moved about with seamless ease while a pianist played a beautiful, haunting lilt in the corner.

It was money on money, and the only reason she didn't bolt was because of Ben. How much effort had he gone to in order to secure their reservation? She appreciated it, she really did. Problem was, she stood out like a seagull in a murder of crows. She was dressed appropriately, definitely looked the part. She just didn't *feel* it. Who was she supposed to be in a place like that?

"Welcome to Prime. May I have your reservation name?" the hostess whose name tag read Haidar, asked.

"Jones," Ben replied.

"Can I take your coat, ma'am?" Haidar said.

Grace unbuttoned her ivory wool jacket. "Thank you."

Ben slipped it from her shoulders and passed it off. When he moved around in front of her, his eyes widened. "You look beautiful."

She blushed and smoothed her palms over her white, deep V-neck shirt before she adjusted her scarlet, wide-banded waist belt. The navy-blue pencil skirt she wore flattered her curves where it slinked to her knees.

Ben's hand settled on the small of her back while Haidar led them to their table. Several patrons fell silent as they passed, their eyes like spotlights, fixed on them.

Grace trailed a finger over the tight braid that wrapped delicately around her left ear. Would crawling under a table be weird? Because the attention was a lot, and that's exactly what she wanted to do.

They stopped in the center of the restaurant, and Ben pulled out her chair. She slipped into the seat and a second later, he took his own and then ordered a bottle of wine. Haidar left the menu for them to mull over before she sauntered away.

Grace pursed her lips as she perused the dinner options because she didn't recognize a single thing on the list. "Are you sure Rodan's not angry?"

He laughed. "It'll do him good. I've never seen him date anyone."

"Never?" Her eyebrows nearly slipped from her forehead because Rodan was an intelligent, good-looking guy, and a doctor to boot, a catch by anyone's standards.

"I guess once, ages ago. He was with some Lesser Demon girl when we were still allowed to socialize at the Hall of Shepherds. If he's seen anyone since then, he's kept it quiet." Ben's Adam's apple dipped, and he changed the subject, completely derailing her train of thought. "I wouldn't finish consecrating the hospital, if I were you."

"What? Why?"

"Because after the patients die, it'll only shunt the souls outside of the building and put everyone entering at risk."

Her heart sank, and she cursed. She'd counted on helping, on doing *something* useful there. Realizing all her work had been for nothing was like a sucker punch that stole her breath.

Ben's phone buzzed, and he frowned as he pulled it from his pocket. "It's Elijah. Give me a minute." She nodded and he stood, then headed outside, because Lord knew the Agent wouldn't abide their conversation being overheard.

A waitress arrived with wine glasses. She placed them down gracefully before she filled them and indicated the menus. "Do you need more time?"

"Yes, please," Grace replied. When the woman left, she picked up her wine and took a sip. There were several eyes angled her way, but one pair in particular stopped her in her tracks. Her tongue trailed her lips, and she swallowed hard.

Gideon's amber stare held hers from across the room. He was seated with several older businessmen and women. Folders and spreadsheets were laid out on the table, along with expensive looking bottles of liquor. His arm was frozen halfway to his mouth, his crystal glass hovering midair as he stared at her. With slow precision, he set it down, then pushed himself up. The others at his table watched, mouths agape at his sudden exit.

He was dressed sharp in a form-fitting, navy-blue suit, matching vest, and white dress shirt. The controlled dusting of his beard lined his jaw and made its strong angles even more cutting, while his tattoos edged out from the top rim of his collar. As he walked, he unbuttoned the jacket, straightened its lapel, then pulled back Ben's seat and took it.

He leaned forward and set an elbow on the table. "You're stunning."

His attention was so commanding, heat flared in every corner of her body, chasing through her veins as it rose to her flesh. She looked away. "What are you doing, Gideon?"

"I've come to say hello, Crys."

She twisted the stem of her glass between her fingers. "I'm here with Ben."

"I noticed."

Lifting the wine to her lips, she took another sip.

He smirked. "You don't like it?"

She swallowed her generous mouthful. "I don't like what?"

"Several things, but let's start with the wine."

"I'm not a wine person," she admitted, but at that moment, she definitely needed it.

"And what kind of person would you be?"

That was a loaded question. So loaded, it had the potential to blow up spectacularly in her face if she spoke the answer aloud. She shrugged by way of response.

"You didn't find anything on the menu that interested you," he noted.

Her tongue traced the back of her teeth. "What makes you say that?"

His stare hooded. "I pay attention."

"You were watching me?"

He lifted a single brow. Slow. Methodic.

There was that heat again. "Fine. It's because I don't know what any of this is."

He picked it up, canted close, and pointed to the options. "Grilled fish, chicken stuffed with cheese, Japanese Wagyu Beef, vegetarian option." He replaced it on the table. "No chicken fingers, but I can inform Frank to prepare some for you again if that's what you'd prefer."

Her eyes widened. *Oh, dear God.* He wasn't joking. "Again? You mean to tell me one of the top-rated chefs in the city was the person who made my chicken fingers before?"

His lip tipped up and he answered without an ounce of shame, "Yes."

She looked to the ceiling like it might hold answers...or patience. Anything. "Sweet Lord."

He sat up and draped his arm over the chair's back, settling in. "He was quite put out when he learned you'd had better."

Her mouth dropped. "You did *not* tell him that?"

He grinned.

Horrified. She was utterly horrified. It was a universally accepted truth that insulting a chef was the best way to ensure a bad meal. Groaning, she said, "God, Gideon. He's going to spit in my food."

"And I'd gut him for it."

She twisted several strands of hair around her finger and sighed as she gestured to the menu. "So, what would you suggest I try?"

"The Wagyu," he said without pause.

Setting her wine glass down, she grumbled, "I can't believe you own this place." Of all places.

"And how fortuitous that we would meet here."

She rolled her eyes. "If you own it, it's not really that fortuitous, at all."

"I suppose it isn't, is it?"

Her attention roved to Ben as he made his way back to their table and her blood pressure spiked. When his stare lit on the Head of the Lesser Demon Sect, it turned wild.

"My date is coming," she warned. Gideon sat completely unmoving, and by the relaxed set of his posture, she got the distinct sense he had no intention of leaving. Her voice turned pleading. "I don't want trouble, Gideon."

"What makes you think there'd be trouble?"

The deep frown she plastered on her face told him exactly what she thought of that statement.

He raised his hands in placation and smirked before he pushed himself up. "You have a wonderful evening, Crys," he offered, then made to walk away.

Ben stepped into his path, fists balled at his sides. "What the hell do you think you're doing, Gideon?"

"It's alright, Ben, he's going," Grace said, trying to diffuse the bomb that readied to explode, but if the fury in his eyes was any indication, his fuse was already lit. Turning to Gideon, she linked her hands and offered him a beseeching look because the last thing she wanted was a scene… or a bloodbath.

He inclined his head then responded to Ben. "I was just keeping the lady company while you were occupied."

Ben's arms drew tight to his torso. "I know what you were doing. She belongs to us now. You're supposed to leave her the fuck alone."

Gideon kept his voice low when he reminded, "She's not Marked yet."

"Back off. Stop trying to get to her."

The laugh Gideon offered held a dark edge as he squared himself to Ben. "If you were so concerned about me seeing her, then you probably shouldn't have brought her here, Benjamin." His stare skimmed Grace before he sidestepped Ben and walked away.

Gideon returned to his table where he stayed standing and addressed those gathered, then took his leave.

Ben reclaimed his seat. "I'm sorry about that."

Her gaze narrowed then speared him to the spot while her anger ignited like fire. It burned so hot her good mood crumbled to ash, and it was a wonder she didn't steam. What the hell did Ben think she was? Some kind of weapon to wield? "Why did you bring me here?"

"It's the nicest restaurant in the city," he said. "Loath as I am to admit it."

Not good enough. She crossed her arms over her chest. "And what about Gideon?"

The muscles of his jaw flicked and pulsed as he clenched it. "What about him?"

"Did your decision to bring me here have anything to do with him?" she said, enunciating every word. She suspected the answer but wanted —needed—to hear the truth from his mouth.

He paused, and his knuckle rapped the table. He must've recognized she wasn't playing because he released a heavy exhale and answered, "Yes."

"Why?"

His eyes pinched, and he had the decency to look ashamed. "Because he took someone from me before. I needed him to know you were with me."

She sliced her hand through the air. "I'm not some pawn in whatever war you *think* you two have going."

He lowered his head. "You're right. I wasn't thinking. I'm just proud that you're with me." He shrugged. "I wanted to show you off."

"I'd like to leave." She began pushing her chair back.

His arm shot out, and he took her wrist. "I'm sorry, Grace. Really, I am. It was a stupid move."

She forced herself to relax because if she didn't, she was liable to lose grip of her tightly tethered leash. "Whatever happened between you and Leah in the past is just that, the past. I'm not her. I won't be paraded around like a trophy."

"No, you're not her." His thumb traced a gentle line across her skin as he threaded his fingers with hers. "You're much more than her. So much more. I've got some baggage, and I shouldn't have dragged you into it."

Her lips pursed so hard they ached. She understood baggage, she had plenty of her own. Hers got in the way all the time. It held her back as they spoke. She had no idea what she was doing. Didn't know what a normal, functioning relationship looked like. It wasn't like she'd grown up around one. In a messed-up way, she got his logic. Didn't agree with it, but got it. Gideon was a magnet. He pulled women in. Any man would be threatened by that, least of all one who'd already lost to him. Her next breath came a little easier. "Listen, if you want this to work, you've got to trust me."

He inclined his head. "I can do that." He cleared his throat. "Did you still want to leave?"

In her anger, she'd been fully prepared to, but with her temper cooling, she was aware leaving would only cause a scene…exactly what she'd been trying to avoid in the first place. He'd admitted what he'd done and apologized. What more could she ask? "No. It's fine. We can stay."

His body slumped, and a slow smile took him as he raised her hand to his lips and kissed it. "At least this won't be a thing after you're Marked tomorrow. I can't wait until you're ours."

A sheen of sweat slicked her skin, and she fumbled to pick up her wine before taking a long, deep drink.

The waitress returned and stepped to Grace's side. "Are we ready to order?"

She exhaled a steadying breath and nodded. "I'll have the Wagyu."

CHAPTER 31
BEN

Ben drove to Grace's before her Marking the next day, his hands fisted around the wheel, his blood pressure through the goddamn roof. He'd barely slept, too busy fantasizing over ways to wipe the smirk from Ryczek's face. It'd taken every ounce of his control to keep cool in front of Grace. He wasn't about to lose her at the eleventh hour. He needed her Marked and bound to the Nephilim. After he was her Sect Leader, stuff would be easier to control.

The way Gideon had looked at her…it was probably the same way he looked at every whore that crossed his path. Not that Grace was one of them. She was a prize. Ben's prize. He'd be her first—there was no doubt about that. He pictured it every time he saw her; her mouth open as she screamed his name, and he came inside her.

He rolled his shoulders as he pulled into her driveway and climbed out. A smile pulled across his lips. Maybe he'd take a picture of his own, one of him and Grace together. He'd pay every penny he had to see Gideon's reaction to it—to watch the knife twist in his gut just like Ben's had with Leah.

His fist thumped against her door, and a few short seconds later, she answered.

"Hey!" She smiled. "You're early."

"I wanted to see my girl." He stepped inside, then leaned down and kissed her.

She pulled back. "I'm still getting ready. I was just about to hop in the shower."

His cock jumped, and he shoved his hands in his pockets to stop himself from dragging her down the hall. They didn't have time for it before the Marking, but later... "Go ahead, I'll wait out here."

"Help yourself if you want anything," she replied, then sauntered away and shut herself in the washroom.

The taps squealed as she turned them on, followed by the rush of water. She was probably taking her clothes off. The shower curtain pulled back. The thought of the water streaming over her tits, ass, and between her legs had him instantly hard.

Her phone pinged on the table in front of him.

He bent forward and picked it up. His stare narrowed, his earlier rage returning with a bullet. "Who the fuck is Jake?"

Jake: *You off tonight? I'm headed to meet Tara and Ivan for a drink? Wanna join? I can pick you up.*

What the hell? Some other guy he'd never even heard of was asking her to go out with another couple, like a double date or some shit? Did this guy not know they were together? He'd fix that real fucking quick.

He clicked on the message. It didn't ask for a passcode. He typed *I have a boyfriend!* then sent it. There, if he didn't figure it out after that, Ben would figure it out for him. He waited for a response, but none came.

Shit. Grace was gonna see that. He fumbled with the buttons when he deleted both his, and Jake's texts. *There. Done.*

If he thought he was pissed before, he'd been wrong. Exiting that conversation, he searched to see who the hell else she'd been talking to. Noah, of course. The two were joined at the goddamn hip. That was gonna change.

He kept scrolling. The list of names had him gripping the phone hard, and he fought not to chuck it across the fucking room. There were women, sure, but all he could focus on were the men. Kyle he'd heard of. Still, why he'd need to text her was beyond Ben. It wasn't like *they* were in a relationship. His vision turned red at the last name he found. Gideon.

He clicked on the conversation.

"Jesus Christ." How many messages were there between them? He kept going, then read.

Grace: *And people?*

Gideon: *Yes, but it's temporary.*

What the hell did that mean? He scrolled back and scrolled and *scrolled.*

Gideon: *Go inside and wait in my office. I'll be there in a few.*

Grace: *Are your spy cameras facing the parking lot too? How do you know where I am?*

Gideon: *Magic. Now go inside.*

Grace: *I'm fine in my car.*

Gideon: *It's winter. Get. Inside.*

So that's why she'd been there alone with the guy. Gideon was goddamn relentless. He'd forced her to go in.

Ben's hands shook as he scrolled further back and landed on the photos she'd sent him. *He* didn't even have a picture of her, but that son of a bitch did? Switching over, he clicked on her call history. Gideon's name…again. And the time lengths showed they'd talked for a while.

The shower turned off, and a few seconds later, the hair dryer started up.

He glared at her phone. He needed to handle this, and he needed to handle it fast. He stabbed Gideon's name to dial the number. It rang.

The prick's voice was smooth when he answered, "Hello, Crys."

"That's not her goddamn name and stop fucking calling her."

"Benjamin. Snooping through her phone the same way you did Leah's. Old habits die hard."

"Go fuck yourself, demon."

"And what would Crys say if she knew?"

"She wouldn't believe you."

"Don't worry yourself, I'm not going to say anything. She's smart enough to figure you out on her own."

He balled his hand into a fist wanting nothing more than to slam it into Ryczek's face just to watch him bleed. The guy needed to feel pain, and Ben needed to be the one to deliver it. "After the Marking, you'll be out of her life. She'll belong to us."

Gideon's voice turned cold. "She'll be Nephilim, Benjamin. But she'll never be yours. You're already fucking that up."

He bared his teeth and stabbed a finger against his chest. "She is *mine!*"

"You keep telling yourself that."

Air burst from him as it pushed through his nose like a bull. "Why the hell have you been talking to her?"

"Why not ask her yourself?"

"I'm asking you."

"Yes. And you're asking me because you know what will happen if she finds out what you're up to right now. But you're mistaken if you think I feel obligated to answer, Benjamin."

"You can't have her, Gideon."

There was a creak as if he'd shifted in a leather chair. "I'm quite well aware of what I can and cannot have when it comes to her."

"You need to get the fuck out of her life."

"What is it about this that bothers you more, Benjamin? That I'm talking to her? Or that she's talking to me?" His tone darkened when he finished, "Do I ruffle your demons?"

Ben's vision narrowed as he readied to lose it but before he could Gideon pushed on.

"Don't worry, there's nothing nefarious. She's not that kind of girl. She understands what boundaries are."

"Do *you* understand boundaries?"

"I understand her. And I also understand that you can't trap this one. She's too strong for you."

The guy's calm façade pissed him off. He wanted him to get it—needed him to. He couldn't risk the two of them talking again. Once the Marking happened, that had to be it. She had to be *Ben's*. "Quit fucking with her."

"That's rich coming from you." There was a tap, then another creak.

"I won't put Crys in a position to face Elijah, but make no mistake, it has nothing to do with you."

Ben slammed his fist down on his knee. "If you don't back the fuck off, I'll make sure you suffer."

"Don't pretend to be brave, Benjamin. If you were brave, you'd be calling to challenge me from your phone, not hiding from Elijah's wrath by using hers. Or I could take it one step further. If you were brave, this wouldn't be a phone call, at all."

The hair dryer stopped, and Ben's head snapped that direction. "Remember what I said, Gideon. Don't mess with me again."

The guy laughed before he offered a threat of his own. "Be careful with Crys, Benjamin. Don't hurt her."

"Fuck you." He hit the end button and cut off the conversation before he threw the phone back on the table where he'd found it. Storming to the couch, he lowered himself down and took a seat.

The bathroom door opened, and Grace stepped into view. Her hair hung in loose waves over her shoulders. She came toward him wearing navy blue dress pants and a pale pink shirt with sleeves that ended above her elbows.

"You look great," he said, working hard as hell to cool himself. Only a few more hours and she'd be his. *Only a few more fucking hours.*

She smiled. "Thank you."

Her phone pinged, and his heart jumped into his throat as she headed for it. *Oh shit. Oh shit. Oh shit.* She picked it up and laughed at whatever was on the screen.

His spine went rigid. Who was that?

"I think Jenna's excited about today," she said as she typed a response.

He rolled his shoulders. "She should be."

Grace tucked her phone into her purse. "I'm nervous."

Only a few more hours. He cleared his throat. "Why?"

"Because my life is going to change."

What was that supposed to mean? Was there something she was upset about losing? Or someone? It didn't matter. He'd fill that void soon enough. He'd fill *every* void. "Is that a bad thing?"

Her brow furrowed as she faced him. "What's wrong?"

"Nothing. Why?"

"You sound off."

His face ached when he forced his lips into a smile. "I have a few things on my mind. I'm just eager to get this done." Have it done and have her far away from that piece of shit Lesser Demon permanently.

She eyed him a few seconds longer before she turned away. "Anything I can help with?"

"It's already taken care of." He rose and closed the distance to her. "We should get going." Slipping his hand around the back of her neck, he pulled her to him and crushed his mouth over hers. She was warm against him, warm and beautiful and *his*.

After her Marking, Gideon's access to her would be blocked. And if he tried to skirt that, Ben meant what he said, he'd make sure the guy paid for it.

CHAPTER 32
GRACE

Grace fell in behind Ben as he led the Nephilim in a single file line toward the front of the catacombs. Her feet were heavy, like someone had strapped a lead weight to them. Every step draining. She pulled her lip between her teeth as her gaze flicked to Gideon where he headed the Lesser Demons to their left, his stride stiff.

His amber gaze found hers, and he offered her a wicked grin. "Goodbye, Crys."

Her heart sank, his words cutting to the quick. That was it. The last thing he'd ever say to her. The last time they'd be permitted to speak. Her shoulders curled as she rubbed the back of her arm. She offered him a trembling smile but didn't have a chance to respond before their groups split off and took their respective sides.

Elijah awaited them at the end of the crypts. A small table with a crisp, white cloth covering it sat beside him. Resting atop it were two gold daggers and three bronze brands of a metal that looked oddly familiar.

An ominous twisting tightened her chest and made it hard to breathe. She offered a silent thanks when their procession stopped, and she swiped her sweaty palms on her pants. Why was she so nervous?

The others had been Marked, and they were all fine. She shook out her shoulders. It didn't help.

The Shepherd lines faced one another, their formation creating a path. Gideon's dominating stare was on her, and her chaotic emotions must've played across her expression, because his brow furrowed.

Ben touched her hand, then shook his head and mouthed *Don't.*

Anger burned like fire through her veins, but she forced her gaze down. The last thing she needed was to draw Elijah's wrath.

The Agent stepped forward. "The unMarked has been blooded Nephilim and will be branded so. She is to face the branding openly, with pride and acceptance of her own free will. This is her destiny, and she must face her destiny alone. The others in attendance will observe but shall not participate. These are the rules of the ceremony." His voice resounded off the walls before reverberating through every cell in her body.

That pit in her stomach rolled like a storm, a savage squall of nausea. She swallowed hard as bile rose in the back of her throat, then swallowed hard again. Why couldn't she shake this feeling?

"Will the unMarked come forward," Elijah said.

Her gaze fell unfocused as she forced herself to take that first step, completely disconnected from her body when she stopped before him.

"Do you understand what it means to be branded? That the Mark is irrevocable? That you will forevermore be tethered to the Nephilim?"

"I do," she said, voice unsteady.

"And do you understand what it means to be Nephilim? To be sworn to a side? A side you are bound to act for. A side you swear your soul to until the end of eternity?"

Her knees weakened, and she swayed but caught herself as she slowly inclined her head. "I do."

"Offer your wrists."

Shouldn't signing herself to Heaven, guaranteeing her seat in the afterlife, have been easy? Her heart drummed in her ears. Something wasn't right. *Stop it, Grace.* She was just nervous. Latching onto that dark feeling, she tried to shove it deep below her surface, but it just kept on breaching.

She raised her arms.

The Agent crossed the Nephilim Absolution brands before him in an x and hovered them a hair above her flesh. "I offer you God's grace." He set them against her.

There was a sharp sting when they touched, and she flinched before a strange sensation crawled over—*through* her. It penetrated her layers as it dove deeper and deeper. It was familiar somehow, yet not. It started as a cool tingling while it chased out, but then it changed, bearing down when it turned to ice in her veins. Cold. It was so unimaginably cold that it burned. Agony pierced every corner of her being, and her vision blurred as she stumbled back. She clawed at her Marks, trying to tear them from her skin and she screamed.

Her mind flashed to the past, jarring another void in her memory into sharp focus.

"Grace?" her mother's unnervingly weak voice said.

"Mom?" She tried to turn her head but was pinned to the dash and couldn't move.

"I love you. I love you more than anything in this world. Everything I've done is for you." There was a rustling, as if her mother had picked something up. "I need you to stay quiet, Grace. Don't let them hear you."

"What?" she mumbled.

"They found me, and they're coming for me now." When next her mother spoke, it was a prayer. "Father, you see all. Please, see me now. See me now!"

There was a clank of metal followed by another rustling. Grace winced when the sharp sting of something touched the back of her neck. It permeated her world. Permeated her soul.

Everything faded, and her eyes fell closed.

The pain snapped her back to the present like a whip. It hurt so damn much it crushed her and stole the air from her lungs. She screamed and screamed again, then collapsed.

"What the hell did you do?" Gideon said.

Elijah released the brands, and they clanked against the ground. He lowered himself before her. "What's happening?"

"It hurts." Her eyes lost focus when tears filled them and spilled over. "Oh, God. IT HURTS!"

"Grace?" Ben said.

"WHAT THE HELL DID YOU DO?" Gideon roared.

It was like a thousand frozen knives cutting her, but she didn't bleed, because it wasn't her body being wounded, it was her soul.

"I've never seen this before." Elijah took up the brands again and inspected them.

Ben's eyes were wide, tone tense when he asked her, "What can I do?"

Her face was soaked with her tears. The world spun as her body grew weak. There was a commotion and people approached, but she had no clue who because she lost focus a second later. The only thing left was the pain.

Her screams faded to a whimper as she sank until her face pressed against the floor. Her breathing grew shallow. Strained voices bellowed around her. People moved in the periphery of her vision. Her sight narrowed, going dim. Her eyes closed, and she welcomed the darkness when it swallowed her whole.

GRACE MOANED. Her body ached like she'd been beaten. It hurt everywhere, not a single corner was left untouched.

"Grace? I need you to look at me, Grace," someone pushed.

Another wave of pain crested, and while it was bad, it'd ebbed enough for her to breathe. When she forced her eyes open, Rodan hovered over her.

"There you are," he said.

She released a pathetic mewl as he checked her pupils, pallor, temperature. Everything. Had everyone lied about what was supposed to happen? If the wide-eyed expressions around her were any indication, the answer was no. But then, what the heck?

"What are you feeling?"

The sensations had morphed into more of a heavy stabbing. That was too much to explain though, so she kept it simple. "Pain."

"Where?"

"Everywhere. It's like knives." She tried to sit up and flinched.

"Stay down and focus on your breathing."

He didn't have to say it twice, not that her body had given her a choice in the matter.

"What the hell was that?" Gideon demanded, and Grace rolled in the direction of his voice.

Elijah shook his head, his face pale. "I do not know."

She swiped away the tears that stained her face. The haze over her mind receded, clearing her thoughts. She'd had a bad feeling. She should've trusted her instincts, told Elijah to stop. *Something.*

Gideon's stare was fixed on her, his voice a hoarse rumble when he asked, "You alright?"

"Back off, demon," Ben snapped. "She's not your concern."

"He's right, Gideon," Elijah warned.

Ben moved into her line of sight to cut her off from the Head of the Lesser Demon Sect. "You scared me."

"You scared everyone," Jenna amended, then turned to the Agent. "Is there anything we can do to help her?"

"Truthfully, I'm unsure. I'll need to speak with a Marksman to seek answers for this."

A Marksman. Something about that was good but Grace couldn't grasp why.

Ben swallowed hard.

"I suggest she rest for now," Rodan put in.

Trevor rolled his eyes. "Her Marking's not done."

Every eye turned his way. *God, he is such an asshole.* If she could've lifted her leg, his outie would've become an innie so damn fast.

"Careful," Gideon warned him.

Trevor looked away.

"I'm not comfortable proceeding with the Passage and soul-sword Marks until I have answers." Elijah took up her daggers and handed them to Ben. "Give her these when she's better."

Trying again, Grace slowly maneuvered into a seated position. The pain aside, she felt...strange. Off-kilter somehow. Not her body, just *her*.

Ben leaned closer. "We should get you out of here."

"I will submit my query to the Marksman and pass along any answers I receive to Benjamin," Elijah told her. "It may take time, but if they require further elaboration or have any questions I cannot answer, I will send for you."

Beyond him, Gideon stood, arms crossed over his chest, imposing. Every line of his body was coiled.

Ben turned to the Agent. "Are we done here?"

"Yes."

Crouching, his hands slid under her, and he scooped her into his arms.

She shook her head. "I think I can walk."

He laughed without humor. "Not a chance."

Her mouth pulled down at the corners before her gaze skimmed Gideon's. In answer to his earlier question, she gave him the subtlest nod she could muster. *I'm alright.*

The wry cock of his brow told her didn't buy it, but anything else between them was lost when Ben angled her away and left.

"THIS ISN'T NECESSARY," Grace told Ben as he drove them toward the compound. Her emotional current churned, threatening to drag her down. All she wanted was to curl up and forget everything. She didn't want to think. Didn't want to talk. Didn't want to do anything except sleep. She could forget with sleep.

He pulled out her daggers and passed them to her. "I want to keep an eye on you tonight."

"I'll be fine, Ben. I'm just feeling sore and…weird," she said as she shoved them in her purse.

"You're weird, alright."

She peered at him askance. Whatever bizarre whim had overtaken him before her Marking was long gone, but his mood swings had gotten harder and harder to keep up with. Shaking her head, she pulled out her phone.

"What are you doing?"

"Letting Noah know I'm not coming home." She punched the message into her texts.

"You two are strange."

Clicking send, she tucked her phone away. "What do you mean?"

"You rely on each other a lot."

"He's my best friend," she said, as if that were answer enough, because it was. Best friends relied on each other. That was how it worked.

"Trevor's my best friend, and we don't check in with one another all the time," he said through a dry laugh.

Unsurprising, considering Trevor was a world-class jackass. She set her elbow on the door's armrest. "Noah and I have been through a lot together. We're family."

He lifted his shoulder in a half-shrug.

What the heck was *that* supposed to mean?

"I hope you get the rules now that this is done. There can't be any contact between sides. None. You need to stop speaking to Gideon. Communication in any form is over."

"Is *over*?" She wasn't an idiot. The seriousness of her situation had been pounded into her head, but the bite in his tone set her teeth on edge.

"Yes. You need to delete him from your phone."

She folded her arms over her chest. "That sounds like an order?"

"You're Nephilim now. You belong to us. If Elijah finds Gideon's number in there, there's nothing I can do to help you."

Her fuse was already short from, well, everything, so she couldn't tell if she read too much into his words, or not enough. Maybe there was a reason he was friends with a guy like Trevor. "And you have no personal motivation behind it?"

"You know how I feel about him. And if I'm being honest, yeah, it bugs me that you're fighting to keep contact with a man you know has screwed me over."

She huffed an exasperated sigh and set her head against the seat. "I intend to follow the rules, Ben. But regardless of Gideon, you need to trust me. Not the others around me, just me."

Her stomach twisted. She'd kept the thought of cutting Gideon out at bay, but the reality of it was hard to swallow, especially when it smacked her in the face. Every defiant cell in her body stood at attention. But his words about the strata of punishment kept knocking around inside her head, quieting the bitter comments at the tip of her tongue.

Ben's eyes shifted to her. "Either way, it's over now."

A white church came into view before they passed under an archway with stone walls that rose on either side. It funnelled them toward a closed, heavy metal gate. A sensor in Ben's vehicle beeped then triggered it to open. They drove into a courtyard surrounded by several brick buildings. Statues of angels dotted the perimeter, their wings and arms spread wide. Ben parked and a cascade of blinding flood lights flicked on, lighting the area like the sun.

Another wave of pain took her, and she winced as they climbed out and he led her into the central building. Compound wasn't a strong enough word for the place. Prison would've sufficed.

"You look tired." He brushed her hair back from her face, and she fought not to flinch. "Let's get you to bed."

There was something in his tone, an edge, or an eagerness, she couldn't tell. She took a half-step back. "I'm fine."

"Rodan said you need rest." Taking her hand, he led her down the hall to his room.

The walls were an aggressive shade of salt-lake blue, while the queen-sized bed in the middle of the room wore a black comforter. The curtains were fire engine red, and the white furniture covered in chips and dents. It looked every inch a bachelor pad.

He closed the door and shut them in.

Her throat tightened. "I'm still pretty sensitive. I should probably sleep alon—"

"I'm staying." He smiled. "Don't worry. I won't hurt you, Grace."

Her gaze darted around like another option might present itself. It didn't. His hands landed on her shoulders, then pulled off her coat and set it and her purse on the floor in the corner. Grace clutched her arms as she headed fully clothed for the bed.

He forced a laugh. "You're wearing that?"

"I don't have any nightclothes."

His brows rose, slow, calculated. "Then don't wear any."

"Ben," she growled because that was *not* on the table. She was a mess on every level, so sex was a hard pass. Pulling back the covers, she climbed underneath and drew her knees to her chest.

He stripped off his shirt, and her eye caught the Mark above his elbow. A gold sword sat at its center, its gilded metal shimmering. His weapon. The room went dark, and the sheets lifted as he set himself down behind her, then moved tight to her back. He slid an arm around her waist, rested his palm against her stomach, and splayed his fingers wide. She tensed.

"Just try and relax," he said, mouth against her ear. His hand moved up and skimmed the underside of her bra. His lips pressed against her neck, his tongue flicking out as his breath brushed over her. Gripping the edge of her shirt, he started to lift.

Her heart leapt into her throat, and she grabbed his forearms. "No, Ben."

His hard length probed her backside. "It feels good, Grace. I promise, it'll help."

"I said no."

He drew in a deep breath, the kind someone did when they were agitated and trying to control it. Every warning bell in her body went off, screaming at her to get the hell outta there. *Oh, God.* What had she gotten herself into? And how was she gonna leave?

His hand slipped to the hem of her pants and dipped under.

Her thighs clamped together as the walls around her closed in. She'd pegged him all wrong. God, how had she pegged him so goddamn wrong? She hadn't seen anyone else on her way in to call for help, and feeble as she was, running wasn't an option. Her new daggers were in her purse across the room, but she had no idea how to use them. What could she do? What could she say?

"I'm bleeding!" she blurted out.

He froze.

She stared straight ahead. "I'm sorry. Believe me, I want this too, it's just not a good idea tonight," she said, the lies like acid on her tongue, but she'd welcome that burn if it got him to stop.

He was quiet for several seconds before he removed his hand. "I just wanted to make you feel better."

"I know. We'll do it soon, I promise. Right now, I think I just need to sleep," she said as her voice quavered.

"Soon," he agreed.

She struggled to keep her breath steady and tears pricked the backs of her eyes before they slipped free, falling into the darkness where no one else could see. Alone, she was so alone.

CHAPTER 33

THIRTY-SEVEN

Thirty-Seven moved quickly down the hall. He needed to contact the Primary, something that wasn't possible while being followed. He'd evaded the woman all night, but she was relentless, and her eyes tracked him like the predator she was. Stalking. Seeking. Wanting.

She trailed about twenty feet behind, lurking around corners while she waited for the opportunity to pounce. He'd pretended to be occupied by his charts in hopes she'd assume he was busy and move on, but she wasn't the kind of woman who gave up on a hunt. Sick of the games, he decided to rip off the bandage and get it over with. He stopped. She made her move.

"Dr. Brookes," she called, feigning surprise.

Rodan forced a smile. "Dixie."

She set the forms she held down, propped her hip against the nurse's station and offered him the full weight of her oppressive attention. "You're a hard man to track down."

"Things have been a bit busy tonight."

"That they have." She took the length of her ponytail between her fingers and stroked it in a suggestive manner. Her lips parted like she was about to say something, and he had no doubt what direction that would go.

He cleared his throat, bit the bullet, and took control. "I spoke with Grace—"

"Your friend must be a strange guy to date someone like her," she scoffed. The words dripped with the bitterness of a woman scorned. "I saw her down in the morgue the other night."

He furrowed his brows, his interest piqued. "What was she doing?"

"I don't know, but with everything going on around here, it made me suspicious. Like, the hospital's under investigation. How dumb can she be?" She crossed her arms over her chest. "I have half a mind to report her."

And here he'd thought Dixie would be a problem, instead she'd gone and presented herself as a solution. He smiled to himself while his stare slid over her, taking her in with new eyes. Grace had practically gift-wrapped her for him. Oh, how the tables had turned.

Regardless of how his conversation with the Primary went, he needed to shore things up with Grace and ensure the problem she presented was rectified—one way or another.

"I APOLOGIZE for taking so long, Primary. I couldn't reach you," Rodan said as he sat on the edge of his bed at the compound.

"The fault is not yours. Word has passed quickly through the Shepherds. I had to lay low to avoid suspicion," he said. "What have you learned of the girl's origins?"

"The mother was a Shepherd." His hand clenched into a fist. "I suspect the name she gave is fake."

There was a long pause. "Is that all?"

His pulse kicked up. "No. Grace figured out what the Claimed can do and shared it with the Agent, Elijah. He's made a request for the Revenant Archives."

"Have they discovered the Claimed Mark's source?"

Rodan rolled his ring until the brand appeared. "No."

"And is there suspicion over where the souls have gone?"

He shook his head. "Not as of yet."

The Primary's voice grew harsh. "The woman's awareness has become problematic. She needs to be dealt with."

"Respectfully, Primary, should we still be proceeding with the plan? Eliminating Crawford won't change what the others already know."

"No, it won't. But they can't defend against what they can't see. We were aware our work would draw attention sooner or later. It just so happened to be sooner. Nonetheless, the girl could be used as a weapon against us, so she's an issue that must be addressed. We need to act."

"Of course," Rodan agreed.

"She'll be weaker on her own."

"Yes, Primary." He smiled. Finally, he'd be done with Grace and the wrench she'd thrown into their progress. "If you're ready, I know exactly when she'll be alone tonight."

There was a dark smile in the Primary's words when he said, "I'll send what's needed."

CHAPTER 34
GRACE

Grace's pulse thrashed in her ears. "Now?"

Angie's lips were pursed when she nodded. "Unfortunately, yes. Now."

God, as if her life wasn't messy enough. Two days had passed since her Marking and for more reason than one, her mind was foggy, thoughts distant, still within reach, but slow to surface. Between Ben, her branding, the Claimed and—she swallowed hard—everything with Gideon, meeting with the investigator for questioning, scheduled or not, was the last thing she needed. Setting her chart aside, she nodded and left.

When she stepped off the elevator, her footsteps echoed, drumming out of time with her heartbeat, as she made her way down the empty hall toward Horace's office. Well, what the hospital called his office anyway. It was more like a musty broom closet in a cold, damp corner of the basement.

Her lungs constricted as she popped her head in the door and offered a tight smile. "Angie informed me this was my allotted time to be interviewed."

The investigator shifted in his seat behind his make-shift desk. He dragged a hand over his gray hair and sucked in his stomach as he rose. "Nurse Crawford, I presume?"

Grace strode the remainder of the way into the room on unsteady feet. "That's me."

He shook her hand. "I'm Horace Redford." The bathroom door to their left popped open. "And this," he indicated the woman in her mid-fifties with dyed, yellow-blonde hair who joined them, "is retired nurse Melina Grant. She'll be sitting in as my expert of reference." He gestured for Grace to take a seat in the orange plastic, cafeteria-style chair across from him.

The three took their respective places. Grace crossed her legs, then uncrossed them and smoothed her scrubs. She was too twitchy. She needed to get it together before she implicated herself in a crime she hadn't committed.

He rested his elbows on the edge of his desk. Picking up his pen, he twisted it and he reset the papers before him. "Do you understand why you're here?"

"I do." She crossed her legs again.

He inclined his head while his stare caught on her trembling hands. "Is it alright if I record the audio of this session?"

"Of course," she said feebly. A permanent record of her words…lovely.

He set the machine down, turned it on, then shifted forward in his seat. "According to the file of patient zero, Laura Gastin, you were the acting nurse for the treatment of her gallstones?"

She swallowed hard. "I was."

"During that treatment, did you notice anything strange with the patient?"

"No." She shook her head. "Her symptoms were standard for the diagnosis."

"Outside of those symptoms, did she behave oddly?"

"Not that I noticed, but a mental health diagnosis would be outside my scope of practice, so I wouldn't be qualified to make that assessment."

He tapped the end of his pen against the desk. "Do you have any suspicions about the outbreak or what could be causing it?"

Ha! Suspicions? She had more than suspicions. Raising her hand, she rubbed the back of her neck. "I'm not sure." It was probably normal for people to be nervous during questionings. It had to be. She prayed it was, otherwise, her fidgety ass would be looking all kinds of guilty.

His head canted, that stare prodding her deep. "You look uncomfortable. Is everything alright, Miss Crawford?"

She stiffened and lowered her arm. Not good. "I'm just, ah, nervous. I've never been through anything like this before."

Horace gave a crisp nod, leaned heavily into his chair and spun the pen around the ends of his fingers as he circled back. "Can you please explain what you did with your patient that night?"

Her throat ran dry. Did he suspect her? Was she some kind of giant red flag? Did he think she knew something? She swallowed hard. "Everything?"

He inclined his head, his voice even when he said, "Yes, Nurse Crawford. *Everything*."

THE FRIGID NIGHT'S air nipped at Grace's skin while she scurried across the hospital's parking lot. She dove into her car and started it. Chucking her purse on the passenger seat, she cranked the heat and left. It probably would've been prudent to wait until the engine warmed, but she was cold as ass, and it'd heat faster in motion.

Her breath came out in short puffs, and she hiked her shoulders to trap what was left of her warmth. Cold shivers that had nothing and everything to do with her Absolution Mark chased through her. The cool bite of pain was constant, and it simmered somewhere deep inside she couldn't place.

A shadow moved in her periphery as she turned down a back road to take a faster route home because faster meant heat. Glorious, glorious heat.

She hadn't seen Ben since she'd practically fled the compound the morning that followed her Marking. They needed to talk but addressing him alone after what'd happened was a hard no. She had to sort herself. To figure out her approach to deal with him. His comment about Noah replayed in her mind like a video on loop. Not because she doubted the need for her best friend but because she doubted the need for him. Noah was her constant—a non-negotiable. Anything that tried to interrupt that friendship was a problem. She'd lost enough joining the Shepherds, she wouldn't be trapped by Ben, too.

Connecting her phone to the car's system, she dialed her best friend.

"Hey," he answered.

"Hey."

Her defeated tone must've tipped him off because his next words were serious, "What's wrong?"

"I just wanted to hear your voice."

"Gracie?"

She let loose a shuddering sigh. "I'm tired." The kind of tired that sleep would never help. It permeated everything. Her body, her thoughts, her emotions. Her wick had burned down to ash and smoke.

He knew her too well for that answer to pass unchecked. "Tired of what?"

"Everything."

"Is this about Ben?"

Her stomach twisted. There were a lot of things that plagued her, and Ben definitely stood at the top of that list. "Yeah."

"Oh. Did you two…?"

"No. I didn't let it get that far." *Thank God.*

"You don't sound happy about how far it went."

Her answering laugh was hollow. Ben was dangerous. She was pissed she hadn't seen it sooner—hadn't seen *him* sooner. She'd been distracted by his pretty words and promises and dismissed every red flag along the way. She'd been a fool.

Grace rubbed her forehead with the heel of her hand.

"Do you want him?"

The answer to that question was simple, but the solution… "He's my Sect Leader, Noah. What do I do?"

"Do you need me to come home so we can figure it out?"

"No. Stay with Kyle. I need to think. At the end of the day, this is on me to deal with. I got myself into this mess, now I've got to find a way through it."

Her shoulders tightened when several patches of black ice reflected off her headlights, partially hidden by the dusting of snow that skittered across the ground. She eased her foot off the gas some.

"Gracie—"

"I should go. The roads are getting bad."

"We're not done here. Call me to let me know you made it home safe."

"Alright. I love you, Noah."

"I love you too."

She ended the call and clenched the steering wheel like it might make her a better driver. The streetlights grew few and far between until the last one lingered up ahead. Something swooped past and blotted out the little light before it vanished. Her foot slapped the brake and her arms locked straight while she fought to keep the car from fishtailing, then thanked all that was holy when she managed.

Swoop.

It whipped by again and she jerked the wheel. The hairs on the back of her neck practically levitated as she corrected the car. Her instincts begged her to go faster, but the road was treacherous, and she couldn't risk—

BOOM.

The vehicle lurched hard to the left when the thing slammed into the back passenger side. Gravel grated beneath her tires as the crunch of metal filled the night. Her head snapped around and caught a flash of black leathered wings.

Grace blinked hard. *No.* She couldn't have seen that right. It wasn't possible. But the alarm bells that blared in the back of her mind begged to differ.

Her chest heaved, eyes drawn to the rear-view mirror. Wings spread wide when a demon descended, and her taillights reflected off its skin, painting it a sinister shade of red.

BOOM.

It hit and knocked the car forward. She screamed as its claws hooked into the trunk then latched on. Its fist smashed against the back window. *Boom. Boom. Boom.* The glass exploded, and its cubes sprayed everywhere, striking her from behind while they tinkled though the car.

How had a demon gotten loose? And why the hell was it trying to kill her?

Bad roads or no, she needed to do something. Cutting the wheel hard to the left, the demon lost its hold and careened off. The car swayed violently, and she whimpered when the wheels caught the rocky shoulder.

Her terror washed over her like a tidal wave, rushing her emotional shore and swallowing everything in its path, her thoughts, her breath, her heart. Her eyes lit on her purse, and she reached for it, clumsily unzipping it with one hand.

BOOM.

The hood of the car bucked violently when a female demon landed on it. It raised its head, and its black eyes locked on Grace's, offering her the promise of a painful death—so much pain.

"WHAT DO YOU WANT?" Grace screamed.

The she-demon tilted its head at an inhuman angle and smiled, baring jagged teeth filed to razored points. Black-tar blood dripped in slow, thick rivulets from its mouth, oozing over its chin. "You."

Grace's throat seized, and she slammed on the brakes. The car fishtailed again and swung left, then right, then left. The beast held on, but its grasp loosened, and it slid down the hood.

BOOM.

Grace's roof caved in as a demon-shaped imprint missed her head by inches. *Oh, God, there are two of them!*

She punched the gas.

The she-demon tore its grip free from the metal as she climbed back into position, then raked its talons across the windshield. The high-pitched keening almost drowned out all other sound before its claws punctured the glass.

Grace shoved her hand inside her purse. *Where are they?*

"How is it you see what you see?" the she-demon snarled, voice carrying over the chaos.

Dread wrapped around her like a tomb. Her eyes widened and flicked to the side as she tried to see around it and keep the damn car on the road. "What?"

"You see differently than the others. You see more than you should. How?" it demanded as it tore the glass away and tossed it aside, giving it a clear path to Grace.

The force of the wind stung her eyes and stole her breath. "I—I don't know!"

A taloned hand broke through the roof as the second demon reached for her. It sliced through her seatbelt, barely missing her chest. Grace's fingers wrapped around a cool handle. Pulling it from her purse, she plunged down and sank her golden dagger into its flesh.

The beast shrieked. Steam rose on the air when its hand crumbled to ash, filling the car and Grace's lungs with its acrid stench. She wretched, then wretched again. With its good hand, it slammed down. A sharp squeal filled the world as the top of the car tore back.

OH, GOD!

When the male demon's rage-filled face appeared, Grace stabbed up and caught it in the eye. Black-blood spurt everywhere, covering her as the thing bucked and snarled and spit. It cracked apart, then fragmented into piece after piece until it was nothing but dust. It left no soul in its wake.

The she-demon hissed.

Grace needed help, and she needed it fast. There were only a handful of people who knew what she could see, which meant there were only a handful of people that information could have come from. One of them had outed her, so who did she call?

She'd convinced herself that good and evil were easily defined. That blood mattered. At every turn, she'd ignored her instincts, shoving them aside in the name of logic, something she wasn't about to do again.

Hitting the call button on the steering wheel, she waited for the Bluetooth system to respond. It didn't. She tried again. Nothing. *No. No. No!*

"WHO ARE YOU?" the she-demon roared.

Grace pointed the dagger at it, shaking so hard, her body rocked in the seat.

SWOOP. SWOOP.

More beastly shadows moved in. A winged silhouette touched down on the road ahead. Waiting.

Grace veered around it. The car's rear end slid out and it headed for the ditch. Please, no! If she lost control, she was done. The tires caught, and the vehicle punched forward as the rubber chirped against the road.

"Who has gifted you?" the she-demon demanded.

Gifted her? Gifted her what?

Metal shrieked as talons tore through her door, nicking her skin. She cried out. Pain. So much pain.

Her chest rose and fell in explosive bursts when she dumped her purse out and grabbed her phone. She waved the knife to keep the she-demon at bay. After several pathetic and quivering attempts, she hit the home button to turn the device on. Would help even come in time? She selected her contacts and searched for—

"Enough of this." The she-demon leaned over and stabbed the side of the car. There was loud pop when it pierced Grace's tire. The car cut a sharp right and careened straight for the ditch. It surged from the road with a horror-inducing silence, then launched airborne before it crashed back to the world. It ground to a painful halt as the demon, metal, and Grace herself went flying. She didn't have the chance to scream before she landed hard, and everything went black.

PAIN EXPLODED behind Grace's eyes as she cracked them open. Her body hurt everywhere as her head fell to the right. A car sat on its side in a crumpled heap about ten feet away. It looked familiar somehow, yet not. Something flickered in her peripheral vision, and she peered toward it. Her phone. She needed it for some reason but couldn't remember why. She groaned as she reached for it.

Her head lolled back when someone latched onto her leg. The first thing she caught sight of was wings.

Wings. Demons! The puzzle pieces clicked together, and everything flooded back to her in a rush.

The she-demon offered her a feral smile. "You're going to answer my questions." It swiped a taloned claw across its flesh and smeared the black blood that surfaced over the Mark on its upper arm. A Mark that matched Gideon's. It flared orange, then molten red. The air wavered as smoke trailed up from the palm of its hand. A second later, flames burst to life.

Hellfire.

Grace stabbed the name on her phone and dialed. Her voice broke on a scream when she was hit by the blaze. Agony was all she knew. It consumed, blinding. She was dying. She had to be. No one could survive this. The fire bore so deep her body bucked, uncontrollable. She gasped for air but couldn't find it.

The she-demon drew back the flame. It crouched, and its face hovered an inch from Grace's while its death and rot-scented breath washed over her. "Now," it said, voice sweet as poison honey, "let's try this again, shall we?"

CHAPTER 35
GIDEON

"For fuck sakes," Gideon snarled as the bass of Bedlam's music thumped in the background. That was the third alcohol order his supplier had screwed up. It'd be one thing if it was just the wrong kinds of liquor, he could've worked with that. Instead, they'd shorted him.

"Again?" Davis asked as he took a seat on a stool across the bar. "How difficult can it be?"

Gideon gave a stiff nod. "Very, apparently." He chucked the bullshit order forms across the counter.

"I'll deal with it."

Gideon shook his head.

"You've got other shit on your mind. Let me take this."

"What's that supposed to mean?"

Davis cocked a brow that said *You know exactly what the fuck that means.*

Gideon rolled his shoulders, then unclenched his jaw. The guy knew him well, sometimes too well. They'd been around each other since they were kids. They could read each other like goddamn books. So, yeah, Davis saw what was up, but like hell Gideon'd ever cop to that.

The sound of dishes smashing had him pivot. He opened his mouth to release a string of epithets, but his phone rang and cut off that trajectory. He glanced down to it where it sat on the bar top.

His expression must've given away something, because Davis asked, "Who is it?"

Gideon stared at the phone screen. "Crys."

"Speak of the devil." Davis paused. "You gonna answer it?"

Ring.

Fuck. All Gideon could think of was Elijah because Crys was playing with fire calling him.

Fuck. Fuck. Fuck.

Gideon had made that clear to her though, and she was a smart woman, so chances were if she called, there was a good goddamn reason for it. At least, that's what he told himself.

Ring.

"Answer the fucking thing," Davis said.

Ring.

She was probably getting set to hang up. Gideon answered. "This is against the rules, Crys," he said, keeping his tone smooth.

There was a scuffle on the other end of the line. *Shit.* She must've dialed him by accident.

Next came the distant, barely audible sound of her voice. The first part was muffled, but the last was good and clear. "—No. Please. NO!"

He went rigid, and his muscles pulled taught, readying. What the fuck he readied for, he had no damn clue, but the one thing he knew was she'd begged someone to stop something, and that someone wasn't him.

"Crys?" he said, voice sharp.

Davis's eyes snapped to him.

"GIDEON!" she screamed, the kind of scream someone let loose when their life was on the line.

His gut twisted. "CRYS?"

Everyone in the bar turned his way, and Davis slid from his stool.

More scuffling, grunting, and a loud, roaring-hiss, followed by her blood-curdling scream.

Gideon jumped over the bar. "Where are you?"

Nothing.

He cut across Bedlam and made for the doors that led to the parkade. "Where are you, Crys?"

"GIDEON!" she cried. "HELP! PLEASE, GOD, HEELLLLLP!"

The roaring hiss sounded again, coupled with her shriek of pain, both blaring across the phone's speaker so loud he had to pull it away from his ear. When it finished, he called out, "Tell me where you are. Just tell me where you are, and I'll find you!" He burst through the exit and beelined for his truck.

"Gideon," she said, weaker.

"I'm here, Crys. Just tell me where you are," he said as he tried to offer her whatever goddamn reassurance he could. *Christ. Just tell me where you are!*

"I'm on Elsh—" The line went dead.

"FUCK!" He ripped the phone forward and called her number. It went straight to voicemail.

"What's happening?" Davis asked from his side.

"Someone has her. She's in trouble."

"Who?"

"I don't know, but whoever it is, they're fucking dead." He ended the call and dialed her again. Straight to voicemail. "You better be alright, woman. Call me." He hung up and called again. Voicemail. *SHIT!*

"Where are we going?" Davis asked as he loosened the cuffs on his coat sleeve.

That's why Gideon liked the guy, no questions asked, he was there, ready for whatever. And he needed to be ready, because they were gonna rain Hell down on whoever hurt that woman. *Christ.* Where was she?

"All I got from her was 'Elsh.'" It wasn't much, but he'd drive every road in the city if he had to. He unlocked the truck doors, then threw his open. He and Davis climbed in. The engine roared to life when Gideon started it and revved even louder when he jammed the thing in reverse and backed out of his spot with a punch. The truck drifted, and he cut the wheel. His tires screeched until it faced the garage doors. Moving forward, he triggered the sensor.

He cursed a thousand curses when the thing lifted with slow

progress like it didn't give two shits about what was going on. When there was barely enough clearance, he stepped on the gas and peeled out as an idea came to him.

"Check those letters in the search engine. See what local street names come up for Arillia with them," he instructed.

"On it." Davis plugged them into his phone. "We've got two options here. Elshaw, and Elshirl. Any clue where she'd be so we can narrow it down?"

Gideon prompted his Hands Free to call her again. *Pick up, Crys. Come on. Just pick up!* He eyed the clock, his head a mess of shit-baked and rage-filled thoughts. It was 7:45 pm. "Tonight's one of her scheduled day shifts. She probably just left work a while ago."

Voicemail.

"I'll search the area surrounding the hospital." Davis dragged his fingers across the map on his device.

Gideon aimed them in that general direction. She couldn't have been far, unless she'd traded a shift or taken a day off, in which case fuck only knew where she was.

"Here! I've got an Elshirl Road a few streets south of the hospital on route to her house." He leaned forward and entered the location into the truck's GPS then hit "Go." The map on the screen highlighted their path.

Gideon just hoped it was the right one.

He called her again. Voicemail.

Davis pulled his phone out and started hitting numbers to make a call of his own. "Hey. You good to talk?" Pause. "Have you heard from Grace tonight?" Pause. "We don't know. She's in trouble, though. We're trying to find her." Pause. "Don't do anything, yet." He turned to Gideon. "I'll call Elijah, he'll officially let the rest of you know." Pause. "I don't know, but whatever's going on sounds bad. The more people looking for her, the better."

Gideon inclined his head. He didn't give a shit who found her, as long as she was found. He'd have a piece of whoever had taken her though. There'd be no stopping him on that front.

"Love you, too." Davis hung up and called Elijah, then relayed everything that'd happened. When that was done, he straightened in his seat. "He's ordering the others to help in the search. He wants us to call if we learn anything."

The GPS showed their ETA was seven minutes out. Too long. He dropped his foot down hard on the pedal and the truck bucked forward. His knuckles were white on the wheel, because the fury that overtook him was a dangerous thing. Whoever had Crys would suffer. And the son-of-a-bitch better hope she was alright, because if she wasn't, he'd feed what was left of them to Hell himself.

They turned onto Elshirl Road, but the direction they approached from would've been the opposite of hers. The streetlights grew sparser until they disappeared altogether. There was black ice all over the road, and it was goddamn deserted. The route would've cut a few minutes off her commute, though, so it'd make sense for her to take it. He fucking hoped.

The only sound that reverberated through the place was the rumble of his truck engine as he pushed it to the limit. That was until another one cut through the night—one that drowned out everything else. It was desperation, agony and pure-fucking-terror rolled into one. It was Crys.

Davis leaned forward. "Holy fucking hell."

Gideon's eyes pushed through the dark, searching for her. He spotted her car first, or at least, what was left of it. The thing was on its side, crumpled to nothing. The roof was torn up, and the driver's side door had long gouges across it where the metal was peeled back.

"What the...?" Davis started.

Gideon stared while his chest constricted, and he tried to figure out how the shit that'd happened. He had his answer a second later when a spray of fire lit the sky. The scream that followed pulled his focus deeper into the field.

"Demons," Davis said.

Hellfire. His stomach clenched. *Christ!* She was Nephilim. She couldn't take the barrage they bore down on her—she couldn't take it and survive.

There were six demons in total; two airborne, two that walked in a wide circle, patrolling the melee like vultures, and the last two that stood over Crys. A female rained flame over her twisted form while a male held her down—not that she put up much of a fight.

How long had they had her? And what in the sweet Jesus did they want? He veered left to take his truck into the field. The demon's heads snapped toward the headlights that aimed their way.

Davis grabbed the holy-shit-handle. "Who the hell let them through?"

Gideon didn't know, but when he found out, there'd be a few more bodies feeding the earth.

"We're gonna need backup." Davis said as his free hand reached for his dagger.

"Make the call."

The guy hit redial on his phone, and whoever answered, answered fast. "We found her—"

Gideon didn't hear anything after that because he shut it out as he honed his focus to pinprick mother-fucking accuracy. He gunned the engine and cut the wheel, kicking up snow and gravel when he sent the truck in a wide arc. Swinging the ass end around, he used it like a battering ram. The demon in his path tried to escape, and its wings snapped out to take flight, but it wasn't quick enough. It went airborne when he hit it though, landing about twenty feet away in an explosion of earth and limbs.

When the vehicle stopped, he whipped his door open, launched out, and drew his dagger as he faced off with the closest demon. It threw its arm up to block the strike, but it wasn't quick enough to stop his fist when it connected with its face. Bones crunched and skin split, whether his or the demon's, he didn't care.

He grabbed it by the hair, then brought its face down, introducing it to his knee. Black blood exploded, painting his leg and the surrounding snow in a satisfying mist. The thing dropped limp to the ground.

He tore his second blade free, spun and squared himself to the other two that moved in. He ducked and feigned right, then dodged their talons and rammed his knife into the gut in front of him. When its Hell-forged metal met flesh, a popping-hiss sounded out. The demon screamed just as Davis entered their fray.

Gideon's stare snapped to Crys. She was on her back. She didn't move. Her eyes were unfocused as the male demon pushed a talon against her throat.

The female who hit her with the hellfire bared jagged teeth. "Tell us what you know."

What the hell would Crys know that was of any consequence to them? "Get the fuck away from her," Gideon said, his voice a low, guttural growl like a pissed off, apex predator.

Davis ripped his blade across his demon's chest, and it roared when it peeled open. Steam filled the air before its body charred and crumbled to ash. Its soul appeared and was gone a second later. Gideon didn't have time to linger on what that meant, and he charged the male beside Crys. The thing raised a hand and loosed its own hellfire at him.

Son of a bitch! He dropped and used his shoulder to roll out of the way before he pushed back to his feet. The thing sidestepped and attacked from behind him. He reached over his shoulder then latched onto the first piece of it he could grab—its wing. The demon's roar boomed through the night when Gideon bent at the hip and hurled it forward. It landed on its back with a hard crack before he plunged a dagger deep into the wing, puncturing it.

Its talons struck for his throat. He twisted away, but not before they slashed the flesh on the side of his neck. Gideon snarled, using everything he had as he gripped the wing and pulled. Bone, tendon, and sinew ripped apart, and the demon screeched, writhing on the ground. He tossed the dismembered piece at it as a shadow passed overhead and drew his eyes up. More. There were more of them coming.

"There's too many," Davis barked.

Fucking hell. He wasn't one to run from a fight, but neither was he stupid enough to stick around when they were outnumbered.

"Tell us who gave you the ability to see it?" the female demon demanded Crys.

Who gave her the ability to see? The only thing Crys could see that no one else could, was the Claimed Mark.

She didn't answer. Didn't even flinch.

His glare locked with the female demon. The smile he offered was a savage promise. "You're mine."

"We're running out of time," the female said to the other Dark Seraphim.

"Then kill her," another beast yelled back.

Lights flashed across the field. Tires screeched, and voices called out.

Gideon ran then whipped his dagger as he beelined for Crys. It caught the female in the stomach, lodging deep. She howled a piercing shriek. Her hand sizzled against the hilt when she tore it free. He slammed into her, took her to the ground, then tore his dagger across her throat and left a gaping hole that sprayed black blood everywhere.

When he twisted toward Crys, another Dark Seraphim moved in. His expression must've matched the sinister fury that coursed through his veins because the thing hesitated. Gideon's chest heaved as grabbed his downed blade and squared himself to it. In the next instant, it made the best decision of its shit existence and fled.

The Nephilim filed onto the field, calling instructions to one another on positioning. Outside of Davis and Jenna, he had no goddamn clue who to trust, which meant no one else would get their hands on Crys.

Ben cut his way to where she lay but Gideon wasn't about to let that happen. Not after the shit he'd pulled. *No. Fucking. Chance.*

Gideon dove and wrapped his arm around Crys's waist, then threw her limp form over his shoulder. "Let's go!" he called to Davis as he made for the truck. A demon stepped in his path, and he planted his booted foot in the center of its chest, knocking it backward. It twisted onto its hands and knees, so he drop-kicked its face when he passed.

"Gid," Davis called.

He turned.

"We should take one for questioning."

He gave a sharp nod. "Do it."

Ben must've figured out what was about to go down because half a second later, he roared, "Give her to me!"

"Not fucking likely," Gideon said, unrelenting. He had half a mind to gut the guy right there, but Crys needed help and she needed it fast. He'd sort Ben later.

"The warehouse," Davis called to the others as he dragged one of the half-dead demons with him, then chucked it into the back of the truck. His stare flicked to Jenna, his brief message clear, *Get the fuck outta here*.

The other Dark Seraphim roared when they spotted their cohort being taken.

"You drive," Gideon said. He opened the passenger side door, shifted Crys's weight so he held her in front of him, then jumped in.

Davis was right behind him. The guy shoved the truck into gear and mowed down one of the idiot demons that stepped in front of it. Its body thudded hard beneath the undercarriage, and something that wasn't the truck popped when they drove over it.

"Crys," Gideon said.

Nothing.

Elijah's car pulled up when they hit the road, but they didn't stop.

"There's only one way she can still be breathing," Davis said.

Gideon's jaw locked down. "I know." While he was glad for that since it meant she was still alive, he was very aware that someone had kept a secret. That they'd lied to everyone about what Crys was. And he also knew that *someone* would answer for it.

CHAPTER 36
GIDEON

"Come on, Crys. Open your eyes," Gideon growled as he bucked his shoulder that her head rested on, trying to jostle her. She didn't respond.

Davis's stare was on the rear-view. "Is she breathing?"

"Yeah, but it's shallow as hell." There was glass in her hair, her jacket was gone, and her clothes were covered in blood. He searched her and found several gashes where the demons had cut her along her forearms and legs. A red stain spread across her stomach, so he lifted her shirt and found one on her abdomen. He pressed his hand over the worst wound on her forearm and glanced at the passenger side view mirror. "Someone outed her."

Elijah and the Nephilim followed behind, while several of the demons had taken flight, trailing them.

"What do you mean?" Davis asked.

"The demons wanted to know who gave her the capacity to see the Mark."

"Wait…they think it was *given*?"

Gideon nodded. His phone rang through the speakers after it auto connected to the truck's hands-free system. Elijah's number appeared on the dash. Davis moved to accept the call.

"Leave it," he told him. Ignoring Elijah was a shit idea, but under the circumstances, he wanted anything that was said to involve every-goddamn-one of them.

"There's only one way something like that can be given, Gid," Davis said, coming to the same conclusion he had.

It might be possible if she'd been given another Mark, one that offered greater Sight. The most common place for additional Marks was on the back of the neck, so he tilted her head forward, then slid her hair aside. Nothing.

He jostled her again, and his gut twisted when she moaned. Her eyes pinched, and her breaths came in short, heavy bursts.

Two of the airborne demon's dove and tried to grab their hostage from the bed of the truck.

"They're trying to get their friend back," Davis gritted out as he cut the wheel hard.

Gideon's hold on Crys locked down while his hand braced against the door. "They're afraid he'll talk."

"Got any guesses on who betrayed her?"

"Only a handful of us knew," he said, then rhymed the list off in his head: Ben, Trevor, Jenna, Rodan, Davis, Elijah, and himself. Noah wasn't even on the list because Crys trusted him, and he'd kept his mouth shut on that front for years.

"Do you think it was an accident?"

Was it possible? Sure. But the demons hadn't just known about Crys's extra Sight, they'd known her location. That was too specific for his liking. He shook his head. "No, I don't."

Davis nodded, because they were on the same wavelength.

They headed further into the city, and the Dark Seraphim moved higher, not that the unSighted could see them, but the buildings would sure as shit slow them down, so the demons still followed in the distant dark.

He felt like shit for touching Crys. He knew what it was like to take the wrath of the hellfire, and it hurt on a level he hadn't known existed. She started to quiver. *Shit.* They needed to get to the warehouse fast. She was alive, but Christ only knew for how long.

"Come on, Crys. Stay with me."

Tears leaked from her closed eyes when her weak voice murmured, "Hurts." Or at least, that's what he thought she'd said. It was too damn soft to know for sure.

Fuck. "We're gonna help, just hold on. It'll get better soon, just hold the fuck on."

She went rigid, and her mouth opened in a silent scream as she curled in on herself and pressed her face against his chest. His head snapped up when Davis whipped them into the warehouse parking lot, with Elijah, and the rest of the Nephilim tight on their tail.

Davis's stare was on the sky. "Get her inside. We'll handle them." He jammed the truck into park, pulled out his daggers, and burst from the vehicle.

Gideon kicked his door open, then bolted for the entrance. Punching his pin into the keypad, he exploded inside. His heavy-booted steps echoed through the place as he ran and headed for the meat locker style door at the far end. The scent of chlorine and cold of the room hit him when he crossed over. The small pool in the center was filled with holy water, so any contact with hellfire would ease the burn. He'd had the thing built for his people, and it'd gotten good goddamn use.

He was halfway to it when something crashed outside the door, which was his only warning before a Dark Seraphim burst inside. He set Crys on the floor by the water, then angled himself in front of her. The demon's eyes slid down to where she lay.

"You can't have her," Gideon said, "But I'll give you a taste."

It snarled. "You will fall. All of you will fall."

The smile that took him was hard. "Lead the way." His hand shot to his blade.

The thing feigned left but dodged right. Its taloned fingers lashed out, trying to distance Gideon from Crys. Not fuck'n likely. He ducked then dropped down. Pain ripped through him as the strike sliced a shallow layer of skin on his back. When he straightened, he plunged his blade into the thing's shoulder. It screamed, the whistling-roar ear-splitting when Gideon tore his knife free, then stabbed out again. The demon dodged, and the blade glanced its side.

The door flew open, and Rodan barrelled forward, body-checking the Dark Seraphim from behind. It lurched then careened headlong toward the water before it caught itself at the edge. Gideon planted his boot in its ribs, helping it in.

Its howl was lost against the sizzle of its flesh, the holy water burning like acid against its hide. Jesus! He'd seen some nasty shit in his time, and while it wasn't the worst of it, it ranked pretty high up there.

"That'll work," he said as he offered Rodan a tight nod. The thing thrashed when it sought a way out, but it was already consumed. The room filled with smoke while it cooked. The rotten-meat smell that filled the space had him throwing his arm over his face.

"Is she alright?" Rodan asked.

Davis burst into the room covered head-to-toe in black blood as he took in the scene. When he spotted the demon's melted body, he grinned. "Well done." He tipped his head toward the exit. "The one we caught is locked up in the next room over."

"Good," Gideon said and made for Crys. She'd gone silent again, her body still as stone. Disturbingly still. He picked her up, then took the stairs into the water.

Davis jumped in, grabbed the twitching piece of shit demon, and flung its mangled carcass onto the tile floor. When he climbed out, he leaned over and stabbed it in the neck. "For good measure."

The thing crumbled to ash. Its soul appeared, and less than a second later, it vanished. Gideon's brow furrowed before he and Davis exchanged a look.

"Someone's got a Gateway open," Davis said, stealing the thought from his mind.

One that was nearby.

The others filed in, and Ben shoved his way through, his expression wild when he charged toward Gideon. "Put her down!"

When Ben reached the pool's second step, Gideon's dagger shot up, aiming with sinister precision center mass at the guy's chest. The point of the blade pushed into his coat and buckled the material. "Don't. Fucking. Move," Gideon said, the words a threat and a promise.

Ben stopped, but that didn't mean he was done. "She's not yours, demon."

With the arm that held Crys, Gideon lowered her into the water. Steam rose from her body like nothing he'd ever seen before. It was so dense, he almost lost sight of Ben. Almost.

Trevor edged forward until Davis stepped up, hand resting on the dagger hilt at his hip.

"Gideon," Elijah said, the calm command in his tone ominous.

Gideon didn't budge, stare locked on Ben. "This is your goddamn fault."

"You think *I* sicced them on her?"

"Oh, we'll get to that." Ben wanted her. He wanted her so bad he'd done something else, something Gideon had never even fathomed. He cocked a brow. "But first, Benjamin, if you could explain to the room how the fuck Crys survived the hellfire?"

CHAPTER 37
GRACE

Everything hurt. Grace's body. Her mind. Even her hair. *Everything*. Something cold touched her skin. So, so cold. The scent of chlorine filled her senses while the crackle of fire still echoed in her mind, dancing in the background. Her heart shuddered a beat. She was alive—barely, but alive.

Gideon had come. She had no clue how he'd found her, but he'd come. He was still there; his voice carried from somewhere close by, strong enough to break through the chaos. He was angry, and there were other voices, but they were distant. Muffled.

She opened her eyes to a slit. She was in a small pool. Why was she in a pool? She floated at the water's surface. It hurt, but there was an odd relief in it, too, like someone had smoothed a salve over her. Gideon towered above her, and steam dissipated around him. One of his arms suspended her in the water while the other pointed a dagger straight at Ben's chest.

If she could've furrowed her brow, she would have.

Someone had betrayed her. Had it been Ben? No. That wasn't what they were saying. Even still, who did she trust? Gideon, Davis, and Jenna, yes, but beyond them, she had no clue.

Elijah advanced to the forefront of everyone gathered. "Someone needs to start talking. Now!"

"Time for confession, Benjamin," Gideon growled.

Her stomach twisted. *Confession?*

"I don't know what you're talking about, asshole. Now let her go, or as her Sect Leader, I'll be forced to intercede," Ben replied.

Gideon's laugh was dark. Disturbing. He shifted, put his back to Ben and faced her. He was covered in a combination of black and red blood. It streaked his hair, his skin, his shredded clothes. His body was coiled, the muscles drawn taught, ready for war.

Their gazes met and he offered her one of his devil-may-care grins. "There you are," he said, but the words were stiff, and the smile didn't touch his eyes.

"Demons," she said, throat raw from screaming.

He inclined his head and said in a low rasp, "You're safe."

There'd been so many she hadn't stood a chance, but he'd come. She'd thought she was dead, that they'd drag her soul to Hell and have their way with her for eternity. But he'd come. Tears stung the backs of her eyes as her hand glided through the water, seeking his.

"Grace!" Ben called. His voice broke on her name, and she froze.

With more effort than should've been necessary, her head fell to the side. He stood at the entrance to the pool where Davis flanked him like the harbinger of death. Her eyes pinched at the corners.

"Grace, please." He advanced a step, but stopped dead when Gideon turned his molten glare on him.

"If you touch her, I'll end you."

"She's not yours."

"Enough!" Elijah bellowed. "Come here, Gideon."

He didn't move and a long, dangerous stare passed between him and the Agent—one that sent a cold dread chasing down Grace's spine. Impressive, since she'd spent God only knew how long being roasted from within. Tensions rose to a perilous precipice. She didn't want him to leave her, but more than that, she didn't want him to face the wrath Elijah might dole out if he didn't comply.

"Go," she said, the words soft, only for his ears.

He offered her a slight, almost imperceptible shake of his head.

Jenna's voice was gentle amidst the storm around them when she moved to the water's edge. "I'll take her."

Gideon hesitated. His eyes flicked to the other woman before they returned to Grace.

Her fingers slipped around his wrist, and she squeezed. "It's okay." *I trust her.*

The exhale he loosed was ragged. "The pain will come in waves, so stay in the water." He motioned Jenna in, then waited until she had Grace. He stripped off his coat and tossed it to the edge of the pool where it landed with a heavy smack. His arms fell to his sides, his broad shoulders and wet shirt displaying every pulsing strand of muscle when he advanced up the stairs, backing Ben up as he stalked from the water like a predator on the hunt.

"Explain yourself," Elijah demanded.

Gideon gave no response and set himself, feet shoulder width apart, arms clasped behind his back.

"I'd say it's pretty obvious," Trevor cut in. "He's the only one in this territory with the ability to open a Gate and release demons. He went there to have her killed."

Elijah's eyes were wild. "EXPLAIN YOURSELF!"

Again, Gideon said nothing.

Speak up! Damn it, just speak up! Trevor was an idiot. They all were if they thought Gideon's silence was for himself. Grace swallowed around the lump in her throat. She'd been the one to breach protocol by contacting him. But she wasn't about to let him take any punishment on her behalf, not after everything he'd done.

With every ounce of strength she could muster, she pushed her feet down, seeking the pool's bottom and stood. Jenna followed as Grace waded to its edge and swallowed around the dread that tightened her throat. "I called him."

Gideon rounded on her, the darkness in his glare roaring, *Keep your mouth shut!*

She shook her head.

He turned back to the Agent. "She panicked and hit the first number she saw."

"Your number should no longer exist on her phone. She is Nephilim."

Gideon cocked his head. "Is she?"

Silence reigned, absolute and heavy. Was she Nephilim? What was he saying? Her head jerked back as she offered him the full weight of her utterly confused attention.

"She was just hit by a torrent of hellfire," Gideon said.

Elijah's eyes widened and snapped to Grace. "Is this true?"

"Yes." Her stomach rolled over itself and bound in a knot so tight, she didn't think it would ever come undone. "What's going on?"

"Care to explain, Benjamin?" Gideon asked.

She found Ben, and when she repeated herself, her voice held a bit more grit. "What's going on?"

"Grace—" he said, her name a plea, one she wasn't about to answer.

Elijah shook his head. "The hellfire and soul-swords are utilized as punishment for their respective peoples because their blood enables them to withstand it. The flame is meant as a weapon against the Nephilim in the war because they *cannot* withstand it."

But she'd withstood it. Her breath left her in a rush when an explanation flashed across her mind, but then…no. It couldn't be. That wasn't possible. She stumbled.

Ben moved as if to help.

"Don't touch me!" Grace recoiled, and Gideon lunged for him.

"No," Elijah threw himself between the two men. But whether the order was for Ben or Gideon, she couldn't tell.

Grace shook so violently, it crept into her words when she spoke. "What am I?"

"She has to be Nephilim. The Absolution Mark wouldn't have taken if she wasn't," Trevor said, face ashen.

"Right. But it sure as shit explains why the Marking hurt her," Gideon said.

Ben dragged his nails down his cheeks. "Grace?"

Davis's hands rolled in and out of fists. "What color was the writing, Grace?"

"Writing? Wha—" She cleared her throat. "What writing?"

Gideon tipped his head to Ben. "When he took you to see *The Chronicle* and spread your blood across the page. What color was the writing that appeared?"

Ben's gaze jumped rapidly between Grace, Gideon, and Elijah, like he didn't know who the bigger threat was. "You don't have to answer that."

Gideon crouched at the water's edge. There was a liquid fire in his amber eyes, one that looked ready to engulf him—one it was clear he used every ounce of his control to contain. "What color was it, Crys?"

Ben shook his head, but he'd lied to her, a lie that'd cost her dearly, so he didn't get a goddamn say. Her fingers dug in when she gripped the edge of the pool. "It was black and gold."

Ben's chest caved before his wild stare slid to the Agent.

"Black and gold?" Trevor turned on Ben. "Jesus Christ. I told you not to do anything stupid!"

Grace had missed something—something big. Her shoulders tightened when she pushed her damp hair back from her face. "What does that mean?"

"The color of the writing indicates which line you belong to; Heaven or Hell," Jenna said. "Black means Lesser Demon, gold means Nephilim."

Grace's heart stopped. She'd had both. She was from *both*. Shaking her head, she sought Gideon who was midway through rising. He came to his full, towering height before he angled himself Ben's way.

Elijah's ire turned hot in an instant. He swung out and backhanded Ben clean across the face. "YOU DECEIVED ME!" He withdrew a black and gold dagger, tore up his sleeve, and sliced his arm. Rodan and Trevor scrambled back as the Agent spread his blood over the gold Mark above his elbow. The air rippled, and the outline of a weapon appeared, materializing in his hands.

Dear, God. The soul-sword.

"YOU LIE AND STEAL WHAT DOES NOT BELONG TO YOU!" Elijah stabbed forward, sending it straight through Ben's chest.

Ben cried out, the sound pain-filled and blood-curdling. The veins in his neck and face strained against his skin, threatening to break loose before the Agent jerked the sword free. Grace took a weak, involuntary step back. This was the Elijah she'd been warned about, the one the others revered.

The Agent turned to her. "Did he take your Collection?"

Somewhere in the hollows of her memory she had a vague recollection of it being mentioned before, but what significance it held was lost on her. She shook her head.

Gideon huffed a sardonic laugh. "Of course, he didn't. That would leave a blood trail, wouldn't it, Benjamin?"

"What is it?" she asked.

The Agent's hand flexed around his hilt. "When Shepherds are taken to *The Chronicle* and their affiliation determined, a vial of their blood is taken to be kept."

Why it needed to be kept was a question for later, because anger, violent and consuming, reignited the fire in her veins.

"I was protecting you, Grace. Lesser Demons are dangerous," Ben said, voice high. Frenzied. His chest rose and fell in rapid pants when he stabbed a trembling finger toward Gideon. "He'll hurt you. You're in danger with him."

"With him? You think I'm in danger with *him*? He's the only reason I'm alive right now. You've lied to me from the moment we met. Used me, weaponized me. The danger to me here isn't him. It's you!" Her doubts, terror, and pain all bottled up into one not-so-neat, rage-filled package. She surged from the water, but her tank had been drained and her body had nothing to give, so she fell.

Gideon's strong arms engulfed her waist before she could crash to the concrete at the pool's edge. He pulled her to him, and his mouth pressed to her ear. "Easy, Crys."

A strangled gasped escaped her when the hellfire's effects reared their agonizing head.

Ben's attention locked on Gideon's touch, and he snarled like a crazed animal. "Let go of her—"

"Back in the water," Gideon said. He passed her off to Jenna before he rolled up his sleeves and bolted across the room. Taking Ben by the throat, he drove him back and slammed him into the wall, splintering the tile at his back.

"See! He's fucking crazy, Grace," Ben said, the words strained.

Jenna trembled as she wrapped an arm around Grace and glided her back in the pool.

The Agent closed in on the men and set a hand on Gideon's shoulder. The Head of the Lesser Demon Sect looked at it for several terrifying seconds. Slowly, he released Ben.

Ben jerked his shirt straight. "I was only saving her from him!"

"Her blood is dual." Elijah snarled. "She wouldn't have belonged to the Lesser Demons, Benjamin."

"He'd have lost me." Grace's heart pulsed in her ears as she came to it. "When I was Marked as something else, he'd have lost access to me." And he couldn't allow that because she was a game he needed to win. But he'd lost in the end. He'd lost badly.

"Grace, please. I love you. I'd never do anything to hurt you. I was just trying to protect you."

Protect? He used that word like he understood what it meant. The only one he knew how to protect was himself. Her blood turned so cold it could have been ice. "You didn't protect me when you watched me suffer during my Marking. You knew what was happening, you knew why, and you did nothing."

"I'm sorry. I just—"

Elijah thrust the soul-sword into Ben's stomach, and he howled. "That was not your decision to make. You are stripped of your position as Sect Leader and will formally receive the first strata of punishment. If you defy me in such a way again, I will not be so lenient." He scanned the Nephilim. "Rodan, you will take his place."

"Yes, Agent," he replied, blanching like he didn't want that privilege. Not that Grace could blame him considering the mess he was about to inherit.

Silence descended, save the sloshing of water.

Elijah withdrew his blade, and Ben collapsed. "When I learn who has betrayed Grace, they will be brought before the Council, and I assure you, I will seek their death."

She might've asked who the Council were, but the fact that death was a punishment option derailed her thoughts and she swallowed hard.

"Gideon, Rodan, stay," Elijah ordered. "I'll speak with the rest of you individually later." He wiped the blood from his arm and the soul-sword vanished. Stepping back, he warned, "Do not cross me again, Benjamin." Then he snapped his chin toward the exit. "You're all dismissed."

"Grace," Ben uttered.

Her name on his tongue was like poison. It made her sick. He didn't deserve to speak it. And she never wanted to hear it from him again. "Goodbye, Ben," she said. Cold. Final. So goddamn final.

Rodan eyed Trevor. "Get him the fuck out of here."

Trevor grabbed Ben's shoulder and shoved him from the room. Jenna helped Grace settle on the pool's stairs before she followed the others out.

Rodan knelt and braced himself against the floor. "Let me see your wounds." He inspected Grace's arm and leg as she fell back against the tile edifice and let it take her weight.

"There's another one on her stomach," Gideon said.

Rodan inclined his head and lifted her shirt. "It's a close call, but they don't need stitches. Just make sure the wounds are scrubbed clean," he said, and edged back.

Elijah's brows drew together. "Why were the demons after you, Grace?"

She twisted the hem of her sleeve. Could she trust the Agent? Her eyes flicked to Gideon, but he offered no indication either way, which she took as a good thing. "Because I can see the Claimed Mark. That's what they called it," she said, getting that off her chest. That strange sensation roiled deep inside her again. She shifted, hoping it would subside. It didn't.

"They wanted to know who gave her the capacity to see it," Gideon cut in.

Elijah's head whipped toward him, eyes sharp. "*Gave* it to her?"

Gideon inclined his head.

Rodan's head canted, eyes narrowing. "Is that even possible?"

Grace was too hot. It simmered under the surface like embers trailed her veins. Even her clothes felt heavy against her skin. *Please no. Not again.*

"I'm not sure. I will ask the Marksman when we make contact," Elijah said.

"What of the demon?" Gideon asked.

"I would like to be present for its questioning."

Questioning? In order to question one that meant… Her gaze darted between them, her voice panicked when she asked, "What demon?" The burning hit full force, and her breath left her in a rush. She fell forward and grabbed the stairs like a lifeline.

"Come on. Back in," Gideon said as he advanced. The water rolled around his lithe frame as he took her deeper.

"What demon?" she feebly demanded.

"The half-dead one locked up down the hall."

A demon was there? Her chest tightened, and she tensed, sucking in a sharp gasp from the pain.

"You're safe," he promised. His stare found Elijah. "I'll be moving it to a different location in case whoever outed Crys decides to come back and keep it from talking."

"Good. Tell no one where it is until the time comes for questioning, not even me." Elijah tipped his head toward Grace. "I'll be in touch."

Rodan offered a stiff smile before he followed the Agent out.

Grace's breathing was labored. "It burns." It hurt, God, it hurt so damn much that her vision waned and a piece of her welcomed it. Maybe when she woke again it'd be over.

"I know." Gideon guided her onto her back. His face filled her sight, eyes strained as he rested a warm hand on her chest. "The more of the water that touches you, the better you'll feel. It'll help if you're submerged."

He'd come. She'd needed him and he'd come. She was alive, battered and seared, but alive because he'd come. With pathetic progress, her fingers threaded through his. and she granted him the permission he sought with a gentle squeeze.

His jaw flicked. "Deep breath," he told her, then pushed her under.

CHAPTER 38
RODAN

Rodan twisted his ring so the Claimed Mark faced his palm. Vicki leaned her elbows against the motel's front counter next to him, the position pushing her breasts up. They were perfect. Grabbable. His. It was as sexy as it got, something the clerk noticed too, because the guy's stare was locked on them when he handed over their room's key card.

Chest burning, Rodan reached into his pocket and pulled out several bills of cash. He tucked them between his fingers, shook they guy's hand, and slipped them to him, branding him.

His brow ticked up and he smiled. *Thank you for your contribution.*

Rodan set his palm against Vicki's low back, then guided her down the hall and into their room. A text dinged on his phone, and he pulled it out. *For fucks sake.*

"Who is it, pet?" Vicki asked.

When the door clicked, sealing them in, he shoved her back until she was pinned against the wall. "Ben." His jaw clenched and he shook his head. The guy was relentless. No wonder he'd dug the hole he found himself in. He didn't understand no. Not that Rodan was about to complain considering it'd pulled the heat off him, but seriously…Ben was an idiot. "He wants to know if I've talked to Grace."

Her soprano laugh tinkled. "Benjamin's been a bad boy."

"He's not good at losing."

She moaned, slipped her arms around his neck, and purred at his ear, "Could he be useful?"

"He's a hair trigger. Temperamental and unpredictable."

"Pity."

Rodan would still watch the guy. Who knew if Ben would do something else stupid and another opportunity would present itself. The more distractions Rodan could place between himself and the Shepherds watchful eyes, the better.

"The Primary is pleased with you."

His stare narrowed. "Grace is still alive."

"For now. Regardless, no one could have predicted what happened. You're doing well, pet. You obviously hold Elijah's trust if he's given you the position. This was the best outcome."

He smirked. It'd been a happy accident. Yeah, he'd taken on more bullshit with the role, but it'd also given him more freedom. More power. "What's our next move?"

"We've been ordered underground for the time being. We'll regroup and deal with Grace when the time is right. But you've been a such good soldier." Her palm settled on his thigh, then grazed higher. "Would you like a reward for all your hard work, Sect Leader?" she said, her smile salacious as she enunciated the title like a prayer.

Fuck yes. He guided her to her knees. She unfastened his jeans, then drew down the zipper, slowly, like she enjoyed the torture. Her hand slipped inside his boxers, and she grabbed his ready cock.

His head fell back, and he hissed. She felt so fucking good, always did.

She took him in her mouth, and he gripped her ponytail to hold her in place. Vicki might've been his recruiter, but it was his turn to control. "Take it," he ordered, rocking his hips and pushing deeper until he hit the back of her throat.

She moaned and sucked harder. Shit, what she did to him, and what he wouldn't do for her. There wasn't anything. He'd raze the dead. Raze the Shepherds. Raze the goddamn world. And as it turned out, the Faction was about to.

CHAPTER 39
GRACE

It took the better part of the next day before Grace's burning subsided. Kind of. Most of that time had been spent between the warehouse's pool and some level of unconsciousness. She'd crashed hard, and at some point she had no recollection of, she'd been brought…wherever she was.

The king-sized bed she occupied had a deep gray upholstered headboard. The sheets were a heavy black satin covered in a thick duvet with pillows in a combination of crisp whites, blacks, and grays. It looked like something out of a showroom—masculine, yet oddly elegant. She wriggled deeper. *And comfortable. So, very comfortable.*

The walls were also gray with one section dedicated to a floor-to-ceiling closet system. A plush, black leather chair sat in the corner by a large window with high-tech black-out blinds drawn, while a door that led to an ensuite stood open across the way.

Noah lay beside her, asleep. She was about to nudge him when the main door to the room opened, and Gideon walked in. His wildfire gaze held hers as he strode to her side of the bed. Tugging the legs of his dark denim jeans, he crouched before her.

She smoothed a hand over her hair as she rolled fully onto her side to face him.

His black T-shirt hugged his chest, the caps of his shoulders outlined through the material. The cut and fabric looked expensive, and while they were casual, he still managed to make them look sharp.

The corner of his lip tipped up and for the first time since everything went down, the smile touched his eyes. She bit her lip as he leaned forward and set his elbows on his knees. "Who knew when I finally got you into my bed it would be with another man?"

She laughed, soft and deep. So deep it reached the torn portion of her soul and stitched it together.

"How are you feeling?"

"Off," she admitted. Between the Absolution Mark and hellfire, she was a mess. Cold and hot, hot and cold. Her body didn't know what was up or down. But the question tripped her memory, and her gaze focused on him when she asked, "If we carry demon blood, why didn't the holy water hurt?"

"Observant as ever, Crys." He linked his hands. "It's not like our weapons, it doesn't come from Heaven or Hell. It's touched by the church, so it's a tool for both sides."

Interesting.

"I've had some brought here if you need it."

Her gaze softened as she angled forward. "Thank you." Her nail trailed the edge of the duvet before she tugged it lower. "So, what was my path supposed to be?"

He lifted a shoulder. "You'd have been tested to determine whether you were best suited to be an Agent, Delphi, or Marksman."

"But my Nephilim Marks are permanent."

He nodded and shifted his weight. "Except you're blooded of both sides and only Marked for one. That interferes with the required balance. Elijah suspects you'll also be branded a Lesser Demon to keep things…equitable."

Grace's gaze flicked to the Scourge on his wrist, and she went rigid. A Lesser Demon. The reality of it, of her soul being Marked again, of being bound to Hell, crashed in around her, paralyzing her mind. She couldn't think, she couldn't—

He shook his head. "Don't go there, Crys. Not yet."

Don't go there. Don't go there. Don't go there. She chanted it like a mantra in her mind and forced her muscles to unknot. He was right, there wasn't anything to be done for it then, which made it a later kind of problem.

His amber stare held hers for several long breaths. Warm. Piercing. He glanced away. "When you were in trouble, you called me." It was a statement, and yet very much not.

She swallowed hard. "Will I be punished for it?" Her voice was steady, which was impressive because the terror of facing that wrath almost made her sick.

"No. Elijah's decided it wasn't technically against the rules since you carry dual blood." His eyes held a rogue smile. "You're lucky he likes you."

Like might've been a strong word, but she'd take it. The relief that washed over her settled into her bones as she dropped her shoulders.

"We'll need to revisit *The Chronicle* when you're better to start the process over." At her questioning glance, he added, "There's concern Ben left out more than just your affiliation."

She frowned. "What do you think?"

The single, sardonic laugh he released was the only answer she needed.

God, she'd missed so much. Everything. How had she been so willfully blind? "Do you think he's the one who outed me?"

He rubbed his jaw, and her brows rose. Gideon's loathing for Ben paralleled her own, so any hesitation on his part spoke volumes. "I wanna blame the guy, but I'd rather find the right person, not the convenient one. He did what he did because he wanted you. Having demons murder you is counter to that purpose."

She hated how logical it was. She wanted an answer, a face, a name. To know who was behind it. Who to blame. She wanted to feel safe. Whoever it was had a hand in the Claimed Mark. It was the only explanation for them siccing the demons on her. "Will they come for me again?" she asked as she fought the tremor that gripped her throat.

He rolled his neck. "I don't think so. By now they'd know they're compromised, especially since we've still got one of them. I doubt they'll risk exposure by coming after you again."

She blew out the heavy breath that rattled around her lungs.

"We'll find them, Crys." His tone was dark. Serious. A promise. He'd find them. He'd kill them. He chucked his chin Noah's way. "He was worried about you."

"I should hope so. I'm his best friend." She stroked her arm and glanced down at herself. "Someone changed my clothes."

"Noah took the honor." A slow, lopsided grin slipped across his face. "But say the word and I'll take the next round."

She rolled her eyes.

His laugh rumbled through her. "There she is."

Oh, but he was proud of himself. A cascade of tingling shivers swept across her body, over her scalp, and through her soul. "So this is your home," she mused. It suited him. Sharp. Stylish. Comfortable with its confidence and swagger. She'd eat dirt before she'd ever tell him that though.

"It is."

She smiled. "I thought you said no one came back here?"

"I guess you must be someone, then."

Heat burned her cheeks, crawling across her flesh before it aimed low. She raked her tongue across the back of her teeth. "Now that it looks like I'll be a Lesser Demon, will I fall under your jurisdiction?"

All mirth left him. "You will."

She wanted that simpering expression back. Needed it for some reason. "Does this mean I'll be forced to submit to your will?"

"Oh, Crys. How I enjoy those words from your lips," he crooned. "But alas, tempting as that may be, as Head of the Sect, I have my own rules to adhere to."

Her fingers trailed the long lines of her throat. "Rules? You?"

He flourished his hand. "Some nonsense about not abusing my power, although your suggestion is tempting."

"That wasn't a suggestion, Gid—"

"From your lips to God's ears."

A phone vibrated and drew her gaze to the bedside table. Her eyes widened when she found the device was her own. Its glass was cracked, but otherwise, it was fine. Her daggers sat next to it. How it'd all survived was beyond her.

Ben's name flashed across the screen, and she scowled so deep she worried it might be permanent. She had half a mind to throw the thing across the room and instead hit decline much more aggressive than necessary.

"The tow truck driver found everything when he retrieved your car," Gideon said.

"At the rate I'm going, you should just give me his number."

"You expect me to introduce you to another man? You're already in my bed with one, Crys. There's only so much a guy can take."

She swallowed her grin.

The roll of his laughter was deep and rich. "Go back to sleep," he said as he readied to stand.

No, he couldn't go. Not yet. Tension built in her chest. It pressed in and crushed her heart, needing to be freed. Her hand shot out and took his. It was warm and calloused, his square knuckles torn. For her. He'd fought for her. Tears stung the backs of her eyes and blurred her vision.

His brow furrowed. "Crys?"

The weight of it all came crashing down, and a sob broke from her. He closed the distance between them with a snap, sheathing her in his arms. His hold was crushing as she buried her face in the curve of his neck.

"You came," she said, voice muffled. Her breath hitched and she clung to him. Safe.

He loosed a rough exhale when his hand knotted in the hair at the base of her neck. She stayed that way until the burning in her lungs subsided. He'd risked everything to come for her. Everything. They still had so many unanswered questions, and the road ahead was long, but he was there.

She withdrew just enough to see him. He didn't yield an inch. She tilted her head, and her pulse quickened. "I suppose I'll have to find a way to pay you back?"

He tracked his thumb under her eye, brushing her tears aside.

"Promises, promises." His voltaic stare dropped to her mouth, and the electricity it kicked off sent a feverish shockwave straight to her core. His heat brushed her sensitive flesh as he leaned closer. And closer.

The bed rustled when Noah moved.

Gideon froze while his gaze flicked past her. His fingers flexed then released. He lowered his hand. "Rest, Crys," he told her, then rose, his stride easy as he headed for the door.

"It wasn't an accident, Gideon."

He stopped, half-turning as he glanced over his shoulder.

Her heart rate kicked up a notch, then another. It took her longer than it should've to figure things out. She'd made a chain of bad choices since she'd joined the Shepherds but trusting him would never be one of them. "When I called you for help," she shook her head, "it wasn't an accident."

His mouth pulled up at the corner. "I'm glad to hear it," he replied, then left and closed her in.

She bit her lip and rolled to face her best friend.

"Did I just interrupt something beautiful?" Noah asked, fluttering his sleep-tired eyes at her.

Fire burned her cheeks when she smacked his shoulder.

"Are you alright?"

She settled her hands under her chin. "Better than I was." So much better. Knowing Gideon was there, that she could trust him, that she wouldn't lose him, soothed her damaged soul. She had people to turn to. People to help. People who'd come, no matter what.

"I'm guessing things with you and Ben are—"

"Over!" So far past over she couldn't believe they'd ever begun. There were mistakes, and then there was Ben. People like him chipped at the foundation of who she was, making her question herself as they stripped her soul piece by piece. He'd tried to hold her back, to interfere, to lock her away. But she'd be damned if he'd take another thing from her.

Every line of tension in Noah's body relaxed when he sagged.

"You knew, didn't you? That something wasn't right with him?"

The smile he offered held no joy. "He had an unnerving edge." He brushed several hairs back from her face before his expression transformed and he beamed. "I'm in Gideon Ryczek's bed."

"Does Kyle know?"

"Kyle knows I'd do anything to help my Gracie."

"Including climbing into Gideon Ryczek's bed?"

He settled his palm over his heart and grinned. "*Anything*!"

Thank you for reading! Did you enjoy? Please add your review because nothing helps an author more and encourages readers to take a chance on a book than a review.

And don't miss the next book of the The Marked series coming soon!

Until then read FOUL IS FAIR, by City Owl Author, Elisse Hay. Turn the page for a sneak peek!

Also be sure to sign up for the City Owl Press newsletter to receive notice of all book releases!

SNEAK PEEK OF FOUL IS FAIR

Half-a-dozen heavily lined faces beamed at me. Why? Why were they *beaming?*

"You must be Aurora," the shortest, roundest one said, her words so fizzy with excitement it made my eyes water.

Oh. Shit. Me. They were excited about *me*. One of them took my arm and towed me further into the room. "Your grandmother told us all about you, dear." Hellfire. I hoped that was an exaggeration. "It's so good to see a young witch coming on board! Look, everyone, Aurora is here!"

"It's Rory." But my protest was lost beneath their effervescent welcome.

I just wanted to get to work, but apparently stage one of my induction involved a spread that could've come off a bake stand at a school fair—and, before witches were legalized, that probably would have been a common side hustle.

Scones, breakfast muffins, slices, cakes—all homemade. The tea was weaker than the water I used to wash my dishes. To top it off was a handwritten banner that read *Welcome to the East Melbourne Coven, Aurora!* It had been decorated with pressed flowers.

"Wominjeka, Rory," said a woman wearing paint-splattered pants and a somewhat wary smile. "I'm Janet."

Trust the First Nations elder to have heard my preferred name. "Hi, Janet." I caught a jar of jam as it slipped from the nicotine-stained fingers of a grinning witch. Grimly amused, I watched the way she turned the situation to her advantage, using my momentary pause as I held the jar to press a plate into my hand.

I felt like a kid while I tried to smile, remember names, respond appropriately, and not drop the scone all at the same time. *Note to self: next time I want a change, I'll get a new hair color, not a new job.*

Behind the veterans, a younger woman with awesome jet-black hair and sapphire-blue highlights sent me a look of sympathy before she quietly removed herself from the fray. Smart woman. I should've gone sapphire blue, too. And also hightailed it out of there.

Some of the cream wilted down the side of my scone to puddle on my saucer as the jam-fumbling witch planted herself beside me, blocking the nearest exit, filling the air with chatter. "Oh, and you really ought to try Suzie's blueberry bar before we get caught up on the humdrum. Suzie's grandson owns a blueberry farm out in Silvan. Brings her fresh berries, doesn't he, Suzie?" Her eyes glittered. "He's a handsome young lad, isn't he, Suzie?" she went on, patting my arm knowingly. "Great butt," she said under her breath in an aside to me. "Looks like he knows how to use his hands, too, if you know what I mean!"

I estimated the likelihood of said grandson knowing the difference between a clitoris and a haemorrhoid as slim to none.

"I should find Arthur," I said firmly, before the grandson idea could gather any momentum. "I'll be back for that slice." Gazes of a half-dozen women, who were all obviously accustomed to people submitting to their affection, swung to me. Well, curse it, if I'd wanted to be fussed over, I'd have gone to work with my own grandmother. "This is such a great welcome. But I won't feel right until I know what I'm doing."

The jar-dropping witch, who might've been Bernie or Becky or even Esmerelda, for all I knew, made a harrumph of disapproval. "Well, you won't get that from Arthur. Half the time, that boy doesn't even know what he's doing, and the other half of the time, he's pulling on his own—"

"Hush, Bernie," another said with a disapproving frown. "I'm sure Aurora knows all about wizards." She cleared her throat, and I tried very hard to smother a grin. "Well, you go on up, dear," she said, her frown melting as she gazed up at me like I was the one grandchild who hadn't spilled food on their party dress at Solstice. "And when you come on back, we'll get you all settled in. Let her go, Bernie. She's quite right. Whether we like it or not, we all have those to-do lists now."

"The old days were much simpler," said a woman whose handmade name badge read *Cici—she/her*. Cool. Pronouns. I could get in on that. "No data or performance reviews. Just you, your wand, some herbs and foci, your coven and your flock. Now there's *paperwork*."

Plus a wage, superannuation, sick leave, holiday pay, and tax deductions.

I kept that to myself, sending them all my warmest, I'm-a-good-kid-with-good-manners smile as I went past the fussily decorated table in the direction I'd been pointed.

There wasn't space to get lost. Budgets being what they were, I hadn't expected a massive, multi-story complex. "Cozy" was a nice description for the little townhouse with its high, old ceiling and narrow rooms overflowing with furniture, plants, and piles of Really Important Stuff. Still, it had character that even the governmental grey paint and grey-flecked grey flooring couldn't overwhelm, vases that overflowed, doilies, donated mismatched furniture, and candles. Of course. Put a coven in a place long enough, it'd become a home, albeit a fussy one, if it was an old-school coven. And this was a very old-school coven.

I kept my face neutral as I went up the stairs. Well, I wanted different. I wasn't going to get anything as different from my last job as this, was I?

Should've gone for the blue streaks. Or maybe purple. I'd look great with purple hair.

A thirty-something, weekend-warrior type looked up from a coffee machine that perched precariously on a hallway table. His expression was equal parts curiosity and commiseration. "Aurora?"

I put out my hand. "Rory," I said, as he took it and shook.

"Arthur. I heard the welcome party banging their drums. Forgive me for not being present, but it sounded like they had you covered." He took an extra coffee cup. Not a flower in sight. "Anyway, word on the grapevine is you're a hard arse, so I figured you'd be okay. Coffee?"

He didn't look at me to deliver any of that. I didn't care, just sighed in pleasure at his offer. "Please."

He smiled down at the coffee machine. He had dimples, and he knew how to work them.

The coffee-making ritual gave me time to look around. He mentioned a few key points of interest: a bathroom, storage, his office—which he didn't share with anyone, I noticed—a meeting room, and the tech hub of the coven, currently unstaffed.

"It's not much," he said with false humility. "But we're two blocks from the local police station, and the tram line right around the corner makes travel a breeze."

"Uh huh." I wasn't here to give a real estate appraisal.

Inside Arthur's office, I was waved towards one of the chairs across from his desk.

I glanced around. Big windows overlooking the neighbour's brickwork. A few framed landscapes. His staff mounted on brackets on the wall.

Old school.

And he definitely had the most space in the building. The rooms I'd passed showed desks and office chairs crowded in so close I'd have my knees in my ears trying to work there.

With some grim thoughts about middle managers, I settled into the chair.

"So, I thought I'd give you a quick rundown of the coven's core values before we get into the nitty gritty of your work."

I folded my hands, reached for patience, found some, and marvelled. "Sure."

"Mutual respect and equality is, of course, the foundation of this coven," he began. This from behind his big desk, sitting in his new leather chair, in the one office that didn't have seven other people crammed into it.

"Mmm." I shifted a little, wishing, not for the first time, wizards came with a *skip* button.

"I know you've heard that before," he said in a way that he probably thought was charmingly self-deprecating. "So, I won't bang on about it. You'll see it in action. Accountability is, of course, critical. Risk assessments and case notes need to be kept updated so I can manage any situation that arises. We aren't police; we're here to tend to our flock, to keep them on the straight and narrow." He nodded at his own wisdom. It was kind of like being near someone sniffing their own farts. "To engage supernaturals in our society, help smooth over any bumps, and to ensure magi use their powers wisely. We're first responders."

So he didn't know what a first responder was. He did know what paperwork was though, obviously. That was the bottom line.

He flashed his dimples again. "And, of course, we need to discuss integrity," he went on, leaning forward.

At that point, I totally zoned him out.

When he finally fell silent, I said, "Thanks, Arthur. So, about the work. I'm assuming I'll get a rundown of my caseload from one of the coven?"

He nodded his agreement. "Unfortunately, you won't be able to do a thorough hand-over due to the nature of your predecessor's departure."

Sure, sour grapes didn't give much juice. I ignored the opportunity to garner gossip. I didn't value this guy's opinion. There would be someone in the know I could talk to. Confidentiality between a coven and the world was sacrament, but I was on the inside now.

"Aurora—"

"Rory."

His smile turned apologetic. "Rory. Most of what you need to know is in the handbook." He pushed the bound manual that had been sitting exactly at right angles to his laptop toward me. *Metro Procedures for Caretaker Witches*. "This is an established coven," he went on. Just what I needed, some light bedtime reading. "Most of the witches here are very…set in their ways."

That was so obvious I had planned on letting it go without saying.

The thing was, as much as their scones and welcome poster amused me, there was a reason the traditions were what they were. We didn't always even know what those reasons were, until we messed with them.

Anyway, they were cute. In a terrifying, grandmother-level-omnipotence sort of way.

Out of nowhere, without any sort of lead-in, Arthur declared, "I'm a feminist." And then he paused.

I met his eye and bit my tongue. He just sat there as if it was my turn to say something. Perhaps dig out a gold star.

When I just waited silently, content to let the awkward pause grow even more awkward, he shuffled a little in his seat and then went on.

"I know you're from the country, and you would be used to wizards getting in your way, telling you to go back to the kitchen and cook love potions."

I had been told exactly that. Still, I wasn't giving him the satisfaction of sharing my righteous indignation.

"Love potions are a Class B substance." My words were brisk.

He grinned at me again, as if trying to get me to share a joke. "Regardless, I want you to know you have my full support." I nodded and went to stand, because surely, this was the end. "I figure a strong, independent woman like yourself wouldn't necessarily want that."

Oh, wow, there was no irony. None. Was that…even possible?

"I just hope you never need it," he said with such concern that I was taken aback.

"I think this should cover me for now, though." I added, holding up the manual. If I ever needed Arthur to bail me out, I was in very dire straits.

As shields went, it might be useful.

He stood and walked me to the door. "Part of your caseload is a local lycanthrope pack," he said with a nod. "They're considered high-risk. I'm the district expert, so you don't need to worry. We'll work that together."

My feet were lead, and ice rushed through my veins. *Sun warming my face as blood began to dry on my hands. Black cockatoos screaming their way across the sky.* I looked down at the floor beneath my feet, drew in air. I was standing on carpet. Not bridge. Not rock. Carpet.

Lycans already? Shit. Suddenly, I didn't care that I'd just been patronized.

"Who's their Alpha?"

"Beo Velvela. Police are investigating them, but we're to keep up our surveillance until charges are laid."

I ignored the clutch of anxiety in my breast. I could deal with lycans.

"Can you email me the name of the officer in charge of the investigation, information on relevant parties, and crimes they could be linked to?"

He nodded. His arm went behind me, his hand resting on the door. I stepped out of that intimate circle without thinking, but he didn't react.

"Betty—your predecessor—and I were going along to where the Alpha works as part of our surveillance. *The Playground,*" he added as I opened my mouth to question him. "Mixed Martial Arts dojo and gym. Beo runs Brazilian Jiu-Jitsu classes, and his whole pack—that we've identified—attend. I've been sparring with them once a week for about two months. Betty sat and knit. She posed as my mother."

Rolling with a lycan pack as undercover surveillance? If this was normal, where the fuck was my hazard pay?

Arthur was either totally ignorant, absolutely amazing, or very brave. I highly doubted he was all three.

"I don't knit. And I don't roll with lycans." *Bones crunched, a splintering, wet sound.* My stomach rolled. Nope-ity, nope, no.

I had goals. One day, I wanted to spend a whole week eating ice cream, chips, and having amazing sex, preferably with someone else.

He shrugged. "So, you can be my girlfriend. Scroll through social media, send some snaps. You and I know you're not that sort of woman, but they'll see what they expect."

There he went again. I was tempted to hit back, but I bit my tongue.

"Is it a mixed class?"

The words popped out of my mouth while my brain held back my ample vitriol. I wondered if he heard my teeth groaning as I clenched my jaw shut.

He nodded, a faint frown appearing on his face. "The pack isn't all male, and there are some human players. It's useful for me to have someone on the sidelines. I'll need you armed and prepared if there's trouble."

On the *sidelines?* "Arthur," I said through my teeth, trying to keep hold of my last shred of patience, "if you're on a mat in the middle of a lycan pack who actually want to hurt you, there's not a damn thing anyone can do, even armed, prepared, and perfectly positioned." Okay.

My vote leaned towards totally ignorant. "I'll get up to date with the information, and we'll figure out how to play it." I emphasised the *we* part, because obviously, Arthur's decision-making skills lent more towards finding opportunities to inflate his own ego rather than keeping his insides on the inside.

His frown deepened, but he nodded his agreement. "I've been going on a Tuesday. Five-thirty until seven."

"We'll keep your pattern." Although why he had a pattern for undercover surveillance, I had no idea. Tuesday night gave me a whole two days, if I counted today, which I absolutely did. Urgency drummed through my veins. *Of* course, *it's lycans. That's just great.* "Any other high-risk cases I should know about?"

"Just Beo. You've got a few moderate threats, but mostly, it's nonviolent."

Well, that was something. I went to leave, then paused; I didn't want to go off half-cocked, even if it was sort of my specialty.

"What belt are you?"

He blinked at me. "With the BJJ? White. It's just a cover."

Because anything he wasn't good at didn't matter, I suspected. Yeah, he was toast if they decided they wanted a snack. Shit. "Any combat training or hand-to-hand combat experience?"

His brows rose. "I'm a wizard, Rory."

My heart sank. Yep, that told me everything I needed to know…and confirmed my worst suspicions.

Lucky for both of us, I was a witch.

Don't miss the next book in The Marked series coming soon, and find more from K.C. Harper at www.kcharper.com

Until then, discover FOUL IS FAIR, by City Owl Author, Elisse Hay!

I like my monsters like my coffee—strong, hot, and not trying to kill me.

I'm done with hunting down supernatural criminals. Fighting for my life everyday gets old. So, career change. Social worker for supernaturals is a way to use my skills in a no risk environment. Right?

Wrong.

It turns out the last witch in my role was slaughtered by a lycanthrope—and the prime suspect is my client who happens to be pure, forbidden deliciousness. Totally irrelevant. I get paid to support the vulnerable, not lust after them. Or assume they're guilty unless proven innocent.

But the cops are outgunned. The wizards are morally bankrupt. And the lycans are concealing information.

There's someone powerful, clever, and armed with inside knowledge who's getting rich running drugs. Someone lurking behind a network of faeries and lycanthropes. Someone corrupt enough to kill to keep their secrets.

I'm a witch. I'm not going down without a fight.

Please sign up for the City Owl Press newsletter for chances to win special subscriber-only contests and giveaways as well as receiving information on upcoming releases and special excerpts.

All reviews are **welcome** and **appreciated**. Please consider leaving one on your favorite social media and book buying sites.

For books in the world of romance and speculative fiction that embody Innovation, Creativity, and Affordability, check out City Owl Press at www.cityowlpress.com.

ACKNOWLEDGMENTS

To my husband for showing me what it is to dream. Thank you for never saying *if* I'd make it, and always saying when. You are my heart.

To mom and dad, thank you for raising me to be strong, to trust my instincts, to care about how I affect the world, and for proving that one person can make a difference. There aren't enough words to express the depth and breadth of my love and gratitude.

To Rob and Natasha for the laughter. I will destroy you at Mariokart...someday.

To my Gram for showing me that strength can be graceful.

To the best group of writers a girl could ask for, Keri, May, Tara, Eilene, Regina, Nicole. If it weren't for your eyes, I wouldn't be here.

To my editor, Lisa for opening the door to publishing and taking me on this journey.

Finally, thank you to anyone who has picked up this book. I hope it's all that you anticipated.

ABOUT THE AUTHOR

K.C. HARPER grew up on Canada's east coast and now resides with her husband in the nation's capital. She spends her time plotting to destroy the happiness of the imaginary people that live in her head. She's an avid reader, developmental editor, and a full-time human servant to a 4.5lb teacup Chihuahua.

www.kcharper.com

twitter.com/kcharper613
instagram.com/kcharper_author
tiktok.com/@kcharperwriter

ABOUT THE PUBLISHER

City Owl Press is a cutting edge indie publishing company, bringing the world of romance and speculative fiction to discerning readers.

Escape Your World. Get Lost in Ours!

www.cityowlpress.com

facebook.com/YourCityOwlPress
twitter.com/cityowlpress
instagram.com/cityowlbooks
pinterest.com/cityowlpress

Made in the USA
Monee, IL
05 March 2023